THE DREAMS OF CARDINAL VITTORINI AND OTHER STRANGE STORIES

By the same author

Plays

Imaginary Lines

Put Some Clothes on, Clarisse!

The Music Lovers

Winner Takes All

Once Bitten

Love Unknown

Biography

Out of the Woodshed, the Life of Stella Gibbons

Story Collections

The Dreams of Cardinal Vittorini and Other Strange Stories

The Complete Symphonies of Adof Hitler

Masques of Satan

Madder Mysteries

Mrs Midnight and Other Stories

Flowers of the Sea

Collected and Selected Editions

Dramas from the Depths

Shadow Plays

The Sea of Blood

Novels

The Dracula Papers

Virtue in Danger

THE DREAMS OF CARDINAL VITTORINI

& Other Strange Stories

Reggie Oliver

Tartarus Press

The Dreams of Cardinal Vittorini
& Other Strange Stories
by Reggie Oliver

First published 2003

First paperback edition published 2012 at
Coverley House, Carlton-in-Coverdale, Leyburn,
North Yorkshire, DL8 4AY, UK
Reprinted 2016

ISBN 978-1-905784-47-9

The publishers would like to thank
Jim Rockhill and Richard Dalby

CONTENTS

AUTHOR'S NOTE

The Dreams of Cardinal Vittorini was first published in 2003. It is the first of my collections of 'strange' stories. After receiving very favourable notices and a nomination for best collection from the International Horror Guild its limited run of 300 copies soon sold out and it has since been very difficult and expensive to obtain. Of the stories only the title story and 'Beside the Shrill Sea' have been printed elsewhere. 'The Dreams of Cardinal Vittorini' was first published in the journal *Weirdly Supernatural* (January 2002); 'Beside the Shrill Sea' appeared first in *Supernatural Tales* No. 5 (April 2003) and subsequently in *Brighton Shock!* (PS Publishing, 2010), for the World Horror Convention of that year. For this edition a few minimal corrections have been made to the text and I have decided to omit one story. This is 'A Warning to the Antiquary' which was written as a *jeu d'esprit*, but the jest, for me at any rate, has rather outlived its charm, and there are those who have found it distasteful. Its omission is no loss to the reader.

I have redrawn many of the vignette illustrations because the earlier ones were either the wrong shape or inadequate or both. It gives me great pleasure to see this collection available again, in an accessible, attractive and reasonably-priced edition. I hope that very soon my second collection, *The Complete Symphonies of Adolf Hitler*, at present as hard and even more expensive to obtain as *Vittorini*, will also appear in a similar edition.

Reggie Oliver
May 2012

BESIDE THE SHRILL SEA

Like a ballerina's arm, the white sweep of Victorian terraced houses curled gracefully around a sandy bay with high moss-green promontories standing guard over it at either end; a little filigree pier jutted out into the sea; wooded hills and a distant grey castle made up the background. That is how I remember Tudno Bay. The place has a romance about it for me because it was the scene of my professional debut as an actor. I loved Tudno Bay, and even attempted to express my feelings for it in verse, but never really got beyond the first lines which were:

'Beside the shrill sea!
Where learned mermaids sing to me!'

They were an arresting pair of lines, I thought; unfortunately I could never think of anything as good to follow them, and so they remained, an isolated, fragmentary tribute to the summer of my apprenticeship.

Admittedly the season for which I was engaged at the Grand Theatre, Tudno Bay was not very stimulating artistically. The repertoire consisted of thrillers and comedies, West End cast-offs two decades old; the direction was routine, the company no more than averagely competent. But in those days the sheer joy of acting transcended more pretentious considerations; and the challenge of making something interesting out of uninspired material had its own peculiar excitement. I was never bored because we did a new play every week and never felt over-worked because my young memory absorbed words easily.

It was the cloudless Summer of 1976 and Tudno Bay was as sun-struck as any Riviera resort. In the mornings we rehearsed; in the afternoons I found some deserted spot where I could spout my lines to the open air; or I would go on expeditions with a fellow performer, Jane, to find props for the show. (Jane and I were the most junior members of the company and were employed as assistant stage managers as well as actors.) In the evenings after the show most of the company would find a bar where we could drink late into the night. Tudno Bay was a respectable place, and the only establishment prepared to accommodate us was Saxon's Bar.

Saxon's was situated in the basement of one of the big Tudno Bay hotels. I was never quite sure whether it was officially a public bar or a drinking club. Whatever it was, nobody seemed to mind its being open at all hours. It consisted of a single, long, low room with a bar at one end. Its decor was nondescript, but the presence of an upright piano and the covering of its walls with framed and signed photographs of minor show-business celebrities gave it a certain atmosphere. It was the meeting place for the more raffish element of Tudno Bay society.

We went there initially because one of our company, a middle-aged character actor called Howard, was living with its proprietor, Ray. Howard was a gentle, frog-faced man, one of those modestly gifted, utterly dependable performers destined to be made redundant by the decline of repertory theatre. He had acted in five successive seasons at Tudno Bay during which he had formed a relationship with Ray, and three years previously he had taken up permanent residence at Tudno Bay in Ray's flat.

If it had not been for Howard, we might not have gone so often to Saxon's despite the appeal of its liberal hours. The fact was, none of us liked Ray except Howard, who was besotted by him. Once, perhaps, Ray had been a fine looking man, but he had long since run to seed. He was in his fifties, tall, heavily built, fat, his features regular but coarsely made. His face seemed to glisten unhealthily from the thin slicked boot-black hair on his cranium to the rounded red bumps of his aggressively dimpled chin. His small eyes were curtained by folds of shiny pink flesh. Every evening he was behind the bar at Saxon's drinking, and though his capacity for alcohol was considerable, he regularly exceeded it. Up to a certain point he exuded bonhomie, artificial perhaps and over-effusive, but acceptable; then one drink would tip the scale: the mask slipped and the creature behind it was revealed.

One sensed rather than consciously recognised the moment when this change took place because it was only towards the very end of a night's session that he became overtly aggressive. He might begin by retailing some outrageously malicious tale about a local Tudno Bay worthy. Had we heard that the Headmistress of Tudno High was having an affair with two of her sixth formers, or that the Mayor had exposed himself to a young boy in the Pier toilets? He would then invite one's reaction to this piece of news. If it was muted Ray would accuse you of prudishness; incredulity was seen as tantamount to calling him a liar; a flippant approach was heartless and shallow. There must have been a way of reacting to him which would have defeated his desire to create tension and anguish, but I never discovered it. Ray had a subtlety of technique in such matters which his appearance belied.

But this was not the worst of it: when he turned his attention to Howard he was a demon. There was, it is true, some scope for his mockery. Howard cultivated certain eccentricities of dress which might have seemed odd even on someone less ungainly than him. He wore suits which were too tight for him and quite out of style. He believed in every kind of psychic nonsense and attended a Spiritualist church in the town. His good-natured credulity was such that he would believe almost anything one told him. Ray took full advantage of all these and other weaknesses, so skilfully sometimes that you laughed, only to feel guilty about it afterwards. If you protested, Ray would say he was only having a bit of fun: what business was it of yours? Anyway, old Howie didn't mind, did he? Howard, who clearly did mind, would put on a ghastly pretence of enjoying it all. Perhaps he knew that if he didn't pretend Ray would make it hell for him when they were alone.

Many times Jane and I would agonise over whether we should go to Saxon's after the show. We often decided we should not, but then Howard would beg us to come. Perhaps he derived some relief from having his humiliations witnessed by sympathetic friends. I hope so, but the memory of those times is still painful to me. Once Jane, who was bolder and more direct than I was, asked Howard why he put up with Ray. Howard said: 'Oh, I know, he can be a bit of a—well, I don't like to use the word, but a bit of a so-and-so sometimes. But when we're in the flat he can be quite different.'

'The flat', as he invariably called it, featured largely in Howard's conversation. Every lunchtime, however inconvenient it was, he had to get back from rehearsals to the flat to make Ray's lunch. He would tell us if he had been cleaning the flat, or if some minor improvement, always suggested by Ray, had been made to its appointments. If one of the company jokingly asked how the flat was that day, Howard would answer the question solemnly, as if 'the flat' were an ailing elderly relative. Some of us once expressed a great desire to see the flat, but Howard mumbled something about Ray and turned our request aside. Evidently Ray had put the place out of bounds to anyone not directly sanctioned by him.

Our season was long: it began in May and ended in October. Towards the end of June we noticed that Ray's behaviour was worsening appreciably. After one night at Saxon's when Ray had reduced Howard to tears Jane and I decided not to set foot inside the bar again. The following morning at rehearsals Howard took it upon himself to apologise to us for Ray.

'It's the drink,' he said. 'I try to tell him to keep it moderate, but he won't. The doctor said he had six months to live if he went on like this. He said the doctors are always saying you've got six months. And he won't listen to me. He says I'm an old woman. I think Trevor encourages him.'

Trevor, or 'Trev' as Ray called him, was a new figure on the scene and another reason why we no longer visited Saxon's. Ray had picked him up somewhere and he had become part of the *ménage* at the flat. He was barely out of his teens with lank black hair and a white face that had seen more than it should have at his age. He dressed in black leather and barely spoke a word. At Saxon's he would stand behind the bar with Ray and occasionally whisper in his ear. Jane, in particular, found his presence troubling; and it was true that since his arrival Ray's teasing of Howard had become even more poisonous.

The month of July had almost passed before the company experienced a sequence of events which changed our lives. For Jane and me these happenings had a prelude which may or may not have a bearing on the story.

It was Sunday evening, our one night off of the week, and Jane and I were walking along the front. We had vague plans of going to a concert at the Pier Pavilion, the weather was fine and we were full of youthful well-being. Suddenly Jane stopped. Turning to look at her I had the curious experience of seeing the colour quite literally vanish from her face within a matter of seconds. Before my eyes she turned from a robust twenty-four year old to a frightened girl of sixteen. When I asked what was the matter she shuddered and said that a man—or something—in black had just walked through her. Jane often had psychic moments like this about which I was puzzled but not resolutely sceptical because her approach to them was too matter-of-fact to excite scorn. The experience so disturbed her that she said she no longer felt like going to the concert.

We turned back towards our digs. The sun was beginning to lower itself into the sea behind a raft of dusky pink cloud. Few people were about, as this was the time in the evening when the holidaymakers were eating their tea. We could see their pink faces bent over the sauce bottles in the windows of small hotels and boarding houses all along the front. The tide was in and the shore almost deserted. A few hundred yards away from us a solitary male figure was hurling stones violently into the sea.

Some trick of the light, or perhaps our troubled imaginations, made the figure, dressed all in black, seem unnaturally tall and thin. As we came closer we could hear that he was singing to himself some kind of unidentifiable rock tune in a high sexless whine. As the song reached a crescendo he threw a stone high into the air. We watched as the stone described its arc then dropped with barely a splash into the dark sea. For a moment the whining stopped; then it began again.

'My God, that's Trevor,' said Jane. 'Let's get out of here.'

The following morning I arrived at the theatre for rehearsal to find that Howard was not there. This was unusual because, though I was early, Howard was invariably earlier. There he would be, sitting in the Green Room sipping a coffee and studying his stars in the *Daily Mirror.* As the rest of the company trickled in each of them asked jocularly what had happened to Howard? They missed him. They needed him to read out their stars as he always did. But he did not come, and our director Len was also late.

When Len did arrive he had on his serious face: 'Boys and girls, I had a telephone call this morning. Yesterday evening our friend Ray had a stroke. Apparently he'd been drinking all day. He was rushed to hospital but he got worse. He died last night. As you can imagine Howard is pretty distressed about it all. I have let him off this morning's rehearsal, so we'll just have to work round him, but he's coming down to do the show in the evening. I think that is for the best. Howard is a professional. The show must go on.'

Len's philosophy of life was based entirely on such tired theatrical clichés. His religion was 'professionalism'. 'I may not be the most brilliant innovative director in the world,' he used to say, 'but I am a professional, and I could teach some of these arty-farty types a thing or two about theatre.' Jane and I liked to imagine those mythical 'arty-farty types' sitting at his feet, imbibing his advice on how to make an entrance through a French window.

That morning Len rehearsed all the scenes in which Howard did not appear with the air of someone who had been dealt a grave personal injury but was bearing up manfully under the strain. At about midday, much to everyone's discomfort, Howard put in an appearance, saying that he wanted to rehearse. Everyone gathered round to console him and, as a result, rehearsals were abandoned.

Howard sat in the Green Room, sipping coffee and recalling Ray's last hours in minute and repetitive detail: how he had started drinking early that day and would not listen to Howard's call for moderation; how the stroke had happened and Howard had called the ambulance; how before Ray finally lost consciousness his last word was the faint utterance of Howard's name. To our embarrassment Howard gave us an impression of Ray's last words:

'How . . . ard. . . . How . . . ard. . . . Like that,' he said.

It turned out that Ray had drifted into death at about the time when Jane had her uncanny experience.

'Where was Trevor during all this?' she asked. For the first time Howard, who had been telling his story in a numbed monotone, became animated.

'Well, when Ray had his stroke, Trevor just sat there in the flat. He didn't do anything. He looked at Ray, sort of laughing, and he said: "Told you so." Just that. Then I telephoned the ambulance, and when it came he was gone. I got back to the flat—oh, I don't know—sometime this morning, and he'd been and *taken things*.'

The last two words, sobbed out, opened the floodgates of grief and Howard wept in Jane's arms.

The rest of us became indignant about Trevor. What had he taken? Apparently the missing items included some small pieces of antique silver and the gold bracelet with *Ray* engraved on it which Howard had given his dead lover. We must phone the police, we said, but Howard had lapsed again into indifference and said they would never catch him. Nonsense, we said, who was this Trevor? Where did he come from? Howard had no idea. He didn't even know his surname. He was just Trevor.

That night Howard gave a word perfect and acceptable performance as the police inspector in *Murder Must Out*. We were all relieved and Len, who had been disgruntled all day, seemed mollified. He offered Howard's conduct to Jane and me as an instance of 'what professionalism is all about'.

Howard never broke down or failed to perform adequately on stage; he merely settled into a state of inert gloom, and his misery was compounded by a number of unpleasant shocks. As he repeatedly insisted to us, he had never expected anything from Ray's will, but to be left nothing except Ray's portrait in oils was obviously a disappointment. Other more substantial bequests were made to various friends in the town, and the bulk of Ray's fortune, including the lease on Saxon's and the flat, was left to Ray's son, Terry. Howard, like the rest of us, had known nothing of Terry's existence but he was soon to be made painfully aware of it when Terry and his wife arrived for the funeral. They treated Howard as a miscellaneous nuisance and he was blamed for the theft of the silver which apparently 'belonged to the family'. He was given twenty-four hours in which to vacate the flat.

At the height of the holiday season it was hard to find somewhere to stay, but a number of unexpected people, indignant about his treatment, offered Howard a room in their houses. He refused them all. Howard felt he needed solitude rather than sympathy, so, with his few possessions and the portrait in oils of Ray, he took up residence in one of the unused dressing rooms of the Grand Theatre, sleeping on a mattress on the floor.

This was strictly speaking not allowed, but the management of the company was based in London and Len, who was its representative, did not have the heart to forbid him the theatre. Though none of us admitted as much, we all found Howard's decision to sleep at the Grand disquieting. A theatre is a place to visit and perform in; to live there is to inhabit a limbo. We would happily talk to him on the stairs or in the Green Room, but we avoided visiting him in his dressing room. The cause of our reluctance was the portrait.

It was a three-quarter length of Ray as a young man at the zenith of his coarse good looks. There was a slight smile on his parted lips and a vacancy in the blue eyes which seemed to look out of the canvas, over the shoulder of a viewer, like a social climber at a cocktail party. With its gaudy flesh tones, confident brush strokes and bright blue background the painting was clearly the work of a journeyman artist of some accomplishment and no talent. Yet, for all its slick vacuity, the painting held one's reluctant attention, perhaps because the manner of its execution so clearly complemented the nature of its subject. In its elaborate gilded frame it hung on the wall of Howard's dressing room, presiding over his few sombre possessions.

'He was the love of my life and I'll never see him again,' said Howard when he first showed me the picture. I tried hard to keep my prejudices in abeyance, but I found Ray's domination over Howard's thoughts even more repulsive in death than it was in life. Howard seemed to make no effort to work through his grief; he was held in suspension. His conversation, never lively at the best of times, trod the same dreadful circle of mourning and memory day after day. It was inevitable perhaps that some clairvoyant at his spiritualist church would vouchsafe him the information that Ray had passed safely over and was 'watching over him'. Howard repeated this phrase to us with melancholy satisfaction, but we thought of the picture and shuddered.

Some weeks went by during which I became used to Howard's peculiar way of life and stopped worrying about it. I was young and the sun shone. The adventure of acting engrossed me and his tragedy became little more than the sombre shade which threw the hopeful colours of my existence into greater relief.

Towards the end of July I began to notice that there was sometimes alcohol on Howard's breath when I was on stage with him. This was disturbing in someone whose avowed rule was never to take a drink before a show, but, as his performance did not seem to suffer, I took little notice. One evening I came into the theatre early and heard voices coming from Howard's dressing room, which was the one nearest the stage door entrance. One of the voices was Howard's, the other—unintelligible—was a hissing whisper. I thought Howard might have been going through his lines, but the words he spoke were not from any play. Interspersed with the strange indecipherable whisper they were:

'No . . . No, don't . . . No, don't say that . . . No don't . . .'

Feeling acutely embarrassed I turned back and shut the stage door loudly, coughing as I did so, to make Howard believe that I had just come in. The voice and the whisper stopped abruptly. Howard came out of his dressing room and asked me how I was. He did not seem unduly agitated, just a little dazed. Peering through his open door I noticed that the taps of his dressing room basin were on. The pipes hissed, and I reassured myself that this was the whispering I had heard.

ꕥ

My digs were not far from the theatre. I occupied a single roomed 'holiday flatlet' on the top floor of a block of similar rooms. My window looked down the street towards the Grand Theatre. One hot, airless night in early August it was open. I went to sleep to the familiar sounds of desultory traffic and the occasional late reveller; then at about two in the morning I awoke suddenly. I thought I had heard a cry of alarm, though it was hard to say of what kind because I had woken out of a tangle of dreams.

I went to the window and looked out. The street was deserted; no voices were to be heard, but there was something unnatural about what I saw. It was the light. There seemed to be a glow where there should not have been. I looked further out of the window and smelt something acrid on the night air. I could just see one of the windows of the theatre brightly lit from the inside by a yellow flickering light. Slowly my waking mind gathered these impressions together and formed a conclusion. The Grand Theatre was on fire.

I ran down three flights of stairs and had just got to the pay phone in the hall when I heard the ring of fire engine bells sweeping down the road to the theatre. Howard was inside the building and I knew where he was. The next moment I was running down the road towards the fire.

The hours that followed are a confused memory. I have no idea what I did most of the time but I know that it was seven o'clock and the sun was well up when someone drove me back to my digs from the hospital and I was still wearing pyjamas and dressing gown. It all seems more of a dream to me as I remember it, because, as in a dream, I was helpless and inappropriately dressed.

I remember the black acrid smoke billowing out of a first floor dressing room window, the steam and spray of the hoses. I remember shouting in a fireman's ear for what seemed like minutes, trying to make him understand that there was someone in the building, the long agonising moments before Howard's unconscious body was dragged out, the ride to the hospital, attempts to resuscitate him and their failure. Even now it is only my reason which can place these events in their true sequence.

When the dawn came the theatre was a blackened smoking shell and Howard was dead. His presence in the theatre that night caused infinite trouble. The insurance company refused to pay up because, they argued, he was there illegally, and his presence may have caused the fire. The Tudno Bay Council who owned the theatre sued the management of our theatre company, and the management contemplated suing us. As it happened no-one paid up because the cause of the fire was never definitively established. All that was certain was that it had not begun in Howard's dressing room. He had died of suffocation from the smoke fumes.

A few days after the fire the company dispersed. Jane and I alone stayed on to go to Howard's funeral. It was a deeply melancholy affair because, apart from an elderly aunt who had travelled over from Liverpool, Howard appeared to have no close relatives and Jane and I were the only friends present. The only other person to attend the cremation was one of the firemen. After the service he came over to speak to me. It was clear that something was on his mind. After some moments of inconsequential talk, I asked if he was the one who had carried Howard out of the burning building.

'No,' said the fireman, 'I was there, but that was Dafydd. He can't be here. Off sick. Funny thing, you know. Dafydd's a good man, a strong man: not much upsets him, but that fire did. It was something he saw when he was getting your man out. There was a lot of smoke, as you know, and the things in his room were all smoke-damaged. You know what I mean? When everything gets covered with this thin layer of soot. You can never get the smell out of things when they've been smoke-damaged. Terrible. But Dafydd could see that there was one thing in that room that was not smoke-damaged at all, and he couldn't find no explanation, see. It upset him no end, and I for one don't blame him. It's all very odd, you see.'

When I asked him what item it was that had escaped the smoke damage I had already guessed, but I wanted to be wrong.

'It was this painting. Portrait it was. Good piece of art, I'd say. A young man, kind of smiling. Handsome face, not nice though. Forensics have it and they can't explain no smoke-damage either. Another funny thing. Your man, he'd not died asleep, as he might have done had he been suffocated with that smoke. He'd woken up and tried to get out. Now it's natural for people to get confused in smoke-filled rooms, but he'd found the door all right. There was blood on the handle and his hands were all bloody too. But why didn't he manage to get out? The door was never locked or anything.'

The fireman paused and looked into the distance at nothing in particular. I sensed that he had more to tell.

'You know, there was this old lady who lived over the road. She was the one who rang the fire brigade. She swears she heard voices coming from that building. From two people, not just the one. One was frantic, screaming like, but there was another, sort of slow, a bit drunk like, laughing almost. She said that voice fair gave her the horrors, much more even than the screaming, which was bad enough.'

'Did she hear what the voice was saying?'

'Nothing much. Just "How . . . ard! . . . How . . . ard! . . . How . . . ard!" Like that. Fair gave me a fright even to hear her saying it. Wasn't that the name of your friend who died?'

We were incapable of responding. When the fireman had left us Jane and I walked for a while in the dreary crematorium garden without speaking.

'Well, at least he's free of Ray now,' I said eventually.

'Not unless he wants to be,' Jane replied.

FENG SHUI

When Mr Pearmain discovered irregularities in some of the overseas accounts of Stolz International, the firm for which he worked, he went straight to his superior and reported the fact. The superior thanked Mr Pearmain politely and said that this was a serious matter which would receive his immediate attention. Some weeks went by before Mr Pearmain went to his superior again. Irregularities were still occurring: what was being done? The superior said that the situation was being dealt with 'through the appropriate channels'. Once again he thanked Mr Pearmain politely, and if there was a touch of frostiness about his courtesy Pearmain, who was not sensitive to such nuances, failed to notice. Months passed; further irregularities were discovered and reported by Mr Pearmain. By this time even he had begun to notice that he was being shunned by his colleagues. One of them hinted to Mr Pearmain that he would be well advised to drop the matter of the overseas accounts, but Mr Pearmain did not understand. He was an accountant; it was his job to see that the company accounts were in good order. He would be failing in his duty to Stolz International if he did nothing.

Pearmain began to find that he was put under pressure at work; he was made to fulfil impossible and unnecessary deadlines. As a result his health suffered and for the first time in his life he found himself having to take days off work. His superior spoke to him kindly: was this the right job for him? Would he not feel more comfortable in a less stressful and high-powered environment? Perhaps it would be best if they were to let him go? Pearmain, whose powers of resistance had been carefully eroded, agreed and he left Stolz International.

His wife Alice received the news with mingled irritation and relief. She was glad that he was no longer under pressure; at the same time she was aware that it was his scrupulous, unimaginative honesty which had brought them to this pass. The very quality for which she loved him was the one which she now found most exasperating. They had two sons, both at expensive schools, what were they to do? Pearmain could get freelance work, but it would not be nearly so well paid as his position with Stolz.

The Pearmains lived at Lime House, a handsome, detached Victorian mansion in a street of similar mansions on the outskirts of Cheltenham where Stolz, which manufactured electronic guidance systems for aircraft, was located. The house was a little too large and too expensive for them, but they had bought it when Pearmain joined the firm because Alice had loved it at first sight and Pearmain always trusted her instincts as a blind man trusts a sighted person to guide him across the road. However, in their newly straitened circumstances, a large sacrifice was necessary, and selling Lime House was the obvious one to make.

Of course, it was the wrong time to sell, or so the estate agent told them, and Alice spent long, dispiriting afternoons that Spring showing indifferent couples around those high-ceilinged well-proportioned rooms. The couples looked at all that space and remarked that it must cost an awful lot to heat, mustn't it? Alice, whose honesty was, in its own way, as scrupulous as her husband's, admitted that it did. But never had she loved the house more than in those dismal days: its comfortable bay windows in which you could sit and look out onto the world, the big unpretentious entrance hall where bicycles and boots could be kept without there being any danger of tripping over them, its intricately moulded plaster cornices and ceiling roses, its plain marble fireplaces and the long-lawned garden shaded by a great lime which gave the house its name. Lime House was a place where you had room to think.

One day Alice opened the door to another prospective buyer, a tall, ginger-haired woman in her late thirties. She was wearing a very smart purple tracksuit and looked slim and fit. She announced herself as Heather Billing. Alice, who had a habit of forming instant likes and dislikes to people, took against Heather Billing at once, not violently, but enough to make her constantly ill-at-ease in Heather's presence. The unease was compounded when she discovered that Heather's husband worked for the very firm that Mr Pearmain had just left, Stolz International.

In her favour, Heather was the first of the would-be buyers to express unqualified enthusiasm for the house. She just loved it. She thought that the spaces were 'amazingly energising'; then she said that she thought the house had 'great possibilities'. Alice stiffened at this: to her the house was a place of actualities not possibilities. She asked Heather politely what she meant.

'I'm sorry,' said Heather, 'you must think that's awfully rude, Alice.' Her accent and the speed with which she had progressed to Christian name terms betrayed transatlantic origins. 'You see I was talking from my own personal viewpoint. My chart told me it was favourable to move into this area. We're coming from Winchcombe so we'd be moving towards the horse, which happens to be my sign.' Alice raised her eyebrows in enquiry. 'Chinese astrology,' Heather explained.

'How interesting,' said Alice whose attendance at the local parish church every Sunday was the limit of her spiritual voyaging.

'There's lots of Chi energy in this house. It could flow really well.'

'Really?'Alice had adopted that condescending would-be-interested manner which members of royalty assume when talking to ballet dancers. Heather, who detected the hauteur in Alice's voice, decided to demonstrate her own brand of superiority.

'I expect you haven't a clue what I'm talking about, have you?' she said. 'Feng Shui. It's the traditional ancient Chinese art of geomancy. I've made quite a study of it. As a matter of fact, I'm a qualified Feng Shui consultant.'

'Ah, yes, I know!' said Alice. 'You go into people's houses and rearrange their furniture.'

'There's a little more to it than that—Oh, isn't this the neatest little room!'

It was fortunate that the tour of the house had brought them just then to this particular room on the ground floor because the discussion might otherwise have become acrimonious. The charm of their surroundings, however, distracted them both.

It was a square parlour off the main drawing room with a window overlooking the garden. Alice had adopted it as her private sanctum. Thinking the word 'study' too grandiose, she called it her 'little office'. In it she dealt with household matters, telephoned her friends and kept her favourite books, together with the few mementoes of her life before she had married Pearmain. Along the window sill were seedlings germinating in trays and cuttings in pots. On the walls were framed family photographs.

'I guess this is your favourite room too,' said Heather.

'Yes.'

Heather nodded with satisfaction and surveyed the room carefully. Alice felt that an intimate part of herself was being scrutinised by strange eyes. It was uncomfortable and she tried to distract Heather by pointing out the view over the garden. Heather paid no attention to this. She was observing the family photographs, the kind of books Alice read; she was absorbing information and making deductions. Then she noticed against the wall by the door a carved oak cabinet, standing on bulbous legs, black with age.

'That's an interesting old piece,' she said.

'Yes,' said Alice, putting on her condescending voice again. 'It's what they call a muniment cupboard. For storing documents.'

'Yes, I know,' said Heather, one of whose previous enthusiasms had been restoring antique furniture. 'Is it genuine seventeenth century?'

'Quite possibly. I'm sure the central panel is. Rather wonderful, don't you think? Adam and Eve in the garden.'

The front of the cupboard was a single rectangular piece of wood which opened down to the horizontal, like the lid of a desk. There it was held in place by a light metal chain. Unopened it presented to the viewer a panel in crude, vigorous low relief inside a broad border of carved leaves. The scene in low relief depicted Adam and Eve, naked, standing on either side of the tree. Round the tree was twined a serpent which was almost as big as the tree itself. It was looking intently at Eve who held a large apple in her hand, hesitantly, as if she wanted to return it to the snake.

'Forgive me,' said Heather. 'I know this sounds strange, but your cupboard kind of looks out of place in this room.'

'Ah, there speaks the Feng Shui expert!' said Alice. Heather was beginning to find this very ordinary looking woman with her twinkling dowager manner intensely annoying. Like most people with little sense of humour Heather was suspicious of those who possessed it, especially when the humour seemed to be directed against her. Alice, sensing from her tight smile that Heather might not enjoy being teased, modified her manner.

'As a matter of fact,' she went on, 'it belongs here more than I do in a sense. It was the only piece of furniture left behind by the previous occupants, and they left it here because it was there when *they* came. Before that the house was owned by an old bachelor called Mr Abney who lived here with a housekeeper. This is going back before the war. There are still people around who remember him. Not fondly, I'm afraid. No particular reason, just that he was eccentric. "Queer" was the word used, though, of course, in the old traditional sense of odd. Not, you know . . .'

Alice stopped herself. She knew she had been rattling on in her usual way without noticing if Heather was listening or not. She often did this to her husband, but it was embarrassing with a stranger. Heather, however, was watching her intently.

'Don't stop. This is fascinating!'

Alice resumed her story more self-consciously. 'Well, all I was going to say is that I'm pretty sure that the cupboard was old Abney's, because when I opened it up, inside I found all these . . . "pamphlets", I suppose you'd call them. They're still there.'

She turned the key in the lock of the cupboard and let down the Adam and Eve panel. Inside was a double arcade of pigeon holes separated by little wooden Tuscan pilasters. Each of the pigeon holes was stuffed with yellowing paper booklets.

'I'm afraid I've never bothered to clear them out,' said Alice apologetically. 'I don't quite know why.' She took out one of the booklets and read out the title on its front cover.

'*Alchemical Symbols Explained: Their Application in Modern Science* by Ignatius Abney B.A. Oxon. Hyperion Press 1934. I think he obviously printed them privately. I doubt if they were great sellers.' She picked up another. '*Eugenius: or the True Cult of the Race Soul*. Oh, dear! Now, wait a minute, here's something which is more in your line: *Matter and Daemon: On the direction of Spirit Force through Physical Objects*. Isn't that a bit like your Feng Shui?'

'No,' said Heather decisively. 'Nothing like. This stuff is just weird.'

After that, the viewing of the house was conducted in a brisk, businesslike way and when Heather asked Alice if the place did not cost a lot to heat she replied 'Not really'. Two days later the estate agent rang up to tell Alice that Mr and Mrs Billing had made an offer for the house which was not insultingly below the asking price. The Pearmains accepted.

Feng Shui

&

Heather's husband, Jack, was a little disturbed to hear that they were buying a house off the Pearmains. He had heard of Mr Pearmain's exit from the firm and was uneasy about it. Nevertheless, he had felt it best that Pearmain should go because, as he had remarked to a colleague, Pearmain was 'not fully in tune with the prevailing culture of a leading-edge firm like Stolz.' Jack Billing had an effortless command of such language which was why he was near the top of the ladder in Marketing.

When the Billings and their three children moved in to Lime House Heather appropriated Alice's 'little office' as her 'private space'. She found, as she had expected, that Alice had left the old muniment cupboard behind. This pleased her. Heather, not being a sentimentalist, had decided to sell it. In the meanwhile it had to be moved from where it was because it was trapping all the Chi energies in the room.

It was some weeks, however, before Heather was able to do anything about her little space because she was so busy arranging everyone else's. Organising other people's lives was Heather's passion in life, which was one of the reasons why she had taken up Feng Shui. (Before Feng Shui she had done counselling, but this had not been a success because she discovered that, strangely, listening rather than advising was thought to be the main task of the counsellor.) Heather's family consented to her bossiness because they recognised the essential benevolence behind the urge to dominate. Her arrangements, whether of furniture or feelings, were nearly always convenient and comfortable.

At last one afternoon Heather was able to start work on her own room, bare except for one object, the muniment cupboard. The room needed painting (blue for meditation) and the cupboard needed moving. She opened the door of the cupboard and found, to her surprise, that all the pamphlets were gone from their pigeon holes. Heather had been planning to burn them, but Alice must have anticipated her wishes. The cupboard really needed to be moved out of the room altogether—black was quite the wrong colour for her space—but Heather had no help that afternoon, so she decided simply to shift it from its present position to the opposite corner of the room where it would be less conspicuous. Heather was strong and fit but she had great difficulty in moving the cupboard. It was unusually heavy for its size and on several occasions threatened to topple over. At last it was done; the cupboard was in a place where it would not dominate the whole room. It was not an ideal solution but it would do.

Heather, exhausted, surveyed the result of her efforts for some time. She speculated that the cupboard would fetch a good sum at auction, four figures certainly, perhaps even five. The carving on the panel was, in its primitive way, remarkable. The faces of Adam and Eve were too worn to be very distinct; it was their attitudes that were so striking. Adam's body was bent and tense, the arms held up as if to ward off an unseen assailant. The whole posture suggested extreme fear. Eve seemed merely transfixed, held from returning the apple to the tree by the gaze of the snake. As in some late medieval paintings that Heather had seen, the face of the serpent was not snakelike, but almost human. It was a powerful and interesting piece of work which Heather would have liked to see in a gallery, but not every day as she worked, planning wholesome Feng Shui for her clients.

Heather decided next to move in some of her reference books to put on the shelves. With this object she left the room. As she did so she heard a loud thump behind her, as of something falling heavily onto the carpet. She turned round and looked back into the room. Nothing had changed. The cupboard stood where it was. It was odd.

Two weeks passed without much happening. Heather moved her things into the room, which she now called her study, and arranged them according to the principles of Feng Shui. She could never settle things quite to her satisfaction, however, and the muniment cupboard, even in its new position, remained strangely intrusive. But the new house was, on the whole, a success, though one night the Billings' youngest daughter Jessica, aged ten, woke up screaming that there was an old man in her room. Jessica was not prone to nightmares.

Three mornings after Jessica's nightmare Heather went to her study. She had seen her husband off and taken Jessica to school (the two older children, Brad and Beth, boarded); the weekly shop was done, the meals planned, the house cleaned: she had earned some time for her own activities. The moment she entered the study she was conscious of something being wrong. Several seconds went by before she was able to recognise what was amiss, since everything seemed in good order; then she realised that the muniment cupboard was not where she had put it. It was back in its old position, and the architect's drawing board which she had placed there was where she had put the cupboard: the two pieces of furniture had been neatly swapped round. Heather stood in the middle of the room. Having understood what had happened, her task now was to understand why. A practical joke? But who would want to play it? Brad and Beth were away. Jessica was too young and too meek to do anything like that. Her husband Jack lacked both the opportunity and the will. Who else was there? Burglars? But nothing had been stolen. As the minutes passed and she still could find no possible rational explanation, Heather's heart began to thump; she was conscious of panic as a palpable physical sensation rising in her.

She tried yoga breathing exercises to calm herself down, but her normally compliant body refused to obey. Her mouth was going dry; the racing blood in her veins made her feel giddy. She ran from the room and into the garden. The sun was shining and, in the lime tree's shade, she regained some composure. From somewhere nearby she heard a soft laugh, but this did not worry her too much: it could easily have been a passer-by, though she did not care to verify this supposition.

That evening Heather made tentative enquiries of her daughter and her husband about the moving of the furniture. As she had feared, her questions were met with genuine bewilderment. Neither of them had ever been in her room, Jessica stating, with a decisiveness unusual for her, that she 'never went into mum's room'. Besides, Heather was forced to acknowledge that the cupboard was simply too heavy for Jessica to have moved on her own. She toyed briefly with paranoid notions of her husband and daughter being in some sort of conspiracy against her before psychological self-defence mechanisms shut off all speculation on the subject.

For some days Heather did not go into the room either, and when she did she half expected her whole experience to have been an illusion and to find the cupboard back where she had put it, but it was not. She spent the day going in and out of her study trying to ignore the cupboard, but it would not be ignored. By the evening she had conceived a hatred for the object more virulent and concentrated than she had felt for any living human being, even her first husband. She wanted to do it harm. She thought of taking it into the garden and burning it, but, apart from the difficulty of moving it, she did not want to provoke the suspicion of her neighbours. She did not want to be thought 'queer'. Besides, to destroy the thing would be to admit defeat. She would sell it, as she had originally planned.

The idea made her more cheerful than she had been for days and she went at once to the telephone in the sitting room to ring Gilchrist's, the local auctioneers. A frustrating time followed. She had wrong numbers, crossed lines, interference, engaged signals. In the end she went into the garden with her mobile phone, and got straight through to Gilchrist's on it. Mr Gilchrist would come the very next morning to look at her muniment cupboard.

As she walked back into the house the telephone rang. It was someone who wanted to book her for a Feng Shui consultancy. Heather put her off quite abruptly. Clients were rare, but she could concentrate on nothing until she had solved her own little Feng Shui problem.

Despite this, it would have been a most satisfactory day for Heather had it not been for something that happened that evening which disturbed her more than anything that had previously occurred. And yet it was so apparently trivial.

She was sitting in the drawing room enjoying a drink with her husband before dinner. Jessica, having had tea, had gone upstairs to her room to do homework. Suddenly they heard her scream. Jack and Heather rushed upstairs to find Jessica standing in the doorway of her room. She seemed rigid, transfixed. In her hand she held a small piece of card. It was as if she wanted to get rid of it but somehow couldn't. (Like Eve and the apple on the panel, thought Heather.) As soon as Jessica saw her parents the spell was broken, she dropped the card and rushed sobbing into her mother's arms.

It was some time before Jessica was able to explain coherently what had happened. She had gone upstairs and, on the chest of drawers by the door, she had seen this card. Jack picked it up and examined it. It was an old fashioned sepia portrait photograph, the back of which was made up as a postcard, dating from the 1920s. The picture showed the head and shoulders of a respectable, commonplace looking man in his thirties. The features were regular, if heavy, and might have been thought handsome, but for a blank, sexless quality about them. The lips, a little too thin, were smiling primly; the eyes were partially concealed behind small round spectacles. He wore a stiff little turned down collar and a suit of some heavy tweed material. Certainly there was nothing in this image to excite fear, apart from its inexplicable appearance.

'But why did you scream, darling?' asked Heather.

'Because it was *him,*' sobbed Jessica. 'The old man I saw in my room that night.'

'He doesn't look all that old to me,' said Jack.

'No, but it *was* him. It was!'

Heather turned the postcard over to the blank side. Very faintly in pencil was written: 'Ignatius Abney M.A. 1926'. That night Jessica slept in her parents' room.

The following morning, after delivering Jessica to school, Heather went into her study. Her mind no longer balked at the improbable events which had taken place; she was filled with determination. Her first task was to empty the cupboard of the few items of hers which it contained, mostly envelopes and writing paper. She opened the panel. There in one of the pigeon holes was her stationary. The other pigeon holes were stuffed with Abney's pamphlets. There had been none there when she had put her things in: she was sure of it. Heather suppressed a scream; but she was now so near winning a victory that she was able to summon up reserves of strength. She went to fetch a cardboard box which she filled with the pamphlets.

Having done so she felt easy enough to be able to satisfy a reluctant curiosity. She picked up one or two of the pamphlets and looked through them. They seemed dull, nonsensical things full of strange symbols and unexplained terms. Idly she flipped open a copy of *Eugenius: or the True Cult of the Race Soul* and read:

> 'Racial Purity is to be preserved not only physically, in the Blood, but also spiritually, in the Culture. Thus a White Aryan can no more practise Obeah or Voodoo, than the Negro can seek initiation into the Rites of Saturn or Pan, let alone perform the Greater Ritual of Abre-Melin. There are some Filthy Dabblers who would fuse and meld magical systems, who fall for the hot embraces of Shiva while running after the slant-eyed blandishments of Pu Yi; but I have seen these *Eclectomaniacs* (as I call them) confounded and fall into the Pit.'

Heather shuddered and shut the booklet. She had read enough to know Ignatius Abney, and the knowledge did her no good. Those dreadful capital letters spoke all too eloquently of the man. She remembered his face from the photograph and could see the prim smile of satisfaction as he coined the word *eclectomaniac.*

༄

Mr Gilchrist was the youngest partner in the firm of Gilchrist Auctioneers, a great grandson of its founder. He was in his early thirties, chubby, personable, ex-public school and a furniture enthusiast. He admired the muniment cupboard enormously. Yes, early seventeenth, possibly even late sixteenth century, and the carving was remarkable: it would excite great interest. There must be a photograph in the catalogue, of course. He would ring up some dealers he knew in London. After examining the carving again he turned to Heather and asked her if he might ask why she was selling the piece.

'Oh, not that we need the money. No. It just doesn't go with anything here. Not our style.'

Gilchrist nodded. In his brief passage through the house he had seen no other piece of antique furniture. It was all modern or reproduction, all colour co-ordinated: expensive, insipidly tasteful, not his style. He asked where the cupboard had come from and Heather told him that it had come with the house and had belonged to a man called Abney. Gilchrist reacted; he knew the name. Heather pressed him for further information.

It was evidently an often-told family story and it had all happened just after the war when his grandfather was head of the firm. On Abney's death Gilchrist's Auctioneers had been called in to clear Lime House. It contained some fine antique furniture and a remarkable collection of books and pictures, some of which, for reasons of decency, had to be sold privately. It had been a splendid opportunity, but, in the event, it caused the firm nothing but problems, the difficulty being that old Abney had died leaving everything to his housekeeper. Unfortunately she had also died at roughly the same time. They had both been discovered lying in their separate rooms some days after their death by anxious neighbours. Post mortems could not determine for certain which one of them had perished first; and Abney's will had stated that, in the event of the housekeeper predeceasing him, the estate was to be divided up among his cousins. Relatives of the two deceased descended on Cheltenham; there were lawyers involved and unpleasant scenes in the auction rooms. Lots had to be withdrawn, and generally, in Mr Gilchrist's phrase, 'all hell broke loose'. The Gilchrists had not forgotten the Abney Sale.

Mr Gilchrist left Lime House not quite so eager to sell the muniment cupboard as he had been. He wished he did not know it was an Abney piece, but he had been compelled to ask about its provenance. The reason was that, as he was examining the carving of Adam and Eve he had noticed that the head of the serpent bore a crude but distinct resemblance to his would-be client, Heather Billing.

In the end Gilchrist's sent a letter declining to sell the muniment cupboard, giving as the rather vague reason for their refusal 'certain unresolved questions as to the provenance'. But by this time Heather had lost all interest in the thing as she was in the throes of a move. Jack had been posted to Stolz's Hong Kong office. It was not exactly a promotion, but it had its attractions. There being no call for a Western Feng Shui expert in Hong Kong, Heather began to study the healing powers of crystals. She sometimes called herself an 'eclectomaniac' and was thought very witty for doing so.

༄

Lime Tree House went up for sale and was bought for considerably below the asking price by the Pearmains, who had enjoyed a reversal of fortune. Before he left Stolz Mr Pearmain had taken copies of the disputed overseas accounts and these incriminating papers formed the basis of his subsequent employment tribunal claim for constructive dismissal. Stolz International tried desperately to negotiate an out-of-court settlement with their former employee but, once he had been persuaded by his wife that this was the right thing to do, Mr Pearmain exhibited the same irritating and dogged determination to see the matter through as he had all those months ago when he had first tried to raise the issue internally. This unswerving integrity was highly praised by the tribunal chairman when awarding Pearmain record compensation and resulted in his being recruited by a new government agency to lead an initiative against offshore corporate fraud.

Pearmain's new position involved a great deal of travel but provided commensurate financial reward. Alice had made the repurchase of Lime House her condition for his acceptance of the job. It would compensate for his frequent absences from home. Alice was pleased but not surprised to find that the Billings had decided to leave the muniment cupboard behind. It was there in her little office where it always had been. She patted it, not perhaps affectionately, but with respect, and studied that strangely evocative relief panel of Adam and Eve. Then she noticed something she had not noticed before: the head of the serpent looked strangely like the head of their new cat, Peter, who had that morning sharpened his claws on the muniment cupboard's bulbous legs. It was the last time he did it, though, and the last time he went into the room. Thereafter Peter sharpened his claws on the lime tree in the garden.

IN ARCADIA

Jason Willis had never imagined that he resembled Horace Walpole until his agent rang him up. Having looked at a few portraits in the reference books in his local library, he was still not convinced. Perhaps it was something about the jaw line, or the long thin nose that had decided them. Jason examined his photograph in the *Spotlight* actor's directory, and realised that it was probably little more than a facial expression which had made him their choice. He had put in a picture of himself looking sideways with a half smile on his face. He had intended the smile to be charming in a reticent way, but he could see now that it was sly; and in all his portraits, from youth to extreme old age, Horace Walpole always looked sly.

The BBC History Channel was producing a series of programmes on *18th Century Men of Letters*, a mildly punning title since it featured some of the great letter writers of that epoch. Each hour-long programme featured two contrasting writers—Horace Walpole was to be paired with Lord Chesterfield—and was to consist of a few scholarly talking heads interspersing extracts from the letters recited by actors in costume. The series was intended to be elegant, prestigious and cheap. Jason was an actor in his thirties with a distinguished record at the National and R.S.C., but he was no household name. His agent told him that this television role would 'really put you on the map'. Jason, who had long ago stopped believing in his agent's manufactured optimism, was content to do an interesting job which would not harm his career.

There were moments, however—brief ones admittedly—when he wished he hadn't taken the part. Letters are intended to be read silently and Walpole's sinuous sentences were as hard to speak out loud as they were to learn by heart. Nevertheless, they had their fascination: *Shall I even confess to you what was the origin of this romance? I waked one morning in the beginning of last June from a dream, of which all I could recover was, that I had thought myself in an ancient castle (a very natural dream for a head filled like mine with Gothic story) and that on the uppermost banister of a great staircase I saw a gigantic hand in armour. In the evening I sat down and began to write, without knowing in the least what I intended to say or relate . . .*

As befitting Walpole's fascination with the Gothic, the filming was to take place over two days at Charnley Abbey in Worcestershire. The building, which had begun life as a monastery, was handed over at the time of the Dissolution by Henry

VIII to one Barnaby Gedge for unknown 'services rendered'. The Gedge family began to rise in the world and took the more aristocratic sounding name of Gauge. In 1610 Nicholas Gauge, now a considerable landowner, had bought a baronetcy from James I, and the family saw the apogee of its splendour—if not its wealth—in the mid to late eighteenth century with Sir Augustus Gauge. Sir Augustus, known as 'Gothic Gauge', had taken the Grand Tour, bought art and antiquities, had himself painted by Batoni in Rome reclining pensively on a fallen column, and returned to beautify Charnley Abbey. But Charnley, being an ancient, rambling structure, did not take kindly to the Italianate Baroque, so it was a source of relief to Sir Augustus when Horace Walpole and his *Castle of Otranto* ushered in a taste for the medieval. The Abbey was refurbished in this fashionable style, and very charming and picturesque and expensive it all was.

Thereafter the Gauge family declined into undistinguished hard-hunting squirearchy. The Abbey became increasingly costly to maintain, and the National Trust did not think it sufficiently important to take on. In the late twentieth century various schemes had been tried to keep the building in the family (and vice versa) with varying degrees of success. Since the mid 1970s Charnley Abbey had been a gourmet restaurant, a religious retreat house, a garden centre, and an exhibition space for local crafts. Wedding receptions were held in its Great Hall and films were shot in and around it. As a result, the Abbey, despite its venerable antiquity, gave off an aura of scruffy impermanence. The Gauges kept themselves to a small and reasonably commodious portion of the West Wing which had been rebuilt after a fire in the 1920s, while the rest of the house, a wilderness of dusty chambers full of mildewed furniture and neglected pictures, was left to those who paid for the privilege of using it.

On the first day of filming Jason was summoned at five o'clock from his Fulham flat and driven down by hired car to Charnley. He slept most of the way and when he arrived, a little after seven on a fresh June morning, the Abbey was looking its best. It sprawled along a fold in the land, like an old grey cat sleeping out its remaining days in the sun. The park, laid out by Repton in 1790, with its lake and picturesque clumps of woodland, afforded a perfect setting. The rolling lawns flashed emerald in the sharp morning light and the high clouds chased each other across a blue sky full of lark song. This was immemorial England. Jason's heart rose. A deep, romantic love of beauty was one of the beacons of his life, but he kept it hidden, believing that such things became fragile when exposed to the scrutiny of others.

The effect was a little marred when, as the car came down the drive, Jason could see a cluster of vehicles in front of the Abbey's main entrance: a catering van, the Director's Saab, a 'people carrier', and two BBC lorries vomiting cable onto the gravel. As soon as Jason got out of the car he was accosted by the Production Assistant, a dumpy girl with large breasts and an intense expression, called Mo. She immediately bustled him away to be dressed, wigged and made up. Jason would have preferred a few moments in the sun with a coffee and a bacon sandwich from the catering van, but he knew that the waiting would have to be done in costume. Production Assistants can be shouted at if their charges are not ready whenever the Director needs them. In the Production Assistant's ideal world actors will be chained to railings ready for use, like bicycles.

Forty-five minutes later Jason came out of the scullery, which had been made into a temporary dressing and make-up room. He was wearing a powdered wig and a suit of plum coloured velvet with white stockings and diamanté buckled shoes. He strutted around a little muttering his lines and tentatively ate his bacon sandwich with a paper napkin covering the lace at his throat. Mo told him that the director would not need him for another half hour, as he was just getting some outside establishing shots, but that Jason was not to move. Jason smiled pleasantly at Mo and, as soon as she was out of sight, decided to take a walk.

The air was still and the sun was already hot even though it was just after eight. Jason had begun to itch and sweat in his velvet, so he wondered if he might not be cooler indoors. This was the case. He was soothed by the chill which pervaded Charnley Abbey even in the hottest months of the year. Outside on the gravel among the vans and the electric cable he felt out of place in his velvet; inside among the dusty remnants of the past his buckled shoes gave off an authentic echo. He wandered from room to room of the old Abbey, sometimes mumbling his lines, sometimes taking in the atmosphere, always alone. In one of the long galleries he got a shock as he inadvertently caught sight of himself far off in a dusky Venetian mirror. In the silvery archipelagos which still clung to the inside of the ancient bevelled glass, he saw a man with a long, clever face under a white wig, one hand holding his script in a scroll, the other resting nonchalantly on his hip. Unconsciously he had been imitating the pose of a grandee in some portrait by Reynolds or Ramsay. The very authenticity of his appearance gave him another start. It was as if he had seen a ghost, and then the ghost had turned out to be himself.

In his wanderings Jason found a small room at the end of the house which seemed even more dusty and neglected than the rest. A single window looked onto the back lawn where the director was filming an academic who was explaining how

Horace Walpole had helped to usher in the Romantic movement.

Jason guessed that the room he had entered had once been a dressing room or boudoir since it gave onto a larger chamber which contained nothing but the grey carcass of a four-poster bed. The room itself was crammed with unwanted furniture and other objects, but not quite crammed enough to make it seem like a mere lumber-room. Jason could see that some of the objects so unceremoniously stored there were valuable and wondered how they had come to be so neglected. He knew a little about antiques because one of his part-time jobs when out of work was to help a friend with a stall in the Portobello Road market.

There was a Georgian tallboy and several elegant chairs whose upholstery had exploded. Some fine but faded damask hangings had been bundled carelessly into a corner; a packing case held a complete leather bound edition of Voltaire. Propped against one wall was a stack of framed pictures. They were mostly eighteenth century engravings and mezzotints, all of quality but most of them torn and foxed, but under these was a small oil painting in an elaborate gilt frame, no more than eighteen inches by twelve. Age had encrusted the canvas with grime and a small wooden plaque on the frame proclaimed its title: *IN ARCADIA.*

For all the dirt Jason could see that it was a good painting. The scene depicted was a woodland glade through which wound a serpentine path. To one side an old man in a brown tunic and sandals reclined, resting against a rock. A crook on the ground beside him indicated that he was a shepherd. He was staring intently at the other side of the path where stood a grey slab of stone on which something indecipherable had been written. The trees were restless and wild, and behind them a dark blue sky threatened by grey thunderclouds could be seen. The landscape, at once both idyllic and menacing, was clearly the work of a master.

Turning the picture over he found a label on which in faint sepia ink had been written the words: *Gaspr Poussin pinxit Roma Ao MDCLXXV*. The inscription puzzled Jason. He knew Poussin to have been a famous painter, but he had a vague recollection that his Christian name was Nicolas, not the mysterious 'Gaspr'. But it was old. The Roman numerals gave him the date 1675.

A crack in the frame at the bottom and two broken lengths of wire attached to the back suggested that the painting had fallen off a wall and no-one had taken the small trouble to replace the wire and hang it up again.

Suddenly Jason heard his name being called. He put the picture back where it had been hidden behind the engravings and left the room. When Mo asked him crossly where he had been Jason replied evasively that he had been rehearsing his lines.

The first day went well. Most of the time Jason was filmed seated at a desk, chewing a quill pen and looking quizzically at the camera. He remembered his lines and made the most of his sly, sidelong glance. There was very little left for Jason to do on the second day except some shots of Walpole with a few extras showing them his cabinets of curios, expatiating on the delights of the Gothic and gossiping with dowagers.

As he was driven to the hotel where he was to be put up that night Jason ought to have felt complete satisfaction, but the painting he had discovered kept clawing at his mind. It annoyed him that something of such artistic merit should have been left, dirty and discarded, in an upper room. Perhaps he ought to tell the owners about it, but this would mean having to admit that he had been snooping around. His slender knowledge of the upper classes told him that such an intrusion would be treated with scornful resentment. It was at that point that the notion of taking the painting for himself began to form in his mind. (The word 'stealing' was kept at bay.) Nobody might ever notice that it had gone, or care if they did notice.

That was as far as his thinking went that night. He put the issue to the back of his mind and concentrated on enjoying the luxuries of his hotel. He would have liked to have spent some time making friends with the Director, but the Director was otherwise occupied. Jason had the unpleasant but fascinating experience of watching the Director make a long and affectionate mobile phone call to his wife and children in the bar, followed almost immediately by the successful seduction of Mo, with whom he soon disappeared for an early night. The actor-observer in Jason compelled him to watch, as, of course, did the prurient voyeur.

The weather held the following morning, but there was a good deal of waiting around. The extras, who had arrived late by coach, had to be dressed and grouped and regimented. For all the authenticity of their costume, there was something insistently twentieth century about their appearance. Jason took care not to wander off too far, but his thoughts kept returning to the picture. His overnight bag was stowed in the dressing room at the Abbey and there was room in it for the picture.

Everyone broke for an early lunch. The extras crowded up to the catering van, but Jason held back. He did not want to be part of the herd. His aloofness was rewarded because the Director, who happened to be passing, introduced him to a man in a tweed jacket and fawn corduroy trousers. The man was in his fifties, balding and run to seed, but he gave the impression of someone who still thought of himself as young and attractive.

This, said the Director, was Sir Ralph Gauge, present owner of Charnley Abbey. Jason took an instant dislike to him.

Sir Ralph's manner towards Jason was offhandedly condescending to the point of rudeness. When Jason explained that he had been speaking to the camera extracts from Horace Walpole's letters which he had learned by heart, Sir Ralph laughed knowingly. He knew that television actors never learned their lines, they just read them off a screen—what was it called?—the 'autocue', that was it. Jason patiently told him that it was not the case, but Sir Ralph said that he couldn't fool him. At this point, the Director, observing a rather dangerous look in Jason's eye, intervened to say that, as a matter of fact, in this case, they weren't using autocues on the production. Pretending to ignore the Director's interruption, Sir Ralph then felt Jason's velvet costume and said that you could really pull the girls wearing this sort of thing, couldn't you? Very sixties. Jason smiled and said what a fascinating place Charnley Abbey was.

'Bloody nightmare to keep going,' said Sir Ralph, stifling a yawn. 'Well, must be off to see a man about a horse.' And he walked away. A few minutes later there was a roar and Sir Ralph wearing a tweed cap swept up the drive in an open-topped sports car. He must have been very dashing thirty years ago, Jason thought sourly.

It was this encounter, Jason decided later, that had compelled him to go and take the little painting. Sir Ralph was a philistine and he did not deserve it, whereas Jason, who had no intention of selling it, would cherish the object. So, before the lunch hour was over, Jason had fetched his over-night bag from his dressing room, slung it carelessly by the strap over his shoulder, strolled up to the little antechamber, taken the painting out from behind the pile of old engravings, put it in the bag with barely a glance at it and strolled downstairs again. As he did so, he found himself trembling violently, but otherwise he felt cool and collected. He returned the bag to his dressing room unobserved.

The last shots after lunch were so hectic that Jason barely had time to think of his acquisition until he was in the car being driven back to London. Then he was compelled to face the fact that for the first time in his adult life he had committed a blatantly illegal act. Jason tried to analyse his feelings dispassionately, as he often did in times of high emotional tension. He felt keyed-up, more than usually alive, but he also felt the fear of possible discovery and some guilt. There were plenty of arguments to be made against his feeling guilt, but he could not help feeling it. He had broken one of the commandments; he was a thief.

He would have liked to discuss the whole affair with someone, but he could not think of anybody suitable. Jason was going through a period of solitude having broken up with a girl two months ago. In any case, he knew what they would say. 'Take it back,' they would say, and he was damned if he was going to.

When he got home, he took the painting out of his bag, wrapped it carefully in some bubble wrap and put it in a drawer. He had thought too much about it and was not going to do any more of that until the next morning. That night he managed to distract himself with a visit to the pub and a film on television. He even slept well enough except that once he woke up with a phrase repeating itself over and over in his head: *Et in Arcadia Ego*. The phrase nagged at him as words do when they come at one from the other side of consciousness.

'And I too am in Arcadia': that was the literal meaning. The inner meaning, said Jason's dictionary of quotations, was obscure, but this anonymous saying was to be found on tombs. 'Even I am in Arcadia', was another rendering. It was clear to

Jason, if not the dictionary of quotations, who or rather what the 'I' was.

Jason took the painting out of the drawer and propped it up on his mantelpiece. He fetched some warm soapy water and with a damp cloth gently began to wipe away the dirt. Where the paint had been applied more thickly he used cotton buds in the same solution. The cleaning of the picture was a delightful, absorbing task which occupied the whole morning. Slowly the work revealed itself, gem-like in its vividness. Never had Jason seen such an intensely dark blue sky, such green and gold in the trees which sparkled in a slanted afternoon sun. (It could have been early morning, but Jason was sure it was meant to be late afternoon. There was something in the attitude of the old shepherd which suggested rest after a long day.) Jason's apprehension and guilt were drowned in the wonder of holding in his hands an authentic masterpiece. The artist had captured a moment, not a single frozen instant, as in a photograph, but a fragment of time just long enough to contain a tiny vibration of real life. The watching mind oscillated within the picture between repose and anxiety.

One moment you felt the melancholy calm of an old man resting in a forest glade enjoying the rays of a declining sun; the next moment the twisted trees and glittering leaves suggested a sudden gust of wind and you saw the dark grey cloud in the blue sky beyond. The air seemed to crackle with the electricity of an approaching storm; then your mind reverted once more to melancholy calm.

Jason was glad now that he had appropriated the picture. Nothing would ever take away from him the intense experience he had just enjoyed with this three hundred year old piece of wood and canvas, not even a prison sentence. But there was one small frustration. He had hoped that careful cleaning would have revealed the inscription on the grey stone which the old shepherd was staring at in the picture, but he could not make it out. Tiny dark strokes of paint suggested lettering vividly without being in any way comprehensible. *Et in Arcadia Ego* perhaps? No, he could not make that fit.

In two weeks time Jason had a part in *The Bill*, so he felt entitled to a break, and he had decided that what he must do was to find out as much as he could about the picture and its painter. The desire came partly from guilt—if he knew more about it he would be able to persuade himself that he deserved the object—partly from a wholly unspecified compulsion which seemed to emanate from the picture itself.

As an actor, Jason was someone whose powers of concentration were above average, but he was surprised by the length of time he could spend simply looking at the picture. It began to alarm him that an hour or two might pass in this way, at the end of which he had only a very indistinct memory of what he had been thinking. After one or two of these sessions, he found that the picture's image was etched onto his mind and formed an almost permanent background to his thought. It was like the tune that keeps playing itself inside one's head.

Researches in the library of the Victoria and Albert Museum, revealed Gaspr. Poussin to have been Gaspard Dughet, sometimes known as Gaspard Poussin, who worked mainly in Italy and died at Rome in 1675. He had painted classical landscapes, somewhat in the manner of the more famous Nicolas Poussin, to whom he had been apprenticed, but often with stormy or overcast skies. The books spoke of him with respect, but essentially as a somewhat derivative minor figure. Jason could find no reference to *In Arcadia*.

The information he had gathered did not satisfy Jason as he had hoped it would. The one fact which haunted him was that

In Arcadia was, if the label on the back was correct, painted in the year of the artist's death. Could it have been his last work? Could the old shepherd, sitting exhausted by the roadside have been Gaspard himself? Jason was aware that this was the kind of gloss an old-fashioned art critic might have put upon it, attributing all kinds of personal references to a public work with an accepted iconography. He had read that in the seventeenth century artists were not individualists as they are now, and therefore *In Arcadia* need not be Gaspard contemplating his own death any more than Prospero drowning his book was Shakespeare renouncing the stage.

He was aware of this intellectually, but he could not deny that the picture had a power of suggestion quite beyond that of conventional classical imagery. Was it perhaps his own state of mind which had induced the extraordinarily intense relationship he had developed with the painting?

On the evening of his return from the Victoria and Albert Museum, Jason sat down before the painting, much as, on another lonely evening, he might have sat down in front of the television. For the first hour or so, he contemplated the picture as he had before, his thoughts slowing almost to a standstill before it. Then something started to happen, something which, even in his hypnotic state, disturbed him. Though he remained seated, a part of him began to move towards the painting. He might have thought that he was dreaming except that his mental faculties seemed fully alive. In fact he felt more fully conscious of himself than ever before.

That consciousness presented him with a choice. He could either draw himself back into his body, his flat in Fulham and the twenty-first century, or he could move forward. He chose the unsafe option and drifted forward, as if pushed by a gentle breeze.

When he reached the surface of the painting, he halted. He had reached a two dimensional plane and he knew he could go no further. For a space of time which could not be calculated in minutes or seconds he studied the canvas in detail. Every brush stroke, every tiny gradation of pigment was revealed to him. But even as he studied these minutiae, he was conscious of waiting for something. A change was about to take place. Then it happened.

Slowly the varnished surface of the canvas began to soften. Jason was aware that the source of light had changed too. Instead of coming from outside the picture and striking its pigmented surface, the light now seemed to come from within. Colours glowed. The next thing he noticed was that objects on the surface of the plane had begun to move in a strange way, shifting somehow and yet remaining in the same place. He could not understand it until he realised that the two dimensional surface was being transformed into a three dimensional space. Very soon he would be able to walk into the picture.

Once again he was presented with a choice. He could stay outside looking into the picture like a spectator in a darkened auditorium gazing at a lighted stage set, or he could move forward. He chose the unsafe option.

The landscape into which he moved was absolutely familiar, except that it was solid and three-dimensional. It was quite static, but not as a statue is: Jason felt that the animation of its trees and the old shepherd, who was some distance away from him on the path, was merely suspended. It was an entrancing prospect. Moments in a normal life succeed each other relentlessly without pausing to allow themselves to be considered. Here Jason could bite this moment to the core.

Before he could do so he was made aware of his own state. Up till this point, he had thought of himself as a disembodied being, as when, in a waking dream, one seems to float bodiless over wide miles of vivid scenery. Now he appeared to be recovering some physical senses besides that of sight. He could hear, though a great way off, the sound of London traffic which pervaded his flat. He began to feel a faint breeze on what he thought was his cheek. A numb pins-and-needles sensation affected him, as if he had some kind of body. Looking down he saw a pair of bare legs, identifiably his, and feet shod with sandals, standing on the yellow dust of the road. He was dressed in a rough brown tunic, like the ancient shepherd in the picture.

As he took his first steps down the path two things happened. Firstly, the faint noise of London traffic vanished; secondly, he began to acquire sensation in all his limbs. His hands seemed particularly sensitive: he could feel a tiny speck of dust and roll it between his thumb and forefinger.

The silence was complete; everything about him was still unmoving. The only movement came from him, because, as he moved down the path, he began to see things from a different angle. The trees were bent and their leaves twisted as if in a wind but they were still. Only the glint of the low sun which Jason could now see had an animated quality to it. The beauty which surrounded him both entranced and oppressed him. He felt that it was his task to bring it to life.

The sheer oddity of what he was experiencing struck him and he turned round to see if his room in Fulham was still behind him. He saw nothing, only a white mist. How was he to get back? The question did not disturb him too much. Apart from his role in *The Bill* (of an ex-public school drug addict) he had little to return to. How puzzled people would be by his disappearance! The idea amused him.

He turned back to his landscape and walked quickly down the path towards the old man. The path snaked so that his journey took him longer than he expected. When he reached the old man he bent down to look at him. The man was motionless but his eyes shone. Jason touched the man's tunic and immediately he began to stir. Jason, suddenly full of an almost unbearable fear, stayed quite still. All around him he could hear things stirring into life, wind blowing, branches creaking, leaves rustling, a distant murmur of thunder, the song of a strange bird. The old man blinked and stared at him without curiosity. The face was old and grey bearded, but the deep-sunk eyes betrayed nothing. Jason felt he could animate him by speech, so he addressed him:

'Who are you?'

The old man stretched out a hand and pointed to a spot behind Jason, who turned round to see what was being pointed out. It was the grey slab, like a tombstone, on the other side of the path. He crossed over to examine the slab and saw the letters carved on it:

> βουλοιμην κ επαρουρος εων θητευεμεν αλλω
> η πασιν νεκυεσσι καταφθιμενοισιν ανασσειν

Though normally the letters would have meant nothing to him, in his heightened state he understood, but their inner meaning still baffled him:

> I would rather be a serf working by the day for another
> than be the prince of all the dead.

He looked back at the shepherd resting by the roadside, but the figure had gone. This disturbed him, because the old man had been a stable physical presence in this strange world that he had entered. Moreover when he looked behind him at the way by which he had entered the painting, there was no longer a white mist but yet more Elysian landscape. Twisted trees fluttered their golden leaves in the declining sun. The snaking path wound up a gentle slope to where stood a white marble temple on a mound before a grove of oak.

Jason decided to walk to the temple. It was the only recognisably human element that he could see, and even that possessed a certain inhuman perfection. It occurred to him that he might be trapped forever in this beautiful but somehow threatening world. He did not think that he would wake up and find himself again in Fulham; he felt too alive for that. As far as he could understand it he had found his way into another dimension of existence; but whose?

It was an odd question, that 'whose?', because as long as he lived in one world—the Fulham world—such curiosity had not existed. The question would have been meaningless, because there was nothing else. Now it seemed full of significance, even though its answer was quite beyond him.

At each step he took, the view seemed to compose itself into another classical landscape. It was as if he had walked into not one but an infinity of pictures, each one a subtly varying depiction of the same exquisite but melancholy mood. No one scene in the Fulham world had the same monolithic intensity; a hundred moods competed for attention within it.

Sounds were slight and precious to his ears. The breeze fumbled at his skin and rustled the trees. No animal noises could be heard, beyond that one invisible bird. His own feet on the path were loud and jarring. When he stopped he listened intently and could just discern, behind the wind, another very faint sound. It was a twittering, that was the only way he could describe it, but he was sure that it was not birds. Could it have been bats or insects? A moment of synaesthesia gave him a mental image of thousands of tiny sparks of light, each of a distinct shape and colour, each with its distinctive tone, whirling in a black void. Then the moment passed and he could barely hear the twittering. He continued on his way to the temple.

In the declining sun the temple's white crystalline marble shone almost like gold. It was of Roman design with an ionic porch attached to a plain rotunda domed with dull green copper which indicated the occasional presence of rain in this strange land. Jason could make out two bronze coffered doors standing ajar under the porch. The inscription on the cornice under the pediment was: ET IN ARCADIA EGO.

He mounted the marble steps and entered the cool portico. As he did so he was invaded by a strong sensation of loneliness, an intensification of melancholy so extreme that it was no longer pleasant. However something drove him on to penetrate the mystery of the place and he walked through the bronze doors into the rotunda.

The coffered ceiling had a circular opening at the apex which let in a slanted column of light from the sky above. At the very centre of the rotunda under the opening stood a gigantic sarcophagus of black marble on a granite dais. It was highly polished and its shape was that of a giant bath with a dome-like lid on top of it. The walls were of polished marble and, at eye level, around the inner circumference of the building there ran a circular frieze in bas relief, crisply and exquisitely carved. The stone from which it was carved was grey, delicately veined with streaks of silver that seemed to heighten details.

The scenes depicted at first made no sense until he found that it was possible to read the sequence of events starting to the right of the door and working round in an anti-clockwise direction.

It began with a naked man lying apparently on his deathbed. Around him men and women in classical dress stood or knelt in traditional attitudes of mourning. The carving had the decorous correctness of a Flaxman, except for a figure to be glimpsed behind the others who was half hiding a laughing mouth behind his hand. Standing apart from this group to the left, a tall veiled figure beckoned a bony finger.

In the next tableau the same man who had been lying on his deathbed was being dragged down a rocky path by the veiled figure now stooping. Its face, half hidden was sunken and skull-like, the eye sockets empty.

As Jason moved round the frieze he saw that the man had now reached the banks of a river where a number of other naked souls stood disconsolately, waiting for the boat. This vessel, punted by a misshapen giant, was propelled through the turbulent waters of Styx in which indistinct figures swam or floundered. One of these clutched at the side of the boat with a weak arm, but it was clear that one of the men in the boat was about to strike at the arm with a stone.

On the other side of the water stood Cerberus, the three headed dog with his tail of snakes, and beyond this a group stood before two masked figures on thrones carved with their names, Minos and Rhadamanthus, the judges of the underworld. One held a pair of scales, the other a sword.

Up till this point, the carvings had been expressive in a somewhat detached way, but the sequence of events seemed orderly and comprehensible. A propriety had been observed. About half way round the rotunda, events depicted became increasingly chaotic and bizarre, even though the classical style of execution had not altered.

Behind Minos and Rhadamanthus a tight mass of people were being pushed into a tiny aperture between two great blocks of dressed stone. The people were being moved by strange creatures, human in the composition of their limbs but so thin and elongated they looked more like insects. These same beings were pushing the blocks of stone together to crush the people they had driven into the aperture. In another scene a group of men and women, emaciated and hungry-looking, sat around a stone table, staring in horror at a single plate. On the plate was an amorphous mass, out of which projected something like an arm which waved a podgy mocking hand at them. Then came a grove of trees through which naked men and women were running in fear pursued by creatures with human heads that went on all fours. Other scenes followed in which people were apparently being forced to enact futile and repetitive tasks. A scene that struck Jason with quite unreasonable horror was one in which a man and woman were being measured by birds with long arms instead of wings. Every intimate part of their bodies was being inspected. On their faces was a look of agonised resignation and despair.

In the last quarter of the relief there was more tranquillity. It was signalled by the depiction of a field of long grass, each blade sharply delineated on the stone, as thin as threads. A few tall plants of asphodel relieved the monotony of the landscape, and the carver had cunningly managed to indicate infinite distance, despite the monochrome of his material. One or two figures were walking through this field though most sat or reclined.

The walkers, predominantly male, wore classical armour and carried weapons. They seemed to represent enthusiasts for the active life, and their faces showed vigour and determination as they wandered about, all in different directions. Those seated or reclining wore flowing classical robes. There were senators in togas, matrons with their heads decorously covered. Their features were serenely regular, but maintained a tenuous individuality. A little apart, a group of bearded men sat on thrones disputing with each other; while a similar collection of women span, sewed and embroidered. Some figures seemed sunk in deep thought while others gazed about them vacantly. None of those depicted had anguish on their faces, but none seemed actively happy. Resignation and boredom were the predominant moods. Jason found the scene so lifeless and oppressive that he almost preferred the depictions of torment and chaos which had preceded it.

At the very end of the frieze near the door was a final figure in higher relief than the rest of the carvings. It was the image of a man seated on a stone and facing the viewer directly. He was elderly and clean-shaven, with hair almost down to his shoulders. He was not in classical dress like the rest, but wore a loose shirt with a wide collar, baggy breaches and buckled shoes. He looked like a skilled artisan of the seventeenth or early eighteenth century. His stare was almost alive and Jason recognised a powerful similarity between it and the look of the figure on the path that he had met when he first entered the painting. In the man's lap lay a scroll on which four lines of Latin were written whose sound and rhythm alone were like the tolling of a melancholy bell:

Omnes eodem cogimur, omnium
versatur urna serius ocius
sors exitura et nos in aeternum
exsilium impositura cumbae.

'All of us are thither compelled. Everyone's lot tumbles in the urn, destined sooner or later to fall out, and then we are bundled onto the boat of eternal exile.'

Horace, *Odes*, thought Jason, wondering slightly that he had remembered his long forgotten Latin so well. But at that moment a noise distracted him, so loud and violent it sounded like the whole fabric of the world being torn apart.

It was the grating and screeching of stone grinding against stone. Jason turned and saw that the lid of the great sarcophagus in the middle of the temple was moving. He ran to the bronze doors which, with a sudden gust of evening wind from the landscape beyond, blew shut. No force could open them. Jason turned to face the dreadful noise which re-echoed round the building, high pitched, almost like human agony.

The lid of the sarcophagus had slid far enough to reveal a small black hole, but not what was moving it. Then a thing emerged that looked at first like a great metal worm, then another, and another, until he saw that they were the fingers of a huge hand covered in some dull pewter-like metal. The hand pushed aside the lid of the sarcophagus which crashed onto the floor and shivered into great sharp fragments. One of them shot across the floor and stopped a few inches away from Jason's feet. The hand seemed to feel blindly about the edges of the sarcophagus. Jason could see now that it was like the hand of a medieval knight in plate armour. It groped vainly for a few more moments, then withdrew into the dark interior of its tomb. Jason stood transfixed, hardly daring to think, let alone move; then he remembered the passage from Horace Walpole's letters about dreaming of the 'gigantic hand in armour', and it reassured him. It meant that whatever he was experiencing, at least some of it belonged to his own subconscious. If he was living through a peculiarly vivid 'lucid dream' experience, then he could presumably control it. And yet the reality of what he had experienced so far had seemed peculiarly unsubjective. Perhaps this was insanity. On balance, however, Jason was encouraged and he contemplated the image of the great hand and the broken tomb with less fear. He even speculated on its

Jungian archetypal significance, as the iron fist of Romanticism breaking out of the classical sarcophagus, and he remembered how during a brief period of his life when he was under the spell of Jung he had started to have Jungian dreams.

But it was hard to maintain complete calm because what he felt was so vivid. The thought that he might actually be dead occurred to him, and he was filled again with fear. What could have killed him then? You don't die from looking at a picture.

There was a time of paralysis during which fear retreated, but also all hope. He felt overwhelmed by the strangeness of his situation and reacted to it by withdrawing into himself so that he began to feel like a tiny prisoner trapped in his own body. His legs started to shake and he wondered if he could stand up much longer. This was the turning point. He realised that he had nothing to lose by action, everything to lose by the despairing torpor into which he was drifting.

His first task was to get out of the temple. He tried the bronze doors several times, but they were irrevocably shut and had no handles on the inside. He tried the surrounding walls for secret entrances, or some concealed instrument to open the doors, but found nothing. Evening was coming on apace and the sky visible through the circular hole above the sarcophagus was turning to a star-strewn violet.

One world may have no meaning, but two must have, because a meaning is a relationship. The world in which Jason found himself was somehow contingent on the other one, the one which he still called, with increasing lack of conviction, 'the real world'. There had been a way in; there must be a way out. At this point in his reasoning, Jason realised that he must try the only way out which was open to him and that was to enter the broken sarcophagus.

For a long while he paused, suspended in the classical calm of his surroundings, knowing that he must not stay, and not wishing to. Darkness was falling and soon he would be barely able to see where to go. The atmosphere oppressed him so that he knew he had to escape; at the same time it weighed him down and kept him from taking action. Fear held him too until he was able to detach himself sufficiently from his feelings to drag his body towards the tomb.

When he had climbed onto the broken sarcophagus he stared down into it. What he saw beneath him was a restless darkness, a blackness in which tides of even greater blackness were eddying to and fro. The air was full of shiftings and whisperings. He leaned over still further in an agony of indecision, then suddenly out of the black came the giant iron hand, seized him and dragged him down into the void.

After the initial shock, Jason became calmer. He was held securely, though not without some discomfort and he was moving. He could not tell in what direction he was moving, only that he was, because he felt a wind rushing against him and presently he saw tiny spots of light moving past, like the sparks of a bonfire on the evening breeze. They eddied and swirled slightly and seemed to be of all kinds of colours, sometimes, small as they were, of many colours together.

After a while he became aware that these sparks had sounds attached to them and that their tones mingled and blended together in a curious harmony whose shape he almost caught, but which remained elusive. Then it seemed to him that the spark sounds were not mere things but animated thoughts and that if only all these fragments could be bound together they would become one single thought. He heard them crying out together for unity, yet never achieving it in the hurrying dark. As he strained his eyes to focus on one of them it seemed to him that these sparks were not near to him but very far off and that the nearest of them had a shape. What shape he could not tell until one of them happened to come by close enough for him to see, no more than a mile or so he guessed. It had a human shape.

Suddenly he was flung down on the ground. It was not very hard, but yielding, almost soft and composed of huge flakes of something. Above him the sparks still swirled and twittered in the cosmic winds while at his feet he was conscious of a faint grey light like the beginning of dawn.

The flakes on which he had fallen seemed to be sheets of paper and he could walk across them with some difficulty. As he looked about him, his world began to take shape. The faint grey light seemed to originate from one source towards which Jason began to walk.

It was a long walk, that was all Jason could say afterwards, because time in this universe had lost its precise meaning. As he experienced it, it could have been months, years or centuries, and in that time he exhausted every thought and memory that he possessed. He wondered if, like those legendary enraptured monks, or the seven sleepers of Ephesus, he would emerge into his world again years after he had left it with everyone thinking he was dead.

Slowly, slowly the light grew until he could see what he was walking on. They were pieces of paper, thousands, millions of them stretching out to the dim horizon in all directions. Picking one up he saw that it had been drawn on, an exquisite little sketch of a rock and two silver birches, their branches intertwined, their leaves blowing slightly in the wind. He held onto it and picked up another. Here was a drawing in sanguine of a valley at evening with a classical temple and some shepherds feeding their flocks, another beautiful thing. He picked up another piece of paper and another, each one of which had a drawing on it of extraordinary excellence. All the drawings showed either fragments of nature, or classical scenes and figures. Jason could have spent hours, years with them, but he felt the need to press on towards the light. He dropped the other drawings, and kept the one he had picked up of the rock and the silver birches, remembering that in some other life Anthony Blunt, scholar and traitor, had called Gaspard Dughet 'the Silver Birch Master'.

On, on towards the light, and in the light Jason saw a seated figure, the original of the seated figure he had seen at the end of the frieze in the temple. As he sat the figure drew on a piece of paper and when he had finished it to his satisfaction he let it fall and then picked up another piece of paper to draw on. He never stopped; he seemed compelled to draw and draw until time itself had an end. When Jason had come close to him he at last looked up.

Jason wanted to speak but could not. His eyes met those of the Silver Birch Master—Jason was sure it was him—and rested for a long time in them. The man's eyes were infinitely tired and Jason felt a wave of pity for him so strong it seemed to be both inside and outside him at the same time. It blew like the wind and as his compassion raged, the million drawings which carpeted the landscape were swept upwards into the surrounding air like a blizzard. Thunder rumbled in the distance.

As Jason's passion subsided, so did the turbulence. The drawings fell to the ground and the air became brighter. The Old Master whom Jason knew to be Dughet rose up from his seat. There seemed to be a new gleam of purpose in his eye. He pointed to his right and there through the white mist Jason could see the scene which he had originally entered, the picture *In Arcadia.* Then the Master pointed to his left and there, dim, very distant, Jason could see the living room of his absurd little Fulham flat.

The Master seemed to be offering him a choice: to go back into the glow of Arcadia, or to return to his flat, flat in more than one sense of the word. Jason did not hesitate, however; he turned right towards Fulham. Once he looked back and saw that the Master had left his seat. Where he had gone he did not see.

Many years later it seemed to Jason that he was awake once again in his own London room, seated in front of the painting, and the clock had only ticked on half an hour or so. He would have believed that he had experienced little more than a peculiarly vivid dream. That was what he urgently wanted to believe, but he was prevented from doing so by the fact that he found he was still holding a piece of paper on which was an exquisite drawing of a rock and some silver birches.

He decided at that moment that he must return *In Arcadia* to its rightful owner as soon as possible.

℘

The only question was how. Eventually he took the simplest, most cowardly course. He wrapped the picture up, wearing gloves the whole time, and sent the parcel off to Sir Ralph Gauge at Charnley Abbey from a busy post office in North London, far from his Fulham flat. He even put on a light disguise to do so. Together with the picture he had included a note written in capitals on a blank sheet of paper.

> 'I found this at the Abbey and am returning it to you. It is a fine example of the work of Gaspard Dughet—sometimes known as Gaspard Poussin—1615-1675.'

On receiving his picture back, Sir Ralph immediately put it up for sale at Christie's where it fetched a handsome price, as it recommended itself to potential buyers both by its artistic merit and by the publicity which it had attracted. A good deal was made of its mysterious discovery and return in the newspapers. THIEF WITH A CONSCIENCE read one of the headlines, though some more cynical commentators thought that the thief was returning the picture because he couldn't sell it. Suspicion fell briefly on the academic who had been filmed at Charnley Abbey talking about Walpole, but no action was taken as no crime had been reported at the time. Jason was neither mentioned, nor interviewed by the press, as he was an unknown actor and obviously ignorant of everything except acting.

With the money he got from the picture Sir Ralph bought a steeplechaser which broke a leg in the Grand National and had to be destroyed. But Jason's career flourished after a fashion. The small success of his Horace Walpole convinced the casting directors (an unimaginative breed) that he was an expert at eighteenth century roles. Consequently, the following year found him playing Sir Joshua Reynolds in a Channel 4 film about his alleged rivalry with Gainsborough.

While researching for the role Jason read Reynolds' *Discourses to the Royal Academy*. In the famous 'Sixteenth Discourse' he came across the following passage written in Reynolds's typically lumbering, Johnsonian prose:

> . . . or like the celebrated Roman artist Gaspard Poussin, who believed, not solely that his fame would be immortalised in his work, but that he himself, soul and body, might mysteriously live for ever in it. He assured himself that, by means of certain occult operations, his spirit might enter one of his own sylvan idylls, and there dwell through all eternity, pleasantly enjoying the fruits of his artful imagination. It is credulously believed by

some that he achieved this, for the death of this Master was indeed attended by no little mystery, and there is said to be a work in which he eternally resides, though no man has determined which. I am obliged to that learned virtuoso, my friend Sir Augustus Gauge Bt., for this curious legend.

EVIL EYE

A week after he had returned from the States Alex invited me out for a drink at Freek's, the wine bar nearest our office. Alex was a high flyer and one of the youngest art directors in DH Associates; I was just a humble copywriter, but we got on, sort of. I don't mind being patronised.

When we got to Freek's Alex ordered a bottle of Bollinger. It was not that unusual: Alex tended to go over the top. Work hard, play hard, he used to say and it showed. Not that he was bad looking; according to some of the girls in the office he was definitely fanciable. He was dark—very shiny gelled black hair—

and dressed sharp in dark suits. Big brown eyes with long lashes which the girls liked; but he was a bit podgy. He was pale and puffy and sweated a lot. On the other hand he was smart, no question, and everyone predicted a brilliant future.

I could tell at once he was worked up, bursting to confide in someone, and I suppose I was the nearest available dumping ground. For a few minutes we talked about the States where he'd been for six months working with DH's parent company, learning management strategies, new marketing techniques, all that stuff. I could see he was just delaying the inevitable. At last he revealed what was on his mind:

'You remember that video surveillance system we did a campaign for last year?'

'*Hidden Eye*?'

'That's the one.' I remembered it well. As copywriter, I had come up with literally hundreds of different lines for them, all to do with eyes, though ears came into it as well. I won't embarrass you with the results. Hidden Eye was the very latest in home security. It was a state-of-the-art 'intelligent' surveillance system which could be programmed just like an alarm. Movement, light or noise acting as the trigger, as soon as something in the room changed, it would start recording. It would only stop when the thing that had made it start, stopped and then after half an hour of immobility. The sound system had the intelligent capacity for editing out background and traffic noise and concentrating on the human voice. The pictures it produced were of high quality, even in dim light, and it had a number of Unique Selling Points. One was that the images were immediately transmitted to a computer, thus providing an almost infinite and totally silent storage capacity, since there was no need to keep switching over DVDs or videotapes. Another USP was that the whole system had its own back-up power reserve in the event of a power cut.

Once it had picked up the moving object it would track it round the room maintaining focus on it and picking up its sound with directional microphones. Above all, it was so miniaturised that the camera—just a tiny lens on the end of a fibre optic cable—could be easily hidden. When you wanted to access the recordings, you simply did so by watching them on your personal computer. Alternatively you could make your own discs and watch them through a DVD player.

'Well,' said Alex, 'they liked the ads so much I managed to wangle a freebie out of them. I got them to set one of their systems up in my flat. Said I wanted to test drive it, that sort of crap.'

'Whereabouts in your flat?'

'Guess.'

'Bedroom?'

'Got it in one.' Alex smiled, then wiped the sweat off his face with a handkerchief. He looked at me almost nervously, as if he was unsure how I would react. I was unsure how I should react. 'Then came the call to America. Quite unexpected. Apparently several people in the office were up for it, but I got it. So I was going to be away for six months and I thought I'd let the flat out. So I did.'

'Who to?'

'This girl called Carol. I saw quite a few before I decided on her. Twenties, blonde, gorgeous legs, nice pair of tits. Nice face. She was just a temp somewhere, but she had this lah-di-dah accent. Very Cheltenham Ladies. She sort of took my fancy. I dropped the rent quite a bit for her.'

'You don't mean—'

'That's right,' said Alex looking away and pouring himself another glass, 'I left the Hidden Eye on.'

'Did you tell her about it?'

'Good God no!' Alex managed to dig up some moral indignation from somewhere. 'No. I mean, I don't want you to think that this was just some sort of sleazy voyeurist trip for me. No. It was more like research. A unique insight into another life.'

'If she ever finds out . . .'

'She won't. I haven't seen her since I came back. She'd left the place immaculate, rent paid, bills paid, everything. I wish I could always have a tenant like her. I'm glad now I lowered the rent for her.'

'You lowered the rent because she had nice tits.'

'Yes. Well . . . I mean, I really wanted to find out. What do they do when no-one is looking; or rather, when they think no-one is looking? I could really get inside the psyche of this person. Could be useful for business. The insights you get. You know the Heisenberg principle: the presence of an observer alters the course of an experiment? That may be true in physics, but in human experiments it only counts if the humans involved know they're being observed. Don't you see? This is the real thing. All these fly on the wall docu-soaps are rubbish compared to this.'

'Bollocks. You just wanted to see her tits.'

'Do you have to be so crude? Anyway, aren't you just a little bit curious to know what I found out?'

'What did you find out?'

'You'd be amazed. I haven't looked at it all. Christ, there's hours of the stuff, but you would be amazed.'

'In what way?'

'Come and see for yourself. Don't tell me you wouldn't walk over red hot coals to see it.'

'Well . . .'

'We could analyse it together. What d'you say? Friday evening after work. We'll pick up a take-away and make a night of it.'

I wish I'd said no. Jesus, Christ, God! I wish I'd said no.

ꝏ

Alex's flat was in a converted warehouse at Canary Wharf. It was one of those apartments that people like Alex chose to refer to as a 'pad', all black leather and chrome and sliding doors, with the clutter of everyday life kept firmly out of sight behind them.

The evening seemed potentially an enjoyable one. We had bought a lavish Chinese takeaway which we spread out on the low coffee table in front of the television and there were plenty of cold beers in the fridge. Our entertainment promised to be both titillating and psychologically fascinating. I wish I could say that I felt guiltier about the intrusion we were making into a private life. Now, it seems horrible that I could have consented to participate, but perhaps that is because of what happened. I did feel uneasy, which may not be very much to record in my favour, but I did. I asked Alex why he had chosen me to watch with him.

'Because you're an artist; you're serious about writing,' he said. The basis for this was that I had once told him that I was trying to write a novel. 'You'll understand. The others would either leer or disapprove.' Of course I was flattered and this stifled my anxieties.

Alex had spent the intervening few days burning the recordings onto a disc for us to watch. For about an hour or so, we watched Carol getting up and going to bed and having long conversations with someone called 'Tishy' or 'Tish'. It did not take me long to forget that I was invading a private world because it was not long before I felt myself part of it. Carol's universe did not appear to be a very exciting one, but its very banality had a certain charm. There was the clumsy, uncoordinated little dance that she sometimes did in her underwear when she played a favourite CD. There was the wrapt absorption with which she examined her slender naked body in the mirror, wondering perhaps how desirable she was, little knowing that her vulnerability made her very desirable. There was the pert way in which she stuck her bottom out before farting and then flapped the smell away with a little wave of the hand. I suppose in someone older or less pretty all these things would have seemed grotesque, even pathetic.

She appeared to be a good girl, if not perhaps aggressively intelligent. She went home to her parents in Gloucestershire every weekend; her gossip on the phone to Tishy was giggling and unmalicious; if she brought men back to the flat they did not enter her bedroom in which she slept every night of the working week. I began to fantasise about meeting her, taking her out and, armed with my secret knowledge, seducing her. In the middle of this reverie Alex stopped the DVD player. 'Well,' he said. 'That sort of thing goes on for several weeks and then there's a change. This is where it gets really weird.' He began to scan through the DVD while I contemplated going home. I did not want there to be a change. I wanted her to continue in the same sweet innocent ways, and I dreaded the prospect of something sleazier.

It began with her return one evening, drunk or stoned, and collapsing onto the bed in convulsive sobs. That night she did not undress to sleep. After that her life seemed to become more frantic: the room became messier, she was frequently drunk, she got up and went to bed at odd times. The talks with Tishy seemed the same as ever, but there were other calls more subdued and intense in which painful relationships were discussed and explored.

There was someone in particular called Kel whom she rang up from time to time. This Kel—one could not tell if it was male or female—seemed to act as a confidant. To Kel she would retail, with some reluctance at first, her secret feelings and fantasies. She was so ashamed of them and yet they were like the thoughts that come to all of us. She occasionally felt resentful of people she loved and who loved her. She was irritated by her parents when she ought to have been grateful. She had sexual fantasies of a mildly masochistic kind. She spoke to Kel with greater frequency and each time she did she was made to repeat the accounts of her fantasies, and, as she did so, the fantasies became gradually more extreme.

Then she began bringing men into her bedroom. They were joyless sexual encounters with men indiscriminately chosen. Sometimes there was brutality and she would cry out in pain, but she offered no resistance. I wanted to shout out and tell her to stop; either that or stop watching, but I could do neither. I looked over at Alex and he was transfixed. The phone calls to Kel continued. She told him about the men, always ending a graphic account with the pathetic words: 'I think I'm beginning to learn.'

Then these one-night stands stopped abruptly. For a week or so a semblance of normality was restored. Alex said: 'This is where I stopped watching.' It was now three in the morning, but we were still wide awake. Alex turned the DVD player off and went to make some coffee.

'We ought to know what happened to her,' I said. 'Okay,' said Alex. 'I sort of feel I shouldn't go on, but you're right. We have to see it through to the end now.'

Was I right? I wasn't sure. We drank coffee in silence then Alex turned the DVD player on again. She was still seeing no men, but the phone calls were changing. She was talking less and listening more. Sometimes the phone would ring and you knew it was Kel just from the solemn way she would reply:

'Yes . . . yes . . . yes . . . yes . . .'

Then one evening the bedroom door opened and Carol walked in, turned and said: 'Come in, Kel.' A man entered. He was well built, of medium height, and in his fifties, perhaps older. He was bald except for a light frizz of white hair around his cranium. The features were strong, a short straight nose, a firm chin and a small thin-lipped mouth. He had an aura of purpose and power, and he had obviously kept himself in shape. There was something undeniably magnetic about him, but also repulsive. Wherever he looked he looked with unblinking intensity.

Alex almost shouted: 'Christ, she's not going to bed with him!'

'Some girls like older men.'

'But my God, him!'

'Perhaps she's not going to bed with him,' I said, not believing but hoping. 'He could be just a sort of father figure, or something.'

Carol did not seem to be afraid of Kel so much as utterly submissive. He told her to take off her clothes, which she did mechanically, without any eagerness, keeping her eyes on him. He, meanwhile, was looking at her raptly with that intense, impersonal stare of his.

When she had finished she stood ankle-deep in discarded clothes. Kel stepped onto them and reached out with his left hand to touch one of her breasts. Just before he touched them, his shoulders suddenly raised themselves and he became rigidly still. For a few moments he remained like this while Carol continued to gaze at him, bewildered.

Suddenly he turned his head to stare directly at the camera. Alex and I both jumped. He might have been in the room, the look was so immediate and intense. It seemed to leap at us across the barriers of technology and time. His extraordinary pale blue eyes were filled with concentrated loathing. Like everything about him, there was something purposeful in his look. It was not rage, or hatred merely for the sake of rage, it was the performance of some indefinable act.

'My God, he's seen us!' said Alex involuntarily.

'Turn it off,' I said.

'No! No! This is ridiculous. He can't do anything. We must see what happens.'

The man was still staring directly into the lens, but now he was mouthing something. We listened intently but could hear no words. Then the screen snowed over. Wild colours flashed across it so vivid that they hurt our eyes: acid greens, electric blues, fire reds. Then the screen cleared and we were in the bedroom again. It was a clear picture except that from time to time the whole image quivered in a strange way, as if the camera were looking upwards through the troubled surface of a pool of water.

There was a figure in the bed, but no-one that either of us at first recognised. It was a man, pale and horribly thin. He had lost most of his hair, but what was left of it was black and clammy. Two days of black stubble covered his sunken cheeks. His pale bony hands fumbled convulsively at the duvet. His breath came in short moaning gasps. It looked as if he was in the last stages of some hideous wasting disease.

'My God!' said Alex. 'What the hell is that bloke doing in my bed?'

I could not speak. It is the only time in my life that I have ever been paralysed by fear, but of what? An image on a screen?

One of the hands lifted itself from the duvet and started to make clawing movements as if trying to ward something off in the vicinity of the camera's eye. The man started to moan words which I could not understand. He repeated the same syllables again and again. It sounded like: 'Hurninaw, hurninaw, hurninaw.' Then the face which had been in gaunt profile turned itself towards the camera, and I received the last terrible shock of the evening. I recognised the eyes. They were large and brown, and the lashes, though gummed and slimed with disease, were long.

'Christ, who the hell is he?' Alex muttered.

'Don't you recognise him?' I asked.

'No! Do you?'

'No.' But I lied.

༄

I can't remember now how or when I left Alex's flat. I know I did not sleep that night and the next day, which was a Saturday, is a complete blank in my memory. On Sunday I lunched with my parents and got some sleep in the afternoon. When I went back to work on Monday I did see Alex. He avoided my glance, but otherwise seemed perfectly normal. In the following weeks our contact was minimal. We both stuck to an unspoken agreement that the evening when we watched the recordings was not to be mentioned.

As it happened, my days at DH Associates were numbered. The firm decided to go in for downsizing, or streamlining, or whatever they call sacking people, and I was out. I was not all that sorry to leave and it seemed that nobody was particularly sorry to see me do so. Alex, in particular, made no effort to commiserate.

I spent two months in the limbo of the workless. It was a dark period in which I began to believe I would never work again. At last, through a good friend, I landed a brilliant job at a new up-and-coming PR firm called Murray-Thomson. Alex and DH Associates soon became very distant memories. Then, one evening, about a year later, I happened to find myself in Freek's wine bar where I had met Alex for a drink that night. I had been meeting a client and, after he had gone, I lingered, idly finishing the bottle of Chilean Chardonnay we had ordered between us. I was in a contented unreflective mood when suddenly I heard my name called. It was Sally, one of the art directors at DH Associates. Though we had never been particularly friendly at DH she greeted me effusively and accepted my offer of a drink.

'We hear you're doing great things at Murray-Thomson,' she said. I smiled. So that was it. Success had conferred status on me. 'A lot of us were very sorry to see you go. One of our best copywriters. The Management at DH is just so crass. Do you know if Murray-Thomson is looking around for new young blood?'

I made a noncommittal answer and asked after my old associates. Sally said:

'You heard about Alex, I suppose.'

'No. What about him?'

'Oh, God! He's dead. Didn't you know? I thought you and Alex were great mates.'

'No. Not specially. Not at all really.'

'Thank Christ for that. No. Sorry. I mean it's just that none of us really liked Alex.'

'What happened?'

'It was incredibly quick. He got this terrible disease. Lost weight; lost his hair. The doctors were baffled. Some sort of virus. AIDS maybe.'

'But Alex wasn't gay.'

'You don't have to be gay to get AIDS, you know.'

'Sorry. No. Quite. Go on.'

'Well, they tried everything, but he just kept going down hill. Eventually he discharged himself from hospital because the doctors were getting nowhere. I did go and visit him. The last time I saw him at his flat it was awful. He was delirious. He was in bed and he kept staring at this spot on the bedroom wall and waving something away with his hand. And he kept screaming the same thing. It took me a long time to figure out what it was. It was: "Turn it off! Turn it off! *Turn it off!*"'

MISS MARCHANT'S CAUSE

I can't understand how I came to do 'The Dare', as it was called. Though not exactly shy, I was a timid, cautious boy at school, with no great ambitions other than to get by and not be punished. My memory of events leading up to the incident is hazy, but I am sure it had a lot to do with what is now called 'peer pressure'. I was twelve years old and in my last year at Stone Court preparatory school in Thanet.

Just outside the school premises, and strictly out of bounds, was a large, derelict, red brick building standing in a wilderness, surrounded by a high wall. This was in the early 1960s, before the age of the developer, when such ruins were not so unusual. The building, called Grove House, exerted a powerful influence on our young imaginations. Of course, it was said to be haunted, but how and by what was never specified. Masters when interrogated on the subject of Grove House were invariably vague, but whether through ignorance or a reluctance to impart information I could never tell.

The whole school used to take a walk every Sunday afternoon and frequently passed its rusty, padlocked front gates. Through these one glimpsed what had once been a park with fir trees and rhododendrons, lawns and herbaceous borders, now thoroughly wild and weed-ridden. Beyond this was the house, vast and rambling, the colour of dried blood. It was on three floors, and along its front ran a glass-roofed verandah, smashed and crazed by years of vandalism and neglect. The style was plain mid-Victorian institutional with touches of Gothic and, as I now know, it had been built in 1870.

The Dare was to enter the grounds, get into the building and return with some memento of the expedition. One Sunday Summer evening a friend called Farr and I decided to do it. I remember that we climbed over a broken section of the wall and entered the grounds with no great misgivings. The evening was pleasantly warm from the sun which had shone all day and the overgrown park was mysterious without being threatening. However, the Dare was to enter the house. The front door was locked, but we knew from previous darers that we could get in through a window on the verandah. This we did and entered a large white room empty except for a single wicker chair. The evening sun shot great dust-filled bolts of light across the room. Farr suggested we take the chair back as a souvenir and I laughed, as much to reassure myself with the sound of my voice as for any other reason. We tried the only door in the room and it opened. It was darker beyond, but I said we must go on. We still had to find our souvenir, and I felt that our dare was not complete until we had entered the bowels of the building.

We went through the door into a long gloomy corridor into which some light filtered from a window at one end. The floor of black and maroon encaustic tiles was littered with debris, so that every step we took crackled like a fusillade. The feeling that we should get out of here as soon as possible became very insistent. I stooped to pick up a little loose square of tile for my souvenir, and, as I did so, something happened which for a few brief seconds gave me an odd feeling of reassurance. I became aware of a smell with which I was intensely familiar, the smell of my own school, Stone Court, on the mornings when it was being cleaned: carbolic, soapy water, wax polish on wood. Then it occurred to me that this was not a natural smell to find in a derelict building. I turned round to look at my friend Farr.

In the gloom I could see that his round, freckled face was whiter than usual and he was looking at something over my shoulder with a blank expression. It was as if his face was losing the thing that made him Farr and no-one else. I turned back and looked towards the window at the end of the corridor.

There, etched against the light was the figure of a woman in a long dress. She was facing towards us, tall, with a slender, and, as I now think, a voluptuous figure. I could distinguish no features, only a black unmoving silhouette. It was enough. We were off at a run, howling as we went.

After that I only remember that we got back into our own school grounds without further adventure, that we did not boast about our escapade and that I kept the little square of dark red encaustic tile from Grove House.

Very soon the Grove House adventure faded in my memory until I almost began to doubt its reality. The tile was kept at the back of a drawer. Each time I came across it I thought of throwing it away, but I didn't. It was not that I wanted to remember the incident, but something told me I should not forget.

Then, when I was eighteen, I happened to find myself at Paddington Station about to board a train to Oxford with nothing to read. The selection of paperbacks at W.H. Smith's was limited, but I chose what seemed to me the most interesting, a compilation volume called *Victorian Scandals*.

I was on the train before I was able to examine the book. I turned first to the thin, smudged spread of photographs sandwiched between the pages of print. There were pictures of Oscar Wilde and Bosie, of Florence Bravo and Dr Gully, of Tranby Croft and Sir William Gordon Cumming. With all of these and the scandals attached to them I was more or less familiar. Then I turned a page and received a shock. It surprises me now to think that a dingy photograph of a drab Victorian building could make my heart beat faster and turn me hot and then cold. I looked round at my fellow passengers to see if they had noticed anything abnormal about me, but they were absorbed in their own affairs. The photograph was of Grove House, and the caption read:

> Grove House, the private asylum run by Eleanor Marchant, where over thirty patients died *in mysterious circumstances*.

On the same page was a half-length photograph in an oval of a woman dressed plainly in the costume of the 1880s. Under it the caption read:

> Eleanor Marchant, pioneer in the treatment of the insane, who murdered her own patients. Was she mad herself?

The face in the photograph had that strange, stony inscrutability you often see in Victorian photographs, the product in part of the early camera's long exposure times. The features were severe but handsome, the only unattractive element being a wide thin-lipped mouth. Beneath the stiff bodice one detected a voluptuous figure. My eighteen year old mind scented a powerfully sexual being behind the façade; it returned with a jolting vividness to the silhouette in the corridor. I was enthralled.

The piece on The Grove House Mystery, as it was called, was not well written. *Victorian Scandals* was the work of a hack who specialised in the genre of 'true life crimes'. One was aware of a straining after sensation which, paradoxically, seemed rather to rob the story of its strangeness. Nevertheless, the bare bones were interesting enough.

Eleanor Marchant had been the daughter of well-off parents. From an early age she exhibited a zealous, crusading nature, a genuine desire to 'do good', combined, as it sometimes is, with an exhibitionist streak. Her inspiration was Florence Nightingale, but the sphere in which she proposed to shine was the treatment of the insane. The writer implied that Eleanor's choice of this field may have been prompted by the fact that there was a record of insanity in her family; though it is just as likely to have been simply that a more humane treatment of mental illness was beginning to be a fashionable cause by the middle of the nineteenth century.

Using family money Eleanor Marchant had Grove House built and set herself up as the superintendent of a private asylum for the insane. At the outset Grove House was run on the most enlightened lines. Inmates had their own rooms and recreations of all kinds were available to them. Exercise in the spacious and attractive grounds was encouraged. Patients had their own small plots of land where they could grow what they wanted. There was a small menagerie of animals which they looked after. The institution was a model of its kind, so that articles appeared in magazines praising Grove House and Miss Marchant's regime. She herself wrote a highly acclaimed work, *On the Care and Cure of the Insane*.

This state of affairs lasted for about ten years until the middle of the 1880s when a change began to take place. Miss Marchant, always a powerful personality, became more arbitrary and dictatorial. The overall atmosphere remained as enlightened as before, but there was an increase in petty regulations. Patients had to be inside Grove House by certain times, take prescribed amounts of exercise, and dress in a more uniform manner. A system of punishments or 'forfeits', as they were called, was imposed on those who infringed the regulations. Some of the hitherto devoted staff left and were replaced by less capable and dedicated employees.

What caused this change is a matter for speculation. It was said that Eleanor Marchant craved attention and that when interest in her waned, as it inevitably did, she resented it. Local inhabitants started to complain that the tone of their neighbourhood had been diminished by the presence of Grove House and that the occasional escape of an inmate threatened their safety. These murmurings embittered Miss Marchant who tended to react violently to any form of criticism.

Another possible agent of change was less known about at the time, but much talked of later. In 1882 a male patient named Bradley had been admitted to Grove House. Bradley had been a doctor and the general consensus was that a combination of drink, laudanum from his dispensary and the tragic death of his wife had affected his mind. There were rumours of assaults on patients, but Bradley's family had spirited him away to Miss Marchant's asylum before prosecutions could be instituted.

Within two years, the regime of Grove House, together with abstinence from drink and drugs, had apparently wrought a total cure on Dr Bradley. Miss Marchant had become, in the course of his stay, very close to Bradley, though whether their relationship extended to physical intimacy is not known. Photographs of Bradley show a short, stout man with dark eyes and a wealth of black whisker. It was generally thought, however, that she made a catastrophic mistake when, in 1886, she decided to dismiss the local doctor and employ Bradley as a resident physician to Grove House.

It was shortly after Bradley's appointment that mysterious deaths began to occur among the patients. There were falls down stairs and from windows, suicides by hanging and self-mutilations. One woman was found burned to death in the summerhouse. Others merely died suddenly for no discernible reason, and the death certificates, invariably written out by Dr Bradley, showed 'apoplectic seizure' and 'heart failure' as the cause of death.

It took some time for the enormity of these occurrences to become apparent, and in the end it was human greed which exposed it. The relatives of a female patient who had suddenly died became suspicious when they discovered that some jewellery belonging to her had disappeared. Miss Marchant, when questioned as to its whereabouts, felt that her integrity had been impugned and was rude to them. The relatives, who were not used to being spoken to in this way by someone whom they considered to be an employee, reacted by initiating an investigation into the death. Strychnine was discovered in the corpse, and this led to enquiries into other deaths at Grove House. Members of staff, who had become resentful of Miss Marchant's increasingly despotic ways, aired their suspicions. Miss Marchant and Dr Bradley were arrested.

As it happened, the jewellery whose disappearance started the whole affair, was found to have been taken away to be 'put in safe keeping' at a previous date by another relative of the deceased.

In the end, it was only Miss Marchant who was put on trial. There was not a strong enough case against Dr Bradley, who gave evidence against her in court. She was found guilty of murdering six of her patients and of inflicting grievous bodily harm on a further seven, but the number of her victims was generally thought to be far higher. Condemned to death, she was found subsequently to be insane and sent to Broadmoor. Dr Bradley committed suicide in abject poverty a year after the trial.

The story haunted my imagination, and I tried to find out more about the subject. Very little of substance came my way, except that, a year after I had read the account in *Victorian Scandals*, I found another photograph of Eleanor Marchant.

It was in a book about the criminally insane which I discovered while browsing idly through a second-hand bookshop in Oxford. There were pictures from Broadmoor records, and among them a double portrait of Eleanor Marchant from 1905. In many ways, I wish I had never seen the picture.

It showed her in full face and profile lit uncompromisingly against a white background. In each of the pictures her chin was raised and she was looking downwards. This gave her an air of defiance which was accentuated by the eyes, now sunken, but still smouldering with the will to power. The long gash of a mouth was wrenched down at the ends in a rictus of misery and despair. It was the look of a defeated tyrant fighting a last despairing battle in the burning citadel. Behind the rage the fear of death could plainly be seen. A note under the photograph stated that she died shortly after it was taken. After that I lost the desire to discover any more about Eleanor Marchant; the ending of the story was so entirely without hope.

Eleven years later I wrote a play for Radio 4 which was accepted. After it had been broadcast and noticed favourably, the Head of Drama took me out to lunch. She wanted to commission another play from me: had I any ideas? I had not expected this offer and my mind was a blank until into it, unbidden, came the Broadmoor photograph, that vision of Hell. I began to tell the Head of Drama the story of Eleanor Marchant and why it obsessed me. She was intrigued: if I could give her a brief outline she would commission me. Before I was fully conscious of the fact that Miss Marchant and Grove House were entering my life again, I had agreed.

My synopsis was accepted and I began work. I was both elated and reluctant. I think that initially I went on with the project because I was afraid to turn down work. At a deeper level, though the subject was in some ways repugnant to me, I felt the need to purge myself of its subconscious vibrations. To do this I had to research the story more thoroughly.

I was relieved to find that the London Library had the books on the Marchant Case mentioned in the bibliography of *Victorian Scandals*, but when I looked on the shelves all of them were out. I was filled with indignation: somehow the Marchant affair had become my property; and I resented anyone who wanted to appropriate the subject for their own purposes. So it was partly out of vindictiveness that I put in an order for all the books I wanted to be returned and sent to me as soon as the borrower's time was up.

Three weeks later a parcel arrived at my flat in Tufnell Park. In it were the books I had asked for and with them was a letter from the London Library saying that they were passing on a note from the previous borrower to whom naturally they had not given my address. The note was on a postcard headed: Monica Freede MA PhD, Department of Women's Studies, Dorset University; together with a telephone number. It read:

> I was a little concerned when I was asked for these books back. Are you also writing a book on the Marchant case? If not, what is your interest? Could you contact me on this number? Monica Freede.

It amused me to think that this Monica Freede was suffering from the same jealous, proprietorial feelings that I was, but I was happy to be able to put her mind at rest. A book and a play were not going to compete; they might even complement one another.

I called her number several times without getting a reply. Eventually the telephone was picked up by 'Monica's assistant', as she described herself. She sounded suspicious and asked for my name and business. Giving her my name and number I said: 'Tell Dr Freede that it's about Eleanor Marchant.'

Within ten minutes the phone rang and I was speaking to Monica Freede. The voice, breathy and with no definable accent, sounded anxious, almost accusing.

'You said it was about Eleanor.' Anyone listening in might have thought she was talking about a close friend who had been involved in a road accident.

I explained about the books from the London Library and when she spoke again, I was conscious of increased tension.

'I'm writing a book about her, you know. I've got a publisher. My work's nearly finished.'

I reassured her that I was only writing a play on the subject not a book.

'Ah.' The tension slacked but did not disappear altogether. She asked how I had come to be interested in the case and I told her that I had been at school near Grove House, though not about my adventure there. She was intrigued.

'My God! So you actually saw it! That's absolutely incredible. You know it was destroyed in 1969. Some bloody developer bought the land and just flattened it. It's a housing estate now. Planning permission granted just like that. Local council got a kickback, I shouldn't wonder. Nobody made any effort to preserve the building; it was an absolute disgrace.'

'It wasn't exactly a thing of beauty.'

'That's a matter of opinion, but, my God, it was a historic building! I mean, Eleanor was a pioneer in the treatment of mental illness. Read her book *On the Care and Cure of the Insane*. It's incredible. She was so far ahead of her time.'

'Yes...'

'Of course, you do realise that she was completely innocent of those deaths.'

'Do you think so?'

'Oh, yes. It's so obvious. She was shielding Dr Bradley out of misplaced loyalty. He was a complete psychopath. And of course the male establishment had been out to get her for a long time, and they saw their chance. They were quite canny about it. They knew that if she was hanged there'd be an outcry, so they had her committed to Broadmoor. So ironic.'

'Why were they out to get her?'

'Because she was a pioneer. Because she had made them all look incredibly out of date. A woman too! My God!'

'Is there evidence for her innocence?'

'Oh, yes! My God. I mean it's obvious!' But she offered no proof more concrete than that. I was in no position to argue with her, and I felt that even the mildest scepticism would be taken as an affront. So, with exchanged wishes of good luck, we ended our telephone conversation on amicable terms.

As I continued with my research, which, admittedly, consisted simply in reading the books from the London Library, I could find nothing to support Dr Freede's belief in Eleanor Marchant's innocence. On the contrary, a clear pattern of events emerged: the increase in petty regulations, outbursts of temper with patients and staff, followed in the early stages by abject remorse; then the occasional assault on a patient—nothing serious to begin with, just a 'box on the ear'; then the institution of severe punishments for the recalcitrant, the appearance of mysterious injuries on the inmates, and finally the unexpected deaths. Everything pointed to a slow loss of internal control in Miss Marchant which manifested itself in a growing obsession with imposing external control on those around her.

Perhaps the most valuable book as far as I was concerned was one produced in the 1920s as part of the *Notable British Trials* series. There, without the adornment of external interpretation, the words and actions of the principal characters were laid bare. In particular, I read and re-read the cross-examination of Miss Marchant herself. It seemed to me that she was in the grip of a profound moral disease. The words 'mad' or 'insane' were somehow inappropriate. The intellectual faculties were in good order: she was reasonable and restrained, and she showed considerable adroitness in her replies to Sir Stanford Rivers Q.C., who led for the crown; but there was something unsettling about the way she appeared to be unaware of the gravity of the charges. She had no sense of how ordinary people might react to what had gone on. A short extract from the cross-examination illustrates:

RIVERS: Miss Marchant, do you remember a female patient named Powell?
MARCHANT: I do. Yes. An elderly woman.
RIVERS: Was she subject to fits?

MARCHANT: She had all kinds of abnormal behaviour, yes.

RIVERS: Including fits?

MARCHANT: Seizures, fits, tantrums . . .

RIVERS: Call them what you will, Miss Marchant. For the convenience of this court we will call them fits. And did she, in the course of these fits, lose control of her limbs and roll about on the floor, muttering and foaming at the mouth?

MARCHANT: That may have been something she did.

RIVERS: Did she or did she not, Miss Marchant?

MARCHANT: Yes.

RIVERS: And were not these fits the very reason why Powell was placed in your care?

MARCHANT: The fits were but one outward sign of her mind sickness.

JUDGE: Miss Marchant, will you please answer counsel's questions directly.

MARCHANT: She was sent to me because of the fits, yes.

RIVERS: And did you, in the presence of witnesses, say to Dr Bradley on one occasion, 'we must beat the fits out of her'?

MARCHANT: What I meant was—

RIVERS: Never mind what you meant, Miss Marchant, did you say those words?

MARCHANT: I may have done. I really cannot recall.

RIVERS: And did you, or did you not, personally administer a beating to Powell when she next had a fit?

MARCHANT: That was a different matter.

RIVERS: Will you answer the question, Miss Marchant?

MARCHANT: At that time her mind sickness was cured and it was my conviction that the fits were not involuntary. Any physical act on my part was done to make her aware that she was no longer helpless and sick. The patient who has

> recovered from mind sickness must be made aware of the moral responsibility which that recovery bestows. Powell had failed to show that responsibility as her deliberate falling into the fits demonstrated . . .

There was much more of this casuistry, through which one could see that Miss Marchant was convinced of her own rightness on all occasions. The consequence of this was that everything she did must be correct; and all those who opposed her must be crushed or eliminated. 'Powell' was the one who was burned to death in the summerhouse.

The phrase 'mind sickness' recurred often in her testimony and in her book *On the Care and Cure of the Insane*. The fact that she used it in preference to a more common word, like insanity, showed a desire to carve out an individual approach to mental illness. I could not say what exactly she meant by the words, but I recognised the egoism with which she insisted on them. She was claiming mind sickness as her territory, just as Dr Freede and I were claiming Miss Marchant as ours.

I wrote my play easily, but without the ecstatic satisfaction that usually comes over me when a piece of writing goes well. The trouble was, there was no redeeming feature: the story of Miss Marchant was a relentless downward slide into murder, madness and oblivion. It was the pure tragedy of someone with a great capacity for goodness brought down by the flaw of hubris. I experimented with altering the chronology of the scenes so that the play ended with an image of Miss Marchant at her best, but it did not work. There was no honest way of deviating from the descent; that was the power and the truth of the work.

While I was working on the final draft, I received an invitation through the post to a lecture in London at the Fawcett Society. Dr Freede was speaking on 'Eleanor Marchant,

Villainess or Victim?' On the back of the card Dr Freede had written: 'Do come. Important new information will revise your idea of Eleanor.' The word 'Do' was underlined several times.

Three questions occurred to me. How had she got hold of my address? Not through the London Library, I was sure of that. She must have traced it painstakingly from the knowledge of my name and telephone number. But then, why hadn't she simply rung me? Secondly, how did she know what my 'idea of Eleanor' was? Thirdly, why was she so anxious for me to attend the lecture?

The Fawcett Society is named after Millicent Fawcett, the pioneer suffragist and is dedicated to the promotion of feminist studies. It has premises in Beech Street EC2 which house a library and other facilities including a lecture room, where I found myself at the appointed time. As I had expected, I was one of very few men present, and, curiously enough, just about the only one (of the men) without a beard. Perhaps the men who moved in these circles felt the need to establish their gender difference by this decisive but unthreatening means. I myself did not feel awkward or particularly embarrassed because everyone seemed so cheerful and friendly. An elderly lady sitting next to the gangway on my immediate right asked my interest in the lecture and I explained.

'Ah,' she said. 'So you've fallen under the spell too, have you?'

I wanted to ask her what she meant, but just then two women walked onto the platform. One of them, the elder of the two, announced herself as the Secretary of the Fawcett Society. The other, who was carrying a neat leather folder, I took to be Dr Freede.

Of course, I had previously constructed a mental picture in my head of Dr Monica Freede, and, of course, it was quite wrong. I had expected someone with glasses, small, dumpy and intense with cropped black hair: only the glasses were correct. She was in her early thirties, six foot tall and willowy with an unselfconscious grace in her movements. She had long auburn hair and her slightly freckled, unmade-up face was beautiful. I was reminded of pictures of Janey Morris or some other Pre-Raphaelite 'stunner'.

At the time I was unattached and I did feel a frisson of sexual interest, but it was muted. Something told me that I would be out of my depth with her; though intimations of that kind had not stopped me from drowning on previous occasions. Besides, I knew that she had other things on her mind.

Dr Freede's lecture began with an efficient and concise summary of Miss Marchant's career up to the mid 1880s. She naturally put the best construction on the facts, but I found her use of 'Eleanor' in referring to Miss Marchant unsettling. It suggested to me a lack of objectivity, and a familiarity of which I doubt Miss Marchant would have approved. But she spoke well, with vitality and plenty of mordant wit directed at 'the male establishment'.

When Dr Freede began to tackle what she called the 'difficult phase' in Miss Marchant's life, I found her less satisfactory. It must have been plain to all present that she was offering an ingenious case for the defence rather than a dispassionate assessment. Inconvenient evidence was ignored or dismissed as hearsay. Her theory, which had some plausibility, was that Miss Marchant became infatuated with Dr Bradley and that this blinded her to the fact that he was a psychopath. He committed the murders and she refused to believe that he was doing anything wrong until it was too late. At the trial, she adopted 'what she believed to be the Victorian male code of honour' and refused to say anything that would incriminate her lover. As to the acts of brutality that members of staff alleged they saw her commit on patients, these were the fabrications of employees who resented her 'admittedly authoritarian management style'.

Finally, Dr Freede dealt with the question of insanity, and here she was more convincing, contending that Miss Marchant had not suffered from mental illness in the accepted sense, merely from the stress to which her relationship with Dr Bradley had put her. She pointed to Miss Marchant's impressive conduct during the trial. She claimed that because the idea of a totally sane woman committing such atrocities was unthinkable, the 'establishment' had decided that she must be mad and had committed her to Broadmoor.

Then, with considerable flair, Dr Freede produced her *coup de théatre*. She had found new evidence which established beyond doubt both the innocence and sanity of Eleanor Marchant. There was a murmur and then a greater stillness in the audience.

Dr Freede had managed to trace the descendants of Eleanor's younger sister Margaret. They still had papers relating to Eleanor, among them a number of letters written by her from Broadmoor to her sister. They demanded that efforts be made to re-open the case, claiming that Bradley had been responsible for the deaths. Dr Freede read extracts from the letters which, as far as one could tell, were coherent and no more repetitive than anyone's might have been under the circumstances. Perhaps the references to Dr Bradley as 'that fiend Bradley', or sometimes simply as 'the fiend' could be judged as intemperate, but even that was understandable.

The letters were impressive, as far as one could tell from the extracts, except for one thing. All the material had to do with self-exoneration: there were no expressions of regret for the suffering and deaths of her charges. When the patients were mentioned they did not merit a single epithet such as 'poor' or 'unhappy'; their deaths were not called 'terrible', they were just deaths.

Among the family papers Dr Freede had also discovered a letter to Margaret Marchant from one of the doctors in Broadmoor from which she read the following extract.

> I became acquainted with your sister in 1903 when I first came as a doctor to Broadmoor. I have made it my unvarying practice never to come to any patient with a preconceived notion of their state. Accordingly, when I went to see Miss Marchant, I put aside from my mind all thoughts of the unhappy circumstances under which she had entered the asylum. My unbiased impressions were of someone not unnaturally in acute mental distress, but otherwise in full possession of her rational faculties. As I slowly began to win her confidence, I found her a most interesting and delightful conversationalist and—dare I say it?—companion. There came a time when I found myself confiding some of my own difficulties to her, and her advice was always very much to the point as well as morally bracing. There were moments when I wondered which was the doctor and which the patient! After an initial reluctance she began to talk of The Case. Her recollections of the circumstances which led to her trial and conviction were clear and coherent, and I gradually became convinced that she was wholly innocent of the charges brought against her, and that her sole misdeed was to allow herself to be duped by the man Bradley. This she freely acknowledged and reproached herself most bitterly for it. She urged me to make representations to the Home Office on her behalf and this I was very willing to do, even though it was a most distressing thing for me to see her great agony every time my petitions failed. It will always be a regret to me that Miss Marchant died at the moment when I believe I had at last persuaded the authorities to

> re-open the case. She will ever remain in my mind as a beacon of inspiration, a true friend to me, I may venture to say, and a wise counsellor who bore injustice with fortitude and disappointment with a determination to overcome it.

Dr Freede then brought her lecture to the following conclusion: 'Here at last, it seems to me, we have a true picture of Eleanor in the last days of her life. She remained at heart as she always was, wise, sympathetic, understanding, but also a great campaigner. She was fighting now not for the sufferings of others, but for justice itself, and she died when it was almost in her grasp. Her great heart gave out before she could restore her reputation. As a result she has remained for over half a century a byword for mad wickedness, a sort of female "Jack the Ripper". But now the time has come to ask the question again: Eleanor Marchant, Victorian Villainess, or Victorian Victim? I know what my answer is; I leave it to you to answer in your own way.'

It was a splendid flourish and fully deserved the applause it received. I turned to the elderly woman on my right for her opinion, but she had gone. Suddenly I felt curiously alone. It seemed to me, quite irrationally, that everyone was now convinced of Miss Marchant's innocence except me, for whom the Broadmoor doctor's letter was simply evidence of her remarkably powerful and manipulative personality, no more.

The secretary invited questions from the floor, but none were of any great interest. I wished the elderly lady was still there. She might have known enough to question Dr Freede's thesis. As for me, I simply did not have the courage to challenge her in front of such a sympathetic audience; besides, though I disagreed with it, I thought her lecture a splendid forensic achievement and did not want to cloud her moment of glory.

After questions the meeting broke up; coffee was served from the back of the hall, and everyone milled around. Quite a crowd surrounded Dr Freede, but I felt it was my duty to make myself known to her. She spotted my approach and waved. Her admirers let me through into the presence.

'You're the playwright, aren't you?' she said. 'I somehow knew you must be.' She smiled with unexpected warmth. I congratulated her sincerely on her lecture. She nodded, almost impatiently, as if this was no more than her due.

'You're still not convinced of Eleanor's innocence, though, are you?'

'No,' I said. 'But you've given me a lot to think about.' Dr Freede made a little grimace. Perhaps she thought I was being condescending. Perhaps I was.

'I'll ring you in a couple of days. I think I might be able to convince you.'

'Why do you want to?' I asked.

'Don't you want to know the truth?'

With that, it seemed my interview was at an end, and I went off to get a cup of coffee. To my surprise I found that the elderly lady who had spoken to me was serving drinks behind the refreshment table. Her sudden disappearance at the end of the lecture was explained. I asked her what she thought of Dr Freede.

'I think Eleanor Marchant is a very persuasive woman.'

'Don't you mean Dr Freede?'

'No, I mean Eleanor Marchant.'

I asked her what she had meant when she had asked me if I had fallen under her spell too. She said that she had once researched the Marchant case for a book she was writing. She said: 'I found that if you get too close to her you can get burnt.' I tried to ask her to explain further, but she deliberately ignored me and busied herself with serving coffee to others.

The next day there were one or two small articles in the papers about Dr Freede having found fresh evidence vindicating the notorious Miss Marchant, but they contained so many inaccuracies as to be worthless. The Head of Drama rang me up and I reassured her that I knew all about the so-called 'fresh evidence' and she seemed satisfied. I spent a day re-writing the final scene to include the Broadmoor doctor and then felt that it was time to type the final draft and deliver it to the BBC.

A week passed during which I typed the play. When it was done I was reluctant, as I sometimes am with a new work, to let it go. I re-read and revised it obsessively, then, one night at eleven thirty, just as I had finally decided to send it off to the BBC, the telephone rang. My mind was still so full of what I was writing about that I was not surprised to find myself talking about Eleanor Marchant with Dr Freede. Slowly, however, I became aware of the oddness of our conversation. Dr Freede had begun talking to me as if we had only just left off our discussion at the Fawcett Society over a week ago.

'You're still not convinced that Eleanor's innocent, are you?'

I explained in the most emollient way possible that, persuasive as her arguments were, the evidence against Miss Marchant was too strong for me. On the other end of the telephone I could sense rather than hear a growing exasperation with my obstinacy. She asked if I had finished my play and I explained that I had and was about to deliver it to the BBC.

'Then you have to come down and see me. I'll show you you're wrong about Eleanor. You needn't worry about the expense. If you can get yourself down here I'll put you up in a guest room on campus.' I would not exactly say that I was afraid to refuse Dr Freede, but I was convinced that life would be a lot easier for me if I accepted.

We arranged a date and the following Friday I found myself driving down to Dorset. In the intervening days I had undergone a change of heart, not about Miss Marchant's guilt, but about the whole nature of her story. It had seemed to me before that, though few narratives in real life had a beginning and an end, the story of a human life certainly did: birth began it; death ended it. But now I was not so sure: Miss Marchant was still alive in my mind and that of Dr Freede, and our respective versions of her career were in conflict. There had been no resolution and no dissolution. Just before I set out I looked for the piece of tile from Grove House, found it and put it in my pocket.

☙

Dorset University campus is situated just outside Dorchester. It is a product of the 1970s, sculpted elegantly into landscaped parkland, its architectural beauties only slightly marred by the mildewed tinge which its concrete is acquiring. I arrived, as arranged, at six in the evening and met Dr Freede in a little office just off the Thomas Hardy Library. She seemed surprised to see me.

'I was wondering whether you'd come,' she said. 'I thought you might bottle out.' I detected an element of disappointment that I had not fulfilled her expectations. The phrase 'bottle out' did not quite belong to her: her nerves had borrowed it for the occasion from a younger colleague, perhaps even a student. She evidently realised that her reception of me was a little frosty, because she then became more animated and friendly, but I sensed that an effort was involved.

'We'll have something to eat earlyish. Can you stand Indian? Then there's someone I want you to meet. Is that okay? Have you been here before? Come along, I'll show you the campus.'

We spent a pleasant hour during which Monica lost much of her inhibition. She was amusing in a caustic way about the university and at one point we found ourselves giggling together in front of the very bad portrait of a recent benefactor. Even then I did not feel quite at my ease because I remembered that on her desk I had seen a silver framed photograph of Eleanor Marchant. Others had relatives, or pets, or loved ones; she had Miss Marchant.

At the Indian restaurant we continued to enjoy each other's company, though I noticed that whenever I tried to bring the conversation near to the reason for our meeting she veered away from it. This, however, gave me the opportunity to get to know something of Monica Freede's mind. She had a keen analytical intelligence and her wit was the sharp, sardonic kind that goes with it. Her specialist area of knowledge was social history from the seventeenth century onwards and, within these confines its depth was considerable. Outside its limits she showed scant interest or understanding. For example, she knew the themes and plots of many Victorian novels (particularly those by women) but had no views at all on their literary merits. A work of fiction to her was merely 'interesting' for the light it shed on social attitudes and conditions. She knew all about the privations which men and women suffered in the Crimean War, but little of its causes or principal battles.

More significantly, her understanding of human character seemed to me rudimentary. People to her belonged in unalterable categories: victim or oppressor, pioneer or reactionary, reformer or reprobate. She found it hard to grasp that a person could be both or neither, or could change over time from one to the other.

But my feelings of superiority towards her were checked by the knowledge that Monica's mind as a whole was finer and more disciplined than my own. I was also conscious of something in her which I could barely comprehend, let alone emulate. She had a kind of daring, a willingness to think the unthinkable, reach out for the unattainable. Perhaps it was her very narrowness of vision which gave her the speed and energy to touch distant heights. I only knew that such brilliance had its dangers.

After the meal, at which she had barely touched her vegetable byriani, Monica announced abruptly that we were going to see someone who lived a little way out of Dorchester, and that I was to drive her in my car while she gave directions. When I asked who we were to see she simply said: 'Her name is Maeve Bush. I think you'll find her interesting.'

Monica's habit of always thinking she knew how I would feel irritated me. I asked her who Maeve Bush was and what she did, but she smiled and said: 'You'll see.'

Half an hour later we found ourselves in front of a cottage on the outskirts of the village of Wolfeton. 'This is where my friend Maeve lives,' said Monica in an oddly girlish tone of voice.

Before we had got to the front door it was opened by a heavy woman in her forties with a frizz of red hair. She wore a loose shift dress of dark green on which were superimposed several layers of richly coloured clothing and a fair amount of handmade jewellery. She greeted Monica effusively.

The front door opened directly into the main living room. 'Maeve,' said Monica when we had got inside. 'This is my playwright that I told you about.'

I extended my hand which Maeve took in both of hers. They were damp and almost unbearably hot. She stared at me, smiling quizzically. She had a longish but handsome nose, strong chin and large green eyes. She must once have been the toast of the Glastonbury Festival before she put on weight.

'Hmm, yes,' she said after a short pause. 'You have quite a way to go, but I think you'll get there.'

There is always a smart answer to this kind of gnomic remark; unfortunately, I never manage to think of it at the time. In fact I was lost for words. I stared at Maeve's ample cleavage on which, among other ornaments, rested a pendant consisting of a silver bat clutching a brilliant purple gem.

'That's wonderful,' I said. 'Is it an amethyst?'

Maeve seemed pleased. 'Yes, it is. I'm glad you like it. It's a bit too witchy for some people.'

'Not for me,' I said fatuously.

'Good! Good!' said Maeve laughing and, to my great relief, letting go of my hand. 'Now then, what about some black-currant leaf tea?'

Monica and Maeve went into the kitchen to make the tea while I looked round. It was a low, oak beamed room warmed by an open fire. Maeve's taste for richly coloured fabrics manifested itself in wall hangings, rugs, cushions and drapings over furniture. A collection of crystals, quartzes and semi-precious stones was ranged along the mantelpiece; books on the occult crammed the bookcase. Over the mantelpiece hung an astrological chart. I guessed why I was there and braced myself for the ordeal ahead.

When Maeve and Monica came back into the room with the tea, Monica said: 'You may as well know. Maeve is a psychic.' I nodded.

'I think he realised that,' said Maeve.

'You can leave now if you want to. I won't mind,' said Monica.

'Why?' I said. 'Do you want me to?'

This challenge seemed to amuse Maeve; behind Monica's back she made silent clapping gestures at me. 'I think you've underestimated your writer friend,' she said. I was not sure that she had because I was beginning to feel very uncomfortable.

As we drank our blackcurrant leaf tea (odd but palatable) the talk ranged over a number of esoteric subjects: tarot cards, astrology, crystals. I did my best to hide my scepticism, but not my ignorance, while Monica revealed herself as an eager disciple and Maeve played the expert. Eventually the moment came when Monica said: 'Maeve has helped me to contact Eleanor on the other side.'

Though I knew that something like this was coming it was still a shock. However much we read, whatever we believe, the idea of death as the impenetrable barrier persists in most of us. Any apparent breach excites horror or incredulity, or, as in my case, a confused mixture of the two.

Having absorbed the shock I asked what evidence there was that it was Eleanor. Monica said that the messages, transmitted to her by Maeve, either by automatic writing or by reported speech through a spirit guide, had given her details about Eleanor's life which only Eleanor could give. I had no chance to ask what that meant because Monica then announced that Maeve would be trying to contact Eleanor tonight.

'Right, well, let's get going, shall we?' said Maeve briskly as she settled herself into an armchair. She asked Monica to light some candles and extinguish the lights. The room became warmer and the atmosphere almost suffocating because the candles—great fat hand-made things—were heavily scented. Maeve was wedged into her chair, her hands gripping the arms and her head thrust back. Her eyes were screwed shut, her mouth half open, a look of intense concentration on her face. Her breathing was stertorous, but I did not feel she was asleep. Monica knelt beside her, holding one of her hands, looking intently into her face. Twenty minutes passed; I found myself on the point of falling asleep.

What prevented me was a sudden and pronounced fall in the room's temperature. It was extraordinarily disquieting because there was nothing to indicate its cause. The temperature drop did not come from anywhere; there was no draught. The candles burned with a steady flame, still giving off their heavy scent, now made nauseous by the chill; logs still glowed in the open fire. Every sense except one told me that it should be warm. Monica looked at me triumphantly.

When Maeve began to talk, her voice was lower than it had been before her trance but otherwise no different. At first came a mere jumble of words and syllables, slurred and indistinct. Gradually the words began to form themselves into sentences, but there seemed to be very little sense in them. They might have come out of a dream. I remember her saying: 'The Devil was on the wrong side, or rather the other side of the water, but he came right by the well-known favourite miracle of changing his faces.' That sentence, like so many others, seemed to hover on the brink of meaning, even profundity. I saw that Monica was concentrating hard, as if she was trying to capture its evasive significance. I wanted to keep the words out of my mind, as I had the feeling that if I paid them too much attention they would suck all the sense out of my head and leave behind an imbecile.

Maeve's enunciation became more distinct as what she said became more comprehensible. Her voice started to describe the situation in which it found itself. The description it gave was at once detailed and bafflingly vague. It said that she was on a ledge of black rock half way down a deep 'hole'. The voice said it was a hole, but from other things she said, it would seem to be more like a chasm several miles wide. There were people at the top of the hole who were shouting at her. These people the voice interpreted as hostile though she admitted that they said they wanted to help her. The voice said she was not going to listen to these 'shouters', as she called them, until she had communicated a message to the world. There was a pause and I asked the voice who she was.

'Eleanor,' she said.

'Is there anything you want to say to us?'

'Justice,' said Eleanor. 'The shouters want me to go, but I can't go until I have my justice. They call me guilty. I was not guilty. I have been abused. My name has been abused. I will not let go until they stop abusing me. There's a man here abusing me. His play. His play is abusing me. Get out! Get out!' The last words were spoken in a sort of guttural bark, like a savage animal. I immediately walked out of the room into the night outside.

After the strange unnatural chill indoors, it was warm in the garden. The air was free of human (and inhuman) tensions. I wandered about inhaling the soothing scents of Maeve's herb garden. When I had done this I walked back to the cottage and looked through the window. I was relieved to see that Maeve was no longer in a trance, but sitting up and being given sips of blackcurrant leaf tea by Monica. She seemed pale and disturbed. When I walked back into the cottage she looked at me resentfully.

'Where have you been?' she said. The room was stiflingly hot again.

'I had to get out.'

Monica refused to look at me, but sniffed her contempt; Maeve merely nodded. She said: 'Something bad happened, didn't it? I don't remember anything. That's unusual. I generally remember something. What happened?'

'Nothing really, said Monica. 'Eleanor got mad at him, that's all.'

'Why?' asked Maeve.

'Because he's going to slag her off,' said Monica. 'In this play he's writing. He's going to abuse her.' It struck me then that Eleanor's voice had talked a lot about 'abuse', employing the word in a strangely modern way.

Maeve asked me if I was going to abuse Eleanor in my play and I said I was going to tell the truth. There was a pause and then I added the words: 'as I see it.'

'I don't think we'd better hold any more sessions,' said Maeve. 'This is getting out of hand. We may already have gone too far.' I asked Maeve what she meant by her last comment, but she refused to be drawn.

Monica drove me back to my guest room at the university in silence. It seemed to me that the séance with Maeve had brought to an end my relationship, such as it was, with Monica. She had taken Eleanor Marchant's side and made me into the enemy. I did not think this fair, and I wanted us to part on friendly terms; so, when Monica had stopped the car to drop me off, I said I had a present for her.

They were the first words to be spoken since we had left Maeve's and Monica shrank back from me as if I had made a pass at her. I took the piece of tile from Grove House out of my pocket, explained its origin and gave it to her. Monica looked at the little square object in her hand suspiciously.

'Why are you giving this to me?'

'I thought you'd like to have it. You could use it as a paperweight while you're writing your book.

'But what is it you're trying to say?'

'I hoped we could still be friends.'

Monica said 'Okay', then bent over and kissed my cheek. I was startled. Suddenly the time and the place became very vivid. The warm impression of her lips remained. I thanked her, got out of the car and made my way to the guest room.

ஐ

This is a story of false endings. I delivered my script to the BBC and it was accepted. I thought that my involvement with Monica and Miss Marchant was now over. That is what I thought; what I felt was different. I cannot claim that this was some kind of psychic intuition of what was to come; it is much more likely to have been connected with sex plain and simple. Monica's kiss had stayed with me. Of course, it was absurd, but that is how it is. If we had gone to bed together I might have got her out of my system. It was the fragility of the connection we had made which captivated my mind.

A new term had begun—I taught English to foreign students to keep body and soul together—and I was walking back one evening to my flat from Tufnell Park tube. I had washed the day's events out of my mind and I was planning an evening of reading and writing. My eye was caught by a car which was parked opposite the entrance to my flat because someone was sitting in it. I have always been slightly disturbed by the sight of people sitting in parked cars. I suspect that they are spying or contemplating suicide, or otherwise up to no good. I took a closer look and saw that the occupant of the car was Monica. I went over and tapped on the window.

She was staring straight ahead, a slight frown on her face and did not respond immediately to my tapping. When she did she seemed indignant and wound down the window.

'What are you doing?' she asked querulously. I replied by asking her the same question. She looked confused for a moment, then she said: 'I want to know what you're doing about Eleanor. I want to read your play. I know you're slagging her off.'

She looked up at me with tears in her eyes. I felt ashamed and helpless. I lied to her, saying that all copies of the play were either with my agent or the BBC, and that my computer was down so I could not print her out a copy at the moment.

'You must send a copy to me as soon as possible,' she said. 'Will you do that?' I hesitated. 'Please! It's terribly important.'

'Did you drive all the way down from Dorset to tell me this?' I asked. Monica looked confused.

'This is very important,' she said.

'Come in and have a cup of tea. Let's talk about this.'

'No. I can't stop.'

'Please, Monica!' I tried to open the car door. She screamed and started the car. I let go of the door just in time to prevent myself being dragged into the road. The next moment the car had gone.

A week passed. I did not send Monica my script and sustained myself with the futile hope that everything would 'blow over'. It did not.

One afternoon, as I was teaching, I was called out of my class. It was the police on the phone. A young woman had been seen breaking into my flat and had been apprehended. She was claiming that I knew her. I asked if the woman's name was Monica Freede and was surprised to be told that it was not.

'She says her name is Eleanor Marchant,' came the matter-of-fact voice on the end of the phone. 'Would you know her, sir?'

'Yes,' I said. 'I know Eleanor Marchant. I'm coming over.' I felt like a man drowning.

When I arrived at the police station Monica was sitting in an interview room. At first I recognised her only from the clothes she was wearing. Her auburn hair had been scraped back into a crude bun; it was greasy and almost dark brown in colour. Something had happened to her face too. It was as if a hand had taken hold of it and subtly twisted it out of shape. I noticed that her mouth, wider than before, was pulled down at the corners in a way that reminded me of the photograph of Eleanor Marchant in Broadmoor.

When she saw me a brief look of recognition and relief registered on her face, to be replaced a moment later by a sullen glare.

'We caught her with a tin of lighter fuel,' said the W.P.C. in charge of her. 'It looked as if she was going to burn the place down.'

'Hello, Monica,' I said, but there was no reply.

I told the police that I had no wish to press any charges, and that I would take responsibility for her. They made no objections; in fact they seemed positively relieved to have her off their hands. A sympathetic officer took me aside and told me rather superfluously that 'Miss Marchant' needed help. I heard another officer mutter something which included the phrase 'gives me the creeps'.

Monica came with me silently and without resistance. I drove her back to my flat, gave her coffee which she drank and asked her questions to which she failed to reply. Sometimes she stared at me balefully; sometimes her face assumed a distracted expression, her eyes wandering uncontrollably, as if she was engaged in some deep mental conflict. At the end of one of these fits she quite suddenly fell asleep. As she did so her face relaxed and took on something of its normal beauty. With difficulty I carried her through into the next room and laid her on my bed.

The sight of her so helpless filled me with a feeling very like love, but I still had no idea how to help her. Only one idea occurred to me which was that Maeve, whom I was beginning to tell myself was responsible for 'all this', should find us a way out. Fortunately Monica's address book was in her bag which had been left at the flat when she was caught. Though I had not remembered Maeve's surname it did not take long to find her: she was under 'M' and, besides, the address book was quite sparsely populated.

With one eye on the sleeping shape of Monica in the next room I telephoned Maeve. She answered the telephone eventually in a drugged voice as if she had been asleep. It was four in the afternoon and she appeared to be irritated by my call. I said I was worried about Monica.

'What's that got to do with me?' she said.

'I thought you were her friend.'

'So are you.'

'I think she's possessed.'

There was a long pause, then: 'Are you serious?'

I replied irritably that of course I was serious, though looking at the peacefully sleeping Monica in my bedroom I began to doubt. After a little further argument we agreed that I should drive Monica down to Maeve's cottage that night. I received the distinct impression that Maeve had no more idea of what to do than I.

I had difficulty in waking Monica, and even then she remained in a semi-comatose state while I got her to the car. By this time it was getting dark. Monica was disposed to sleep during the journey and I was happy to let her, but it was a strange, lonely drive down to Dorset.

As we were approaching the village of Wolfeton Monica woke up. She was confused and asked me where she was and what was happening. I tried to give her soothing answers but she was obviously troubled. Though I wondered whether I should stop the car and offer her more detailed reassurance my instinct was to go on as we were nearly at Maeve's.

We were driving along a comparatively narrow stretch of road. Ahead I could see the lights of a lorry approaching. Suddenly Monica grasped the wheel and steered my car into the path of the oncoming vehicle. It was a strong cold grip. The lorry hooted. I wrenched control of the steering wheel and pushed the car back to the other side of the road. The lorry grazed the bumper; Monica screamed and I drove on. I was not going to stop until I reached Maeve's.

I glanced at Monica in the car mirror. She was in some kind of fit. Tears were starting from her eyes and the mouth was being held down in that terrible rictus.

It was instinct or perhaps Providence which took me to Maeve's cottage. My brakes screeched as I stopped beside the gate. I saw Maeve running out. Monica was sobbing uncontrollably beside me. When she noticed Maeve she scrambled out of the car and rushed into her arms. I let them go into the cottage together.

For about ten minutes I sat in the car recovering from the delayed shock of the incident with the lorry. My mind was clear but my body was incapable of movement. I can remember debating with myself quite rationally whether my paralysis was mental or physical, and whether such a Cartesian distinction between mind and body was valid in the circumstances. I wanted to move but knew I could not: all my impulses were stillborn.

Slowly, will and movement returned, beginning with the extremities. At last I was able to get out of the car and walk to the cottage. When I came through the door I saw Maeve facing me at the end of the room. Her big, slightly comic face had assumed a serious expression. I knew what it meant: indignation and the secret pleasure that accompanies feelings of moral superiority.

'What have you been doing to her?' she asked.

'Where is she?'

'Never mind that. She's upstairs on my bed resting. She doesn't want to see you ever again, and quite frankly I don't blame her. First of all she comes down to see you to talk about the play and you try to have her arrested; then, while she's asleep on the way down you start groping her. She wakes up and tries to hold you off, and in the struggle you bloody nearly drive into a lorry and kill her. And quite frankly, I don't want to listen to any explanations or excuses, because I've had it up to here with you. Just get out.'

I stood my ground and told her what had really happened while she listened with an impenetrable face.

'D'you expect me to believe that bullshit?' she asked when I had finished.

'Why would I have brought her down to you in the first place?' I asked. After a pause I said. 'She's got to you, hasn't she?' This last question seemed to shake her.

'What do you mean?'

I wasn't sure what I meant, or even who I meant by 'she'; I had spoken without thinking. Then I said: 'You must admit there's something about Monica that's not quite right.' Maeve did not reply, but I knew she had seen a little of what I had seen. The silence that followed was broken by a creak and then another. Maeve and I started violently.

The creaks came from the staircase which opened into the main living room through a door. Monica was coming down from the bedroom. We heard her fumbling with the latch; then she entered.

She was wearing nothing except one of Maeve's dressing gowns which was hanging open. Her eyes were wandering and unfocussed. The corners of her mouth twitched as if they were being pinched by unseen fingers. When she saw me she let out a hiss. Her eyes became fixed on mine with that cold predatory stare that you sometimes see in cats. I thought Maeve would do something but she made no move. Desperate, I let my mind empty itself of all thought in the hope that inspiration would fill the vacuum.

The next moment—perhaps the most extraordinary to me of the whole affair—I stepped forward and hit her hard across the cheek, at the same time shouting her name. The light of humane recognition entered her eyes and I held her close to me calling to her again and again. Her body entered a convulsive phase but I still held on to her and together we were propelled about the room in a strange involuntary dance.

The convulsions were replaced by trembling, then she became still. I laid her down in a chair, thinking the worst was over, but Eleanor Marchant had one more trick to play. With a sudden movement Monica launched herself at me. I cannot remember what happened but Maeve told me afterwards that Monica had butted me in the stomach; I had been thrown back and knocked myself out on the coal scuttle.

I can recall that period of unconsciousness as a kind of dream. Yet it was unlike any other dream I have had. The events in it were coherent, simple and stripped of surrounding detail; my mental faculties were sharply rational.

I found myself in a grey mist. I imagined myself to be standing, but I could feel no solid ground beneath my feet and I seemed to be suspended in vacancy. The sensation—or rather the absence of it—would have been disquieting if I didn't have the feeling that I was there for a purpose.

A black speck appeared in the mist and seemed to get larger or come closer: in the absence of any surroundings it was impossible to tell which. The speck formed itself into the silhouette of a tall woman in a long dress. I recognised the shape as the one I had seen long ago in the ruins of Grove House. Though the shape became more sharply defined it remained only a shape; no details or features revealed themselves. It was as though I was looking into a black hole in the shape of Miss Eleanor Marchant.

What happened next, although it remains transcendently vivid to me, is almost impossible to describe. I can only say that my mind and that of Miss Marchant came together and fought. Perhaps the word 'soul' would be better than 'mind' because this was in no sense a contest of intellects. It was a battle for possession and though that possession involved ideas, it was more fundamental and psychic than that. A force that turned the edges of my thought soft was bearing down on me. The sensation was like being just on the conscious side of sleep when one is trying to stay awake, but in this case the sleep was not a pleasant one but full of nightmares. I felt I was being invaded by a mind trapped within its own space, which had no means of survival except by trapping and absorbing others. One lucid idea came to me in this confusion: that the absorption of another mind would offer it no liberty, only a bloated continuation of its former existence. It would be a fatter rat in the same small cage.

Though my thinking was clear, the space in which it had its being was getting smaller. I was losing the battle because, though I could defend, I had no means and somehow no wish to attack. I had a shield but no sword and so I was constantly on the retreat. Two things saved me.

The first was an extension of the thought I had about Miss Marchant's attempt to possess me, and that was that my resistance was as much for her benefit as for mine. But more than that, my resistance was an attempt to preserve something that was natural, correct, just—any one of those three adjectives would be inadequate on its own—and that her efforts at conquest were the opposite. I would stress that this did not seem to me like a moral conflict in the sense that we normally understand it, a fight against corruption or cruelty. It was the opposition of what conformed with universal harmony—simply another way of saying 'the way things are'—with what rebelled against it. The force that was trying to possess was doing so in order to remain separate, and that aim was not so much 'evil' as self-defeating.

The second element which turned the tide in my favour was a simple phrase: 'Go in Peace.' Insofar as one can hear without ears, I heard this; it did not come from inside me. I think I recognised the voice of Maeve speaking it first, but the phrase was taken up by a thousand other voices unknown to me. It was not long before I knew that phrase to be my salvation and I was speaking it as well. The phrase swelled into a chorus, each expression of it woven into a clear yet complex pattern, like a Bach fugue. I felt the pressure being lifted from my mind and the dark silhouette begin to withdraw. I became a very small part of what was now happening, barely more than a spectator, as the phrase: 'Go in Peace' reverberated all around me. Its meaning seemed to become richer and more complex as it was taken up by more voices higher and deeper. Each of the three words contained a universe.

The last thing I remember of this visionary part of my experience was witnessing some subtle transformation taking place in what had previously been the black silhouette of Miss Marchant. Streaks of silver were appearing in it and turning it from a flat dark surface into a three-dimensional figure in grisaille. Light was moulding the head and I began to see those familiar Marchant features, scored still with lines of pain but somehow more real and realistic than before. Then the head turned away and the figure began to move off towards an unknown destination.

I woke up to find both Monica and Maeve bending over me. I said: 'She's gone.' They said: 'We know.' After that there seemed to be nothing more to say. I slept on the sofa at the cottage and drove back alone the following morning to London.

ၹ

About a month later Monica and I went down to Broadstairs. We visited my old school, Stone Court, now an old people's home, and walked around the housing estate which had been built over Grove House and its grounds. It was a Sunday: children were riding around on bicycles and fathers were cleaning cars or mowing front lawns. Then we walked to the North Foreland and threw the tile from Grove House into the sea.

That was not the end, of course, but it was a kind of beginning. As for the danger, it had merely entered a new phase, but for us it did not come again from beyond ourselves.

TIGER IN THE SNOW

It was not perfect, but it was her own. As a site for an art gallery it had the advantage of being just off New Bond Street, comprising two large airy rooms together with a small office. On the other hand it was on the third floor and the rent was ridiculous; but for Sally Cochrane it was to be the start of her great career. For some years she had earned a very good living running galleries for other people: she had done it well; she had built up a superb list of contacts. The glory, however, had belonged to others and, though the owners may have listened to her suggestions, she had never been allowed to choose her own artists.

Sally had decided views on the work she wanted to display. She wanted the newest, the freshest, the most adventurous. She wanted to take risks, a thing her employers talked about but very rarely did. And for her first exhibition at the Sally Cochrane Gallery she wanted one of the Young Wreckers.

The Young Wreckers were so called because *Young Wreckers* was the title of the highly publicised exhibition this group of artists had held jointly just after they had left Bermondsey Art School. They explained the title by saying that they were bent on wrecking the preconceived notions of the current art world. They were wise enough not to specify what these preconceived notions were, just in case some killjoy critic were to tell them that such ideas had long ago been abandoned and nobody took any notice of them anyway. Whatever else they were, the Young Wreckers were shrewd, and their talent for showmanship was formidable.

Their leader Kevin Spooner was well known for his 'bar-code paintings', huge enlargements of supermarket bar-codes painted on canvas in vivid colours which sold well to the boardrooms of retail companies. His bust of the late Princess Diana made entirely from his own frozen semen aroused great indignation and much desirable publicity. There was Anna Frend who made the famous Butter Bridge. Her representation of a human penis constructed entirely from smashed light bulbs is a curiously beautiful thing. It is also, of course, a wittily ironic comment on the current fragility of male sexuality. The O'Bogan brothers specialised in video art with banks of screens simultaneously showing slightly different versions of one person performing a mundane task. Their most startling piece at the *Young Wreckers* exhibition was their video installation, 'Breakfast for the Third

World'. A bank of a hundred screens showed a hundred different bottoms all defecating at the same time. These films were run repeatedly to the tune of 'The Star Spangled Banner'. It was the title, of course, that created the furore and it drew outraged condemnation from the prime minister of Bangladesh, then visiting the country. Naturally the work was intended to be a mordantly ironic attack on Western consumerism and waste, but representatives of impoverished countries are not always as sensitive to irony as they should be.

It was generally agreed, by the critics if not by the Young Wreckers, that the most talented of this group was Tina Lukas. She specialised in meticulously detailed installations with a strongly autobiographical slant. For *Young Wreckers* she produced an extraordinary reconstruction of the hotel room in which she had been conceived. The walls, of which she had taken casts, were made from a transparent resin into which photographs of herself and her parents at various ages had been set. The bed bore the distinct impression of two naked bodies facing one another but not touching. The critics described this piece as tender and poignant which perhaps it was, though it has to be said that Tina Lukas's parents did not like it at all.

She went on to produce a number of smaller installations which were bought by the Tate Modern and other major galleries, and her commissioned memorial to the victims of the Brighton Rail Disaster won almost universal acclaim. She had cast in a translucent amber resin some random objects found in one of the ruined carriages. These she arranged in an airtight glass case through which wound tendrils of smoke lit by gently varying beams of light. The effect, which in cruder hands might have seemed mawkish or merely vulgar, was haunting and pathetic. Even some relatives of the victims approved.

Tina had just been announced as being on the short list of the Turner Prize when she also agreed to open the Sally Cochrane Gallery with a one-woman exhibition. Sally felt that her career was made. It had taken her months of patient negotiation, because Tina, despite her Young Wrecker image, had a deeply reclusive streak.

Only one small cloud hovered on the horizon for Sally: Tina had not thought of anything to exhibit. With three months until the opening, this was serious, for Tina was a slow worker; and only a new piece of hers was going to command the publicity Sally needed. Sally kept in touch with Tina by telephone; she visited her workshop in Whitechapel. She tried to keep up a gentle, tactful pressure, knowing that anything remotely resembling intimidation would send Tina bounding into the undergrowth like a frightened gazelle.

Tina's creative block was simply explained. She was having an unhappy love affair with a sculptor called Jake Pomorski who made large, unsold, unattractive pieces out of rusty scrap metal. His resentment of Tina's success took the form of an intensely critical approach to everything she did. He told her and himself that he was critical of her work only because he cared deeply about it and wanted to improve it. The result for Tina however was creative paralysis.

Sally began to hate Jake with a passion. She was intelligent enough to realise that she would damage her cause if she were rude about him in front of Tina, so she treated him with glacial politeness and praised his work very faintly indeed. 'Interesting' was the adjective she used; even, when she was feeling particularly vicious, 'quite interesting'. Jake, who fully returned the hatred, would tease Sally about the approaching date of her gallery's opening. 'What are you going to do?' he would say.

'Have an exhibition of empty space? That would be quite interesting.'

The situation was becoming intolerable. Then one day Sally visited Tina in Whitechapel and found for once that Jake was absent. He was usually there when Tina had visitors because his fanatical jealousy extended even to women friends. Sally noticed a slight bruising around Tina's left eye and asked about it. Tina swept a pale lock of hair over it and gave an evasive reply about a fall in the kitchen but Sally knew that Jake had done it. The anger Sally felt was so great that for almost half a minute it stopped her from speaking. Even after that she could not trust herself to approach the subject directly.

On her way to visit Tina Sally had bought an *Evening Standard*. The front page had a report of a woman convicted of stabbing her husband to death. The case had aroused some controversy because though the woman, Jean Miller, had killed her husband while he was asleep on the sofa of their living room she had pleaded not guilty on the grounds of provocation and self-defence, maintaining that he had physically abused her over several years. However, her counsel had not convinced the jury and Jean Miller was found guilty of murder. Sally drew Tina's attention to the story. It was the nearest she could get to a direct reference to Jake's behaviour.

Tina showed interest: 'Look at their house,' she said. On one of the inside pages there was a photograph of the house in which the killing had taken place, a large modern, detached dwelling on a new estate outside St Albans. It was described in the paper as a 'dream home' ('but the dream became a nightmare' it inevitably added). The victim, Ken Miller, had been the personnel manager of a large pharmaceutical company.

' "Dream Home",' said Tina. 'I love that phrase. Isn't it extraordinary? Of course a real dream home would only exist when you were asleep. A real dream home would be unreal, wouldn't it? The rain would fall through. Can I keep your paper? I'd better see this dream home; it might give me some ideas.'

Sally left soon after. She could see that Tina did not need her; her own thoughts were becoming far more interesting companions. But Sally was very pleased with what had happened. She had set Tina's mind working, and maybe the exhibition would not have to be postponed after all.

For a week Sally did not ring Tina, much as she wanted to. At the end of it she was longing to know what Tina had been doing. Several times she found her hand poised over the telephone. On one of these occasions the phone rang, but it was Jake.

'What the fuck have you been playing at, Sally? What the . . .' and so on. Sally was subjected to a monotonously obscene battery of insults. The burden of Jake's complaint was that Sally had set Tina off on a project of which he personally did not approve and to which he had been denied what he called 'input'.

'She's refusing to take any constructive criticism. That's bad news. I'm beginning to worry that she's going down the tubes as an artist, I really am.' A note of sentimental compassion had come into his voice, self-pity masquerading as pity.

'Has she chucked you out then?' asked Sally.

'What the fuck has it got to do with you?'

'Everything, it would seem,' was the smart reply that Sally thought of but did not give. Her father was in the Royal Navy and she had absorbed some of his disciplined decency.

'I know what you're thinking, but it's not what you think,' said Jake confusingly and rang off.

The next day Tina telephoned to announce that she had one or two ideas and would Sally come round to Whitechapel and discuss them? There was a suppressed excitement in Tina's voice which implied: 'Come now!'—so Sally did.

ꟹ

Tina's studio flat in Whitechapel was almost as big as Sally's gallery. It was situated at the top of a warehouse just off Brick Lane and consisted of a large studio with a sloping roof, most of which was made of glass, and a little warren of smaller rooms off it. Everything was painted white. Sally noticed a new tidiness and discipline about the place.

'Jake's gone, then?' she asked.

'Oh . . . yeah . . .' said Tina carelessly, and that was the last time she mentioned him. She went over to a plan chest, opened a drawer and took out a folder. Sally wondered if she was going to be offered a cup of tea—she would have liked one—but Tina was oblivious to such niceties.

'Now then,' she said. 'You remember that house I was talking about? Where Jean Miller murdered her husband Ken? Well, I went to see it. You can't imagine the trouble I had to get in there, just to photograph the place. They didn't know who I was. They obviously haven't heard of the Turner Prize in St Albans. Anyway, luckily I've got an uncle who's quite high up in the police, so I managed to get into the place. I even managed to see the sofa on which Ken Miller was murdered. I took a picture, but they wouldn't sell the sofa to me. The bloodstains are still on it. Anyway, the house was amazing.'

Tina opened the folder and took out a set of large colour photographs of the interior of the murder house. It looked much as Sally had expected it to look: expense had not been spared on its embellishment but taste had; or rather what Sally and those like her understood as taste. There were ruched curtains of glazed chintz, wallpapers of simulated watered silk, onyx-covered tables, carpets with patterns like an explosion in a paint factory. The furniture, when it was not aping the worst excesses of Louis XVI, was bloated, bulbous and upholstered in violent-hued velvet or leather. And the ornaments! And the pictures!

'Incredible, isn't it?' said Tina who gave the impression that she had seen nothing like it before. Where has she been? thought Sally. Tina took out another set of colour pictures.

'Now, this is the murder room itself.'

It was the main lounge, lavishly appointed like the rest of the house. There was a bar in one corner. There were brown bloodstains on the white carpet and the sofa which was upholstered in gold brocade. Those stains infected the whole room with desolation and horror. Sally thought she saw the way Tina's mind was working, but she was mistaken.

'And look at that picture on the wall. Isn't it incredible?' said Tina pointing. Sally peered at the photograph. On the wall behind the fatal sofa was a modern framed print. She couldn't quite see what it was.

'Look. I took a close-up of it.' Tina handed Sally an enlarged photograph of the picture. It was a signed, limited edition print representing a tiger padding through the snow on a bleak mountain top, the legend in barely legible italics was *Tiger in the Snow*. The original painting was obviously the work of a highly accomplished professional artist.

'It looks like a Roger Banbury,' said Sally.

'Yes, that was the name,' said Tina, surprised. 'Do you know him?'

'He's famous. His originals sell for thousands, and he makes a fortune out of these limited edition prints. Specialises in African wildlife. You must have heard of him.'

'He's crap.'

'Yes . . . well . . . he caters for a market. Not ours. When I was working for the Carlton Galleries they had an exhibition of his work. I met him. Actually, he's a very nice bloke. Professional, you know. Believes absolutely in what he does.'

This aspect of Roger Banbury did not interest Tina at all. She said: 'But it's the image that's so amazing. This awful cheesy image of aggression and violence in the very place where a violent act took place. That's going to be the focus of the work. Images of violence. Actual violence. How they relate. I've got an idea for this installation. I'm going to recreate the room, but with variations. This tiger image is going to cover an entire wall.'

'Wait a minute, Tina. You're going to have trouble with the copyright.'

'Oh no I'm not. I've bought it.' Tina saw Sally's astonishment and laughed with delight. 'Yes, you see Roger Banbury didn't own it. He'd actually donated it to the Wildlife Preservation League who produced the limited edition print.'

'Very generous of him.'

'Yeah, well apparently he's potty about all those jungly creatures. Anyway the WPL have made their pile out of the *Tiger in the Snow* prints, so they were only too pleased sell the copyright on.'

'How much for?'

'You don't need to worry about that. I managed to beat them down.'

'Roger Banbury won't be pleased.'

'Actually, he's fallen out with the WPL for some reason. That's how I managed to get the copyright so easily. If he kicks up a fuss it won't be bad for our publicity.'

This conversation increased Sally's admiration for Tina. At the same time a ruthless streak had been revealed. Sally tried to dignify it in her mind with the phrase 'the single-minded dedication of the artist', but it still made her uneasy. She pressed Tina for more details about her installation, but got no more out of her. 'Wait and see,' said Tina.

Murder Rooms was the title of Tina Lukas's show at the Sally Cochrane Gallery, and it was subtitled *Violent Image and Violent Reality.* Sally was not alone in thinking that it was Tina's best work to date. The main part of the first room of the gallery was occupied by a replica of the room in which Jean Miller had stabbed her husband to death. Tina had taken the proportions of the room and reproduced them in plywood and plaster at about eighty percent of their actual size. The furniture consisted of exact copies of those in the original room, and the fact that they were disproportionately large by comparison with the room's overall dimensions created an eerie, claustrophobic effect. The stains on the carpet and sofa were bright red and freshly painted each day so as to remain sticky and glutinous. The back wall was entirely covered with a crudely coloured reproduction of *Tiger in the Snow*. From this single installation, which resembled some bizarre stage set, emanated two serpentine lines of objects ranged along the floor which flowed into the second room of the gallery. These objects were items connected with other famous domestic murders of the past all neatly and voluminously labelled in Tina's exquisite copperplate hand. There was a plaster cast of William Corder's death mask; Dr Buck Ruxton's actual stethoscope; an arsenical flypaper of the kind used by Florence Maybrick to kill her husband (believed by some to be Jack the Ripper); a little miniature model of the trunk into which Patrick Mahon put the dismembered remains of his mistress, and so on. All these grisly relics and pseudo relics, together with their elegantly hand-written labels, were for sale. In the second room the two lines of objects snaked across the floor, crossing each other several times and finally wound up in opposite corners of the room where two further installations stood. One was a life size replica of a bath in which George Joseph Smith had drowned one of his victims. It was filled to the brim with what looked like blood, on which floated a female tailor's dummy in full Victorian walking costume. The effect was bizarre and disturbing.

Even more alarming was the installation in the opposite corner of the room. It was a quarter size model of the cellar beneath which Dr Crippen had buried the body of his wife Cora. Taken from photographs and executed with minute and scrupulous accuracy, it seemed as if every patch of grime on its dingy walls, every smear of dirt on its dusty floor had been faithfully reproduced. The little model was lit by a tiny naked bulb which swung to and fro from the ceiling, throwing strange shadows about the enclosed space which could be observed from two vantage points: at eye level through three glass panels cut in the wainscot, and down the cellar steps from a raised platform.

At deliberately calculated irregular intervals an event occurred which many visitors described as quite unusually sinister. One of the flagstones of the cellar would flip up and through it, like an old Jack-in-the-box, would come a doll in the ample shape of the murdered Cora Crippen. Its mouth would open and through it, seemingly, would come the ancient, scratchy recording of a contralto voice singing 'The Lost Chord'. (No recording of Cora Crippen survives so the voice used was that of Dame Clara Butt, but this in no way diminished the peculiar horror of it.)

It was an extraordinary feat. Tina Lukas had done it all in little more than two months. She had used assistants, but much of the handiwork and all of the ideas had been hers.

The private view was a huge success. Nicholas Serota put in an offer for the 'Bride in the Bath' for the Tate Modern and

Charles Saatchi had snapped up the Crippen Cellar even before he heard Cora Crippen's rendition of 'The Lost Chord'. Many of the smaller items sold, despite their exorbitant prices and the critics were enthusiastic. They nearly all claimed to have been deeply disturbed by it which is a very high accolade indeed in the modern critical lexicon. Ladbrokes made Tina Lukas odds on favourite for the Turner Prize.

Only one event marred this triumphant opening: Jake turned up, drunk and uninvited. Fortunately Sally had installed a large doorman at the entrance of the gallery in anticipation of his arrival. Nevertheless there was an ugly scene. Several celebrities and a cabinet minister were jostled. A critic who had his glasses knocked off in the affray assumed that the whole business had been staged as a first night stunt for his benefit and pronounced it 'frighteningly realistic', as indeed it was.

Two other people intimately connected with the exhibition took violent exception to the show. One was Roger Banbury, original begetter of *Tiger in the Snow,* who was outraged to discover that his copyright now belonged to Tina. The other was Jean Miller, the convicted murderess whose front room was the focus and starting point of the whole exhibition. From her prison cell she sent out letters to anyone who might conceivably be interested in her plight. A few tabloid newspapers registered her hurt, but the more serious periodicals failed to see that this woman's feelings had any relevance to anything. Mrs Miller's solicitor put up a rather half-hearted protest that the exhibition might prejudice the outcome of her appeal, but this was rightly disregarded. Public sympathy towards Mrs Miller had begun to wane in the light of various revelations about her private life. Whether her husband Ken beat her up or not remained disputed, but she herself had been found to be drunken, promiscuous and unpopular with her neighbours. 'She has lowered the tone of the area,' they said.

One morning, a week after the exhibition had opened, Sally read a small paragraph in her *Guardian* to the effect that Mrs Miller had hanged herself in her cell. Disturbed by the news she rang up Tina who, although she had not heard, still registered no great interest. She was beginning to develop a series of works for her Turner Prize exhibits in the Tate. They were all to be based around Roger Banbury's *Tiger in the Snow*.

'I'm trying to see how far you can develop one banal image so that it stops being banal and becomes significant. In the same way that the Renaissance artists did it with the Madonna and Child. That's just as banal in its way. But I'm saying you can do it with any image. Even one with no cultural or religious significance at all. Just as the sublime can become ridiculous in one short step, so there's also one short step from the ridiculous to the sublime.'

'Samuel Butler.'

'What?'

'Didn't Samuel Butler say roughly the same thing?'

'Did he? Well, I said it first.'

༄

A few days after Mrs Miller's suicide one of Sally's assistants at the gallery asked to be relieved immediately from her duties. Sally was not greatly disturbed, as she was being inundated with requests from young art students to 'help out' at the gallery, but she was surprised. She asked the girl, called Ingrid, why she was leaving and received a rather incoherent answer.

'It's only recently,' said Ingrid, 'but it's the crowds. They get to me.'

'Well, it's a very popular exhibition,' said Sally.

'I know, but they sort of . . . they like . . . mess with my head.'

'Mess with your head? What do you mean "mess with your head"?' Sally heard herself adopting the tones of her old headmistress. It must be the onset of middle age, she thought. Ingrid looked pained as she had expected sympathy.

'I don't know, but it's funny. It's like the place is always full but I haven't seen them come in. And there aren't many signing the visitors book. And they dress funny.'

'In what way "funny"?' Visitors to modern art galleries are not known for their sartorial conformity.

'Old fashioned. Like stiff collars and that. Really weird. And they never say anything to me. Thank me and that.'

Sally let Ingrid go more in sorrow than in anger and rang up an eager art student who wanted to take over the following day, but Sally put her off. Sally had not been into the gallery for some days and decided to investigate Ingrid's nebulous complaint for herself the following morning.

Sally arrived at the gallery half an hour before its ten o'clock opening with no particular sense of foreboding. As she walked up the stairs to the third floor she felt, if anything, eager to re-experience the show alone, and see if its admittedly macabre atmosphere would 'get to her' in the same way that it had obviously done to Ingrid.

She stopped on the landing just before the final flight of stairs to the gallery for no reason other than a slight feeling of weariness. This was unusual enough—Sally was known for her unflagging energy—but what was odder was the sensation she then had that there were whispering voices coming from the gallery. She could not say exactly that she could hear them, as they came to her in a muffled way, more like a tinnitus inside the ear than a normal auditory sensation. She crept up the final steps to the gallery hoping to gain a clearer impression of what she thought she heard, but the 'sound' remained muffled and stopped altogether the moment she touched the gallery's door.

Sally shrugged off the sensation as a mere physical aberration, unlocked the door and entered the gallery. She found nothing unusual other than a peculiarly stuffy atmosphere. She opened some windows and switched on a fan in the inner gallery where the *Crippen Cellar* and the *Bride in the Bath* were installed. Silly Ingrid, thought Sally, she wasn't getting enough air; that was what had been 'messing with her head'. Sally hated the phrase, but it kept re-entering her mind, like an annoyingly insistent tune.

Soon after ten the first visitors of the day arrived, an enthusiastic, art-loving couple called the Kramers from New York. They were not there to buy, but had read the reviews and gave the impression that almost their sole reason for coming to London, England was to visit Sally's gallery. 'Of course, we went to the Tate Modern, as well,' they said, almost in parenthesis. While Mrs Kramer engaged Sally in a serious discussion about whether she thought Jeff Koons was radical enough these days, her husband wandered through into the inner gallery. When he emerged Sally was still talking to Mrs Kramer.

'Hey,' said Mr Kramer. 'That guy in there. Is he part of the installation too?'

'No,' said Sally. 'What guy?' She was sure that the Kramers were the only people who had come into the gallery so far.

'This weird guy. Like he's wearing these weird heavy clothes, you know.' The upward inflection at the end of the sentence gave it a hint of interrogation. 'Like he's got this strange hard collar, and a droopy mustache, and these weird glasses with kind of no handles on a string?'

The word 'pince-nez' entered Sally's mind and then she dismissed it. No-one wore pince-nez these days. 'No,' she said politely to Mr Kramer. 'I haven't seen anyone like that, I'm afraid.' She got up from behind her desk to look for herself, but just then a group of art students came in and she was distracted.

'This is some crazy gallery,' she heard Mr Kramer say. 'That guy really bugged me. Like I'd come in on his party and he didn't want me there.'

The rest of the morning passed without incident. There was a steady stream of visitors, but Sally reluctantly had to agree with Ingrid over one issue: she also had the impression on several occasions that there seemed to be more people in the gallery than she had observed coming in. Out of the corner of her eye she was aware of little groups of people, huddled together, apparently discussing the exhibits; but when she looked fully in their direction they were not so many as she thought, and they dispersed quickly. Perhaps more tantalisingly, when she was attending to the needs of one of her less elusive visitors she would overhear above an almost constant murmur of conversation, strange little fragments of talk, of the kind one does not usually hear in an art gallery.

'Marshall Hall was splendid . . .' 'Scales of justice . . .' 'The hyoscin was not intended...' 'Getting rid of it was the problem...' '*Nearer My God to Thee* on the harmonium . . .' All these were spoken in hushed tones but were quite clearly heard by Sally. One remark in particular stuck in her mind, partly for its strangeness, partly because it recalled something that she had heard recently, she could not quite remember what. It was a male voice speaking, a very charming voice, with a lilting Irish accent. It was saying: 'Her head was staring at me out of the fire.'

In the afternoon Beth, Sally's part-time secretary who handled the money side of the gallery, called in; then the art student came to be instructed in her duties as an invigilator.

Both were welcome company, but neither stayed as long as Sally would have liked. They seemed strangely anxious to leave as soon as possible, especially the art student whose initial enthusiasm about working for Sally was not so evident by the end of their interview. Sally had wanted to close the gallery with the student, but the student said she had to be somewhere else urgently.

So when the gallery officially closed at five, Sally once more found herself alone. After the bustle of the day, everything had now fallen silent. Sally went round the gallery doing her usual checks. It was then that something very disturbing happened.

She was in the far gallery turning off the mechanism which sprang the Cora Crippen Jack-in-the-box when she distinctly heard a female voice in the main room say:

'That bloody tiger! Ken loved it, but I always hated it.'

Sally ran into the next room but no-one was there. For the first time she felt fear. Being naturally strong-willed and brave she hated herself for being afraid so she deliberately took her time to leave the gallery. Having locked the door behind her and walked down to the first landing she stopped to listen for a long time. Nothing. Then, as soon as she had put her foot on the next step down, the whispering started, just as she had heard it before, coming from her gallery. Sally ran down the stairs and did not stop running until she was out in New Bond Street with the dear sweet traffic.

That evening Sally met her sister and some friends and went out to dinner. When she got back to her flat she went straight to bed and fell asleep. Three hours later, at four in the morning, she woke up suddenly. She was not particularly alarmed, but she knew she had woken up because she had thought of something. A connection had been made in her brain during the hours of sleep which she must now recall. It had to do with that odd remark she had overheard: 'Her head was staring at me out of the fire.' Then suddenly she remembered.

When Tina was constructing the installation, she had told Sally all kinds of stories about the murderers whose relics she was placing in little trails across the gallery floor. One story concerning the trunk murderer Patrick Mahon was particularly memorable. When Mahon finally confessed after being sentenced to death, he recalled how he had dismembered his mistress to put her in the trunk. He did this in the living room of a small seaside bungalow. When he cut off the head he threw it on the fire to see if it would burn. The heat of the fire caused the eyes of the corpse to open and it seemed to him that they had looked straight at him. That was the story. Sally did not sleep again that night. Towards morning her turning, troubled mind did find some tranquillity out of sheer exhaustion, but not for long. At eight o'clock the telephone rang and it was the police.

The office below Sally's gallery employed overnight cleaners. At about four in the morning one of these had heard a sudden commotion from the floor above. He can't have been very courageous because it was some time before he and a fellow cleaner had ventured upstairs to see what had happened. They found that the door of the gallery had been broken open. They entered and looked round. It was some time before they realised (or were willing to realise) that the figure sprawled across the bloodstained sofa in the main installation was not a sculpture but the real corpse of a man.

Who was it? The police said that they didn't know, but the body had been removed to the police mortuary and would she try to identify it and make a statement? A car would be calling for her shortly. She asked how had the man died. The police said enigmatically that there were no obvious signs of a violent death.

Sally did not recognise the body at first, the features were so distorted; it was the signet ring that did it. One of Jake's affectations—and he had had many—was that he was the scion of an ancient and immensely aristocratic Polish family. The family crest, an eagle devouring a hare, was engraved on a gold ring which he wore on the little finger of the left hand. Once she had recognised the ring Sally was able to identify the face as Jake's. The mouth was agape and the eyes stared: it was like a statue of Fear personified. After explaining who he was Sally asked again how had he died? The police would go no further than to say that it appeared to be some kind of heart seizure and that 'foul play was not suspected'. Sally had difficulty in preventing herself from laughing hysterically: the words 'foul play' seemed so hideously inappropriate.

Later that morning Sally gave the news to Tina who broke down and wept convulsively. Whether it was grief or remorse, the reaction was terrible. Apparently, that very morning Tina had been told in confidence that she had won the Turner Prize. How she wished Jake could have been there to share it with her, she wailed. Sally took advantage of this moment to say that in view of all the circumstances she would like to close the exhibition early, in fact as soon as possible, in fact that very day. Most of the art objects for sale had, after all, been bought. Tina impulsively agreed.

Sally had the exhibition dismantled the same afternoon. When she had seen to the despatch of the artefacts to their various buyers, she closed the gallery and went to stay with her godmother in the Dordogne.

The celebrations surrounding the award of the Turner Prize that year were rendered even more unpleasant than they usually are by a group of Animal Rights protesters who claimed that Tina's variations on *Tiger in the Snow* were 'speciesist', an ugly word. By this, presumably, they meant that her work was insulting to tigers. One commentator observed that, after all, no tigers had protested and anyway it was not the tiger which had been insulted but the intelligence of the art-loving public. Generally, however, Tina's award was reckoned to be well deserved, and everyone was touched by the moving tribute she made in the acceptance speech to her 'late partner', Jake Pomorski.

ꕥ

Roger Banbury no longer paints wildlife, but his income is not diminished. His talents are now concentrated on the representation of Spitfires and steam engines, and he never relinquishes his copyrights.

Tina Lukas's work now consists entirely of copies of *Tiger in the Snow*, often with bizarre variations. Sometimes the tiger is shown wearing Wellington boots, or a rakish Trilby hat; sometimes he holds in his mouth a coat hanger on which is a blood-stained cardigan; sometimes the face of the tiger carries the lugubrious features of the Prince of Wales. Many critics are fascinated by the turn Tina's art has taken; they say that her work is an ironic commentary on . . . well, opinions differ, but irony always comes into it somewhere.

There are others, of course, who simply say that Tina is mad. But in the Art World today what is sane and what is mad? Indeed, are such antiquated categories relevant at all to the modern cultural scene? Sally Cochrane has decided that these questions are not worth asking, let alone answering, and now runs a highly successful craft shop in Nuneaton.

GARDEN GODS

Julian and Antonia (Jules and Tonia) Paige were a notoriously successful London couple. They were tall and attractive and in their late thirties; they had highly paid jobs as financial analysts in merchant banks; they had two daughters of eight and ten, both, like their parents, gifted and bright. They also had a wide and admiring circle of friends to whom it came as a shock when they decided to give up their jobs and live permanently in the country. A cottage in the Cotswolds, or even Suffolk, for weekends was acceptable, but 'going the whole hog' was looked at askance. Reactions ranged from anxious warnings and downright disapproval to grudging envy.

The decision Jules and Tonia had made was not an impulsive one. It had been contemplated over several years while they saved large sums from their salaries; and they knew what they were going to do with their rustication. They would buy a substantial property and create a garden of great beauty from which visitors could buy plants. Workshops and residential courses on horticultural matters would be run from the house. The Paiges flattered themselves on having green fingers: Tonia was the plantswoman and Jules the designer.

At weekends they would set off in search of their ideal property which was to be an old house, spacious and stylish but not grandiose, set in several acres of well drained soil. Jules and Tonia had the reputation among their friends of being lucky, a reputation which appeared to be well deserved when, sooner even than they expected, they came across exactly the right place for a surprisingly modest price.

Wyvern Manor, not far from Westhill in the heart of the Cotswolds, was an eighteenth-century house of compact elegance set in seventeen acres of ground on the crest of a gentle slope. Its natural advantages were enhanced for the Paiges by the fact that it already possessed a horticultural reputation, albeit a faded one.

In the 1920s it had come into the hands of the Honourable Adrian Clavering, the younger son of Lord Swinbrook. Adrian Clavering had the misfortune to have been born the one artistic member of a very conventional aristocratic family. After Eton and Oxford he had shunned a traditional Clavering career in the army or the diplomatic service in favour of the arts. Which one of them he could never quite decide, for his gifts, though various, were thinly spread.

He scraped an acquaintance with the Sitwells and contributed a couple of pale poems ('Harlequin in Montmartre' and 'Pan on the Saxophone') to their journal *Wheels.* He painted for a while in the Cubist manner, and was nearly commissioned to design a ballet for Diaghilev. He played the piano prettily enough and might, with more application, have become a distinguished professional interpreter of Ravel and Debussy. But nothing quite stuck—he had the sensitivity but not the steel of the true artist—and so he drifted, living the life of a mildly impoverished but socially acceptable bachelor-about-town.

When a favourite aunt died leaving him Wyvern Manor and a substantial sum of money, Clavering found his vocation. He emptied the house of its Victorian accretions and filled it with good Georgian furniture and well-chosen modern paintings. He completely redesigned the garden, turning it into a place of delicate neo-classical fantasy, full of lichened statues, fountains and eccentric topiary. At the end of a long yew walk he built a folly in the form of a classical temple to the god Pan. He gathered strange botanical specimens from all corners of the globe and planted them with taste. His garden became famous to many (open to the public on the first Sunday of the month from May to October) and his hospitality was enjoyed by a select few.

In 1931 he published his first book, *Green Thoughts* ('Decorated by Rex Whistler'), about the making of the Wyvern garden. The elegant if mannered prose together with its combination of wit, recondite horticultural scholarship and practical advice made the book a distinct though minor success. *In a Green Shade,* the sequel, and other works of a similar nature followed. The golden years for Adrian Clavering were the early 1930s when he was esteemed, fulfilled and still young. They were marred only by an unsatisfactory private life whose main theme was a febrile, at times self-destructive quest for the perfect partner. A number of young men came and went, some taking with them substantial amounts of his money when they left.

The war years were lean ones in which Clavering was forced to give over some of his acres to the growing of potatoes and other unattractive but useful vegetation. After the war Clavering re-made his garden, but he was older, less energetic, and yet no wiser in his choice of companions. Visitors still came from far and wide to see the Wyvern garden; Clavering still wrote occasional articles in *Country Life*, but everyone who knew agreed that it was 'not what it was'.

Adrian Clavering was found dead in his Temple of Pan one bitter January morning in 1971. There were mysterious circumstances surrounding his death which the police never cleared up. The property was inherited by a great nephew who, being a normal philistine Clavering, sold the Georgian furniture with the modern paintings, and neglected the garden. When he left his wife, she was allowed to live at Wyvern rent-free as part of the divorce settlement, and there she drank herself into an early grave. By an odd coincidence she too was found dead one morning in the Temple of Pan. It was on her death that Wyvern was sold to Jules and Tonia Paige.

After essential repairs to the fabric had been made the Paige family arrived with their removal van one bright, cool morning in April. The yellow Cotswold stone of Wyvern Manor shone almost like gold. Its beauty struck all of them, but to Jules it did not seem an altogether friendly kind of beauty. Tonia walked up to the house and tore down some of the ivy which was masking its architectural beauties. Their two daughters, Emilia and Tamsyn, began to run about in a great state of excitement.

'Millie, Tam, don't go too far away. We've got a lot to do,' said Jules, who was seized by an irrational fear that they would lose themselves in the overgrown garden. The family cat, Hermes, lolloped cautiously out of the car, walked a few paces towards the house and then sat down on the gravel drive to stare at the building. His gaze was the still, intense one he usually reserved for potential prey.

The hall was empty except for a large thin rectangular package wrapped in brown paper leaning against a pillar. Jules smiled at his wife.

'Tonia, darling,' he said. 'I think it's for you.'

'What?'

'A house-warming present from me to you. Open it.'

'Oh how sweet! Thank you, darling.'

Tonia began to unwrap the package with slight feelings of irritation. Jules had on what she secretly called his 'Clever Me' expression, a little schoolboyish smirk. He often wore it when he was giving her something which he really wanted for himself.

It was a picture, the head and shoulders of a man in his mid twenties set against a black background, superbly painted.

'It's a Glyn Philpott,' said Jules, half reading his wife's thoughts.

'Yes, I can see. He *was* good, wasn't he?' said Tonia, a little grudgingly. 'But who's it of?'

'Can't you guess? Adrian Clavering, of course. I thought we had to have him with us, so to speak, if we were going to restore his garden. To inspire us.'

'Oh, brilliant! Thank you, darling. How did you get hold of it?'

As the removal men brought in their furniture and effects Jules told his family the story. He had known the picture existed from a reproduction he had seen in a book. When he found out that the Clavering great nephew from whom they bought Wyvern owned the painting, Jules had persuaded him to part with it for only three thousand pounds. Of course, the great nephew had not known who Glyn Philpott was and so Jules was able to get it for less than he should have paid, but that, Jules implied, was the great nephew's fault for being a philistine. Tonia was troubled by her husband's story: it was not that she felt any qualms about the great nephew, but she did not like Jules glorying in his smart deal. They were, after all, supposed to be leaving all that sort of thing behind.

The picture had the rich, old-masterish glamour which Philpott managed to impart to his best work. Superficially it was just a society portrait, but it had depth. Clavering in half profile was staring out of the picture to his right. An orchid in his buttonhole suggested an earlier, more dandified age than the 1930s. The head was narrow, the hair black and sleek, the eyes large, dark brown, long lashed. Elegantly almost-handsome was the first impression; the second impression was less easy to define.

There was something about the tilt of the head, the half smile, the nervous intensity of the glance that suggested unease. Poise was aimed at but not wholly achieved. He seemed to be hungry for something which he could not quite grasp or define. That was Tonia's impression, and she hoped that his picture would not be put in too prominent a position because its presence might become unsettling.

The Paiges' first few weeks at Wyvern were spent on the house, redecorating and generally, as Tonia put it, 'making it our own'. Though he never said so Jules began to feel that they would never make Wyvern entirely their own; nor did he want them to. The legacy of the past should continue to weave its spell. Nevertheless, this settling in period was an exciting time despite all the hard work.

There were, inevitably, one or two elements in their situation which made for unease. The first of them, trivial but disturbing nonetheless, were the empty bottles. There were hundreds of them: some were wine bottles, but they were mostly gin and vodka bottles, and the Paige family found them in every conceivable space not immediately visible to the eye. They were the only traces to be found of Wyvern's previous occupant, the divorced, alcoholic Mrs Clavering. Hardly a day went by without a new cache being found. 'I honestly think they breed,' said Tonia who, with Jules, strenuously tried to make a joke of it in front of the children. Alone, when Millie and Tam were in bed, they confessed to finding these discoveries depressing.

'Poor wretched woman,' said Tonia. 'What a bastard that husband of hers must be.'

'It makes me gladder than ever that I did him over the Glyn Philpott,' said Jules.

Tonia grimaced and turned her head away from him. 'But why on earth didn't she just put them in the dustbin?' she asked. 'Why keep the damn things?'

'Her way of making a mark. We all have to leave a mark.'

'But this isn't an unhappy house. Is it?'

'Oh no. It's going to be a very happy house indeed.'

⁂

Tonia got the girls into a good nearby primary school and set about making herself part of the community. She made use of what local shops there were, even though the supermarkets at Evesham were far cheaper, and for purely social purposes she went to church. Everyone was perfectly pleasant, though she was irritated by the fact that whenever she mentioned that she and Jules were remaking the Wyvern garden, the reply was always: 'Oh. Good luck!' spoken in such a way as to imply that it was an impossible task, but they were welcome to try.

They found that, after London, society in that part of Gloucestershire seemed a little restricted. Of course, they missed their metropolitan friends, but it was more than that. There were in the main only two social classes: the commercial and agricultural workers and those loosely described as 'landed gentry'. Though Jules and Tonia considered themselves and were considered to be in the latter group, they did not find many sympathetic spirits among them. In London, social categories tended to be less rigid and had more to do with interest and occupation than lineage and wealth. The gentry still held fast to feudal beliefs and pursuits which revolved around horses and hunting. Gardening was looked on as a secondary activity; music and literature, Jules and Tonia's other passions, were barely thought of at all. The Sunday morning drinks parties, common forms of entertainment in that part of the world, had an extraordinary sameness about them: the same white wine—or Pimms in Summer—the same canapés made and served by the same catering firm, the same Snaffles and Munnings prints on the walls (or originals in the case of the 'seriously' rich), the same chintz covers, the same people. Jules and Tonia, however, were not too worried about this lack of social diversity, as they were too busy creating their own world at Wyvern.

By the end of May the house had been fitted up more or less to their satisfaction and they were ready to devote all their efforts to the garden. A first serious inspection revealed that they had a huge task ahead of them. Large areas of the grounds had become impassable thickets of bramble and nettles; in the walled garden every glass pane of the Victorian greenhouses was smashed; all the ponds and water features, of which there had been many, were dried up or choked with mud and reeds. Only the Temple of Pan remained undamaged, though its bronze doors absolutely refused to open. Irritated by this they began to refer to the Temple as 'The Folly', and it became to them a symbol of the difficult and possibly foolhardy task which they had undertaken. If, as was their plan, they were going to open to the public the following June, Jules and Tonia would need assistance.

They had found someone to come in and help clean the house twice a week, but met with unexpected difficulties when looking for someone to work in the garden. The locals would shake their heads and say they didn't know of anyone. Their tone of voice implied that Jules and Tonia were asking a lot.

'Anyone would think we were looking for a tight-rope walker,' said Jules irritably. Their gentry acquaintances were even more annoying.

'Of course,' they would say, 'we have George who's an absolute treasure, but he wouldn't want to work for anyone except us.' 'We can ask, if you like,' added the more friendly ones, 'but I'm afraid he won't take you on.'

Advertisements put up in shop windows had no response whatever. 'So much for this so-called rural unemployment,' said Jules one day with a contemptuous little sniff. God, thought Tonia, he's beginning to sound like his awful old father.

Relief came from an unexpected quarter. One morning their vicar called unannounced. The Reverend Herbert Somers looked after several parishes in a group ministry with the aid of a curate. Tonia did not like the perfunctory way he had conducted the services at Westhill church. Most of the congregation were already in their pews when he would arrive carrying a suitcase containing his vestments. Five minutes later, he would emerge into the choir from the vestry in stole and surplice and launch into the old prayer book matins. He read it efficiently, speedily and without enthusiasm, often obscuring his face behind part of the rood screen as he did so. His sermon was always ten minutes long and barely intelligible. It was a lamentable performance. The curate when he came to Westhill was better, though timid and sometimes scarcely audible, but mostly they got the Reverend Herbert Somers, because he lived next to the church at Westhill Rectory.

He was a big, loosely built, white haired man in his sixties who walked in a strange, awkward way as if he were limping on both legs at the same time. His face was pink and flabby. Everything about him suggested a withdrawal from the world into a private sphere; yet the pale blue eyes could still flash with angry life. There were moments in his brief but rambling sermons which showed that he had once had a good mind. He quoted widely, though nearly always irrelevantly, from the Church Fathers and the Greek and Roman Classics. Julia heard rumours of a brilliant ecclesiastical career ruined by a mysterious scandal, but she put this down to malicious speculation. Somers was not liked, and his parishioners had tried unsuccessfully on several occasions to get rid of him. In his turn Somers did not disguise the fact that the dislike was fully reciprocated which was why Tonia was so surprised to receive a pastoral visit.

But as soon as Somers had bustled into the hall of Wyvern Tonia knew why he had come: it was sheer naked curiosity. Even while she was suggesting coffee and biscuits in the drawing room he was peering around, barely taking in what she was saying. Tonia was amused rather than offended by his rudeness: it would be something funny to tell Jules when he got back from looking at rotivators in Evesham. She went into the kitchen to make the coffee and when she returned with it he was in the drawing room staring at the Philpott portrait of Adrian Clavering above the fireplace.

He had his back to her when she came in with the tray and, as she set it down, she said: 'Did you know him?'

Somers gave a start, then said irritably: 'Of course!'

'Yes. How silly of me!' said Tonia soothingly. She was thinking: he obviously doesn't like women, why do I bother? She poured the coffee. He took it milky with several spoonfuls of sugar, and when she offered him a biscuit he put three on his plate. 'So you know this house of old?' she said encouragingly.

'I first came here in the fifties with a friend from Oxford.'

'Did he have some lovely things? Furniture and pictures?'

'Of course!' Again, the undisguised irritability.

'We're doing our best to return house and garden to something like its former glory. With rather limited resources, I'm afraid,' said Tonia. Why was she apologising to this man?

'Hmm.'

By this time Tonia was beginning to tire of his brusqueness, so she decided to provoke him. 'I gather Adrian Clavering died in rather mysterious circumstances,' she said. It had the desired effect: the pale blue eyes became fierce.

'What do you know about that?' he snapped.

Tonia said coolly: 'I was going to ask you precisely the same question.' Got him, she thought. He's an old bully and you just have to stand up to him. Somers nodded, acknowledging the smart riposte. When he spoke again, his speech was slower, more hesitant.

'He was found in the Temple of Pan.'

'The Folly.'

'Adrian wouldn't have called it that. In fact he hated the word being applied to that building; but, yes, as it happens, Folly is *le mot juste.*'

'What happened?'

Somers ate a biscuit before replying: 'Adrian was an amateur, you see, in everything. Gifted, of course, but essentially a dabbler because he was rich and spoilt all his life. Very charming, though, and a delightful host. I dined with him the night before he died. I tried to warn him, from bitter experience as it happens, but he wouldn't listen. I do hope you are not a dabbler, Mrs Paige.'

'What happened?'

'Good heavens, is that the time? I must be away.' Somers got up, pocketing the last biscuit on his plate as he did so.

'Thank you for your hospitality, Mrs Paige. If there is anything I can do for you, naturally, please don't hesitate . . .' As he said these last perfunctory lines, he was on his way out, so that Tonia had to run after him to stop him from going.

'As a matter of fact,' she said, 'I don't know if you could possibly . . . but we're having terrible trouble finding someone to help out with the garden.'

Somers stopped and turned to look at her. For the first time since she had known him Tonia saw him smile. 'Ah. Yes. Well . . . Naturally,' he said. He made a little 'Hm-hm' sound in his throat that was almost a laugh. The Paiges' inability to find a gardener was a source of malicious amusement to him. Then he nodded gravely as if correcting himself for his former hilarity.

'Have you tried Quinton?' he asked.

Tonia said no, she had never heard of Quinton, who was he? And how could she get hold of him? Somers told her not to worry, he would sound out Quinton himself; then he left. The following morning at ten a man presented himself at the front door of Wyvern Manor and said that he was Peter Quinton and he understood they were looking for someone to help out in the garden. He was prepared to give them one whole day,

Thursday, every week. It was better than nothing, and his fee was very reasonable.

They called him Quinton, or 'Old Quinton' in private, though he insisted on being called Peter to his face and on addressing the Paiges as Julian and Antonia. Quinton was tall, wiry and of indeterminate age, though certainly over sixty. There was something gipsyish about his appearance: he went in for red and white spotted bandanna handkerchiefs around his neck, and his hair was dyed with Henna. His bushy eyebrows, now almost white, showed traces of ginger; his brown face and arms were freckled. His accent, certainly not local, was not easily identifiable, but Tonia thought it had a South London twang. His eyes were the most striking feature, they were green and could look positively feral at times. Jules swore that the pupils were not round but oblong and slitted, like those of a cat: it was a joke, of course.

Quinton became both indispensable and intensely annoying. On Thursdays he arrived early, left late and worked hard, but he could rarely be contacted outside his working hours. He did not have a telephone and it was a long time before he revealed where he lived. He had a small, rather isolated cottage about four miles away from Wyvern, but when Jules or Tonia tried to call on him he was hardly ever there. On the few occasions that he was, he came to the door of the cottage to talk to them. Beyond that door was an unlit dinginess, and he made it quite clear that they were unwelcome. He would very rarely change the day or the time that he came to Wyvern with the result that if he could not come on Thursday, he could not come at all that week. This inflexibility was infuriating.

He could also be quite irrationally stubborn about what he did and didn't do in the garden. He would prune or plant or weed without complaint, but if he was ever asked to move an established plant from one location to another, he would often argue against it, or simply refuse point blank to do so. His innate conservatism led to many disputes, one of the fiercest of which was over the Herm.

The Herm was discovered one day when Jules was in a remote part of the garden. He had been following one of the many stone paths which wound their way about the property when he found his way barred by a dense patch of briars and undergrowth. He summoned Quinton and they hacked through it to discover that the path opened out into a brick paved oval space surrounded on all sides by yew hedges, now wildly overgrown. In the centre of the paved area was a stone pedestal of the kind that usually carries a sundial. No sundial was evident on its top, only a bronze disk covered in verdigris on which something indecipherable had been engraved. It seemed a gloomy place, though not without romantic charm for some, thought Jules. He looked at Quinton, who was staring about him as if searching for something.

At one apex of the oval, half buried in the yew, Jules spotted a tall object in grey, lichened stone. He turned to Quinton whose gaze had also been directed towards it. Together they attacked the yew until the object was revealed.

It consisted of a flat sided pillar, two feet wide and six feet high, slightly tapering at the bottom where it stood on a stepped pedestal. The top of it consisted of the classical bust of a bearded man which, because of the extra height given to it by the pedestal, stared down on Jules and Quinton. About half way down its flat front surface the erect genitals of a man had been carved in low relief. Jules, who was proud of having had a classical education, pointed at the object and said: 'That's a Herm.'

'Right,' said Quinton.

It was an irritating remark, and somehow typical of Quinton. It implied that he knew perfectly well that it was a Herm, indeed what a Herm was, and was simply endorsing Jules's identification. Regardless of this Jules told Quinton that Herms were votive statues, originally of Hermes, later of other deities, which were common in fifth century BC Athens. He even started to tell him how the mysterious mutilation of their genitals caused a scandal in Athens and led to the exile of Alcibiades with disastrous consequences for the city. All the while Quinton listened to him, nodding from time to time, annoyingly like a schoolmaster approving his pupil's recitation.

'Of course, it will have to go,' said Jules.

When Quinton questioned this decision, Jules explained that he was hoping to attract visitors with families and that some might be offended by the statue's ithyphallic equipment. Quinton seemed unimpressed by the argument and said that it had been put there for a purpose and one shouldn't move things without good reason. Jules left the discussion at that, but thereafter, whenever Jules had devised some scheme of moving the Herm, which inevitably required doughty male assistance, Quinton raised objections. There were times when Jules nearly lost his temper in front of Quinton, but he was afraid to offend him. This fear, as he ruefully admitted to Tonia, did not only stem from the fact that Quinton was their only source of help in the garden. There was something about him, quite indefinable, which made him uneasy. Tonia agreed. She particularly distrusted Quinton's association with the children.

Millie and Tam were fascinated by Quinton, whom they always addressed and referred to for some reason by his full name, 'Peter Quinton'. They would follow him around the garden, chattering to him. He did not slacken in his work, and most of the time he ignored them, but sometimes Jules or Tonia would hear them talking with him. Their attempts to find out what he was saying to their children always failed. He invariably spotted them before they got close enough to make out what he was telling Millie and Tam.

One afternoon in September Tonia happened to be looking out of an upper window of Wyvern onto the back lawn. There she saw Quinton with Millie and Tam. Quinton was crouching down with the girls standing over him, and he was showing them something which he held in his left hand. Tonia could not tell for certain what it was, but it was flat, black and shiny, like an ancient obsidian mirror she had once seen in the British Museum. With his right index finger Quinton began to describe a figure in the air just above its polished surface which he then covered for a while with the red and white bandanna he had taken from his neck. He said something to the children who bent further over his shoulder to look at the thing in his hand, then with a quick deft movement, like a conjurer, he swept away the bandanna. Millie and Tam stared, fascinated, into the black mirror.

Something about the way her daughters were looking at it troubled Tonia, quite apart from the oddness of the whole situation. She opened the sash window and called to Millie and Tam. They reacted by starting back in shock, as if suddenly shoved by an invisible hand. Quinton looked up at Tonia, and for a moment she saw a look of rage and hatred pass across his face. Its intensity was demonic, but it was replaced almost immediately by bland bafflement. He wrapped whatever it was he had been showing the girls in the bandanna and thrust it inside his shirt.

As Tonia descended the stairs Millie and Tam came running in from outside. She asked them what they had been doing with Quinton, to which they said 'Nothing'.

'What was he showing you?'

'Nothing,' said Tam.

Millie, the elder, felt that some explanation was owed, so she said: 'We were just playing a game.'

'What sort of game?'

'Scrying in the stone,' said Tam. Tonia saw Millie look at her sister with annoyance. Evidently Tam had said more than she should have.

'And what on earth is "scrying in the stone"?'

'Oh, just a game,' said Millie, taking Tam by the hand and skipping off with her into the drawing room. Tonia knew she would get nothing more from them, but she was angry. She had a feeling that something bad had been going on. Somehow Quinton had been 'interfering with their young minds'; that was the phrase she used to describe her unease. She went into the garden to have it out with him.

Quinton was tinkering innocently with the lawnmower on the gravel drive. As she approached he looked up casually and said 'Hello, Antonia'. He seemed to be pretending that they had never exchanged glances when she was at the upper window. The word 'insolence' formed in her mind, even as she realised that such a term did not belong to the present egalitarian age. Tonia made a conscious effort not to sound feudal as she spoke.

'Peter, what was it you were showing Millie and Tam just now?'

'Oh, that! Just something I picked up.'

'Can I see?'

Quinton took the bandanna from inside his shirt and unwrapped it to reveal a thin, irregularly shaped slab of black stone with a flat, highly polished surface. He only showed it to her for a few seconds before putting it away again, but in that time Tonia had noticed that it had been finely engraved—so finely you could barely see the lines—with some kind of geometrical figure.

'Where did you pick that up?' she asked.

'Oh, you pick these things up.'

'The girls said you were playing a game with them.'

'A game? Well . . .'

'What is "scrying in the stone", Peter?' She was watching his expression carefully now, but he gave nothing away.

'Oh, that,' he said. 'We were just seeing if they could see theirselves, like in a mirror. Just a game.' Tonia paused before replying, hoping that the pause and the quizzical look she gave him would imply scepticism without her having to express it verbally.

'I'm not at all sure about these games of yours, Peter,' she said eventually. Tonia's intention was to make it quite clear, without being heavy handed, that she was telling him off, but she failed. She managed only to sound petulant and condescending.

'Right you are, Antonia,' said Quinton starting up the lawnmower and thereby putting an end to all further conversation. Later in the day he left a note in the hall to say that he would be unavailable the following Thursday.

That night Millie and Tam had nightmares. This was not unusual as they were both highly strung, imaginative children. What was odd was that their nightmares were almost identical. They said that in their dream they were running through the garden at nightfall and wherever they went faces would suddenly poke out at them from the hedges and undergrowth. What kind of faces? White faces, said Tam. Old-fashioned faces, said Millie. What did she mean, 'old-fashioned'? Like the faces you see in old art books, said Millie, with curly lips and beards, sometimes with little horns. Laughing, said Tam. But not nice laughing, added Millie, horrible laughing, like they were playing a game with you that they knew, but you didn't. Jules read them to sleep again with a story and made a mental note to talk to Quinton when he next came.

But he didn't. Quinton, for all his faults, was invaluable. There was so much clearing and tidying to be done before the Spring. The garden was slowly yielding up its secrets, some of which were agreeable to Jules, others, like the Herm, not. For such a large area it had very few open spaces. Adrian Clavering had gone in for features, most of them, especially those involving water, very decorative. But even these tended to be over-elaborate: water did not merely emerge from a simple aperture, it was belched from the mouth of a grotesque head, or was blown from the conch of a Triton, or cascaded over a shell grotto. Quinton's uncanny ability to restore these and get them flowing and splashing again reconciled Jules, up to a point, to both them and Quinton.

The problem was, as Tonia said to Jules, that Wyvern was not one garden, but many: rose gardens, knot gardens, walled gardens, water gardens. There was also a maze which neither of them liked, though neither said so to each other, even when Millie had run in one afternoon to tell them that there was an old woman with long grey hair crawling about in the maze, carrying a bottle. No such woman was found, of course, and the story was briskly dismissed as fantasy. Millie was a very imaginative child.

And there were statues everywhere, all of fine quality, but none of them entirely likeable. If there was a cherub carrying a basket of fruit, he was, unaccountably, weeping. A faun leered at you aggressively. A serene seated greybeard, in classical robes, was contemplating a skull. Mithras in his Phrygian cap was slitting the bull's throat in a peculiarly violent manner. It goes without saying that there were several representations of Priapus, the god of gardening, with his erect penis, most of them mercifully small and easily concealed, but one of them was a fountain. Even the leaden urns on the terrace were decorated with low relief scenes in which Centaurs carried off struggling Lapith women, or nymphs fled in terror from lustful satyrs. Tonia found a curious marble version of Leda and the Swan in one of the old stable buildings. Zeus in the guise of a swan seemed to be perpetrating a rape rather than a seduction. Tonia locked the outhouse, grateful that this sculpture at least had not seen the light of day.

By the end of that year nearly all the ground had been cleared of its accretion of weeds and superfluous growth. Many parts of the garden had been restored almost to their former picturesque selves, and in this Quinton was invaluable. Though he was still determinedly against innovation, he had a genius for restoration. With the aid of a few old black-and-white photographs, and some sketchy plans, he was able to tell what had been planted where. He even proposed a compromise solution over the Herm. He had been able to find an attractive variegated ivy which would grow fast enough up the Herm to cover its offending appendages before the following Spring.

At the beginning of the following year Tonia and Jules were fairly confident they would be able to open in June, but there was still much to be done. All gardens have a habit of suddenly revealing some hidden area of neglect just as one is beginning to believe that it is at last tamed, but Wyvern had this habit to excess. One Friday in mid March Jules found that he had not really investigated what was to be found at the bottom of the steep bank behind the Temple of Pan which they called the Folly.

He was delighted to find that a meandering path led down to a dell through a thick planting of crocuses. At the bottom was a hollow surrounded by a grove of poplars and sweet briar, in the middle of which, embedded in undergrowth, was an oblong object that looked from a distance like a tomb. Closer inspection showed it to be the statue of a reclining figure on a plinth.

It was a sculpture in lichened marble of a sleeping girl with an exquisite figure and small, beautifully formed breasts. She lay on her side, one arm carelessly thrown over the delicate features of her smiling face. Jules was charmed. This at least was a tasteful addition to the garden. He would make a feature of this one. There was nothing to shock or alarm. But then he saw to his dismay that there was. Between the almost crossed legs the sculptor had carved a penis and testicles. It was a hermaphrodite. When Jules had cleared some moss and ivy from the plinth he found a carved inscription:

HERMAPHRODITUS

And whosoever hath seen thee, being so fair,
Two things turn all his life and blood to fire;
A strong desire begot on great despair,
A great despair cast out by strong desire.

It was at this point that Jules suddenly felt he hated the Wyvern garden. Everywhere he saw beauty, but the beauty always seemed to be twisted out of true, like this hermaphrodite, or pitched towards the grotesque. If this garden was going to live again it could not be restored, it must somehow be reformed.

Jules was surprised by his own thought. Up till then morality to him had been a banal, utilitarian entity to do with loving Tonia and the children, not being ruled by money, donations to charity, offering his seat to pregnant women in the tube. He had been reasonably good at most of these, and he was content that this should remain the limit of his ideal. Now he was seriously considering the idea that an environment could be a force for good or evil: that leaf and stone and water were spiritually charged. If that was the case, where would it all end?

His mind went giddy at the idea.

Suddenly he became aware that he was being watched. He looked about him. The air was still, no leaf stirred, no twig cracked. He looked again up the steep bank to where he could just see the rear of the Temple of Pan. The setting sun behind it threw up a backdrop of gold onto which an intricate tracery of leaves and branches had been printed. Into this another shadow had been inserted, the figure of a man who looked grotesquely large in the waning light. Jules shaded his eyes to see who it was. The figure moved and he saw that it was Quinton.

'Hello, Peter!' said Jules. 'This isn't your usual day.'

'I was wondering if you might be wanting me for an extra one,' said Quinton. 'Seeing as the time is creeping on.'

Jules walked up the serpentine path and onto the lawn behind the Temple of Pan where Quinton stood. If it were not for the odd thoughts he had just been having he would have accepted eagerly. As it was, he was not going to turn the offer down. It was arranged that Quinton should come the following Monday.

Over the weekend Jules and Tonia drew up plans for a new garden at Wyvern. The serpentine paths, the dark shrubberies, the little enclaves and grass theatres were to be cut down in favour of more open borders, more light, broader, more sweeping curves to the paths. The maze would be levelled to make way for a rockery. Perhaps they couldn't do everything that year before the opening in June, but they would try. Both of them thought as one: it was to be transformation not restoration.

'And I'm going to open up the Folly,' said Jules. 'We've neglected it for long enough.'

'Is that wise?' said Tonia.

'What do you mean?'

Tonia did not know what she meant; she felt afraid, but offered no further objection to Jules's decision. She did not want to stand in the way of her husband who seemed to have found a new spirit. She wondered at this. During all the time they had known each other, she had been aware of being the more mature and rounded person. When they met at Oxford, she had been the star: academically brilliant, beautiful, a leading player in OUDS. Emotionally she was far more experienced than the clever, callow ex-Wykehamist who had been lucky enough to catch her eye. She had been the senior partner in the marriage, and initiated the move to Wyvern; but lately she had been conscious of a subtle shift in the balance of power, of which his decision to make the garden more their own was the most striking example. She found to her surprise that she welcomed the change, and that acceptance enhanced rather than diminished her own strength.

That night two occurrences unsettled the family. The first was that Hermes the cat did not come in for his evening meal. Then at eleven, just as Jules and Tonia were going to bed they heard Millie screaming. It was a nightmare. She said she had dreamed that she was being chased through the garden by a man with spindly legs and hooves instead of feet.

&

They looked and asked everywhere for Hermes over the weekend, but he had gone. Millie and Tam, who had paid him little attention when he was around, were distraught. On Monday morning Tonia drove to the station at Moreton-in-

Marsh to fetch her mother who was coming to stay. When Quinton arrived he found Jules standing alone on the steps of the Temple of Pan.

'I want to open up the Folly, Peter,' said Jules.

'You mean the Temple of Pan?'

Something about the way Quinton insisted on the name alerted Jules. What a fool he had been! It was now so obvious to him that Quinton must have known Wyvern in Adrian Clavering's time.

'The doors seem to be locked,' said Jules.

'Ah, well then,' said Quinton turning away. 'Perhaps it's best left alone.'

'No. I want it open.'

'Why would that be?'

'Why not?'

'I don't see no point, that's all. There's other work to do. That brick walk in the rose garden . . .'

'Peter,' said Jules quietly. 'We are going to open the Folly. I want it open. I can't understand why you're so reluctant. I have a sledge hammer here. If we take it in turns, I'm sure we can break the doors down.'

'Don't you think we should try and find the key first?'

'Where would we look? I don't want to waste any more time.'

'I got an idea where it might be. There's a big old key hanging on a hook in the stable building where the statue of that swan and the woman is.'

'Then you'd better fetch it, Peter. And if that doesn't work we try the sledge hammer.'

As Quinton went to fetch the key Jules contemplated his victory. In the past it might have made him light headed; today it simply hardened his determination.

It only needed a small application of oil to the lock for the doors of the Temple of Pan to creak open. The interior was a rectangular space with windows on either side so caked in dust and grime that they barely let in the light. The air was damp and chilly. At the end of the chamber at eye level was a niche in which rested a sculpture of polished black basalt. Unlike the statues in the garden it was not in imitation of the classical style, but had the smooth stylised lines of an artist from the 1930s.

It represented Pan crouched, goatish knees brushing his cheeks, blowing the pipes. His frowning, saturnine features showed enormous concentration on the work of making music, and yet his eyes seemed fixed on the spectator. Jules could not decide about the look, whether it was malign, domineering or merely curious; perhaps a subtle combination of all three. It was a work of art.

An inscription on the base showed that it had been carved by Gilbert Bayes in 1933. Jules decided there and then that he would sell it. It was a fine work by a once eminent artist now coming back into fashion, but it no longer had a place here in the Folly. Jules planned to turn the place into a shop selling postcards and lavender bags and home made jams. The money from the sale would help pay for the garden's transformation. How neat.

'You don't want to get rid of that,' said Quinton.

Jules gave a start at this adroit piece of thought reading, but he remained calm. He asked Quinton what he meant. Quinton mumbled something about leaving things be.

'I fail to see what it has got to do with you,' said Jules who walked up to the statue to feel its polished surface. 'It's far too valuable to stay here.' Something odd struck him as he felt it. How could it have remained so long neglected and yet stayed so pristine. And what was this? As he touched Pan's hair his fingers became slippery, as if there was oil on it.

'Don't touch him!' shrieked Quinton.

The sound was so shocking that both of them remained quite still, staring at each other until the last faint echo of the cry had died away.

As the thoughts came to Jules, he spoke them: 'You've been in here, haven't you? You know it well. You've known it for a long time. You come in here and put oil on it.'

'He's my god! You move him. You lay a finger on him. I'll set him on you and her and the children. I will!'

'Get out!'

Jules thought Quinton was going to jump at him, but perhaps prudence restrained him. Jules was younger and stronger. Instead Quinton let out a series of cries, almost howls, except that they seemed to be in some inarticulate language. Occasionally Jules could distinguish something which sounded like: 'Io Pan! Io Pan! Io Pan Pan Pan! Io Pan!' Then Quinton turned and ran from the Folly.

Jules followed him and watched him go. As Quinton reached the drive he began to walk, bending almost double as he did so from breathlessness. Just then Tonia, who had been fetching her mother from Moreton-in-Marsh station, was driving up to the house, and narrowly missed hitting him. Oblivious of her, he went on stumbling down the drive.

'It's all right,' said Jules, hurrying up to the car. 'We've had an argument. I doubt he'll be coming back.' Tonia merely nodded, noting a new firmness in his tone, and helped her mother from the car.

'Come and see what I found in the Folly,' said Jules, quite ignoring Tonia's mother. Tonia's mother, whose name was Lady

Hope-Gore, and who expected to be greeted with respect and some affection on her arrival, looked at him stonily.

A minute or so later all three were in the Folly standing in front of the glistening black statue of Pan. 'Oh dear,' said Lady Hope-Gore. 'I hope you're not going to keep him.'

'I won't,' replied Jules.

'No. I shouldn't,' said Lady Hope-Gore who liked to have the last word. Jules thought that he had misread the stare of Pan when he first had seen it. Its expression was not ambiguous: the stare was unequivocally malign. As they left the Folly Jules locked it and pocketed the key.

That evening over dinner Lady Hope-Gore, the widow of a senior civil servant, gave the whole family the benefit of her views on a wide variety of subjects with such exhaustless energy that Jules and Tonia had no opportunity to discuss Quinton's departure. Tonia thought: Heavens! She must be lonely to have to talk so much. Jules thought: Tonia must be thinking how lonely her mother is, will she ask her to live with us?

That night when the children had gone to bed, Jules, Tonia and Lady Hope-Gore took coffee in the drawing room. Lady Hope-Gore was still talking but Jules had reached that stage of weariness when he found her conversation soothing rather than irritating. He allowed it to drift across his consciousness while he nodded occasionally to show he had not actually fallen asleep. For Lady Hope-Gore the semblance of attention was always a perfectly adequate substitute for the real thing, especially since most of the time she was unable to distinguish between the two. How many opinions, how little thought, reflected Jules, and then, because his ears had attuned themselves to hearing his mother-in-law's talk as a mere blur of noise, they caught something else. It was a faint sound and yet sharp and clear as faint sounds can be. It was like a wind instrument, as high pitched as a recorder, and yet somehow with a fuller tone. It was playing a continuous melody, or what seemed like one, for it returned to almost the same sequences of notes, but always with a slight variation which led on to some new theme. Fragments of it seemed familiar, but Jules could never quite identify it. It seemed uncannily modern and ancient at the same time. Ravel of *La Valse* could have written some of it; there was a touch of Debussy's *Prélude à l'après-midi d'un faune,* a moment or two from Warlock's *The Curlew,* the vocal line of Britten's *O Rose thou art sick*. All these were hinted at; or was it the other way round? Was it that Britten and Ravel, Debussy and Warlock had all drawn from the well of which this melody was the fountainhead? Jules's mind began to shut out Lady Hope-Gore altogether in order to follow the sound: and the metaphor of following the sound seemed very exact because it seemed to lead his mind out into strange territory.

It was as if he had passed through the dark garden of Wyvern into a wild landscape, scratched and scrubbed, untouched by cultivation, yet oddly like the part of the Cotswolds where they lived. Across the landscape roamed herds of savage creatures whose shape he could not define. The string of notes seemed to wind itself round his brain like a garrotte, strangling every other idea or image except these grotesque and shaggy pictures. He entered a primitive world where vision and feeling were one and by-passed altogether the language of conscious thought. Earth and sky were not dumb objects, but beings with which he held a constant tongueless dialogue.

'Jules!' said Tonia. Jules gave a start. 'Were you asleep?'

'No. Just thinking.'

'Been working too hard, I expect,' said Lady Hope-Gore with reproach.

'Can you hear that music? Sounds like a flute or something.'

'You ought to go to bed if you're so tired,' said Lady Hope-Gore.

Just then they all heard Millie and Tam crying out for their parents. Jules ran up stairs at once. Tonia had to shake off her mother who disapproved of being left alone in the sitting room just for the sake of the children.

Millie and Tam, who shared the same bedroom, were sitting bolt upright in their beds and yelling. What was the matter? asked Jules. There had been a face at the window, pressed against it. It had been black—everything black, hair, teeth, eyes, skin—black and shiny and it had looked at them as if it wanted them. Jules looked out of the window but saw nothing. By the time Tonia arrived her daughters had calmed down, but they were still tearful and afraid. Jules said he would stay with the children until they fell asleep again. Lady Hope-Gore in the doorway said that one shouldn't indulge children who had nightmares, it only made them worse.

'The children or the nightmares?' asked Jules.

'Both!' said Lady Hope-Gore.

'It wasn't a nightmare,' said Millie. 'We saw it.'

'You stay here, then,' said Tonia to her husband. 'Mother and I will go to bed.'

Jules heard them arguing away down the corridor. It was a soothing sound. He sat in the old nursery armchair, quite prepared to read his daughters to sleep, but they settled themselves and were soon at peace again. Jules himself began to drift off. He had listened out for the music, but heard nothing. All was silent outside: no nightingale, not even any cars along the Broadway road. It was almost worryingly quiet.

Jules did not quite fall asleep. Something deep in his brain stayed alert, turning over the day's events. He could not help making connections: the statue, the face at the window, the pipe music, Quinton's rage. It was all very strange, he thought, but his mind balked at a conclusive deduction. Then, into his dozing consciousness came a sound. This time it was close and it was not music. It was a thudding sound, like heavy hooves on the grass outside. But the rhythm beaten out was like no horses' hooves he had ever heard.

Jules roused himself into full alertness and looked out of the window. He could see nothing at first; then he began to make out vague dark shapes on the lawn outside. They seemed to be living forms which belonged to no particular animal or plant. It was as if the whole garden had become restless and was beginning to dance about the house. The thudding grew louder. Millie and Tam woke up screaming. The house was beginning to shake in time with the thundering hooves. Then the banging was on the wall and the doors of the house. Lady Hope-Gore and Tonia came running into the bedroom and clasped Millie and Tam to them. The sound increased until none of the family could hear themselves speak. The banging and thundering became intolerable and then went on increasing in sound.

Jules decided to go downstairs. He did not know why, but he knew he must act. He also knew that if the sound abated he would be able to hear Tonia telling him not to, so he resolved to act immediately. As he came down into the hall he felt himself surrounded by rhythmic thunder, trapped in a universe of pure percussion. Strange shadows, irrationally projected chased each other round the walls of the stairwell. It was as if some pagan orgy was being played in shadow and sound all through the house, and in Jules's head. Each step Jules took down the stairs became more difficult, and yet he dared to go on.

When he reached the bottom step he stood still, wondering what to do next. Every moment the noise and the moving darkness seemed to be increasing its grip on the house. It was threatening to break in unless . . . unless what? Then Jules knew. Instinctively he realised that a victim was being demanded and that if his wife and children—not to mention Lady Hope-Gore—were to be saved, the victim would have to be him. This conclusion was not rational except in the wholly irrational circumstances in which he had come to it. He took a step towards the front door.

As he did so he saw a faint glow coming from the drawing room. If there is such a thing as a grey light, this was it. The light flickered at first and seemed to draw back and move forward in a pulsating movement, but with each pulsation it moved forward more than it drew back. Jules took another step forward and the light seemed to come forward to meet him. By this time the light had formed itself into a shape, long and thin. It had begun to acquire the features of a human being, but fitfully. The fully formed semblance of a hand would appear and then regress into a vague woollen mitten of light. A face appeared several times and then blurred again. At last it achieved the full image of a tall thin man in a grey double-breasted suit with an orchid in the buttonhole. The face was narrow, clever, almost-handsome. Jules recognised the face of Adrian Clavering.

'Did you do this?' said Jules.

The figure held a warning hand up and walked towards the front door, then passed through it. A moment later the thundering stopped. A complete absence of sound invaded the whole house. Nobody dared to break it. Then a scream was heard, a long wail of terror and despair. This was no spirit scream. It had been squeezed viciously from living flesh and blood. It filled an eternity in ten seconds and was cut off by a single, monstrous thud. There was silence again, but this time, it was a normal, natural silence punctuated by the small sounds of a modern Gloucestershire night.

The front door swung open. On the moonlit drive outside Jules saw the tall willowy form of Adrian Clavering. With a thin finger, spectrally attenuated, it pointed in the direction of the Temple of Pan. As if compelled, Jules walked out of Wyvern House and along the yew walk towards the Temple. The doors had been burst open and were hanging limply on their twisted hinges. When he entered the Temple Jules could see that the black basalt Pan had fallen from its niche and shattered into a thousand glassy shards. On the floor of the Temple was another shape, the contorted body of Peter Quinton. Some kind of bizarre rigor mortis had arched his back up from the floor and pulled his staring eyeballs almost from their sockets. In the centre of his forehead was the scorched black imprint of a single cloven hoof.

Jules left the Temple to walk back to the house. He looked for the shape of Clavering on the drive, but it had vanished. In its place stood Hermes the cat, back arched, watchful. For a moment Hermes stared coldly at Jules, then, as cats do, he relented and trotted up to receive attention.

❧

The next few hours were another kind of nightmare, full of policemen and ambulances and interrogations. It was further complicated by Lady Hope-Gore, who had decided that the whole episode was caused by terrorists who had come to kidnap her. She vaguely suggested that her late husband's connections with the Middle East had been the cause of it all. It was absurd, of course, but no more absurd than any other explanation.

One tiny ray of understanding was shone into the darkness when Jules was talking to an elderly police sergeant who had lived all his life in the area. He was one of the few people who knew something about Peter Quinton.

'That's not his real name,' said the Sergeant. 'Peter Quinton was a name Mr Clavering gave him. Some kind of joke, he said. His real name was Jack Bly, I heard, and he had a record.'

'Criminal record?'

'That's right. Long before, though. But there was something nasty at the time Mr Clavering died. Peter Quinton, he claimed Mr C. had left something to him in a will he made. The whole of Wyvern, he said. But there wasn't any will, except the one leaving all to the family. Quinton said there was another will and the Clavering family, they'd destroyed it. He couldn't prove anything so it was dropped.'

Jules and Tonia discussed this new information and decided that the Reverend Herbert Somers owed them an explanation. It was he who had found Quinton for them, and he must have known something of his history. The next morning, leaving the children in the charge of Lady Hope-Gore, they drove over to Westhill Rectory.

The vicar's battered Volvo was in the drive but the front doorbell was not answered. Jules and Tonia walked round the house and found the back door open. They entered an old-fashioned scullery, all gloom and dinginess, not dirty, but dull and melancholy. An open door showed a passageway with doors off it leading to the front hall. No lights were on except for a yellow glow coming from an open door to the right. Tonia and Jules were not deterred. A moment later they were standing in that doorway.

What they saw was a room full of books: books in shelves, books on tables, books in tottering piles on the floor, books on the window ledge and the mantelpiece. What little wall space was not devoted to bookshelves was covered in dark oak panelling. The light came from a naked bulb in a single standard lamp under which the Reverend Herbert Somers sat in a brown leather armchair, reading. He looked up from his book with rage in his eyes.

'How dare you intrude upon my privacy like this?' It was almost funny; Somers' words, choked with arrogance and anger, seemed to belong to another age. Jules and Tonia stood their ground and told him why they thought he owed them an explanation. They insisted he tell them what he knew about Quinton and Adrian Clavering's death. He said scornfully: 'I do not owe you an explanation, as you put it. I really know very little. Please go. I am busy.'

'We are going to stay here in this Rectory until you tell us what you do know,' said Tonia. Somers crumpled himself resentfully into his armchair and tossed aside his book. Jules noted that he had been reading Euripides' *Bacchae* in Greek.

'Yes. Yes,' Somers muttered to himself. It sounded like an admission of defeat. Tonia reminded Somers that he had dined with Adrian Clavering the night before he died. 'What was it you warned him about?'

Somers sighed, as people do when they are about to tell a story for the hundredth time; though Tonia was sure he hadn't told it to anyone else before.

'Adrian had quarrelled with Quinton. It was perfectly silly. About the siting of a statue of a faun in the garden. Naturally Adrian should have had his way, but Quinton was the strong one. You see, Adrian was besotted with Peter Quinton. He used to be very good-looking, believe it or not: I have an idea he was once an artist's model. People even say there was a will leaving everything to him. I doubt it though, but Adrian may have told him there was. He could be such a tease. Well, Adrian wanted his own way over the faun, and so, for some reason did

Quinton. It became very acrimonious. I tried to reconcile them; in fact that's why I went to dinner with Adrian that night, a last ditch effort to patch it up. It was no use. Adrian's love—I suppose that is the word—had turned to hatred. He wanted revenge and he told me what he was going to do.' For almost a minute Somers stared at the ceiling.

'What?'

'He was going to summon Pan.'

'Christ!' said Jules.

'No, Mr Paige. Quite the contrary. And please do not use that name as a vulgar expletive in front of me. I do have some sensibilities left. Yes, Pan. As in Panic. Adrian, had always said that Pan was his favourite God. A childhood reading of *The Wind in the Willows* may have had something to do with it, I suspect. You remember that miraculous chapter, 'The Piper at the Gates of Dawn'? Hence what you call the Folly, Mrs Paige. A bit of an affectation, of course, but . . . He'd found something in a book—I think it was by that awful old charlatan Crowley—it was a summoning and sending ritual. It only needed a few burnt bay leaves and a black cockerel to do it. He had acquired both. I tried to persuade him not to. I really did. I had some personal experience to draw upon. When I left him I honestly believed that he was in a more reasonable frame of mind, but the next morning he was found dead. There was fear all over his face.'

'What had happened?'

'Who knows? All I can say is that Adrian was a dabbler whereas Peter Quinton knew a great deal more than we thought. As you've discovered. These Gods, they can't return to wherever they come from without a victim.'

There was a long pause. Somers' pale blue eyes were watery and distant. He said: 'Summoning Pan. It's a thing you don't do, especially if you're an amateur, a dabbler. You see my hair? When do you think it went white? Five, ten years ago? No. At Oxford, not long after I was ordained. When I was twenty-five. In one night.'

THE BLACK CATHEDRAL

'We are still essentially thinking for the computer,' Jasper Webb would say. 'We should be devising more ways of making the computer think for us.'

The first time we heard him say it we were impressed, but he said it so often it became tedious. These clever ideas stop being clever if you don't actually put them into practice. What none of us knew at the time was how hard Jasper was working to do so.

Our company is called Playtronics and we are inventors of computer games. We're young and we think we're the best in our field, with some justification. We specialise in adult games:

not the usual shoot-em-up crap, but genuinely intelligent stuff that an Oxford don wouldn't be ashamed of playing. You've probably heard of *Austerlitz!*, an amazingly lifelike representation of Napoleon's famous 1805 victory in which you take command of the Austrian and Russian armies and try to defeat the French. Others have done games based on Napoleonic campaigns before, but none have factored in such complex information on weapons, weather, terrain, even the morale and psychology of the opposing forces. Then there is *Faydo!* in which you take on a character in a turn-of-the-century bedroom farce and have to escape from a compromising situation with your reputation and trousers intact.

Jasper Webb at twenty-seven was probably our most brilliant games inventor. I say 'was', though, for all I know, he is still alive, somewhere, in some way. The truth is, he has disappeared, and this is the story of his disappearance. I don't ask you to believe me; I simply present you with the facts as I experienced them and leave you to draw your own conclusions.

࿐

We generally operate in teams at Playtronics, but Jasper liked to work on his own until a fairly late stage of development. Because he was recognised as the resident genius, this was tolerated. He didn't like to let on what sort of game he was thinking up until it was nearly ready. I often knew what he was about before he went public, because I am the computer graphics expert and he used to call me in to put the pictorial detail into his concept.

That August five years ago we all knew that Jasper was working on something big. As usual, we were kept in the dark, but he gave us the impression that it was some kind of architectural game in which one built one's own structure and could thereafter inhabit it 'virtually' and take others on a tour of it via the Internet. It sounded like a promising idea, but whenever we tried to probe further he evaded our questions and went off on an apparent tangent. He would lecture us about the medieval 'Art of Memory'. Apparently some people in the Middle Ages used to create elaborate buildings inside their heads, and within these imaginary palaces they would put pieces of information they had learnt into certain alcoves or rooms. It was a way of enhancing the powers of memory. Jasper said that the computer, being an artificial extension of the brain, could be used in the same way. He would tell us how we, as computer pioneers, were fulfilling old-fashioned theories of magic and how visualisation was the key. All this seemed pretty good nonsense to us. The cliché about madness being akin to genius was often used, though not by me.

One evening Jasper summoned me to meet him at his flat. The time had come for him to reveal to me what he was working on. There was a streak of showmanship in his make-up, so I knew that he was going to put on a display and that my response to it would have to be a mixture of admiration and enthusiasm. Jasper's self-assurance was a thin veneer; he reacted badly to criticism.

In appearance he was slender, small and dark with a pale face and protuberant eyes. Occasional flashes of light-heartedness animated his face in an attractive way. He lived on the seventh floor of a newly built complex of flats on the South Bank near Deptford. It had been designed by one of those architects who go in for bare white walls, chrome steel and concealed lighting, and for whom books and pictures are clutter because they are too narrow minded to appreciate any aesthetic except their own. They flatter their imaginative sterility by calling it 'austere'. Jasper, who had a curiously spiritual turn of mind, called it 'ascetic'. There was something in this. He had deliberately made his surroundings barren in order to concentrate his imaginative life on the computer screen.

Knowing his passion for punctuality, I arrived on the dot of nine p.m. As he opened the door to me Jasper looked at his watch and said 'I very nearly had to wait.' Was this echo of Louis XIV's words deliberate or unconscious? Was irony, or even self-mockery intended? I have no idea. He gave nothing away. He showed me into his living room. Its most striking feature was a long plate-glass window which looked out over London across the Thames.

Without many preliminary courtesies Jasper sat me down on his black leather sofa and started to walk up and down giving me a presentation of his latest idea. They say—or rather Jasper once told me—that Molière used to test out his comedies by reading them to his cook. Well, as far as Jasper was concerned, I was his cook.

'It's a new concept,' he said. 'Something that is both game and personal therapy, and psychological investigation. If you think that electronics can't fulfill those functions you're not thinking imaginatively enough. I've provisionally called it *Know Your Enemy!*' He paused for effect. I looked at him enquiringly.

'Tell me: if I were to give you a photograph of someone, could you devise a programme whereby you could create a fully animated virtual image of that person on the screen?'

You must remember that all this took place some time ago, and that IT has since evolved rapidly. At the time his question was perfectly valid.

I told him that there were already such programmes which had been used by film companies. To fit a programme like that into the compass of a computer game would require some compression and simplification, but it could be done.

'It could be done, right. But could *you* devise a programme which would do it?' Jasper had challenged me. With studied casualness I said that of course I could. Jasper nodded dismissively and went on: 'My idea, in its basic form, is that you use that technology to play a game against the opponent of your choice. You construct a fully-rounded 3D image of your enemy and challenge them. It could, of course, be some public figure like a sportsman or an unpopular politician, but I'm thinking more in personal terms. Someone against whom you feel some personal animus, someone on whom you need to work out your aggression, settle a score.'

'What kind of game are you thinking of?' I asked. 'Something violent?'

For the first time in our conversation, I noticed an element of evasiveness in Jasper's manner. 'Not necessarily,' he said. 'I see a more subtle psychological element entering here. I envisaged some sort of game of pursuit and capture. I've mapped out a few scenarios. You construct the living image of someone you dislike and you pursue him or her. Eventually you get to capture or even destroy them in some way. Nothing too gruesome, naturally. One doesn't want to pander to the baser instincts. Of course there has to be a game element. They have the chance to get away. But you can start the game again. It's like a blood sport without the blood . . . Maybe we should use a dog, or a pack of virtual hounds. That's an idea.'

I said I was uneasy about it. I said that the people who consider it their business to take offence would do so. They would undoubtedly make use of that ill-bred cliché 'the pornography of violence'. They would say it could encourage feelings of hatred, racism even.

'I would argue that it might do the opposite,' said Jasper. 'Purge those feelings. Channel them harmlessly away. Like masturbation over pornography. If, say, you have a grudge against someone at the office, you can get rid of all your animus against him.'

'Like using a picture of his face as a dart board?'

'Exactly. Only infinitely more subtle and satisfying. What do you think?'

I said that it was 'an interesting concept' and tried to suppress the fact that something inside me hated the idea. I turned to look out of his plate glass window. The lights of London below glowed like the embers of a fading bonfire, but the thickness of the glass blocked out almost all sound. It was a silent, safe panorama. A glass clinked behind me. I turned round.

'Would you like a drink?' asked Jasper. He opened a silvery door and revealed a lighted fridge full of beer bottles that glistened with cold sweat. Without waiting for me to reply he opened one and poured it into a glass. This he handed to me; his own beer he drank straight from the bottle. There was some significance in this act which I could not fathom, but I was aware of tension in the room.

'I need you to do something for me.' He took a colour snapshot out of his pocket and threw it down on the coffee table in front of me. The gesture was so deliberately casual, so perfectly executed that I suspect it had been rehearsed. 'See if you can make a fully animated computer image out of that.'

I picked it up and saw that it was a photograph of Sam Prentice, a colleague at the office. Sam was the marketing consultant at Playtronics and ever since he had joined the firm there had been an antipathy between him and Jasper. Sam had never really been able to understand Jasper's working methods—which he branded secretive, volatile and erratic—and he complained that his habits were an extreme expression of the creative mentality. Jasper thought Sam a tiresome pen-pushing bore. On the whole,

I took Jasper's side, but I knew there was a certain naivety as well as arrogance in the assumption that his creations were so great that they did not require marketing. He had made no secret of his contempt for Sam who was just as arrogant as Jasper but with rather less cause. There had also been rumours that Sam and Jasper had been in competition for a girl in the office called Sally, and that Sam had won.

'Why him?' I asked.

'Can you do it, or can't you?' said Jasper. I said I could. Jasper put his hand on my shoulder and said in a gentler voice: 'It's just a bit of fun. Test out your abilities. If you can do that, it would be a major breakthrough.'

I won't go into technical details, but I will give a rough outline of the procedure. Using a template of a male human form, I scanned in the photograph and then worked out a detailed series of proportional measurements which could be wrapped onto the face and body so that the features of the subject could be reproduced in a 3D computerised image. It was surprising how close I got to Sam's likeness just by this method. The programme proved difficult to work out, but wonderfully simple to use. You could hand me a full length photograph of anyone and, in a matter of seconds, I could produce a moving, articulated image of that person, a 'sim' copy, fully dressed, or naked if desired. It was a walking statue on a screen; a talking one too. When Jasper handed me a recording of Sam's voice, edited from a tape made at a meeting, I agreed almost unthinkingly to put a voice to my re-creation. Any scruples I had about its use were drowned in pride over my achievement. I was Pygmalion. Finally I handed the programme over to Jasper and waited for the response.

No praise came from him for my efforts, no criticism, nothing. This was disappointing. Two weeks passed before I heard from Jasper at all, and during that time something happened which may or may not be significant: Sam Prentice had a bad accident.

He was never quite sure what happened, because his memory of the incident was vague. He thinks that he had a fall and suffered concussion as the result of being pursued by 'something like a large dog'. It happened at night, and insult was quite literally added to injury when Sam's girlfriend Sally, who apparently did not believe the dog story, said he must have been drunk. Sam took great exception to this and the two split up, Sally leaving Playtronics soon afterwards.

When Jasper contacted me again it was to prepare a presentation of his new game *Know Your Enemy!* for the board of Playtronics. After much debate they rejected it. There was some vague talk of moral objections, that the game 'might be criticised for encouraging violence or stalking', but apparently it was the possibility of potentially costly lawsuits which sank the project. If Playtronics were to publish the game, thereby encouraging people to make sim copies of other people without their permission, these sim copies might end up being distributed round the world through the internet. People would probably claim intellectual property rights to their own images in cyberspace and sue for defamation if those images were portrayed badly. Playtronics might be held responsible. Even if prosecutions failed the legal fees alone could break the firm.

Jasper seemed to take the rejection well because soon afterwards he presented the board with another game in which I was involved called *ArtTheft!* and this was accepted. It involved stealing famous paintings from a virtual gallery and placing them in your own private virtual gallery. As with most of Jasper's games it required strong nerves, physical skill and a degree of intellectual ability. The player could plan the raid at leisure but he would have to execute it by navigating through a sophisticated alarm system in real-time without attracting the attention of the security guards. It was a very exciting new concept and the subsequent commercial popularity of the game quickly re-established Jasper's status as our leading designer.

Only I knew that Jasper was still working on his most cherished project. He occasionally would call me in for a consultation on some technical detail of graphics. He talked about producing the game himself. It had become an obsession with him. One day, he summoned me to his flat, just to report his progress to me.

'I'm experimenting with a new chip called a Randomised Connector,' he said. 'It allows the computer to simulate the human mind in that it does not always act rationally, but is allowed to make bizarre shapes, or to choose from a number of alternatives. It simulates the activity of the human imagination, but you need to give it enough material to work on. It needs to be educated. The uncanny thing is that it would seem that you can train it to act in accordance with your own thoughts.'

'Or perhaps your thoughts act in accordance with it?' I asked.

'That is a possibility.'

'A frightening one.'

'Is it frightening? I think it's rather exhilarating. But no, I think we can be the controlling partners. You remember Gilbert Ryle's critique of Descartes?' Of course, I didn't. I had barely heard of Descartes, let alone Gilbert Ryle, but that was Jasper's way of establishing his superiority: he pretended to assume that you knew as much as he did. 'Ryle called Descartes' separation of mind and body "the concept of the ghost in the machine." Ryle, being a thoroughgoing materialist, assumed there was no ghost. No soul, in other words, independent of the body; no mind, independent of the brain. But science has proved him wrong. Even, as early as the 1930s, the J.B. Rhine experiments were beginning to show that such things as telepathy and clairvoyance were a scientific reality. As one eminent biologist once said, if a ghost could act on a machine, the brain would be the right instrument to act on. So amazingly sensitive. And if our ghost, soul, spirit—whatever you call it—can act on our brain, and on other people's brains through telepathy, why not the artificial brain of a computer? I tell you, that is the next frontier! We can inhabit cyberspace, not just through remote controls like a mouse or a games console, but directly with our own minds.'

He stopped. His face was flushed, his eyes bright. Were there tears in them? In which case, what was he crying about? At that moment, he looked and sounded like a prophet. He glanced at me to gauge my reaction. It must have been satisfactory because he then said in a quieter, almost furtive tone: 'There's someone I'd like you to meet. Can you come here next Friday evening?' I knew that this was an order not a request.

When he opened the door to me that Friday evening Jasper seemed a different person. The reticent, self-contained character who could be galvanised into high-flown enthusiasm had been replaced by someone anxious, tentative. He told me that Aidan Plimson would be arriving any moment now. The name was spoken as if it were someone I ought to have heard of.

'I very much want you to meet Aidan,' he added redundantly. 'Aidan is an incredible person, absolutely brilliant in his way.'

'As I am in mine,' was the unspoken conclusion to the sentence, because admiration had not entirely deprived him of personal vanity. Actually, I think it had enhanced it: he seemed to look on the discovery and befriending of this Aidan Plimson as a brilliant achievement in itself. He spoke of him in the language of adolescent hero-worship, but I was sure there was no sexual attachment. It was power of intellect and personality that he seemed to be admiring. I asked Jasper who this Aidan Plimson was and what he did.

'He has a bookshop in Coptic Street, near the British Museum. He's a great authority on the occult.'

'Is he a black magician or something, then?'

'Don't mock what you don't understand. You'd be amazed by his intellectual depth. He's opened a whole new world to me. I knew about it theoretically through writers like Frances Yates, but she was just an academic. She didn't dare experience it. Aidan has shown me the reality.'

I wondered what this Plimson might be like, and whether I would be similarly overwhelmed. In my mind I pictured a dark, imposing figure, perhaps wearing a long black cloak lined with scarlet silk, like Count Dracula in the films. Absurd, I know. I suppose I was subconsciously preparing myself to resist his influence. I must have felt that anyone who could reduce a hard-boiled egoist like Jasper to abject subservience was dangerous. On arrival he proved a great disappointment. Plimson was in his late thirties or early forties, of average height, fat with small hands and a shiny, pink skin. An insubstantial frizz of ginger hair crowned the top of his large head. He had cultivated the dandified 'young fogey' look: tweed suit, pearl-buttoned waistcoat, spotted bow tie. He wore glasses and had a habit of constantly adjusting them onto his small nose with his right index finger. His manner was benignly avuncular, or condescending, depending on your point of view. Mine was unfavourable.

He sat down on Jasper's leather sofa and accepted, as he put it, 'a glass of vino bianco, per favore, with just un smidgenette of Perrier.' The fact that Jasper didn't vomit at this was enough to tell you that he was under Plimson's spell. I sat down opposite Plimson who, having accepted his drink, turned his attention on me.

'Young Jasper tells me you're a genius where computer graphics are concerned.'

I made some self-deprecating remark. He smiled and nodded, as if acknowledging that my modesty was a mere formality, albeit an acceptable one. He then went on to interrogate me on my line of work. Unwillingly, I was impressed. He had a good basic understanding of the subject, and his questions were astute and stimulating. Under his sympathetic guidance, I found myself articulating my theories about the future of computer graphics with more fluency than I thought I possessed. Though his appearance was against him, Plimson had an attractive voice, a bit plummy, but mellow and precise with a subtle variety of tone. I was not surprised to learn that he had pursued quite a successful career as a professional singer (light baritone) before devoting his energies to the book trade.

'I still do the odd gig,' he told us, pronouncing the word 'gig' very much in inverted commas, as if holding it metaphorically at arm's length. 'My trouble is, they will have these concerts in churches, and I can't bear singing in a church. The draughts, my dear, and the people! The acoustics and the encaustics! It's all too much for a white woman.'

Jasper even laughed at this. Plimson, without looking at him, held out his glass to be refilled. Jasper obliged. He was treating Jasper like a disciple already in his fold. I had the feeling that the interest he showed in me was that of a cult leader towards a potential convert, flattering but predatory. He made a little performance out of taking me into his confidence in front of Jasper.

'You see, your friend here interests me strangely.' He waved his hand in the direction of Jasper who looked on, stoically embarrassed. 'He is a Renaissance man, that is to say he is both artistic and scientific. And like many of the great Renaissance men, he has the instincts of a Magus.'

'What is a Magus?' I knew this was the question he wanted me to ask, but I couldn't help it.

'A Magus is essentially a man who stands between two worlds, the world of the spirit and the world of appearance which you mistakenly call "the real world". By means of his skill he tries to make the one influence the other and to hold power in both. It requires great discipline and a level head, but it can be done. The Magus is a man of power. He operates in the shadow and the light; that is to say, he uses both good and evil for his own purposes which transcend both good and evil. Have I confused you? I have. Let me put it this way. In all your computer games you rely on the principle of opposites, don't you? You need an opponent to defeat or shoot down. And on the most fundamental level the computer uses a binary system, the zero and the one, positive and negative. The one has no validity or function without the other. It is this essential fact that the Magus has grasped. He uses both the left and right hand paths. The great seventeenth-century witch La Voisin advised her clients to say a Christian Mass for what they desired, and only if that failed to resort to the black variety. She herself was arrested coming out of Mass. So you see the notion of black and white magic is nonsense really. It is all just magic. There is no white without black. They coexist of necessity. The Magus makes use of both. He might have made the Christian pilgrimage to Jerusalem or Compostela, but he went on the Black Pilgrimage too.'

Jasper was listening to all this stuff mesmerised. He asked: 'What was the Black Pilgrimage? Where did they go to?'

'Some went to Jerusalem and worshipped at Golgotha. To them it was the scene of the death of God and the triumph of the Lord of this world. That was rather crude; it was also dangerous. They were all too often found out and torn to pieces by the Christian mob. There were others who went to Chorazin where, according to legend, the Antichrist is to be born. Well, I've been, and believe me, my dear, there's nothing. It's a ruin. Just a few broken stones—black basalt mostly—and some even more broken peasants. But there were others still who were deeper adepts, and they went to the Black Cathedral.'

'Where was that?'

Plimson smiled. You could tell that he had anticipated the question and that he was going to enjoy answering it. His fat body wriggled into a more comfortable position on the sofa and seemed to expand in doing so.

'We tend to think of virtual reality as a modern invention, don't we? One realises that nearly all the scientific discoveries of this century were anticipated by the Renaissance Magi. Look at Leonardo and his flying machines. The idea of creating an alternative virtual world by means of visualisation techniques was known to many of them.'

'So the Black Cathedral was purely imaginary?'

'It was imaginary, but not purely so. This is where we in our twentieth-century so-called scientific mind-set go disastrously wrong. The great maxim of Hermes Trismegistus from which everything else stems is *Ut supra, sicut infra.* "As above, so below." In other words, anything that can be made to operate on what you call the imaginary plane, can be made to act on the physical plane. So the Black Cathedral may have been first conceived in the mind, but it had its reality in the material world. Our ideas of the relationship between spiritual and material are still terribly crude, far cruder in many ways than the old magicians. Look at Ryle's facile sneer at the "ghost in the machine." '

I glanced at Jasper who smirked. I asked: 'What was the purpose of this Black Pilgrimage?'

'Power, naturally. You went alone but you would return with someone or something.'

'What?'

'A talismanic object of power or a familiar which would do your bidding. But that thing bound you to the Black Cathedral. When you possessed something from the Black Cathedral, the Black Cathedral would begin to possess something of you. Of course, that might be a sacrifice one is willing to pay, but you don't get "out for nowt", as they say in the North.'

This man was appalling. I was finding it difficult to stay in the same room with him; nevertheless a guilty fascination held me.

'How do you get to this cathedral?' I asked. 'Or how does this cathedral get to you?'

'Yes,' said Plimson, nodding with schoolmasterish approval, 'the latter question is the more appropriate. There are certain rituals and symbols to be adhered to. Power attaches to them by virtue of their antiquity and frequent use. Some, like poor old Jack Parsons, favour the so-called Babalon Working. You can find it in his *Book of the Antichrist*. Pretty crude stuff, though, but what do you expect from an American whose principal acolyte was L. Ron Hubbard? The real strategy is visualisation. Remember the saying of Paracelsus: "Resolute imagination is the beginning of all magical operations"—and that is where computer graphics are so useful. It is an artificial interior space. We have the means of constructing our own Black Cathedral.'

'Why should we want to?'

'Because it is a vessel of power,' said Plimson. 'And the one thing needful is power. Power over our own lives, and power over others.'

After that the conversation was diverted into less controversial areas. Once or twice, I caught Jasper and Plimson exchange a questioning glance. I thought that they might have been wondering whether I was a possible recruit to their cause. When Plimson rose to go he came over to me and put his hand heavily on my shoulder.

'These are stirring times,' he said portentously. I very nearly laughed. 'Yes. Stirring times. Will you be part of them?'

I did not answer; I just sat there, longing for him to take his hand off me.

When he had gone, I wanted to question Jasper more about Plimson and how much he believed in all that stuff he had been giving us, but Jasper had reverted to his old self. He was once more secretive, aloof. 'I'll be in touch,' he said. 'There are some things I want you to do for me.'

During the next few weeks Jasper kept me busy. We did not meet, but he sent me a constant stream of e-mails and scans of old engravings. Some of these were of architectural details; others of cabalistic symbols, others of grotesque figures half-human, half animal. He was, he said, designing a 'new version of an old game'. He wanted me to turn these engravings into computer graphics which could be used for the construction and decoration of a vast virtual structure. Let me admit that I guessed very soon that he was working on Plimson's notion of the Black Cathedral, though how seriously and with what object, I had no idea. I did not ask; I simply told myself that it was all nonsense.

I should have taken it more seriously because I was disturbed by Jasper's increasingly troubled relations with the management of Playtronics. His previous aloofness had been replaced by an active arrogance, and his aggression was matched by that of Sam Prentice, now on the board of directors, who, since his encounter with the mysterious dog, had revealed an edgy, paranoid side to his character. Most people in the firm recognised that Jasper's waywardness had to be tolerated because of his creative brilliance, but Sam did not. 'Talent is a privilege, not an excuse,' he used to say. This may be true, but it doesn't help you to deal with someone like Jasper.

My work for Jasper on the Cathedral had just finished when I heard that he had been sacked from Playtronics. I immediately rang him up and e-mailed him, but there was no response. Eventually, one bright Saturday morning, I went round to see him. He answered the door immediately, but seemed reluctant to let me in when he saw me. I think he had been expecting Plimson.

Instead of letting me into his flat in the normal way by simply turning and allowing me to pass through, he retreated, walking backwards so that I was facing him the whole time. He was perhaps even paler and more emaciated than usual, but what struck me most were his eyes. They seemed to be focused on some distant point beyond me, even when he appeared to be looking into my face. I told him how sorry I was that he had left Playtronics and that they shouldn't have let him go. He responded to what I said with only half a mind. He claimed he wasn't bothered about being sacked from Playtronics because he had been going to resign anyway, but I did not believe him. I saw resentment behind the distracted, wandering eyes.

Very soon I began to suspect that he was desperate for me to go. This became obvious when my glance strayed towards a glass table on which stood an ornament that I had not seen before. Perhaps 'ornament' is not quite the right word. It was a little statuette about four inches high standing on a polished cube of polished black basalt. The statuette, of blackened bronze, its slightly rough texture suggesting great age, was of a hooded and cloaked figure crouching or squatting. The figure was humanoid, stunted in growth and hump-backed. One long-fingered hand emerged from the folds of its cloak to grasp its knee, but the most striking aspect of it was the head. The hood put all its features in shadow, but the posture was quite eloquent enough. It was thrust forward from the body in an intensely watchful way. One did not need to see anything of the features to know that it was looking, and looking hard.

When Jasper saw that I had noticed the statuette, he started to bundle me unceremoniously out of the flat, muttering something vague about having a lot to do. I did not resist. I was glad to go, because the whole experience of visiting him had disturbed me. On leaving the flat I spent quite some time just walking the streets before I was calm enough to gather my thoughts. I had reached the terrace in front of the Royal Festival Hall on the South Bank of the Thames before I could begin to articulate what had worried me. It was a bright September day and the sun glittered on the choppy, tawny waters of the great river.

The brilliance of the light made me remember Jasper's flat. The living room had white walls; it had a huge window facing north east; the sun had been shining. Yet all the lights were on in the flat and it was still quite dark. The light was somehow dull and, as I remembered, there were curious and inexplicable shadows in the corners of the room. The impression was of sombreness where there ought not to have been light.

There was another thing that disturbed me. The statuette of the crouching figure was very like something I had seen before. One of the images Jasper had sent me when we were working on the Black Cathedral was an old engraving of just such a hooded creature. I remember the engraving had a name scrawled under it in antique script: Asmodeus. The statuette was an exact realisation of that engraving. I knew that because I had turned the engraving into a 3D computer graphic.

I tried to dismiss Jasper from my mind by telling myself that he was taking drugs, or had wrapped himself up with that disgusting Plimson man and there was nothing to be done for him. He was lost. But I couldn't stop being concerned. Several times I tried to contact him again without success. Having done my best to keep in touch, I tried to forget him; but conscience has a nasty habit of not allowing you merely to do enough; you have to do more than enough to satisfy it; you have to go right over the top.

One morning, a week after my last face-to-face meeting with Jasper, I was in the Playtronics building having a 'creative session'. Actually a group of us were thinking of ways we could improve an old game so that we could bring out a new edition of it. There was no doubt about it: the firm had lost its edge since Jasper had left. Sam Prentice's personal assistant came into the room and asked if I could see him urgently. She looked troubled, and I wondered if this meant that my days at Playtronics were numbered. Sam's status in the firm meant that he could cause trouble, and I sensed that he liked me as little as I liked him. He had all the egoism of Jasper but without any of the genius.

Apart from a conference room where our creative session had been taking place, the main office is all open plan, so there is no knocking on doors or anything, and the great advantage is that you can often spy out what sort of mood the person you're going to see is in. I managed to get a look at Sam in this way without his seeing me. His part of the office was partly hidden by a screen but his face was in full view, though sideways on. He looked thoughtful, puzzled but not potentially hostile. Then he saw me and beckoned me over.

Sam had ginger hair and went in for brown leather and designer spectacles. His booted feet were on his desk. The man behind the pose was difficult to make out. He cultivated an energetic no-nonsense approach which he put into practice by addressing me as soon as I was within earshot.

'I've just had something delivered to me in the post,' he said. 'It came anonymously. Do you know anything about it?' It was such a bizarre question that I simply looked at him in astonishment. 'I'm not accusing you; I just want to know. You being on the artistic side, you might have seen this before. Have you?' He walked over and took something out of a cardboard box. It was Jasper's statuette of the crouching figure.

'What the hell is it?'

The reason why I don't tell lies is that I never believe I can get away with it, so I simply said: 'I think it's Asmodeus.' Sam looked at me as if I had given him a very stupid answer. I explained and there was a pause.

'Jasper,' he said at last. 'I might have known. Well, if you see your friend Jasper you can tell him from me that I am not impressed. He can't play head games with me. This is what I think of his rubbish.' So saying, he picked up the statuette and dropped it into the waste paper bin. As he did so I saw a sudden look of pain pass over his face. It seemed to me that he had let the object go a fraction before he meant to. 'Fucking thing,' he said, waving me away. As I left him he was nursing under one arm the hand which had dropped the statuette.

In the lunch hour when Sam was out of the office I went to look for the statuette in his bin. I can't explain why. When I looked in the bin, Asmodeus was gone, and it was nowhere in his office.

What happened next I have from various colleagues at Playtronics, because I was away at a computer graphics conference which, like most conferences, was one tenth useful gossip, and nine tenths useless boredom. Apparently, Sam's behaviour became increasingly erratic and irascible. He nearly got into serious trouble with the police for attacking a young beggar who had taken up residence in a cardboard box not far from the office. The beggar was a thin boy who often wore the hood of his anorak up and would crouch in doorways holding out his long emaciated hand for coins. Sam had to apologise profusely and pay him quite a lot of money to stop the prosecution going ahead. According to Sam he had mistaken the boy for someone who was following him. Everyone thought this was just paranoia, except for Julie (his personal assistant). This was because of something she had seen the day before Sam's attack on the beggar.

That evening Sam had decided to go home early, leaving Julie to sort out the notes of a meeting he had just attended. Julie was in his section of office on the third floor and had wandered to the window to watch Sam leave the building. She liked to do her work alone and needed to be sure Sam would not suddenly come back and surprise her. From the third-floor window she saw him open the great glass doors of the office building and step into the little piazza outside. As he did so, he glanced anxiously from left to right, once, twice, three times, then his eyes scanned slowly round the piazza. Julie told me that his posture—slightly hunched, head thrust forward—had that aggressive-defensive look of a cat whose territory has been invaded by a fellow feline. Having done this, he seemed satisfied and began to stride purposefully across the piazza.

Just before he disappeared round a corner Julie saw something detach itself from the dark recess of a building opposite her. The way she described the 'something' was 'half way between a shadow and a living thing', then, to cover herself, she added: 'I know that sounds stupid.' She said it was like a dwarf or a small child in black with a hood over its head. It might have been crawling except it moved too fast for that. 'It sort of scuttled, slightly sideways, like a crab,' she said. 'And I knew it was following Sam. Don't ask me why. I just knew.'

After the beggar incident, Sam seemed reluctant to be left alone. He took to going with colleagues to a wine bar after work. The trouble was, he didn't add much to the jollity: he just sat there drinking. The rest got tired of this, so they used to try to tease him out of his gloom. Their efforts were unsuccessful until one night when they started to needle him about telling the police he was being followed. One bright idiot said he remembered a bit of poetry about it that he had learnt at school:

> Like one that on a lonesome road
> Doth walk in fear and dread,
> And having once turned round, walks on,
> And turns no more his head;
> Because he knows a frightful fiend
> Doth close behind him tread.

The effect was immediate, Sam went berserk and started to attack the bright idiot, screaming gibberish at the top of his voice. It took all the other five colleagues there to restrain him and get him out of the wine bar. The following day Sam rang in to say he was sick and the day after that his cleaner found Sam lying dead in the bath. He had cut his throat with a kitchen knife and the water was red with his own blood. The police took it to be a straight case of suicide, but were puzzled by the fact that his body was covered back and front with a strange series of parallel scratches, as if from the long nails of a hand.

When I heard these stories on my return from the conference, I tried to get in touch with Jasper, but again with no success. I went to his flat, rang the bell and got no reply. Then one evening the phone rang and someone at the other end announced herself as Jasper's sister. (She was unknown to me because Jasper had never given anything away about his background.) She said that she had been trying to contact her brother but having no luck. Apparently I was the only person Jasper had ever mentioned to her as being a friend. I was moved and saddened because I had never felt very much for Jasper except detached admiration. The sister, whose name was Jenny, had a set of keys to his flat. Would I meet her there, and go into the flat with her, just in case . . . ?

Half an hour later Jenny and I solemnly shook hands at the door of Jasper's flat. I would have recognised her instantly as a relative of Jasper's. She had the same dark hair, closely cropped, and the same narrow, interesting, not-quite-beautiful face. I detected the same nervous energy too, but more focused, less frantic. Jenny was an osteopath.

We went into the flat and turned the lights on. Once again, I had the sensation that the place was darker than it ought to have been. It was also cold, with the deadening, slightly musty chill of a place which has not been occupied for some time. Jasper was not there. The unspoken fear of finding his body proved to be groundless, but this only deepened the mystery. The place was in perfect order. When we searched the bedroom there were no signs that he had packed and left. I went into the adjoining bathroom. His shaver was on charge and his toothbrush stood at ease in its glass tumbler. Suddenly Jenny said from the bedroom: 'My God, what's that?'

I came out of the bathroom and saw her pointing at a little chest of drawers in the corner. On it was the statuette of Asmodeus. Instinctively I told her not to touch it. She looked at me curiously and said she had no intention of doing so, but why . . . ? I said nothing and we went back into the living room.

There, on a long shelf, above a radiator was an object we were sure had not been there when we entered the flat. It was a candlestick in which a black candle with a black wick had been placed. The candlestick itself seemed to be made of some greyish lustreless metal, possibly pewter. It was in the form of a column with a heavy pedestal base and a capital composed of four grinning imps. I realised with a shock that its design was one which I had made for a computer graphic to Jasper's specifications. Around the base in Roman capitals were incised the words FANVM EIVS QVI SPECTAT IN CALIGINE. Translated this meant: 'The Temple of He who Watches in Darkness'. I knew that because Jasper had told me in an email. But the word 'caligo', according to Jasper, means more than simply darkness, it means more a thick black fog, or a deep shadow. I picked up the candlestick. Though it was not much more than a foot in height and its main body two inches in diameter it was so heavy I could barely lift it. Its surface was smooth, slippery and uncannily cold.

I dropped it. The thing was a horror, so we left it lying on the floor. We then began a more systematic search of the flat for some message or clue as to Jasper's whereabouts. On the huge screen above his PC was a post-it note with some writing on it in green biro. It read: 'You must get rid of Asmodeus. Avoid touching it if at all possible. For Christ's sake don't try to trace me.'

Not knowing what to do next, I switched on the computer. Jasper had a large plasma screen the size of a dressing table mirror which totally absorbed my entire field of vision, and it was operated by a state-of-the-art touch-screen control system. As soon as the machine booted up I began to look for clues. My eye was attracted to an unusual desktop icon. It was a sinister little black gothic arch under which the word 'BlackCath' was written. I touched the icon and found I had entered a version of Jasper's *Know Your Enemy!* game. I was then presented with a large virtual simulation of Jasper himself, requesting that a preferred enemy be chosen. Hearing his voice speak out loud in that lonely room was an unnerving experience, especially as I was unable to locate any speakers. Jasper's hand trailed across a selection of enemies, each one represented by the iconic reproduction of someone's head. One further icon allowed the player to programme in a new enemy of his or her choice.

I almost shut the system down there and then, but something urged me on. Under Jasper's baleful stare, I looked closely at the icons. Two depicted individuals unknown to me; one other was clearly that of Sam Prentice, although it seemed to have been scrawled through with a dark cross; the last was of Jasper himself. I touched the Jasper head.

As I remember, the game begins with the approach through a wood to a great gothic doorway. Over it—and this was new—had been written the words ALL HOPE ABANDON YE WHO ENTER HERE. Some skill is required to open the door: I had to move carefully through a circle that described a five-pointed star with its apex facing downwards. Once that had been done, the head of a horned goat appears in the pentacle for a brief flash and the doors open.

The game of *Know Your Enemy!* consists initially in making one's way through a maze of stone corridors in such a way that one surprises one's quarry. (A small map in the top right hand corner of the screen tells you where you are and where your prey is.) I negotiated this first part with practised ease and found what I was looking for. There was Jasper again, fully and accurately represented on the screen by means of my own graphic art. Everything about him seemed real and alive, even the facial expression. The image of Jasper looked round at me and there again was the pleading look in his eyes. He was being compelled by an irresistible force towards something dreadful. There was something about the whole experience of the game which shocked me. It was somehow more real than virtual, not just 'virtually' real.

The fleeing figure of Jasper tried in vain to escape me. Eventually I cornered him in front of a dark entrance on either side of which two monstrous hooded figures in stone held up the lintel. What was beyond the entrance I half guessed because I had designed its building blocks myself. This was going to be the Black Cathedral. I touched the screen on a point in the black opening and suddenly we were inside. It was a vast windowless Gothic structure with ribbed vaulting. The decorations on the capitals of the piers and the bosses of the vaults were grotesque, crooked, grimacing figures and masks, all of them twisted into a separate agony of desire or rage. They were all my designs, but somehow, in some subtle way, hideously enhanced. In the centre of a vast space stood a black draped altar on which stood two candlesticks of the kind we had found in Jasper's sitting room and which I, for my sins, had also designed. Between the two candlesticks on the altar crouched the all too familiar hooded figure of Asmodeus. I saw the image of Jasper turn to me and I swear that there was a pleading look in his virtual eyes. He was still being compelled forwards against his will, this time towards the altar.

'Stop! Stop!' screamed Jenny. 'Don't do any more! Switch it off! Get out of the game now!' I touched the Escape icon but nothing happened. I pressed it again frantically and the game froze but I could not get out of the game. There was nothing for it but to switch off the whole computer. The whole system went down with a strange, melancholy moan, in which I thought I heard a faint but distinctly human cry.

Jenny and I looked at each other, stupefied. She said she would tell the police of Jasper's disappearance, though I think we both knew this was useless.

What I did next was my own initiative. Whether it was right or wrong I don't know. I borrowed Jenny's keys and returned to the flat next day. Wearing gloves, I took the statuette of Asmodeus, wrapped it in a cloth and placed it in a cardboard box. I then looked through the section entitled Antiquarian Booksellers in *Yellow Pages*.

ꟼ

Plimson's establishment was in one of those little streets by the British Museum full of old fashioned glass-fronted shops selling specialist books and prints, or oriental curios. His shop had a kind of inn sign hanging over the door with the words 'A.J. PLIMSON—OCCULT BOOKS AND CURIOSA' in dull gold letters on a background of midnight blue gloss paint. 'Curiosa and curiosa,' I remember thinking childishly, as I went in. The place was lined from floor to ceiling with books. Apart from me it contained a solitary browser and Plimson who was installed behind a desk on my immediate right as I came in. Hearing the shop-door bell, which clanked rather than tinkled, Plimson looked up. To my relief he did not recognise me. I was wearing the light but effective disguise of a woolly hat. Woolly hats, in my experience, especially when pulled well down over the forehead, give even the sanest looking man an air of mental derangement.

Plimson seemed rather greyer in complexion than when I had last seen him and had lost that deceptively cherubic look. When I approached him he seemed irritated. I put on my most timid manner. I said that I had with me an object which I believed to be of some occult significance, but I had no idea what it was. I had heard he was an expert in such matters: perhaps he could help me? Perhaps he might even be able to sell it for me? Plimson relaxed. He shifted the spectacles on his nose and his lips began to curve into the familiar condescending smile. I handed over the cardboard box. He opened it and took out the statuette wrapped in a cloth. As soon as he had removed the cloth I saw his skin turn from greyish pink to bone white. He gripped the little image of Asmodeus, trembling violently, then turned his terrified eyes on me.

'How the hell did you get hold of this?'

'I'm a friend of Jasper Webb's.'

'Take it back!'

I put my hands in my pockets.

'It's yours,' I said. 'A gift.'

'Take it back!' shrieked Plimson. The browser, an old man who had been looking at books on astrology in the corner, stared at us with a kind of vacant curiosity, as if he were watching television. Plimson was still holding onto the statuette. He was screaming. I don't know how it was, but his hands seemed somehow to have become stuck to the object and his attempts to tear them off it were causing him intense agony. The old man continued to stare in passive fascination, blinking his watery grey eyes.

Plimson began to whimper, begging me to take the statuette back. I said I would take it back if he told me where Jasper was. He wailed that he didn't know. I said that I thought he did know, that he was in the Black Cathedral, and that he must get him out of there. Then Plimson started screaming again.

'But don't you understand! I can't! The Black Cathedral is nowhere. It's everywhere! It's here! Oh, God it's here! Let me out!'

I told him that if he couldn't get Jasper out, I certainly couldn't get *him* out. I was sorry for him now, but there was nothing I could do. I walked out of the shop and went on walking, leaving Plimson with Asmodeus and the old browser. I stopped my ears and mind to the screams. Next day I read in the papers that Plimson had died that afternoon of heart failure. No reference to a little black statuette was made. One gathered from the reports that Aidan Plimson was a well-known character but that his passing, for various reasons, was unlamented; so why do I still feel guilty?

Know Your Enemy! was never put on the market, but I know that people have somehow managed to get hold of unofficial copies of the game. A website known as Blackcath.com has mysteriously appeared, though I have not been able to find out who hosts it or how it is maintained. I have visited it several times in the hope of picking up some clue to Jasper's whereabouts, even for a mention of his name. The messages to be found there are densely cryptic so that anyone lacking the inside knowledge would think the site was dotty but harmless. On one occasion I visited the site with my speakers switched on, a precaution I now carefully guard against. Initially I was intrigued, as the background noise at first seemed to be very similar to that found in a large cathedral—whispered invocations, distant choral recitals, the echoing clack of leather shoes on stone floors—but there was something wrong. Listening to the choir I found that the sequences of chords were always unresolved and the end of each phrase was unnaturally swallowed up in silence. Then I understood: everything was being played backwards, everything, that is, but the faint cries of utter despair which could be heard behind the other noises. My hand went to the volume control to turn off the dreadful noise. As I fumbled desperately with the dial a simple sentence among the usual litter of cabalistic signs and phrases flashed up onto the screen. The sentence read:

'Do not try to trace me.'

THE BOY IN GREEN VELVET

I met Uncle Alfred for the first time at my father's funeral. I was eight years old and just about to go to a preparatory school in Oxford. I had known that my father had a brother and that his name was Alfred—never Alf—but further than that, nothing. I was an inquisitive boy and might well have asked my parents about him had I not been somehow aware that enquiries about Uncle Alfred were not welcome.

My father had been a chemistry don at St Saviour's College, Oxford and my mother, at the time of his death, was on the point of becoming Headmistress of a girls' high school in

Banbury. They were brisk, kind people who had organised their lives with immaculate good sense and efficiency, so it seemed like an affront to their rational world when my father died very unexpectedly of a cerebral haemorrhage at the age of forty-three. I remember people saying that my father's death was 'so unfair,' but I did not think like this. It was horrible and it happened: that was all there was to be said, as far as I was concerned.

A pompous funeral service in St Saviour's College chapel was followed by a short committal at a crematorium and it was here that my Uncle Alfred put in his appearance. I was first aware of him from my mother's reaction. Throughout the day she had been in a state of uncontrollable, almost hysterical grief. It had surprised and worried me, because my mother was a calm, disciplined person, and, even when she first received the news of my father's death, her reaction had been more stoical. I was barely beginning to understand the processes of my own bereavement, let alone anyone else's. In retrospect I realise that she was suffering from delayed reaction: only on the day of the funeral did the full enormity of a life without my father hit her.

We had taken our places in the crematorium chapel, waiting for the service to begin. I was on one side of my mother in the pew; her sister Margaret was supporting her on the other. I was studying the stuff of my mother's black coat and watching it quiver and shake from the sobbing body inside it. I had no idea what to do, so I left it all to my Aunt Margaret whose line in clucking and soothing noises seemed to me more suitable to a sick animal than my mother. I kept my eyes on the black coat, not wishing to see any more of my mother's red-rimmed eyes and collapsed face. Suddenly the black coat seemed to stiffen; the body inside had stopped shaking. My mother sat upright and I heard her say: 'Good God! What's he doing here?'

'Isn't that Alfred?' said Aunt Margaret.

'Sssh!' said my mother, and then to me, 'Don't look round!'

But it was too late; I already had. Standing in the aisle was a tall man in a dark blue velvet-collared overcoat. I think I would have known it was my Uncle Alfred even if I had not been told. The resemblance to my father was not in anything obvious, except perhaps for the shape of the mouth; it was more in the way he held himself, his head thrust forward, chin raised, blinking watchfully at the assembled mourners. It had been absolutely my father's stance in moments of deep abstracted thought, except that Alfred's version was more pronounced, like a caricature of my father's mannerism.

In the few seconds allowed to me before my mother told me sharply to stop staring, I took him in greedily, vividly. That first sight of him is still my clearest visual memory of Uncle Alfred.

He was some seven years older than my father and approaching fifty, but his skin was smooth and shiny. He had virtually no hair and his head was an almost perfect oval. I wondered later whether my father's beard, his general shagginess of dress and grooming, had been a calculated antithesis to his brother's sleekness. The beakiness of Uncle Alfred's nose, together with his habit of making small quick movements with his head (another characteristic shared with my father), gave him a bird-like appearance. For a fleeting moment our glances met and I was aware of two pale grey eyes searching mine with a look of intense but utterly detached interest.

After the service everyone stood around in the crematorium courtyard, pretending to admire the flowers and exchanging awkward banalities. My mother by this time no longer needed her sister. Calm and smiling she thanked people politely for their attendance, but when she saw Alfred approach she stiffened and seemed to make herself a couple of inches taller by an act of will.

'Alfred!' she said when he was about four feet away from her. Her tone was that of a teacher addressing a disobedient pupil and the intention was to stop him in his tracks, but it had no effect. He came right up to her and before she could take evasive action he had sandwiched her hand between his two, which were gloved in pearl grey suede. I saw her jerk her head back in anticipation of a kiss which he did not proffer.

'I came because I saw the notice in the *Times*,' he said. 'Nobody had informed me.' If there was an implied rebuke it was in the words, not in his tone of voice which betrayed nothing. His speech was low and well-modulated.

My mother said defensively: 'I'm afraid I had no idea what your address was, otherwise . . .'

'It was on the card I sent you at Christmas.'

'Was it? I didn't know . . . Anyway, what with everything . . .'

'I quite understand. I wasn't in any way . . .'

'No. Naturally.' There was a pause and I became aware of my mother struggling with herself. Eventually she said: 'I do hope you can come back to the house.'

'Of course I will,' said Uncle Alfred in an unctuous tone, as if he were conferring a great kindness. My mother merely sniffed. I think for the first time in my life I became aware that a conversation can signify more than the literal meaning of its sentences.

'Hell!' said my mother when he had withdrawn from earshot.

In the car on the way back to the house I pestered my mother and Aunt Margaret for information about Uncle Alfred. I felt I was entitled to it now that I had seen him in the flesh. What was his job? Apparently he was a musician, but he did not need to work because he had 'inherited all the family money'. I detected no envy or resentment in these words, only scorn at his drone status. Aunt Margaret, who was rather more neutrally disposed towards Uncle Alfred than my mother, told me that some of his compositions had been performed and he had once written a ballet score for Covent Garden. (Called *Olabolika,* and based on the drawings done in Bedlam by Richard Dadd, with a scenario by Osbert Sitwell, it was one of Frederic Ashton's least successful ventures.) 'He was crazy about the theatre,' my mother added. 'Still is, as far as I know.' With a sophistication beyond my years, I asked if he was unmarried. I knew from snippets I had picked up from adult conversation that people who had to do with theatre and ballet were often 'not the marrying kind'. No, he was not married. 'But he did live for quite a while with that little ballerina,' my Aunt added carelessly. 'What was her name? She was rather sweet, as I remember. Now what happened to her? Didn't she—'

'George,' broke in my mother. 'When we get home, would you mind making yourself useful by handing round sandwiches and things? It's a dreadful bore, I know, but I think it's best to keep busy on these occasions. All right, darling?'

Poor mother. I think she genuinely thought I was as grief-stricken over my father's death as she was. At that moment I was still too bewildered to feel anything except perhaps the vaguely comforting sensation that I was now the most important person in my mother's life.

By the time Uncle Alfred arrived at the house I was busily handing round refreshments. It was a good thing to be doing because it kept me from being stuck with one person. I suspected everyone of wanting to smother me with sympathy which was what I least wanted. Suddenly I found myself face to face, or rather face to paunch with Uncle Alfred. Even the superb tailoring of his dark blue double-breasted suit could not disguise the ungainliness of his figure.

He took a glass of sherry from my proffered tray and sniffed it. Putting it to one side, he took the tray from me and set it down on a nearby table, keeping his eyes on me the whole time. I did not feel intimidated so much as disquieted by the interest he took in me.

'So. George . . .' he said in his round theatrical voice. He paused, as if expecting me to respond.

'Hello, Uncle Alfred,' I said feebly. This amused him for some reason.

'Hello, indeed!' Then he remembered the occasion. 'This is a sad day. Sad day. Your father and I . . . We didn't . . . communicate, perhaps, as often as we should have done. Different worlds.' He waved his hand at the room and looked round, as if to illustrate the fact that he was in alien territory. No secret was made of his disdain at the functional furnishings, and the pictures which were all reproductions of well-known masterpieces in cheap frames. Suddenly, as his gaze took in the mantelpiece, his expression changed. For a moment there was a look of shock and guilt on his face, like that of a child who has been caught rifling through the drawers in an adult's bedroom. A second later the mask was on again.

'Ah,' he said very casually. 'You have the Boulle clock, I see.' I had not heard the name before, but I knew what he meant: an elegant eighteenth-century clock decorated with brass and tortoiseshell marquetry which stood proudly in the centre of our mantelpiece. It was known to us as 'the antique' because it was the only old thing in the house.

'It's an antique,' I told him.

'It is indeed,' said Alfred condescendingly. 'And did you know it was quite a family heirloom? By rights it should be . . . I must talk to your mother about it. Perhaps now would not be the best moment. You must both come and visit me in London.

Would you like that? I could show you *my* antiques. I have quite a collection. Here's my card.'

He presented me with a visiting card. His name, Alfred Vilier, Esq., was on it, his Chelsea address and his telephone number. I was impressed.

'Feel the surface of the card,' he commanded. I felt the smooth silky pasteboard and the slight roughness of the raised lettering. 'Can you feel that? Now I'll tell you something. If you can feel the embossed lettering, that means the card has been produced by an engraving process rather than mere printing. You can always tell a gentleman by the fact that his cards have been engraved rather than printed.'

My mother had already tried to imbue me with a steely common sense about matters of class, so I knew this was pretentious rubbish. That is to say, I knew that if I told my mother what he had said (which I did not) she would dismiss it as pretentious rubbish. Soon after that Uncle Alfred left the house, never to visit it again.

ꕥ

A few weeks after the funeral my mother had a letter from Alfred. She did not communicate its contents to me, but I heard her talking to Margaret about it on several occasions. They had a habit of returning again and again to a topic that interested them, mulling it over, looking at it from all angles and, when there was indignation to be expressed, expressing it at enormous length.

The letter concerned the Boulle clock. It began by stating in a roundabout way that because the clock was a Vilier family heirloom, it was technically the property of Uncle Alfred, he having inherited all the family effects on my paternal grandfather's death. However, magnanimously, he was not going to press his claim, but he would like to have it in order to 'keep the family collection together'. Would my mother be prepared to sell it? A generous sum was suggested. My mother and Margaret agreed that Alfred's letter was both insulting and suspicious. They concluded that the clock was obviously worth far more than he had offered, but they took no steps to confirm whether this was so. (I later discovered that he had suggested a very fair price.) After much discussion Mother and Aunt Margaret decided that the best course was not to reply to the letter at all.

More weeks went by before another letter came from Uncle Alfred, again on the subject of the Boulle clock. He perfectly understood if my mother was unwilling to part with the clock, but he was concerned about its safety, it being a family heirloom. Were there proper safety locks on her windows to deter burglars? In addition he had noticed that some of the brass inlay had begun to peel away from the tortoiseshell background. If this was allowed to go on, the clock might become irreparably damaged. He knew an excellent restorer of Boulle work in London and would be very happy to pay for its repair. This time my mother wrote back a curt letter stating that she was perfectly capable of looking after her own clock and that there must be no further correspondence on the subject.

My first term at my preparatory school came and went. The reports were good and, as a reward, my mother decided to treat me to a day in London. We would visit the Science and Natural History museums in the morning, have lunch at the Victoria and Albert and round the day off with the National Gallery later in the afternoon. My mother was a relentless educator, and I was not totally averse to being educated. We were only just beginning to recognise where our paths diverged: she preferred knowledge, I beauty. As it happened, our proposed day out was a good compromise between the two.

We spent longer than we thought we would at the Victoria and Albert. I was entranced by the ceramics and the furniture. It had not really occurred to me before that household objects could be things of beauty, and at one point my mother remarked sourly that I would grow up to be like Uncle Alfred if I wasn't careful. It was past three o'clock before my mother persuaded me that we must move on, but I insisted that we should have one last look at the medieval ivories. I was fascinated by these minute depictions of religious scenes, their breathless, harsh intensity, combined with a kind of purity.

We were so intent on a crucifixion triptych, my mother explaining, I looking, that we were very startled when a voice behind us said: 'Good afternoon!' We turned round to find Uncle Alfred in immaculate Prince of Wales check, leaning on a malacca walking stick and observing us.

'I do apologise,' he said. 'Did I startle you?'

'Not at all,' said my mother. 'What an unexpected pleasure!' This was a little overdone, but my mother never liked to show herself at a loss. Aplomb was a vital part of her armoury as a teacher.

'You like the ivories?' Alfred asked me. I nodded.

'We were just leaving,' said my mother.

'Splendid! In that case you must come and have tea with me. It's not far. We'll take a taxi.' He turned to me. 'Would you like to go in a taxi?' I looked at my mother. She was about to protest, but Alfred stopped her. 'I insist. In fact I would take it very much amiss if you refuse. Young George here obviously has a taste for beauty. He must see some of my things. It would be very instructive for him.' It was a close call, but this last appeal to education just about tipped the balance in his favour, and my mother gave in. I was delighted but chiefly because of the taxi ride: my mother never wasted money on taxis.

In the taxi on the way to Glebe Place Uncle Alfred showed himself to be a man of formidable charm. I wouldn't say that by the end of the journey my mother had been won over, but the edge of her hostility had been blunted. He made no attempt to flatter her directly, knowing that this would be greeted with suspicion. Instead he devoted all his energies to bringing me out of my shell, listening to my opinions, and then developing them in such a way that they sounded wise and mature. It was a brilliant performance, like a man playing tennis on both sides of the net: lobbing over an easy ball, then rushing to the other side to help his opponent play a devastating return. I think my mother was even more beguiled by him than I was.

The house in Glebe Place was, of course, exquisite. The walls, painted in rich dark colours, were covered with pictures, many with a theatrical flavour. There were framed playbills, costume and stage designs, and old coloured prints of actors in extravagant poses, bedecked with tinsel. On shelves and mantels, china harlequins leapt, columbines smirked and pantaloons stooped. It was a visual feast, especially for a child, but I do not think it is merely hindsight that makes me remember the overall effect as somehow oppressive. Those capering clowns and attitudinising tragedians in pottery, print and bronze all seemed to be clamouring for one's attention. It was like walking through a silent, gesticulating crowd.

Uncle Alfred's housekeeper appeared, a thin hollow-eyed woman called Mrs Piercey. Without explaining our presence Alfred ordered tea for us all. Mrs Piercey did not express surprise, or any other emotion; she simply disappeared and re-emerged ten minutes later with tea, cake, biscuits and a plate of thin slices of bread and butter. By this time we were settled in the drawing room whose elegant sash windows looked out on

Glebe Place. Like the other rooms we had been shown it was crammed with curious and beautiful things.

Mrs Piercey, refusing any assistance from my mother, dispensed tea and cakes in silence while Uncle Arthur, who seemed barely to notice her, expatiated on Leon Bakst's costume designs, Callot's Commedia etchings and the sombre, theatrical James Pryde that hung above the fireplace. After she had gone he seemed to relax a little. He asked about my academic progress, a subject my mother was always delighted to discuss. Her report was glowing, if a little exaggerated. Uncle Alfred rubbed his hands

'Excellent!' he said. 'Obviously Master George has inherited the Vilier brains.' My mother gave a tight little smile: it was Alfred's first mistake. He tried to correct himself by adding light-heartedly: 'And yours too, *naturellement*!' He gave a little bow, to which mother gave a curt nod of acknowledgement. There was a short teacup-tinkling pause. Uncle Alfred cleared his throat.

'If I may once more broach a delicate subject. The Boulle clock . . .' He saw my mother stiffen. 'I realise I may have expressed myself poorly in my letters, but I wonder if you have reconsidered my offer with regard to having the clock repaired. I really can't see how you can possibly object—'

'Alfred,' cut in my mother. 'You have been really most kind. The tea was delicious and it was so nice of you to show George all your interesting things. Let's leave it at that, shall we? We don't want to spoil our nice afternoon.'

Uncle Alfred held up his hands to acknowledge defeat and as he did so I saw him give my mother a look of such concentrated loathing and contempt that I dropped my slice of seed cake in astonishment. My mother did not notice his look: her powers of observation, though often acute, were extremely selective in their objects. Not long after this we took our leave. At the door, as he was seeing us off, he suddenly asked when my birthday was. My mother, who tended to answer for me whenever possible, told him that it was on November the 15th. November was three months away, so we thought nothing of it; in fact, by unspoken mutual consent, the subject of Uncle Alfred was not discussed by us on the way back to Oxford.

❧

That November my birthday fell on a Saturday so, though I was at school, I had some leisure to enjoy it at home. A large parcel came by post for me in the morning, but my mother insisted that I should not open it until I came back from school at midday. All through lessons that morning my mind was devoured by curiosity over the package.

One learns fairly early in life that expectations are nearly always disappointed, but this was one of those rare exceptions to the rule. My mother made me wait for the parcel till I had finished lunch, by which time I was in a frenzy of anticipation and indigestion. I tore open the brown paper wrapping to reveal a stout cardboard box on which reposed a little white envelope. In the envelope was one of Uncle Alfred's engraved visiting cards on which the words 'Happy Birthday' had been written in violet ink.

When I opened the box I found it neatly packed with various items in tissue paper on top of which lay a booklet. On the booklet was printed the words: 'Benjamin Pollock Limited, Instructions for Assembly'. It was a kit for a toy theatre. Packed into the box was the stage base with a tiny trap door in it. Then there were strips and struts of wood, little packets of screws, and some sheets of cardboard printed in bright colours. Among these was a long narrow strip showing an orchestra pit and the top halves of a Victorian orchestra in evening dress. There was a pillared and pedimented proscenium frontage with side boxes inset in which men and women were represented as watching a play. There were various swags of gold-fringed scarlet curtain in cardboard, and there was a drop curtain also in cardboard on which in gold had been inscribed the words ROYAL COBURG THEATRE. Everything was in pristine condition, but I had the feeling that it was nevertheless about thirty or forty years old. This for me added to the fascination and beauty of the thing. It filled me with wild delight. Mother was less enthusiastic, but she made me sit down at once and write a letter of thanks to Uncle Alfred.

Over the next days and weeks I devoted every spare moment to the construction of my toy theatre which, when completed, stood two foot wide by eighteen inches high, the stage going back to a depth of nearly three feet. This was fairly standard for the so-called 'large format' toy theatres, but there were one or two oddities about Uncle Alfred's present. In the first place, though I had received the theatre complete in every detail, I had no scenery or characters to go with it. There was only a frame at the back of the stage which accommodated various back cloths made of coloured tissue paper through which a light could be shone. This, I discovered later, was a feature that was generally found only in the Spanish toy theatres of Seix and Barral, but the frontage was pure English with its gaudy decoration and the charming touch of naivety about the drawing.

There were other peculiarities in the design of the stage front which only became apparent on close examination. For example if you looked at the musicians in the 'orchestra strip' you began to notice that several of them had faces which were only half human. One of them had a snout like a pig, another resembled a cat, another a monkey. The conductor, seen only from the back, was so hunched over his podium that he looked deformed. Long strands of black hair snaked over his collar. One of his abnormally long arms was lifted high in the air with the baton in his hand pointing downwards, almost as if he were about to stab someone with it. In the four stage boxes, two on either side of the proscenium, the figures wore Regency dress and stared rigidly in profile at the action on the stage with the exception of the couple in the bottom right hand box. Here a man and a woman were facing outwards, the man with his hands on the woman's shoulders quite close to her neck. The figures were not very subtly drawn but I had the impression when I looked at them sometimes that he was about to strangle her. Then, when I would look at them again, I saw nothing of the kind and wondered how I could have been so fanciful.

These oddities did not disturb me at all; in fact they captivated me. I loved my theatre and spent long hours staring at it. I peopled its bare stage with my imagination. I had it set up beside my bed and, going to sleep with it in my sight, would often dream about it. In my dreams I heard the murmur of the audience and could see shadowy figures moving around the stage, but I never had a clear idea of what they were doing. Once or twice my dreams took an unexpected turn. In them the clamour of the audience would get louder and louder until a piercing scream of agony would bring it to an end. The sound was so vivid and precise that I would wake up with the scream still ringing in my ears. A faint internal echo of the noise would reverberate inside my head for several minutes before fading. When I awoke I did not feel fear, as one normally understands the term, because fear contains expectation. It was much more like the feeling that one has having just been through a fearful experience: emptiness, mental exhaustion, and a morbid sensitivity to the slightest sound or sensation. In those moments the rustle of my sheets was like the crash of storm-tossed waves.

I told nobody about these occasions because I knew that my mother would immediately say that my toy theatre was having a bad effect and would take it away from me. I would suffer anything not to be separated from my passion.

Christmas brought me a further parcel from Uncle Alfred, and an excitement almost equal to the first. Inside the cardboard box were sheets to be cut out on which were printed scenery, characters, and some properties such as tables and chairs. In addition there was a set of operating wires to draw the characters on or off stage and a booklet containing the text of the play for which the scenery and characters had been designed. It was called *The Boy in Green Velvet* and the title page stated that it had been written by someone called Valerie Fridl, an improbable name.

Toy theatres are not quite like puppet theatres in that a character can be moved across the stage, but must remain throughout the scene in the same pose. The same character will be represented in different poses and costumes for different scenes in the play. Thus there was a different cut out figure of Conrad, the eponymous boy, for Act I, Act II and Act III, Scene 1 in various costumes and attitudes. The style of the sheets did not coincide exactly with that of the frontage. The figures had none of that crude histrionic raffishness you find in British prints. They were well-drawn lithographs with rich colours, very much in the mid nineteenth-century German Romantic style.

As I write, I hesitate, even though nearly forty years have passed since the events I am writing about. I find myself skirting round the periphery, describing sets and costumes in general terms and not coming to the play itself. My reluctance to do so even now has a measure of dread about it.

The Boy in Green Velvet began in what was described as the 'Oak Chamber Scene', a dark panelled room with no windows, Jacobean in feel. There were three characters involved, the boy Conrad, a priest called Father Silas, and a curious dwarfish creature called Zamiel. The script of the play began very dully with a dialogue between Conrad and Father Silas in which the priest gave the boy all kinds of moral advice and the boy replied in monosyllables. In a clumsy piece of play construction Father Silas abruptly leaves and is immediately replaced by Zamiel. The conversation between Zamiel and Conrad was more interesting but more baffling. It consisted mainly of a series of questions by Zamiel to which Conrad gave bewildered replies. I can only remember a small sample which went like this:

ZAMIEL: Where are you?
CONRAD: I am here. This is my home.
ZAMIEL: But you have no power in it. Where would you go?
CONRAD: I do not know.
ZAMIEL: Is it mastery that you desire?
CONRAD: Why? Can you give it to me?
ZAMIEL: I can show you. What do you wish to find?
CONRAD: How to be the master.
ZAMIEL: Where do you wish to find this mastery you desire?
CONRAD: Wherever it is.
ZAMIEL: Will you let me take you to it?
CONRAD: If it must be.
ZAMIEL: If you and I are alone, how can it be otherwise?

I have still no idea precisely what this means, but I know that the conversation between the two had a direction and purpose however obscure: Zamiel was persuading Conrad to go with him to some place. I realised even at the time that Zamiel was making Conrad believe that he himself wanted what Zamiel wanted him to want. The subtlety appealed to me, and my very meagre theatrical experience did not tell me that this was a very odd sort of play. The only playwright to which my mother had introduced me was Shakespeare, and he seemed quite as strange as Valerie Fridl.

The second act took place in a rocky glen by moonlight, depicted in a highly romantic German style, not unlike old set designs you see for the Wolf's Glen Scene in *Der Freischütz*. The stage directions called for the effects of a thunderstorm. A light was to be flashed behind the backcloth and a small sheet of metal foil was to be shaken to provide tinny rolls of thunder. The second act figures of Conrad and Zamiel had changed slightly. Conrad was still attired in his improbable knickerbocker suit of green velvet but his hair was dishevelled and his eyes were hollower than they had been. His stance was a traditional melodramatic pose, leaning back, one leg extended, the other bent, his hands raised, palm outwards. It suggested fear, agitation, some sort of tension. The figure of Zamiel had become a little more grotesque. He sported a hat with a feather in it and the ingratiating smile he wore in the first act had become a malignant grin.

The scene which was to be enacted in this Gothic glen was one which I found enthralling. The action was simple: Zamiel in the guise of a magician conjured up seven visions for Conrad's benefit: a beautiful woman, a mountain of food and drink, a luxurious bed, a vast mirror in which Conrad's features were gigantically reflected, an emaciated figure wielding an axe in the middle of a raging fire, a chest spilling over with gold coins, and a curious glass tank in which various richly dressed figures paraded and disported themselves. There was hardly any dialogue in this scene, Zamiel merely announcing each apparition, luxuriantly depicted in coloured cardboard, with the words: 'Lo! Here is yet another vision.' Each of these visions could be made to rise from below the stage, by means of the little trap door.

The finale of this act was the strangest thing of all, and, though it delighted me then, it makes me shudder now. After some obscure banter between Zamiel and Conrad about what people most desired in the world, Zamiel conjured up a final vision, or it may have been a real event. On this the text was obscure. A cart was wheeled onto the stage on which, tied by all four limbs to a sloping wooden grid, was Father Silas being tormented by four demons. The stage directions in the book of the play called for 'agonised screams of terror and pain from Father Silas.'

The final act, designated in the text as Act III, Scene 1, took place in the great hall of a deserted castle, mentioned in the previous act as 'that castle yonder'. The two principal characters were again Zamiel and Conrad to which was added a third simply called Shadow. Shadow was a black draped, stooping figure, its face obscured by a black cowl. The only visible part of its body was a thin grey arm with long taloned fingers. There was no dialogue for Shadow, but stage directions indicated that while Conrad and Zamiel talked he entered and left several times for no explained reason. The dialogue between Conrad and Zamiel in this scene was the most arresting and the most worrying of the whole play. In it Conrad would ask for something, like food, or a fire to be lit, and Zamiel would prevaricate, subtly tormenting the boy with his own unfulfilled desires. When Conrad began to lose his temper and rant the Shadow would enter. His appearance would always subdue Conrad and prompt the horrified question: 'What is that?' to which no answer was given. The scene ended inconclusively with Zamiel leaving the stage and Conrad calling after him vainly. The final stage direction read:

After a short pause SHADOW *enters. Curtain.*

It puzzled me that having had an Act III, Scene 1 there was no Act III, Scene 2. The whole play was unresolved; nevertheless it filled me with enthusiasm and I was determined to perform it before an invited audience. I was not a natural exhibitionist, but from an early age I did have a strong desire to establish myself as a distinct and individual personality, and this play was to me the perfect opportunity to demonstrate my singularity.

I had a school friend called Willis—his Christian name was David, but we never used Christian names in those days—whom I could generally get to do what I wanted. He was slightly younger than I, slightly less academically proficient, and, like me, was the son of an Oxford don. I persuaded him that it would be a wonderful thing if we put on this play, *The Boy in Green Velvet*, before an audience of school friends with myself as producer and doing all the characters apart from the hero, while he acted as my assistant and was the voice of Conrad.

I don't think I bullied him at first, because, though far from unintelligent, Willis was easily led and was willing to submit to the glamour of a more forceful imagination than his; but gradually, as we rehearsed, my taste for theatrical perfection grew. I became a martinet over the precise timings of entrances and exits, curtains, scene changes. I demanded from him the same degree of dedication that I was giving to the project. When he fell short of my exacting standards I was severe. I am amazed now that he tolerated this treatment.

I do not believe that my actions over *The Boy in Green Velvet* were entirely due to normal boyish egoism. I felt that something was reinforcing my natural desire to dominate and driving it in directions against which a part of me rebelled. This is not to excuse what happened; only to say that what happened was not characteristic of me and that there was something mysterious about it.

I became increasingly irritated by Willis for many things, but chiefly for his perplexity over the play itself. Quite reasonably he complained that *The Boy in Green Velvet* was odd and had no proper ending. I replied that it was an excellent play once you understood it properly (which, of course, I didn't), but I was forced to concede that it was incomplete. If there was an Act III, Scene 1, there must perforce be an Act III, Scene 2, but no such scene existed in the text. I thought of writing to Uncle Alfred about it, but something held me back. Willis, partly, I think to flatter me, urged me to write the final scene of the play, but I could think of nothing. Instead I threw myself and him into even more intense and disciplined rehearsals of the truncated script.

I dreamed almost every night that I knew the ending of the play. I watched it played out to perfection on my miniature stage, but when I woke up I could remember nothing of it except the noise that brought the curtain down: that piercing scream which had woken me out of my dreams before. Then I began to dream that I had woken up and remembered the ending, only to wake up in actual fact and find that I had forgotten it.

Two days before my school friends were coming to the house to witness the performance I woke up to find that I had remembered the very end of the play. In my dream the characters were no longer cardboard cut-outs, manipulated by wires, but miniature three dimensional figures, like puppets, animated not by strings but by my own thoughts. The scene was set in a subterranean vault of the castle lit by the glare of torches. Conrad was on stage, his hair wild, his costume stained and torn. He seemed to be waiting for someone or something. Suddenly there was a tremendous sound as a door opened and something slid into the room quickly and scuttled across the floor. It was the Shadow which was now on all fours and moving rapidly. Conrad stood still. There seemed to be no more will in him to escape or resist. The Shadow circled him three times, then suddenly pounced on his back. Two long grey hands grasped Conrad's throat and a mouth from inside the Shadow's dark cowl began to suck at Conrad's throat. At that moment I was no longer watching the play but taking part in it as Conrad. I felt the tightening grip of hands, all sinew and bone, I felt two cold lips on the back of my neck and the pin pricks of hundreds of tiny sharp teeth, then I woke up screaming.

On the morning of the performance a large envelope arrived for me from Uncle Alfred. It contained scenery and characters for the missing final scene of *The Boy in Green Velvet*. In addition, some ancient sheets of typescript held together by a rusty paperclip provided me with the dialogue for the last scene. This threw me into a frenzy. Willis was not due to come until an hour before we were to perform for our friends. There would be no time to rehearse it but I knew I had to include this last scene in our play, so I spent the morning cutting out the characters and arranging the scenery.

In this scene Conrad was shackled to the Shadow. Cursorily I read through the script. It took place, very much as I had dreamed it, in one of the castle vaults. It was evidently some sort of storeroom as various barrels and bales of wood were piled up around the walls. Conrad was beginning a melancholy soliloquy on his captive state when Zamiel enters to announce that 'they' have been seen on the horizon and are approaching rapidly. Who 'they' are is not specified, but it is implied that they are coming for Conrad and are to be feared. Zamiel keeps going out and returning to announce that 'they' are coming nearer. Conrad begins to cry out in fear, but Zamiel warns him that if he screams too loud he will set the castle on fire. Still Conrad screams and his screams mysteriously start a blaze. A quick, ingenious transformation of scenery and characters shows him just before the final curtain engulfed in flames. He is still attached by chains to the Shadow who is now crouched on his back and seems to be sucking the life out of him.

I accepted the ending as dramatically effective, never questioning its logic or propriety. Only later did I realise that the whole play was terribly strange. Its uncanny preconfigurings of the absurdist drama of Beckett, Ionesco and Pinter only heightens the oddity.

By the time Willis arrived an hour before the tea party where we were to perform our play I was in a strange state of exaltation and extreme nervous tension. I was convinced that my young audience (with a smattering of parents) would be as entranced by the play as I was. I have a notion that Willis and my mother tried to disillusion me, but I ignored them. I outlined the final scene that was to be included and was surprised by Willis's extreme reluctance to perform it. He complained that we would be doing it without any real rehearsal, but I brushed all considerations aside.

It is hard even now to describe the sheer disaster of the occasion. My school friends arrived and, after a lavish tea, sat down on the floor of the drawing room to watch the play, very well disposed towards the forthcoming entertainment. My toy theatre stood securely on a stout table in the middle of the room with screens to the right and left of the table and a cloth upon it reaching down to the ground so that, as far as possible, our machinations could be concealed.

Very soon after the curtain had gone up I became aware that the drama was not enthralling its audience. The little sounds of restlessness, boredom and perplexity were all too easily identified. From the few adults present I heard murmurs of disapproval when, in a desperate bid to win back my friends' attention, I began to caricature the prosing boredom of Father Silas, the priest. For the first time, I found myself looking at the play objectively and I began to realise that it was rubbish and, what was worse, nasty rubbish.

I should have abandoned the whole thing at the end of the first scene, but stubbornness, pride, perhaps even a forlorn hope that somehow all would be well kept me going. In my anxiety I began to rush things and this agitated my friend Willis. Mistakes were made, lines were fluffed, characters made unscheduled appearances. I became increasingly irritated by his clumsiness. We stumbled on until the last scene. At this point the show descended into chaos, Having no idea of the lines we were desperately reading from an old, poorly typed script, the scenery was in a muddle, and Willis, who had become progressively paralysed by embarrassment, was saying his lines in a whisper. As we were trying to contrive the final transformation scene in which the castle bursts into flames, Willis managed to make the entire set fall down. The audience laughed heartily for the first time, and the ugly rage which had been boiling up inside me at last erupted.

I have no personal recollection of what happened next. I know now from witnesses that it took several strong adults to tear me off poor Willis. I was roaring at the top of my voice and trying to strangle him. Another ten seconds, apparently, and I would have succeeded in killing him. There was even talk of sending for the police, but moderation prevailed. In the immediate aftermath I felt utter humiliation mixed with astonishment at my own behaviour. The following day my mother made a bonfire in the garden of my toy theatre and took me to see a child psychiatrist who had nothing constructive to offer except to recommend that I should be taken away from my present school and sent to a boarding school outside Oxfordshire. This was done.

Much to my surprise, my mother did not reproach me with the incident. Perhaps she realised that the shame I felt was sufficient punishment. The calm efficiency with which she dealt with its consequences did much to heal the wound. I only once saw that calm exterior crack when one morning a letter dropped onto the front door mat. It was addressed to me and written in Uncle Alfred's familiar violet ink. Before I could get near it my mother had seized the letter and torn it into tiny pieces.

❧

Time passed. After leaving university I took a course at the Courtauld and, fulfilling my mother's direst prophesies, entered the world of art and antiques. When I first got a flat in London mother gave me the Boulle clock as a housewarming present. 'It belonged to your father and I never much liked it anyway,' she said characteristically. I liked it and decided to spend hard earned money on getting it restored. As Uncle Alfred had predicted, neglect and unsympathetic treatment had rendered it almost beyond repair. The brass inlay was coming away from the tortoiseshell and had been broken off in several places. The clock mechanism had never worked since I could remember, so I decided to have that restored as well.

One day I received a call from the restorer to say that he had found something in the clock which I ought to see. He had found a stiff piece of folded paper jammed into the mechanism which was the chief reason for its not working. Unfolded, the paper turned out to be a will made by my paternal grandfather only a week or so before he died in 1947, five years before I was born. It was witnessed by the two nurses who had been looking after him, and, revoking all other wills, it left his entire estate not to my Uncle Alfred, but to my father. It was the briefest of documents and gave no reason for this radical change of heart.

I felt a mixture of emotions, but the principal one was of dismay. I wished I had never seen the will. I decided not to tell my mother, knowing that she would have gone into battle over it on my behalf, and that was not what I wanted. I did feel, however, that Uncle Alfred owed me some answers, so I rang him up at Glebe Place. The telephone was answered in the curtest way possible by his housekeeper Mrs Piercey. Mr Alfred Vilier was seeing nobody; he was ill; he knew nothing about a nephew; goodbye. A few weeks later he died, though I was not informed of this and consequently did not attend the funeral.

About a year after his death I happened to meet one of Alfred's last remaining friends, a dealer in theatrical memorabilia. He told me terrible things about Alfred's last days: how he had become increasingly reclusive, refused to go out, and had come to hate any kind of natural light or scenery. All the curtains in the house were permanently drawn. The dealer told me that in the end he could not bear to go there, the oppression was so tangible, the ever-present Mrs Piercey so unwelcoming. Alfred retreated to his bedroom and was found one morning by Mrs Piercey to have suffocated himself by tying a plastic bag around his head. A bizarre detail given to me by the dealer sticks in my mind: it was a Harrods plastic bag, apparently, of the customary dull green with the word 'Harrods' and the Royal Warrant emblazoned in gold upon it.

I half expected that out of guilt Uncle Alfred might make me heir to his estate, but I was disappointed. The bulk of his fortune and the house in Glebe Place was left to Mrs Piercey. The theatrical memorabilia was left to a museum and I was made the inheritor of one black japanned tin trunk labelled 'Family Papers'. The label did not lie: the trunk was full of family papers of the dullest kind. Only one item was of any interest. It was a smallish mahogany box, with brass corners and decorated with a simple brass inlay, at a guess early nineteenth-century.

In the box which was lined with dark green velvet were two oval miniatures in gold frames. Their quality and the date 1814 engraved on their backs, suggested the work of Richard Cosway or one of his many talented pupils. They were head and shoulders portraits of a man and woman, young, handsome and dressed in the height of fashion. The woman had dark brown hair and delicate features, but there was something not quite likeable about the simpering expression which just showed her teeth: a certain capriciousness was suggested. You had the feeling that this was someone who might do or say anything on a whim, and be totally unaware of the damage she had caused. The picture of the man was much more striking. It was a brooding, Byronic face, not unlike the portraits one sees of the young Beethoven. A curious feature of the miniature was that he seemed to be looking intently at something slightly below his eye level and to his left. What that look meant precisely was unfathomable, but it was not at all pleasant. There were no names engraved on the miniatures and nothing to suggest who their subjects were, except for the only other thing in the box. It was a frail, yellowing copy of a journal called *The Monthly Intellegencer* dated December 1819. The *Intellegencer* was a tabloid-sized scandal sheet, typical of the period, whose longest items consisted of no more than two or three paragraphs. A heavy line in pencil was drawn down beside a paragraph which was headed:

HORRIFIC EVENTS AT THE
ROYAL COBURG THEATRE.

It read as follows:

> On the 10th of this past month of November, during a performance of *Elvira; or the Martyred Bride* at the Royal Coburg Theatre, a startling and most lamentable series of incidents was observed to be taking place in one of the stage boxes. Sir George and Lady Vilier, a couple noted for moving in the most fashionable and elevated circles, having taken the box, appeared to be engaged in a fierce altercation during the performance. Suddenly Sir George was seen to seize his wife Lady Hester by the throat and begin to choke the life out of her. Before effective assistance could be rendered to the unfortunate lady she had expired under her husband's violent assault. Sir George was immediately apprehended and is to stand trial shortly. It is widely believed that Sir George Vilier was possessed by an epileptic seizure in the course of which the balance of his mind was deranged. No other explanation can be found to account for the conduct of a gentleman widely regarded as a model of genteel manners and an ornament to his station in life. It has been said, we know not with what authority, that Sir George had of late lost large sums at cards and that he attributed his ill fortune to the colour green which he ever considered a most unlucky colour, and that on the night of the tragedy Lady Hester had on a new gown of bright green taffeta.

℘

At last the wickedness was unwinding and, one evening, as I was doing the *Times* crossword, I recognised the anagrammatic significance of Valerie Fridl and the final thread was unravelled.

THE GOLDEN BASILICA

'You were at Oxford?'

'Yes.'

'Ah. My son was at Oxford. Before your time. Christ Church. The House, you know.'

'Yes.'

'Were you at The House?'

'No. Oriel.'

'Ah, my son was up at The House, as they say. He lives in Italy. Professor at Venice University. He's written a book, you know.'

'What kind of book?'

'It's a masterpiece. It's called *The Golden Basilica.* I'm going to have it made into a play. Yes.'

This odd fragment of conversation occurred in equally unlikely surroundings. The man with the son who had been at Christ Church was sitting opposite me in a large bare room at the YMCA in Great Russell Street. He was supposedly interviewing me for a Summer repertory season at the Royalty Theatre, Seaburgh and his name was John Digby Phelps. He was a pale, flabby man in his sixties, with the greasy remnants of curly blonde hair clinging to his large cranium. His eyes were grey, protuberant and watery. He brought to mind one of those creatures that fishermen haul up from the dark depths of the sea, accustomed to silent, murky regions of the biosphere, an impression enhanced by a baggy grey suit, shiny with age. Conversation streamed from him in a bubbling monotone, full of dropped names, and mild but insistent self-aggrandisement.

I had gone to see Phelps, the director and owner of the Royalty Theatre, to read for a number of leading roles in his season, but he was more interested in talking about himself than auditioning me. He seemed impressed by the fact that I had been to Oxford and that I talked, as he put it, 'like a gentleman'. This rather relieved me because I felt at the time that these two factors often weighed against me with other more democratically inclined directors. Mr Phelps's snobbery was, objectively speaking, repulsive, but, as far as I was concerned, it was redressing a balance. I read one or two speeches out of various plays, but I could tell he was hardly listening to me. He had made up his mind. A few days later a letter arrived from him offering me a three-month season at Seaburgh. My misgivings about Phelps himself only slightly dampened my pleasure and relief: almost a quarter of the year would be spent in gainful employment.

But the strange conversation about *The Golden Basilica* stayed in my mind and before I went up to Seaburgh I spent a fruitless afternoon looking for a book with such a title in libraries and bookshops. The title appealed to me: I had a vague idea of *The Golden Basilica* being an elegant, witty novel about English expatriates in Italy with perhaps a touch of E.M. Forster or even Henry James about it. I have no idea why I thought that. Out-of-work actors are prone to such ruminative fantasies: they will watch the mannerisms of someone sitting opposite them in the tube and construct whole dramas out of a few simple observations. Actually, I was almost relieved not to find a copy of *The Golden Basilica.* It meant that my fantasy could soar, ungrounded by reality.

About the Seaburgh season itself there is little to say. The company was good and the plays decent. We performed a repertoire of four plays consisting of *Deathtrap*, *Gaslight* and a couple of Alan Ayckbourn comedies. All of them, especially the Ayckbourns, went down well with Seaburgh audiences and were enjoyable to perform. Once the plays were rehearsed and in the repertoire we had a good deal of leisure.

However, there were peculiarities about the way the season was run which made the company uneasy at times. These peculiarities all emanated from John Digby Phelps. Though billed as director of the plays, he did not direct. He would scrawl a few pencilled notes on the printed edition of the plays, underline all the stage directions and then instruct the company stage manager to take rehearsals. The results gained by this method were indistinguishable from those achieved by the average theatre director, but it was evidence of his strange personality. Very occasionally Phelps was seen prowling round the back of the auditorium during a performance, but he rarely stayed for the entire duration of the play. The day after these visits he would deliver notes on the performance via the stage manager and they would be on two subjects only. The first was our appearance. If he took a dislike to an actor or actress's hairstyle or dress, he could be severe, sometimes demanding a dress parade before the show to make sure that the desired adjustments had been made. The other theme of his comments was the curtain speech which thanked the audience and announced the forthcoming attraction. The exact words of the curtain speeches for every play were typed and pinned to a notice board, the slightest deviation from them bringing down sharp reproof, even threats of dismissal. Phelps's conduct was sometimes described as eccentric, but eccentric is a subjective term. An analysis of his behaviour showed a pattern consistent with egocentricity rather than eccentricity.

For some reason, perhaps because of the Oxford connection, Phelps took a liking to me. I did not welcome this favour because it made the other members of the company suspicious that I was somehow 'on his side'. In order to disabuse them I had regularly to make uncomplimentary remarks about him. This was not always safe to do, especially in the theatre, as Mrs Phelps was usually about.

Joy Phelps was Phelps's second wife, a mousy, furtive little woman, twenty years his junior. She ran the box office and the bar. She cleaned and managed the theatre almost single-handedly, sometimes assisted by her elderly mother, a presence even more shadowy and unforthcoming than her inappropriately named daughter. If any repair work was needed on the theatre, Joy's brother, a shrivelled imp called Ron, would turn up in a van that may once have been white. Their presence added to the stuffy, inward-looking atmosphere of the place.

One morning, as I was about to go into rehearsals, I was waylaid by Joy in the theatre foyer. I often came in through the front of house rather than by the stage door because our mail was delivered to the box office. She summoned me so secretively into her sanctum that I began to be afraid that something terrible had happened. Had a phone call come through announcing that my parents had died in an air crash? A hundred ugly possibilities rushed through my mind before she relieved my anxiety. Would I, she asked me almost in a whisper, if I were free, come and have tea with Mr Phelps at about four on Sunday? When I had said yes, she gave me directions to his house which was a short bus ride out of Seaburgh. I would be expected at four. She relayed these instructions in a solemn, urgent tone as if afraid that I would disobey or, worse, misunderstand them. She also intimated, in a roundabout way, that I was not to tell the others in the company about my visit. The implication was that Phelps's invitation was an enormous privilege of which they might be jealous. I had no intention of telling my fellow actors but for the slightly different reason that it would confirm their suspicion that I was Mr Phelps's toady.

Phelps lived in a village called Tiddenham about three miles out of Seaburgh in smooth, unspectacular East Anglian countryside. His house, the Old Rectory, stood by the church in its own grounds, a large grey, early nineteenth-century building on two floors with a severe Doric porch. Buildings provoke an instant reaction from me in a way that people don't, and I disliked the Old Rectory at once. Perhaps it was the day on which I first came to it, humid and threatening rain; perhaps it was the dreary garden which surrounded it, all gravel paths, lawns and laurel bushes; perhaps it was the pretentious austerity of its architecture; or perhaps it was the dread of meeting its occupants socially for the first time. Whatever the cause I was attacked by an almost overwhelming sense of oppression as I was about to ring the front door bell. It was exactly four o'clock.

I must have waited three minutes before I heard shuffling footsteps and the door was opened about half an inch by a hideous old woman in a blue overall with a bright red gash of lipstick around her mouth. I explained who I was.

'You should have come in round the back,' she said brusquely. I started to walk away. In a slightly more conciliatory tone she added: 'You'd better come in.'

I entered a large unlit hallway whose walls were hung with big, uncleaned pictures of dubious quality. To my left a door opened and Phelps emerged palely into the gloom. He wore cavalry twill trousers and a patched sports jacket of yellowish check. In these surroundings he more than ever resembled some dim submarine creature.

'Ah! There you are,' he said. 'Did no-one tell you to come in round the back?'

'No,' I said, wondering guiltily whether Mrs Phelps would suffer for this omission in her instructions.

'*I* told him to go round the back,' said the old woman.

'Ah,' said Phelps. 'Get the tea then, Nanny.' Nanny shuffled off to get the tea, but not before giving me a venomous look.

Phelps summoned me into the drawing room, which was well-proportioned and furnished in the approved country house style with a chintz three piece suite and a few good items of eighteenth-century furniture. Coloured George Morland prints adorned the walls. It was all correct and elegant; the silver on display was Georgian and well-polished, but there was no character. Nothing there had been chosen with love or enthusiasm. It looked like a stage set furnished to create the right impression of gentility: *The drawing room of the Old Rectory,*

Tiddenham, one dull afternoon in July. Over the mantelpiece was an undistinguished early nineteenth-century landscape in oils.

'You see that?' said Phelps. I nodded. 'A Constable. You know how to tell a Constable? He always hides a face in his landscapes. You see. There!' He pointed to a part of the painting. There was indeed a sort of face to be discerned in the configuration of the rocks beside a small stream in which a lumpy, misshapen boy was dully fishing. I had never heard of Constable putting a face in his landscapes, and this was no Constable, but I stayed silent. I had neither the courage to contradict him, nor the cravenness to agree.

Nanny came in with tea and cake on a silver tray, laying it down on a low table in front of the fireplace.

'This is Nanny,' said Phelps gesturing towards her as if exhibiting a prize pig. 'Not my nanny, but my son's. Stayed on after he'd gone. Stayed on to serve me. Loyalty, you see. Yes.' Nanny left the room without indicating by so much as the flicker of an eyelid that she had heard this tribute.

Seeing only two teacups on the tray, I asked if Mrs Phelps would be joining us.

'No, no,' said Phelps who seemed disconcerted by the question. 'She's busy, you know. Visiting her mother . . . or something. She wouldn't understand what we were talking about. She's not a theatre professional like us. Help yourself to tea. And have some of that sponge cake. Made by Nanny. Superb. She wins prizes for it, you know.' The cake was good, but had a suspiciously pristine, shop-bought look about it.

Our conversation during the next two hours consisted largely of a monologue about the theatre from Phelps punctuated by nods and murmurs from me when he seemed to require them. I tried to make these as ambiguous and unacquiescent as courtesy would allow since his views were fairly absurd. Occasionally he would ask me questions about the season and other members of the company. He seemed particularly interested in any rivalry or tension there might be among us, and he asked me my opinion, 'in strictest confidence, of course', of their acting abilities. I made my answers bland, sensing that he would not hesitate to exploit any indiscretion.

One topic recurred again and again in his monologues and this was *The Golden Basilica*, the work written by his son. He had the most grandiose plans for it. It was to be made into a play and performed in his theatre. Then it would be filmed, mostly in his theatre as well, though with a few external shots using the 'magnificent East Anglian scenery'. He made it sound as if this too, like the theatre, was his property. I was intrigued, but every time I tried to find out what was *The Golden Basilica* and what was its story or theme, he became vague or replied simply that it was 'a masterpiece'. Frustrated, I said, teasingly, that *The Golden Basilica* was certainly a splendid title. Phelps showed no awareness of the veiled irony, but seemed immensely gratified by what I had said. He picked up a silver framed photograph from a side table.

'There you are,' he said. 'My son, Peter Digby Phelps. M.A. Oxon. Like you.'

The photograph, at a guess fifteen or twenty years old, showed the head and shoulders of a young man in his twenties. One could see the resemblance to his father in the slightly blunt features and the crinkly blond hair, but he was better looking than Phelps could ever have been. The father must have looked on his son as an idealised version of himself. A touch too of Phelps's pretension was to be found in the ostentatiously large spotted cravat he wore. The expression was vaguely self-important, but gave little away.

'Done while he was up at The House. He was a very popular figure. Joined all the clubs, you know. The Grid, the Bullingdon. Spoke at the Union. Great success. Double first in Economics and so on.'

The picture conjured up of the brilliant all rounder was somehow dated and unconvincing. I did not point out that one could not achieve a double, or even a single first in Economics alone at Oxford. Phelps rambled on with his semi-coherent tirades—Equity, the actor's trade union being a particular bugbear—until the clock on the mantelpiece chimed six. Then a sort of muddled briskness took possession of him.

'Ah. Six. Well. Must be getting on. Expect you have things to do. Lines to revise. I have papers to . . . er . . . go over. Good of you to come. Must do this again. Show yourself out. The back way. Nanny will direct you. We shall consult further. About *The Golden Basilica.* Would value your advice. As an Oxford man, you see.'

As he said this he was shepherding me out of the drawing room into the dim hall. Once there he pointed to two large nineteenth-century vases, decorated with Chinese motifs: commonplace things generally used as repositories for walking sticks and umbrellas. 'Ming vases,' he said impressively, 'decorated with sayings of Confucius.'

❧

I was invited to come again the following Sunday and the next. The visits developed into a ritual, which was especially unwelcome because I had to decline offers of a day out with the rest of the company. When I told them where I was going they were amused, but I felt they were also suspicious.

My visits to Phelps never varied. They began at four and ended at six. Nanny served the same tea with the same sponge cake. Worse still, Phelps treated me to almost the same monologue every week. Like most egoists he was either unconscious of repeating himself, or did not care if he was: in return I gave him the same responses every week. It was uncannily like being in a play.

Why did I continue to go? I was not exactly afraid of Phelps, but I did feel a certain obligation towards him as my employer. He seemed lonely, and I like to think that a kind of detached pity played a part. There was one other factor which seems absurd in retrospect, but which I cannot discount: I wanted to know more about *The Golden Basilica*.

Each time I went Phelps came tantalisingly close to revealing the nature of his son's 'masterpiece'. His praise of it became increasingly extravagant but was always couched in the vaguest of terms: 'brilliant', 'beautiful', 'superb', 'witty'. For one brief moment he did step out into the daylight of exactitude. While talking about his proposed dramatisation of the work he told me that the opening scene would take place in St Mark's Square, Venice. Just that. When I pressed him further, he slipped back into the mists of vagueness.

In the town of Seaburgh I tried to pick up as much information as I could about Phelps and his son. They had begun to obsess me. Many people were either reluctant to discuss Phelps, or treated him as an unpleasant joke. Shopkeepers in particular were wary, as he had a habit of running up bills and then not paying them until threatened with legal action. I heard that he had married his present wife some ten years ago after an acrimonious divorce and that his first wife was still living nearby. About his son Peter, offspring of his first marriage, people had even less to say except that he 'lived abroad' and that relations with his father were distant. I did gather one piece of information from the local chemist, Mr Wendice who took photographs of the productions at the Royalty Theatre and was one of the few people in Seaburgh to be on reasonable terms with Phelps. Wendice told me that before their estrangement Peter Digby Phelps had persuaded his father, who had made a fortune in the garment trade, to buy the Royalty Theatre for him to run.

Phelps's peculiar attitude to the theatre was partly explained. He did not love the Royalty for itself, only as a link, however tenuous, with his absent son. It also explained his obsession with the staging of *The Golden Basilica*.

℘

There came a week towards the end of August when I was not invited by Joy Phelps to take tea with her husband on Sunday. Though this came as a considerable relief, I was also troubled. Had I offended in some way? When Mr Wendice saw me entering his pharmacy, he simply nodded, as if he knew what I was after. He had a bland, watchful face, almost hairless except for a short frizz of sandy hair above each ear. This, combined with his gold-rimmed spectacles and his habitual white coat, gave him an excessively clinical appearance.

'Yes,' he said without further preliminaries. 'I have some news for you. His son Peter is dead.'

The baldness of the announcement shocked me. I remember staring at a shelf full of toothbrushes for about half a minute before I asked for details.

According to Wendice, Peter Phelps had died in Italy of alcoholic poisoning. I asked if there had been any reconciliation with his father before he died. Mr Wendice did not know for sure, but he thought not. Phelps, he said, had been talking of visiting his son in Italy after the end of our theatre season, but Wendice thought nothing would have come of it.

I walked away from the pharmacy full of sadness. It was a bright windy day, and as I walked along the front, the wind that blew against me was the breath of grief. I heard the death rattle in the pebbles on the beach as they were raked by the ebbing tide. I decided that the only thing I could do was to write a letter to Mr Phelps. This I did, and gave it to Joy that evening. She seemed quite frightened by the fact that I knew about Peter: why, I wasn't quite sure. It may have had something to do with what I had seen that morning as I was passing the theatre. Joy's brother Ron had drawn his van up outside the stage door which was open. Out of it Joy and Ron with their mother in attendance were manhandling a large Victorian sideboard. They put the sideboard in the van. When Joy saw that I was watching them she said something to her two familiars, then hurried them inside the theatre. The sideboard was one of many pieces of furniture which were stored in the theatre for use in productions. I suspect that Joy believed that Phelps would soon be disposing of the theatre, and was attempting to salvage something for herself before it had gone.

The following day I received through Joy a large envelope from Phelps containing a letter from him thanking me for my note of condolence. He mentioned the production of *The Golden Basilica* and how he wished to make it a memorial to his son. Also included in the envelope was a rough bundle of notes which, Phelps claimed to have made on the subject. I was intrigued. At last I was about to discover what *The Golden Basilica* was about.

What I read disturbed me as much as it disappointed. There were random jottings of such generality that they were meaningless, such as: 'the scenes must be effective in conveying the action'. There were phrases in quotation marks which appeared to be projections of what the critics might say: '*The Golden*

Basilica is a masterpiece of wit, elegance and profundity.' Interspersed among these were sentences which seemed to have no bearing on anything. Some of them, joined up, seemed to form a dialogue of some sort, but the conversation led nowhere.

'Where are you?'
'Come back.'
'I never meant to.'
'You fell over.'
'Don't have any more.'
'We must talk. Come back.'
'What you did to me.'
'What I did to you.'
'I'm in a pool of blood. You put me there.'

Finally, there were three sheets of paper on which had been written at the top of each:

Act I. St Mark's Square, Venice.
Act II. The Steps of St Mark's, Venice.
Act III. The Interior of St Mark's, Venice.

Under these headings the sheets of paper were blank. I had no idea how to respond. Grief must have cut the last mooring rope connecting John Digby Phelps to reality. I could not share these things with anyone in the company. I did not want others to laugh or talk in some facile way about madness. This was not madness whatever that may mean: it was a self-imposed exile from the real world.

That evening after the show I had lingered in my dressing room. I did not want to go out drinking with the rest of the company. They knew about Peter's death, and had been properly sad for Mr Phelps, but it had not distressed them deeply and they were now beginning to speculate about how it would affect the rest of the season. Would he cancel it? I found myself isolated and laid low by these events in a way I had not expected. I felt a responsibility to grieve with Phelps, but I could not think why. My pondering over this slowed me down. By the time I was ready to leave I was alone in the theatre except for Joy, who would lock up the theatre after we had gone. I could hear the faint chink and clatter of her washing up glasses in the bar.

But there was another sound. As I left my dressing room and passed along the corridor behind the stage I thought I could hear someone singing. It was a man's voice, but high and reedy. I could not make out the words because the voice slurred over them drunkenly, but I knew the tune. It was the Barcarolle from Offenbach's *Contes d'Hoffman.* The tune, romantic and wistful, had always struck me as being somehow desperately lonely; and it never had seemed more lonely than when I heard it that night. Someone in an abyss of solitude was clinging unsteadily onto a last fragment of beauty.

I stopped, trying to locate the sound. It seemed to come from the stage. Obviously a drunk had strayed into the theatre and was lurching about on the set of *Gaslight* which we had played that night. It was my duty to go and get him off before he did any damage.

I went through the pass door to the stage. Everything was in semi-darkness but the singing, though perfectly clear, seemed no closer than it had been. The voice was now half-singing, half-sobbing. The scenery flats prevented me from seeing the stage. I went to open one of the doors onto the set and, as I put my hand on the handle, I heard a thump like a body falling onto the floor. I opened the door and stepped into the heavy Victorian parlour of *Gaslight*. One faint working light illuminated the set. By it I could see that the stage was empty. I stood for some moments waiting for something to happen. As I did so I was aware of a stale, sour smell, like whisky on a drunk's breath. Then something hissed in my ear, hideously close, icily cold. The words were:

'*The Golden Basilica!*'

Panicking, I blundered from the stage and in the corridor almost bumped into Joy.

'Oh, I'm glad I caught you,' she said. 'Mr Phelps wants you on the phone.'

I followed Joy meekly to the box office. It did not strike me as peculiar that she had not asked what I was doing charging about in the gloom, because that was Joy Phelps. To her, the whole world she had entered on marrying Phelps was strange and fearful; an actor stumbling about in a darkened theatre was no odder than anything else.

On the telephone Phelps said: 'Ah. There you are. Yes. Thank you for the letter. I believe I sent you some notes. About *The Golden Basilica*. What did you think?'

'Well . . .'

'Yes. Yes. Come and see me tomorrow. Four o'clock. We'll discuss the whole thing. A tribute to my son. A genius. Yes. Are you coming?' For a moment, a crack had appeared in that monumental self-assurance: he was begging me.

'Yes.'

'Good. . . . Good. . . . He's coming home, you know.'

I suddenly felt very cold. 'I'm sorry . . . ?'

'The body. The body's coming home. For the funeral. I've had it all arranged. Yes.' Then he rang off.

The next afternoon I presented myself at the back door of the Old Rectory at four o'clock. It was a dark, gusty, rainy afternoon. I rang the back door bell and waited for Nanny's familiar figure to shuffle into the scullery and grudgingly let me in. Five minutes passed; nobody came. I tried the door, found it unlocked and went in. I called out, but nobody replied.

The interior was grey and dim, but I had the feeling that it was far from empty. The place seemed to be populated by softly murmuring voices. I did not hear them in the normal sense of the word. They came from the house but they seemed to enter my head without assaulting the outer ear. The tone was that familiar rippling babble that I knew so well from the conversation of John Digby Phelps, but there was more than one of him. It was as if a thousand tracks of his soft, burbling self-aggrandisement had been recorded and were all playing at once. I caught few words, but those I did were familiar: 'genius', 'brilliant', 'masterpiece', 'my son, you know', 'my son . . .' Then these voices were joined by another, similar in timbre but subtly different, sharper, higher, more dissipated. A note of discord entered and the voices began to bicker.

I stood in the hall trying to make sense of this cacophony which surrounded me and threatened to suffocate. It was as if I was wrapped in an invisible sheet of sound. My own thoughts began to slide and lose their power. It was like the sensation one has before drifting off to sleep, except that a part of me remained fully conscious. It was my will that was being withdrawn from me.

The voices began to speak almost together, as if chanting. It was like the sound of a psalm being recited by a cold congregation in a dark church. Phrases were repeated and more and more often I began to hear the words: '*Golden Basilica, Golden Basilica* . . .' With this chanting, I seemed to lose all control over myself. Something soft and insistent was pushing me upstairs to a part of the house. A hideous, mumbling corporate entity was dragging me upwards, urging me to include myself utterly, to immerse myself in a ritual, quite mysterious and unknown except for its name: *The Golden Basilica*.

I reached the landing of the grey house. Soft hands pummelled and pushed me towards the half open door of a bedroom.

I entered the bedroom, drawn by the horrible force. I remember nothing of the room, only the mahogany bed on which was a cream-coloured candlewick bedspread. Something vast and misshapen was writhing and thrashing under it, or it may have been two things because a struggle seemed to be going on beneath the covering. I watched the bedspread heave up and fall like a stormy sea, expecting any moment the thing or things beneath to throw it off and reveal themselves. Apart from the awful rustling of bedclothes which seemed to crackle in my ears like gunfire, the sound was of the continuous murmuring dispute that I had heard before, its pitch now raised to a frantic falsetto. I stood as in a dream, unable to move or look away.

One vast heave and the coverlet was off. On the bed was a vast bag of wiggling, pulsating skin, white but blotched and bloodshot, slimed with mucus. Its shape changed constantly so that occasionally an arm or a leg would emerge from the fleshy chaos, and almost always there were two heads, both male, both with slimy and receding blonde locks, one marginally younger than the other. One I immediately recognised as Phelps; the other, I suppose, I don't know, must have been somehow his son, Peter. The two heads faced one another, mouthing incoherent noises, intimate yet antagonistic. Then one head would launch itself at the other and start to gnaw and suck so that one face would gradually become absorbed in the other. But always the other head would emerge somewhere else out of the great bloated bladder of flesh, and so the struggle went on. It was a parody of passionate love, a war for possession and mastery in one obscene body. But no victory would be won. Down dark avenues of death's eternity they must fight on. Then something merciful crossed between me and the foul bed: a telephone rang in the dark house; I was able to regain some of my own will and tear myself away.

Some hours later a member of the company found me wandering in a daze along the sea front at Seaburgh. He told me that Phelps had had a massive heart attack soon after lunch, was taken to hospital by Nanny and Joy. He had died at about four o'clock, the time I entered the Old Rectory. The telephone had been Joy, ringing me at the house to tell me what had happened.

ℰ𝒪

John Digby Phelps and his son were buried side by side in Tiddenham churchyard. His widow Joy inherited surprisingly little because the Old Rectory was found to be heavily mortgaged and Phelps's other assets did not amount to much. As for the Royalty Theatre, it had been given to Peter Phelps some years previously and was merely managed by John Digby Phelps. Peter Phelps in turn had left the theatre to his mother Vera, Phelps's first wife. The season at the Royalty Theatre continued as before because Vera Phelps ordained that it should be so, not out of sentiment but because she realised that she would have to pay the actors anyway, so they might as well work for their money. She even kept on Joy Phelps to run the box office and the bar.

One Sunday I was invited to visit Vera Phelps at her flat on the outskirts of Seaburgh. It seemed like a strange but inevitable repetition of my former Sunday ritual. Vera was a small, bitter woman with dyed blonde hair who might once have been beautiful. Her flat, on the first floor of a row of terraced houses facing the sea, had pretensions to elegance. She had heard something of my experiences with Phelps and wanted to know more. I in turn wanted to hear about Phelps and their son.

'John and he were incredibly close when Peter was a boy.' she said. 'I know it sounds absurd, but I got quite jealous. Then something went wrong; I never got to the bottom of it. Men. Two big egos, I suppose. Peter was always trying to get away, John wanted him to stay. He even bought the theatre to keep Peter—my darling son was theatre mad at the time. But the big break came when John decided to marry Joy, his box office girl. I don't know how that happened. I mean John had always had his girls before, but there was never a question of him marrying them. She had got her claws into him somehow. I was told she knew some sort of secret involving him and Peter. I don't know. . . . Anyway I was pretty fed up with John by this time, so I wasn't too upset, but Peter, bless him, took it very hard. Championed me, bless him, which he didn't need to do. Anyway there was a big row and Peter moved to Italy. He and I kept in touch, but he never spoke or wrote to John again.'

I asked her about what Peter did in Italy. Was he, as Phelps had said a professor at 'Venice University'?

'No, darling. He taught at a language school. In Venice. Teaching Italians English.'

Of course, I thought, Phelps's fantasies about his son Peter had been as extravagant as they were about other aspects of his life. So I asked Vera if Peter Digby Phelps really had written a book called *The Golden Basilica,* and if he had, had it been published?

Vera gave me a curious look. 'Oh, yes, darling, it's been published, all right,' she said. 'What did the old man tell you?'

She went to a bookshelf, pulled out a slim paper-backed book with a glossy cover and handed it to me. I opened it and read the title page:

> *The Golden Basilica,* A Guide to St Mark's Venice by Professor Francesco Loredan of Padua University, translated by Peter Digby Phelps B.A. (Oxon)

DEATH MASK

Being sent away to boarding school at the age of eight was not regarded as cruel or strange in the 1960s. My parents were enlightened by the standard of their day, but my father, a diplomat, worked abroad, so they had little choice except to abide by this upper middle class convention. I always joined my mother and father for Christmas and the Summer holidays, but I sometimes stayed with an aunt over Easter. Though I was not constantly unhappy, I had an almost permanent feeling of dislocation, of travelling from one place to another, not having a real home.

Most of the year I was at school, which meant that a good deal of my emotional and imaginative life was bound up in it. Stone Court, near Broadstairs in Kent was, even for the early 1960s, an old fashioned place. Its academic standards were modest; its facilities for sport and other activities were no more than adequate. Its advantages lay in the spacious and attractive grounds and the geniality of its headmaster, but even at nine years old I had a vague sense that this was not enough. There was something dusty and Victorian about its atmosphere: comics and sweets were banned; the school library was dominated by the works of Henty, Rider Haggard and Conan Doyle. Works by anyone more contemporary than these Edwardian giants were hard to find. There were lantern slide lectures and the occasional film on Saturday evenings. The only events I ever saw on television there were the Derby and Winston Churchill's funeral.

Despite its general air of benevolence, the school was run with the aid of an infinite number of petty regulations. Infringements were as inevitable as their consequent punishments. One folded clothes a certain way, one went to the lavatory at a certain time, one could talk only in certain parts of the building. Life was needlessly regulated, and rebellion against the restrictions had a pre-adolescent sexual allure. One of the most thrilling experiences of my young life was had scrambling over the school's roof after lights out.

The assistant masters were an odd collection. A few were permanent staff who seemed to our eyes to have been there forever, in other words since before we were born. They were mostly human flotsam who had been washed up into this forgotten creek by an unremembered tide and then stranded. They had few qualifications beyond the obligatory public school education, but they knew the ways of the school and survived by doling out their meagre stock of learning to reluctant boys. They cultivated little eccentricities behind which they could conceal their timid souls. One wore a woollen muffler even on the hottest day; another had an ancient car which he called Bucephalas, after Alexander the Great's horse. The Headmaster and Deputy Head made allowances for them, knowing that their permanence offered a certain stability to the boys, and a somewhat spurious assurance of respectability to their parents.

There was also a floating population of masters who came and went, some with bewildering speed. Those who came from other preparatory schools usually showed why they had been on the move before a term was out. There were the young men seeking temporary employment between public school and university, or between university and life. There was also a small unclassifiable category and, of these, the one I remember most vividly was Gordon Barrymore.

Mr Barrymore managed to cause a sensation among the boys even before we saw him. He had a Jaguar car which appeared on the gravel drive of Stone Court on the first day of term. All the other masters, if they had a car at all, had at best one of the serviceable and second-hand variety, but Mr Barrymore's was new, bright blue and conspicuously luxurious. The gleaming dashboard was of dark walnut veneer; the seats were of real soft leather, with a masculine aroma that one could almost smell through the closed windows. One of the boys examining this work of art knew it to be the new master, Mr Barrymore's car, and we speculated wildly about what he would be like.

Surprisingly perhaps, Mr Barrymore did not disappoint our expectations. He was in his late forties, of middle height, and though he had put on some weight he carried it well. Though not handsome, he had a pleasant face and dark, humorous eyes. His black hair was slicked back and he wore a neat little moustache. He dressed habitually either in a suit, obviously tailor-made, or in a blazer and slacks, always fresh and neatly pressed. A silk handkerchief adorned his breast pocket; he never wore the same tie on successive days. This set him apart from the other assistant masters who kept rigidly to the traditional patched tweed jacket and grey flannels dress code. If we were conscious that there was just a touch of the cad about Mr Barrymore's appearance, it could only have enhanced his appeal: at least he wasn't boring.

Mr Barrymore's charms were not confined to his appearance. He soon became very popular with us by treating us as equals. Not that he allowed us to take liberties. He kept discipline in his classes by the force of his personality and by our anxiety to please him. He taught French with little regard to rules of grammar, but with a fluent and intimate knowledge of its idiomatic usage. By means of jokes, conversations, games and stories in French we picked up much more of the language than we would have done from a text book. He always seemed at ease with us in class and we, at ease with him, learned much.

He also appealed to us for a darker reason. He made it very clear, but by the subtlest means possible, that though he liked us boys, he looked on his fellow masters with contempt. In particular, he showed an active dislike for the Deputy Headmaster, Mr Capstick.

Looking back, one can see that Mr Capstick had his good qualities. To begin with, he virtually ran the school because our amiable Headmaster, Mr Villiers, known to us as J.V., used often to slip away for a few days' shooting or fishing. Capstick had a good academic brain and taught a wide variety of subjects with efficiency and some imagination. He had a genuine love of poetry and inspired a few of us with it by reading to us in his melodious voice from his favourite Victorians: Tennyson,

Browning and Matthew Arnold. But he was one of those people who are instinctively disliked, especially by instinctive creatures, such as pre-adolescent boys.

It is hard now to think of any specific reasons for this dislike, except for an element of pretence, even pretentiousness, in his character. The skill and enthusiasm with which he produced the school play each year revealed the actor in his make-up, and there were signs that it was present in other parts of his life. There was something histrionic in his teaching, and in the exercise of his authority. It was effective perhaps, but to a small boy suspect. Much of the man was hidden, and so potentially dangerous.

He was also, by our boyish standards, an ugly man. Physical appearance played a large part in our judgement of people. Looking back, though, I tend to agree with my mother's judgement that he was a 'joli laid'. He had a bulbous nose, high cheekbones and the general appearance of a satyr which was accentuated by a neat, dark beard and moustache. He cultivated certain dandyisms in his dress, such as bow ties, loud checks and corduroys, which made him look like a fairly successful minor artist. He was married to a woman considerably younger than himself and this too, for some odd reason, did not find favour with us.

Our dislike of Mr Capstick was exploited by Gordon Barrymore to increase his popularity. A mutual antipathy between the two masters soon established itself, Capstick, the dedicated professional, no doubt resenting the easy success of the gifted amateur.

The year Mr Barrymore came, I was twelve and soon in his senior French class. As my early childhood had been spent in France where my father had held a junior post at the Paris Embassy, I was almost bilingual. My facility with French made me a favourite with Mr Barrymore and, when he discovered that I was not often visited at the school, an only child, somewhat isolated from my family, he showed me great kindness.

The second term that Mr Barrymore was there was the Summer term. My memory can only recall long sunny days. It must have rained at some time, but it certainly did not on the school Sports Day which occurred in the middle of that term. It was customary for all parents to visit their offspring on this day, but this was not possible for mine because they were in Athens. The only other available relative was an aunt who very rarely took me out from school because she did not drive. So I was one of the few boys without anyone to take me out to lunch that day until Mr Barrymore offered to do so. He was pleased to hear that I was not in the finals for any of the sporting events. 'We'll slip away early and avoid the whole ghastly shooting match,' he said conspiratorially. I was, I think, a little shocked by this attitude because Sports Day was a sacred event in the school's calendar, but I was also excited and relieved. I had hitherto been rather ashamed of my inadequacies on the playing field, but Mr Barrymore had given me permission to disregard them.

I had no idea where or how Mr Barrymore lived as I stepped into his purring, leather-scented Jaguar at midday. I did not know where we were going, but I did not ask. It was my habit then as now not to ask questions, but simply to watch and let events unfold, allowing ignorance to give me a fresh eye.

'I'll take you home first,' said Mr Barrymore. 'It's not far. We'll pick up my wife. There's a pub in the village which has quite a decent menu and a perfectly acceptable wine list. I thought we'd go there. All right?' He winked at me and I laughed back. 'Right then. Let's get the hell out of here.' He roared his engine and the Jaguar sped off down the drive of Stone Court, scattering gravel to right and left. Half way down the drive we saw Mr Capstick walking up it. He stepped smartly out of our way with a look of severe disapproval. Mr Barrymore laughed.

'Old sourpuss!' he said and switched on the car radio—then something of a novelty. A comedy programme was on the 'Home Service'—*Round the Horne* as I remember—and we laughed our way through the sunlit Kentish lanes.

Gordon Barrymore—I was encouraged to call him Gordon outside the school—lived some twenty or thirty miles from Stone Court in a village called Halton off the Canterbury road. His home was called Halton House, which impressed me, a long, half-timbered two-storey building standing in its own grounds. My first impression of it in the full glare of a high Summer sun was vivid. It was just the kind of home I wished my parents had, rambling and ancient, full of quiet corners and immemorial silences. The lawns that surrounded it were heavily shaded with ancient oaks and the occasional copper beach more recently planted.

When we arrived Mrs Barrymore—Freda—was sitting in a lounger on the terrace, a drink beside her. She waved gaily to us.

'Hullo, sweetie,' said Gordon. 'Started on the G and T already? You naughty girl!'

'Couldn't wait, angel,' said Freda, then, turning to me: 'So, you're the young prodigy. I've heard a lot about you. Come and tell me all about yourself.' Then, to Gordon: 'Be an absolute saint and freshen my drink, would you darling? And get the young prodigy a lemonade or something.' Gordon merely laughed and took her glass through the French windows into the house while I sat down opposite her.

She looked older than Gordon, perhaps because, being fair-skinned and blonde, the wrinkles were more in evidence. A chiffon scarf was elegantly swathed around her neck to conceal the ravages of time, but she still had a good figure. She smoked a cigarette in an amber holder which seemed to me the height of sophistication. She had a low voice with a slight rasp in it, no doubt the product of too many cigarettes. Was she beautiful? She had style and poise which gave an impression of beauty.

'So,' she said, subjecting me to uncomfortably close scrutiny. 'Gordon was right. You are a good looker. One of these days you're going to break all the girls' hearts. What do you think of that?' I smiled. I was twelve, an immature twelve at that, and the idea meant nothing to me. She saw that I was confused, so she began to ask me about Stone Court. She had been well informed by her husband about the subject, though the combination of his prejudice and her imagination had distorted the picture somewhat. I was happy to set her right; and she was content to allow me to do so. Presently Gordon came out of the house with two large gins and tonic, which they always called 'G and T's', and a Britvic orange juice for me.

I remember that we seemed to spend an inordinate amount of time drinking before we set off to the pub for lunch. I remembered that at the pub there was Prawn Cocktail and Duck á l'Orange on the menu, which was quite daring for a country pub in those days. I remember that after lunch we came back to Halton House and that Freda taught me how to play mah-jong. I remember how we left it rather late to drive back to Stone Court, and that Gordon got into some trouble because of it.

I remember most of all that I was happy with them. Freda and Gordon were childless and had not acquired the parent's habit of looking on all children as creatures to be kept out of harm's way and organised. They treated me as a young adult, rather gravely, except when we were all sharing a joke together, which was often. Perhaps it was also the case that by being childless Gordon and Freda had not entirely grown up themselves. I remember thinking how odd it was that I was much more at ease with them than with my parents.

When, later on in the term, my mother and father paid one of their rare visits to England and to me at school I insisted that they should take Freda and Gordon out to lunch. The four got on well together, though my mother and father, both in their ways highly intelligent as well as intuitive, had their reservations. My mother thought that Gordon was 'an absolute charmer', but that Freda was rather 'brittle'. I asked what she meant by the word, but either she could not explain, or I could not understand. My father's reactions were different. He found Freda entirely sympathetic, but though he acknowledged Gordon's charm, he said he felt uneasy about him. 'I'm not sure you can believe a hundred percent what he says. He told me he was "in Spits mostly" during the war and based at Biggin Hill. All very glamorous. I'm not so sure.'

'He was,' I said. 'I've seen an old photograph of him in RAF uniform at their home.'

'That doesn't mean he was in Spitfires though, does it?' said my father. 'I think he's a bit of a romancer.'

Despite misgivings my mother and father came to an arrangement with Gordon and Freda that they should take me out to lunch on one or two week-ends during term-time. In this way my parents relieved some of their guilt at being so distant; and no doubt my non-driving aunt felt happier too.

As I got to know Gordon and Freda some things about their life puzzled me. They behaved not as I had seen other married couples behave, but more like friends. They chattered away to each other and laughed and teased, but they very rarely touched. I was surprised to find that Freda and Gordon had separate bedrooms. There was something odd too about Halton House. It seemed only partly furnished, and what furniture there was, with the exception of a few small pieces, was battered and undistinguished. I noticed that several of the rooms in the house were empty. I later discovered that Freda and Gordon were not the owners of Halton House, but merely its tenants.

One Saturday, on my second or third visit to them from Stone Court, Freda sent me upstairs to her room to fetch some cigarettes. On the dressing table where I had been told her silver cigarette case was to be found were two photographs. One was of a beautiful blonde woman in WAAF uniform, taken obviously in the war. It took me a few moments to realise that it was Freda. The features were hers, but the expression was not one I recognised. It was gentle, wistfully happy, full of quiet joy. Freda could be cheerful and high-spirited, sometimes noisily so when she had had a gin or two, but beatific calm was not one of her moods. There was a restlessness about her even at the best of times.

Beside this, in an identical silver frame and taken by the same photographer, was the picture of a man in RAF uniform. It was not Gordon. This man had crinkly fair hair and the slightly soft good looks of a 1930s matinee idol. His expression was similar to Freda's, but something was lacking. The wistful romance was there, but not the joy. He seemed to be staring out of his golden youth into a very uncertain future.

I wondered whether the man might be her brother, but the kinship of those two faces had nothing to do with physical resemblance. I stored the two images in my imagination and went downstairs with the silver cigarette case. An elegant thing, made by Cartier, with Freda's monogram on the lid picked out in diamonds, it evoked for me an entire vanished world of cocktail bars, luxury liners and Hispano Suiza limousines.

At the end of that Summer term Mr Capstick suggested to my parents that I was clever enough to sit for the scholarship exam to Winchester, my father's old school. This idea found favour. The ambitions of a father for his only son and of Stone Court to improve their honours board coincided. I was bewildered as I had no sense of being more than slightly above average intelligence. Moreover I had no desire to be, because I was aware that exceptional gifts carried their own burden of responsibilities which included the obligation to work hard. But I was also timid and pliable, so I fell in with their plans.

The idea was that I should sit the scholarship exam the following Summer and, with this in mind, my parents decided that I should have some extra coaching for the last four weeks of the Summer holidays. They proposed that I should stay with Freda and Gordon and that I should go over to Stone Court on two days a week for Latin and Greek with Mr Capstick. The rest of my studies were to be supervised by Gordon.

Before this was settled Mr Capstick wrote to my father saying that Gordon Barrymore was a quite unsuitable person for me to stay with and that I should stay with him and Mrs Capstick at Stone Court. Though not by nature strong-willed, I expressed an adamant opposition to this suggestion, and my parents were neither able nor really inclined to overrule me. My father said that it was impertinent of Mr Capstick to interfere with his plans, while my mother murmured something about the Barrymores needing the money. This surprised me. I had always assumed that because Gordon and Freda had two cars (hers was a mini), lived in a splendid house and ate out at good restaurants they must be very rich. My parents lived well within their means, and so, I thought, did everyone we knew.

I arrived back in England after my truncated Summer holiday with a sense of anticipation and adventure. I was going to be with friends; the educational aspect of my stay did not bother me much. I suppose I must have done some academic work that

Summer at Halton House, but it is all erased from my memory. On the other hand, I did get to know the Barrymores very well, and that knowledge has stayed with me. The better I came to know them, the stranger their life seemed.

For such apparently gregarious people they lived a curiously isolated life with few friends. The only ones I met more than once were the Trantings with whom Gordon and Freda played Bridge once a week. I enjoyed these evenings and was allowed to take an intelligent interest in the proceedings with the result that Bridge is the only card game at which I have any proficiency. Tom Tranting was a retired naval Commander, one of those apparently straightforward types who have hidden depths. His wife Venetia, a faded beauty, wrote dull children's books. Gordon and Freda used to apologise to me for them and say that they were 'a bit of a bore', but I did not find them boring.

Once, when we were at their house, I found myself walking in the garden with the Commander. His lawns were immaculate. A characteristic naval neatness determined everything about his domestic arrangements, except his wife, whose occasional waywardness he tolerated with uncomprehending good humour. He asked me several questions about myself to which I gave the shortest answers that courtesy would allow. He did not seem to mind my brevity, but merely nodded, as if he now understood that I was one of those people who did not like to talk about themselves. When he stopped questioning me I had the opportunity to ask him how long he had known the Barrymores.

'Ah,' he said. 'So you want to know about your hosts. Well, we got to know them when they took Halton House about six months ago. Apparently they've moved about a bit. I like them, but they haven't made themselves universally popular in the locality.'

'Why not?'

'This is strictly under your hat, you understand? They don't fit in. People are terribly stupid about that sort of thing, especially round here. I personally don't give a damn, but Gordon and Freda sometimes send out the wrong signals. They're not terribly good at paying their bills sometimes. People don't like it if you're a bad payer, and then they see you swanning around in your Jaguar and having expensive meals in restaurants. I suppose that's unwise, but don't judge them too harshly. They had a tough war, both of them. I'll let them tell you about that themselves.'

Now that I was fully aware of their financial difficulties I began to understand their listless, haphazard approach to household management; their irritation with telephone calls; their frequent nervousness when they saw someone coming up the drive. I also appreciated the tact with which they shielded me from their troubles. As to their 'tough war', I learned about that the day after my talk with the Commander.

On the afternoon of the following day Gordon had to go into Canterbury on some mysterious 'business'. The sun shone and I was deputised to 'help Freda with the garden'. Freda's idea of gardening was to wander about in a large hat, occasionally snipping off dead heads and blowing cigarette smoke at greenfly. There was a gardener who came once a week, but his visits invariably coincided with Gordon and my going out on some ostensibly educational expedition, to Richborough, say, or Walmer Castle.

This afternoon, Freda's attempts at gardening were even vaguer than usual. We had had a rather scrappy lunch 'in' during which Freda had begun drinking gin and she still had a glass in her hand when we went out into the garden. She was not drunk in the sense of being unsteady on her feet or in speech, but her manner was more than usually distracted. She snipped savagely at a rose bush.

'I don't really like roses,' she said. 'I mean in the raw like this. I only really like them when they arrive at your door wrapped in cellophane. I suppose you think that's horribly superficial of me. I suppose it is. . . . You always get rose bushes in cemeteries. Nasty little groups of them in beds with crazy paving all around. They remind me of death. . . . Never get old. Never live longer than you want to. The lucky ones were the ones that died. I saw that even at the time. Oh, God, I'm exhausted; let's sit down.'

We sat down on a teak bench side by side and Freda lit a cigarette. The view across the lawn to a belt of tall trees was peacefully idyllic. I looked at Freda and saw that tears were rolling down her cheeks. She wiped her eyes with a handkerchief.

'Sorry, darling,' she said. 'I don't know what's the matter with me today. Must be the booze. Ought to cut down. My mind goes back. What did your father do in the war?'

I told her that he had been captured by the Japanese at Singapore and had worked on the Railway. Freda drained her glass.

'How ghastly. How simply ghastly. It was all ghastly. Don't let anyone tell you it wasn't. All that smiling through, Dunkirk spirit stuff. It's rubbish. It was sheer bloody hell. That bloody man Hitler. What a shit he was. Excuse my French. No, but he was. An absolute château-bottled shit. I was a WAAF. You've seen that photo in my room, haven't you? I was a stunner, wasn't I?' I nodded. 'Yes. You noticed. You're not as innocent as you look. Well, I was. I was in the ops room at Duxford, and of course one got to know the boys. That's where I met Gordon and Michael. You saw that picture on the dressing table next to mine. That was Michael. You've got a look of Michael sometimes. He was a lamb, an absolute darling. I can't tell you. . . . He and Gordon had been at school together. Best buddies and all that. Inseparable. They were both pilots, in Hurricanes. We used to go round as a threesome, but Michael was the one for me. . . . Michael and I got engaged. Next leave we were going to get married with Gordon as our best man. Then one day I was in the ops room and the news came through that Michael's plane was down and he was killed. It was the most ghastly moment of my life. It broke Gordon up as well. I think Michael was the love of his life too. He couldn't fly solo again after that and it caused no end of trouble. But that's another story. After Michael had gone I thought my life was finished. Perhaps it was. . . . Well, when the bloody war was over, Gordon and I met up again and sort of got together. We married in forty-six. Gordon's terribly sweet, but I wasn't in love with him. He knew that and he didn't seem to mind, as long as I wasn't in love with anyone else which after Michael I couldn't be. Well, we decided we were going to have a good time because we'd earned it, and we jolly well did. Gordon had inherited quite a lot of money and we had a lovely time spending it. We went everywhere: South of France, Monte, Capri, Portofino. Gstaad for the skiing, come the Winter. Great larks. Then the money started to run out, so we came back here and Gordon went into business with a RAF chum who turned out to be a complete swine. Left us practically broke. We still had a bit left and so we came here and Gordon got this funny job at Stone Court, and we met you, so it's not all bad, is it?'

She smiled at me cheerfully and ruffled my hair, but I could tell that she was still upset. Once she had told me her story that afternoon a new level of intimacy grew up between Freda and myself, an intimacy with which I was not entirely comfortable.

Whenever Gordon was away she would confide in me, and it was always the same story that she had told me in the garden that day, but with variations and embellishments. I was possessed by its melancholy; my whole idea of the war became suffused with tragedy. Previously I had taken my unthinkingly heroic concept of it from forbidden comics and the *War Picture Library* because, though my father had had a bad war, he never mentioned it.

Gordon took no part in these reminiscences. Once he came in unexpectedly while Freda was giving me a particularly maudlin and gin-sodden recital. She stopped abruptly. He looked at her angrily and his manner was unusually abrupt for the rest of the evening. Later he apologised to me, adding that I was not to pay too much attention to what Freda said, 'especially when she's had a G and T or two.'

The tensions in Gordon and Freda's relationship which had been revealed made my last week at Halton House an uneasy one. This uneasiness came to a head in a strange way three days before I went back to Stone Court. That afternoon I had gone for a bicycle ride in the woods around Halton and was returning rather late. It was hot and sultry and the sun was beginning to set in a yellow haze behind Halton House. As I approached along the gravel drive I caught sight of something white behind one of the windows on the first floor. The first floor windows lined a gallery which ran the length of the façade. Gordon and Freda's bedrooms opened off the gallery and their windows looked over the back of the house. I had never much liked that bare, dusty gallery for some reason, and was glad that I had been given a bedroom on the ground floor.

I wondered why my attention had been drawn to the object in the window. Perhaps it was because I knew that the gallery was always empty and that it was unusual for something to be there. As I approached the house I kept my eyes on the white thing which did not move. Some mysterious conflict of feelings in me both wanted and did not want me to know what it was. I moved off the drive onto the lawn to a point where I thought I could see it better.

It was a white, roughly oval object wrapped in a sheet which acted as a crude hood. The white oval had three black holes in it shaped like two eyes and a mouth. A faint shadow in the middle indicated a flat misshapen nose. It was unpleasantly both like and unlike a face. The thing was a mask, I concluded; but who would want to wrap a mask in a sheet and put it in a window? Were Freda and Gordon playing some sort of joke on me? They could be childish, but that kind of childishness was beneath them.

The two black holes at the top of the triangle seemed more like eyes the longer I looked at them. I had the feeling that, for all their emptiness, they were staring at me, not in a hostile or friendly way, but simply trying to absorb some part of me into their black depths. I thought I saw something glint in the empty sockets, but this may have been a trick of the light. The hole at the bottom seemed more like a mouth the longer I looked at it. It was elongated and, though lipless, it was surrounded by wrinkles that curved inwards towards the maw. It gaped, like a very old creature trying to catch its breath. The mouth began to work slowly up and down in a gumless chewing movement.

At that moment I managed to wrench my eyes away from the mask. Leaving my bicycle on the lawn, I ran indoors and upstairs to the long gallery. Anger had superseded fear. I wanted to expose the thing for the nasty fraud that it was.

But there was nothing in the long gallery: nothing to be seen or heard except a faint dry rustling sound that could have been a rat under the floorboards. I walked back down the stairs shaking and met Freda coming out of the drawing room. She had a gin and tonic in her hand.

'Hello, darling,' she said. 'You look a bit green about the gills. Anything the matter?' I told her what I had seen. 'Oh that!' she said casually. 'You must have seen the ghost.' What ghost? Whose? 'Just the ghost. That's all I know. It lives here. Only in the long gallery; that's why we made you up a bedroom downstairs. I haven't seen it myself, but plenty of people have. I believe it's rather nasty.' She seemed to find my further enquiries tedious. 'Don't be a bore, darling; I really don't know any more than that. Now, what do you say to a slice of old Mrs Thing's lemon sponge and a touch of the mah-jongs?'

So we played mah-jong, I with half a mind on the game, half on my astonishing encounter and Freda's almost equally astonishing indifference to it. When I later tackled Gordon on the subject he was even more dismissive. I had the impression Freda and Gordon were trying to block the whole ghost idea out of their minds; that their lack of interest was not natural but willed.

When the Trantings came for Bridge the following evening I managed to have a few words in private with the Commander. Remembering it now, I am fairly sure that Commander Tranting had contrived to make himself available to me. I asked him about the ghost of Halton House and described my experience. He nodded.

'I haven't bumped into it myself, though I'm not dismissing it. I've seen too many strange things to be anything but an agnostic. I believe Gordon and Freda got Halton cheap because of it. Well all I know is that it takes many forms. This face or mask that you saw is a new one on me, not that I'm doubting you. But whatever it is it always appears in the same place at the window in that gallery.'

'Who is it?'

'I don't know if ghosts are a "who". They may be just a "what", if you see what I mean. The only thing I do know is that bad things have happened in this house, and that gallery was always part of the story.'

'What sort of bad things?'

'Suicide, I believe. Always a dodgy business, suicide. I've never known a suicide that didn't cause more agony than it cured.'

I wanted to ask him what he meant by this last comment, but just then we were summoned to the Bridge table. Two days later I found myself unexpectedly relieved to be back at school.

ꟹ

At the end of the following term Gordon left Stone Court. He was, in fact, 'asked to leave', but he went quietly. When he told me half way through the term that he was going to be dismissed I wanted to get up a protest, but he forbade anything of the sort. He said that my academic progress was far more important than his career at Stone Court which would have come to an end quite soon anyway.

A fortnight into the term Gordon had been found guilty at Canterbury Magistrates' Court of driving under the influence of drink. Having discovered this Mr Capstick told J.V., the Headmaster. He added that a convicted felon was not fit to be a member of staff and that consequently Gordon must leave at once. J.V. was disposed to be lenient, but Capstick was implacable. A compromise was reached whereby Gordon should leave at the end of term. Even now, though I can appreciate Capstick's position a little better, I cannot help feeling that vindictiveness played a part in his actions. I am also not so sure that Gordon minded going as little as he pretended to.

Out of defiance, and perhaps some loyalty, I wrote to him regularly over the next two terms. He wrote back, always taking care to type the address on the envelope so that no-one at the school would recognise his handwriting and confiscate the letter. His news at first seemed to be excellent. Using some money he had 'scraped together', as he put it, he had set up a small school at Halton House for teaching foreign students English. There were, apparently, plenty of foreign students in need of just such a facility. He sent me an elegant brochure for 'Halton College' which I forwarded to my parents in Athens. In her next letter back my mother wrote: 'Daddy asks if Mr Barrymore has got permission from his landlord to use Halton House as a school.' I passed the warning on, but neither I nor Gordon took it seriously.

The following Summer I took the scholarship exam and, much to my surprise, succeeded. Stone Court granted itself a half holiday to honour the achievement and Gordon wrote me a jubilant letter of congratulation. At the end of the letter, almost as a postscript, he wrote: 'Alas, Halton College has had to close its doors for the time being. Some nonsense in the lease about not using H.H. as a place of business. I'm sure it'll all sort itself out, but at the moment Freda and I are in a bit of a tight spot.'

As I had won my place at Winchester, I was granted a good deal of time off during my last weeks at Stone Court. I decided as a priority that I must visit Freda and Gordon. One Saturday I rang up Halton House and Freda answered the phone. She seemed delighted to hear from me, almost too delighted, and I said I would bicycle over for tea. I remember thinking as I rode over that the weather was as sultry as the day I had seen the face in the window of Halton House. When I came into the drive I did look up at the first floor window and thought I saw not one but two white objects staring at me from behind the glass. It was only for a moment though, because there was Freda in her lounger calling to me from the terrace. It was three in the afternoon and there was a gin and tonic on the table beside her.

She greeted me effusively and sat me down. 'Now, tell me everything,' she said. I did my best. I was as anxious to hear about her and Gordon's 'tight spot', but whenever I tried to turn the conversation towards the subject she demanded more news of Stone Court. She was thinner than when I had last seen her and her hand, as she lit a cigarette, shook a little. I noticed that the wrist was bandaged.

When my news was finally exhausted I asked her where Gordon was.

'Oh, in Canterbury on business, darling. He'll be back shortly. I told him you were coming. He's dying to see you. We're probably going to have to leave Halton quite soon.'

'Why?'

'The money, darling. It's gone!' The withered, fleshless hand which held her cigarette described a vague arc in the air as if she were trying to show how 'the money' had flown. 'It's all been rather ghastly. I don't know what we're going to do.' On an impulse I reached out and grasped her cigarette-free hand, so very small and fragile. I took care not to touch the bandage on her wrist. My action made me suddenly feel years older.

'You are a darling,' said Freda. 'You've got a look of Michael. Did I ever tell you that? He was a love. He really was. Love of my life. . . . You know, when the money runs out I don't know that there's much point in going on. I don't want to live on charity. I've never done that. I know it sounds awful, but I just don't see the point of going on living. I simply don't. Have I shocked you?'

I shook my head in denial, but she had. Not long after this a car came up the drive. It was an old Morris Oxford estate car with the half timbered effect at the back. It lurched to a halt.

'The Jag had to go,' said Freda laconically.

I might not have recognised Gordon as he got out of the car, had Freda not called to him. Like Freda he had lost weight so that his clothes hung loosely on him. The hair had greyed; his face was pale and he had shaved off his moustache, perhaps to avoid being recognised by creditors. But he greeted me with great warmth and we enjoyed half an hour of jokey conversation. It was almost like the old days.

Then, quite suddenly, a silence fell. I sensed that they were tired and didn't want to talk any longer so I got up to go. They made a half-hearted attempt to keep me there, but I said I had to get back. 'Well,' said Freda. 'You know where we are, so do just drop in any time. But give us a ring first.' I said I would certainly come back.

The following week, which was my last at Stone Court, I tried several times to ring them, but their telephone had been cut off. In the end I decided to bicycle to Halton House and find out what had happened. It might be my last chance of seeing them.

The Morris Oxford was in the drive when I got there. It was about three in the afternoon, a dull day with the sky paper white. I rang and knocked several times but there was no reply. I walked onto the terrace and saw that one of the French windows was ajar. Entering the house, I was met with gloom and silence. There were signs that a packing-up operation had been started, then abandoned. A few sticks of furniture remained. Some pictures had been propped against a wall. A crowd of empty bottles were huddled in a corner, as if holding a melancholy meeting.

I walked through the sitting room into the hall where stood three half-filled packing cases. A glass lay smashed beside one of them. On the hall table was a vase and against it leaned a piece of white cardboard on which in red pencil was scrawled the words: DON'T GO UPSTAIRS.

I looked at the message and the message looked at me. Was I its intended recipient? Why should I not go upstairs? I do not know how I arrived at the conclusion that I should disobey the instruction but I did.

It was very quiet in the gallery and the door of Freda's bedroom was open. Looking into the room from the gallery, I could not see the bed because it was behind the door and facing the window which looked out onto the back lawn of Halton House. In front of the window was Freda's dressing table, bare except for the silver framed photograph of Michael which had been positioned so that it faced the bed directly instead of slanting inwards to one side as it usually did. The other photograph, of Freda herself, had been put face down on the floor beneath the table.

I went into the room. A man and a woman, fully dressed, were lying side by side on Freda's bed. Their clothes were those of Gordon and Freda, but their faces were unrecognisable. They were dead white and their gaping mouths were wrinkled, lipless holes. I noticed that on the bedside table were two pairs of false teeth, together with two tumblers, some empty pill bottles and an empty bottle of gin.

As I took in this scene slowly I was at first no more than perplexed until I noticed their eyes. They had sunk so deeply back into their sockets that they were barely visible. They were little more than black holes, like those in the death mask I had seen staring at me from the gallery.

I only have the word of others for what happened next. Apparently Commander Tranting, who had been worried about Gordon and Freda and had come to check up on them, found me wandering in the garden of Halton House. He summoned the authorities, then took me back to his house where I stayed the night. It was he who told me that the Barrymores had committed suicide by taking an overdose and that the phenomenon of the white face and sunken eyes was a known symptom of barbiturate poisoning.

Others were indignant on my behalf against Gordon and Freda. 'How selfish of them,' they said. 'How cruel when they knew he would go looking for them!' But I was not angry with them because they had, after all, tried to warn me.

ꝏ

In the following years I pursued academic excellence with a fanaticism that troubled even my ambitious father. What drove me, I don't exactly know. Many factors may have played their part, but I was conscious, whenever I thought about it, of a fear of the outside world. I was afraid that unless I applied myself I would not be able to control life and that its tides might take me where I did not want to go. It would be neat to conclude that this fear was connected with the fate of Freda and Gordon, but at the time all that seemed part of another life. I hardly ever thought about it, and whenever I began to I stopped myself.

It was after I had finished my final exams at Oxford, had got the required First, and was beginning to research for my doctoral thesis that the dam burst. I became possessed by a feeling of utter futility. I was afraid that even if I were to be offered an academic post I would be unable to take it up because I had no faith in learning, no faith in anything for that matter. I felt tired the whole time and I found it hard to distinguish between reality and my own dreams and visions. My mind created a wall of illusion between myself and the outside world. I called this state my 'inside world' and it contained visible, sometimes tangible horrors.

The worst of these horrors was the white face, the same black-eyed, lipless death mask which I had seen in the window of Halton House. There were days when I could not leave my flat in North Oxford in case I caught sight of the thing gaping at me through some window on the other side of the street. At night it was worse because then it got out from behind the windows and I would spot it peering at me over hedges or between bushes as I walked up the Banbury Road.

One evening I was hurrying back to my flat after a long day in the Bodleian. The need to get home before dark had become an obsession with me so that I was running. When the exertion became too much for me I stopped to lean against a low wall. I remember my right hand reaching out for some support and touching a smooth surface, spongy, and slightly slimy, like the cap of a mushroom that has been kept too long in the fridge. I drew my hand back and saw that I had touched the death mask. There it was, peering at me vacantly over the wall, its mouth working, making vague chewing movements. If it was trying to say something, no sound came. I screamed and ran.

My other visions were less alarming but no less haunting. More than once in that strange borderland between waking and sleeping I saw, or thought I saw something. At first it was no more than a white mist, but I had the impression that, though I knew myself to be in my small flat in the Banbury Road, I was also, on some other level, surrounded by the mist. The sensation filled me with despair, not of a violent, grief-stricken kind, but settled and, in some horrible way, peaceful, like a narcotic sleep.

Slowly, out of the mist, two shapes would emerge. They came towards me out of a great distance. As they came closer, it was not simply their physical presence which encroached on me, but their emotions and agonies. Even before I could see them clearly, I knew them to be Gordon and Freda. They seemed to be asking for my help, but I had no idea what help I could give them, or if there was anything there to help. Each time I confronted their pleadings with my helplessness I could feel their distress and I saw their faces fall into the gaping death masks that I had seen on that almost but never quite forgotten day. As I struggled out of my hideous waking dream, a phrase would keep repeating itself over and over in my head: 'We thought we were going to end it all.'

My mental condition deteriorated. I became more fearful, more withdrawn, more visionary each day. Eventually a kind friend found me a psychiatrist. His name was Bernard and some swore by him, while others said he was a crank. I only discovered later that, in addition to being a qualified shrink, he also belonged to an Anglican religious order. He listened patiently while I described my terrors to him and their probable origin. When I came to my visions of Gordon and Freda Barrymore in the white mist, he nodded as if he recognised the phenomenon.

'A white mist? Yes, that often happens with suicides,' said Bernard.

I was baffled. He seemed to be talking about real events rather than my subconscious. He saw my confusion and explained: 'When people are somehow in touch with suicides they often have this impression that the suicides are walking through a white mist, a sort of "spaceless" space, infinite, but claustrophobic because everything is the same. It's an image, of course, but it's almost certainly a reflection of reality. It means that the suicides have lost their way. They are quite literally lost souls. They don't know where to go, or what to do.'

'Even if that's true, what can I do about it?'

'Oddly enough, you can do quite a lot. You can pray. The prayers of the living are often a great help to suicides, because they're still earthbound, you see.'

This struck me as pure nonsense, but my reaction to Bernard's words was at odds with my impression of him as a person. He was quiet, intelligent, unhysterical. Though I thought what he said was folly, I felt that he was a man whose views should be respected.

'How do I pray?' I asked him.

'I can't tell you. I'm not an expert. To be honest, no-one is. You just have to try it and find out for yourself.'

I cannot draw any conclusions. I can only say what happened. I attempted to do what Bernard suggested. I spent some time of every day thinking about Gordon and Freda and asked some power in which I did not wholly believe to lead them out of their limbo. As I did so my anxieties began to diminish. One night I had a vision of the white mist again, but the figures of Gordon and Freda were walking away from me, and they were not alone. A third figure was with them, and he wore a uniform.

Now in my waking and dreaming thoughts the death mask has gone; and so have Freda and Gordon Barrymore. All that is left behind is my gratitude to them; and that I cherish.

THE SEVENTEENTH SISTER

I have no way of verifying this story. Father Berrigan died a few weeks after telling it to me, and I can only say that I have no reason to doubt it. Father Berrigan was a small, emaciated, wiry man who gave off an aura unique to himself: a combination of extreme, almost febrile spirituality and great toughness. He could look severe, but you discovered that whatever severity there was in his nature was inflicted on himself. He had a narrow, intense face and a thin mouth which, when it smiled, showed a beguiling, mischievous side to his complex personality.

He ran the Catholic chaplaincy at the University of Dorset for which I was the Anglican equivalent. Our relations had always been cordial, but it was only after my wife had died that we became close. If there was a chink in Berrigan's armour, it was the slight unease—I would not exactly call it nervousness—that he exhibited in the presence of women. There was a certain wary respect between my wife and him, but I sensed there could never be anything like a friendship.

Once I was a widower he would come to my house almost every Thursday evening after dinner. He would pour himself and me a large glass of Jameson's Irish whiskey which would then be diluted with an equal measure of water, and we would talk. That the bottle was supplied alternately by one of us was an unspoken part of the ritual, as was the rule that one glass only per evening was allowed. The conversation, while never trivial, was not heavy. University personalities and politics were usually discussed and, as Berrigan's view of life was ironic rather than censorious, we laughed a good deal. I enjoyed our conversations but, about six months before Berrigan died, I began to sense that there was something he wished to tell me. There were moments when he would swallow a large gulp of Jameson's, lean forward and take a deep breath, as if about to embark on some serious topic. Then he would check himself, sit back in his chair and make a general, anodyne comment to fill the gap he had created. I wondered if I should urge him to come out with whatever he wanted to talk about. In fact I found that I was nerving myself to prompt him in the same way that he was nerving himself to tell me.

The moment came one evening when we had been discussing the dismissal of one of the lecturers for sexual harassment. The case was particularly heinous because the lecturer in question—Berrigan noted in passing the homophonic appropriateness of the title—had used academic bribery and blackmail to ensure silence and get his way. I speculated aloud whether that difficult adjective 'evil' was appropriate in this context.

'Oh, no,' said Berrigan with unexpected firmness. 'He was weak and vain and dishonest—as much with himself, as with anyone else. But evil? Oh, no, that's a different kettle of fish.'

'But surely the effect of what he did . . . ?'

'Effects are not relevant. We don't call a drunken coach driver wickeder than a mass murderer because he kills more people in a traffic accident. Effects anyway are ultimately incalculable. Evil, like beauty, is a thing of itself, without cause or justification. It is an entity, independent of those it acts on and through. When you see it, you know it.' Berrigan was leaning forward and I saw that there was a tremor in the hand that held his whiskey. 'Hannah Arendt was wrong when she talked about the banality of evil. Sin is banal. Human weakness is banal. But evil lies beyond human weakness. It preys on human weakness, and it is not banal.'

'There's something you've been wanting to tell me,' I said.

Berrigan leaned back with a sigh. He was grateful for the opportunity, but I detected a residue of reluctance in him. At the time I thought that as a Catholic priest, he may have felt it beneath his dignity to open up to a mere Anglican. I now believe I was mistaken: Berrigan was beyond such trivial sectarian concerns. When a man has stared into the pit as he had, he very properly hesitates to communicate the horror he has experienced.

He made several false starts to his story, and often, during the course of his narration, went into long digressions, fascinating in themselves, but not relevant to the events he described. I will therefore give a précis of what he told me and only set down his exact words when I can remember them and they are of importance.

I must also, for the sake of completeness, make one other observation. The time of year was October, and it had been raining. My house is a modern one, its rooms are small and centrally heated. The radiators were on and the room when he began to tell his story was pleasantly warm, but as he got into his narrative I began to experience something like cold. That is the only way to describe it, because I am sure that, had I looked at a thermometer it would have shown that the temperature had not dropped. It was similar to having a fever when you know that you are perfectly warm but you still shiver, and cold sweat courses over your skin. But the symptoms were not shivering or cold sweat, but the kind of stiffness and paralysis, both mental and physical that you experience if you have to spend a long time in a cold, damp room.

ꟹ

Soon after his ordination Father Berrigan was sent to a parish in the North of England. The work was hard; the poverty he witnessed was distressing, but the sense of fulfilment was great. The period we are talking about was shortly after the Second World War when there was at least almost full employment, and communities had not yet begun to disintegrate. He had been working in this parish for about a year when he was summoned by his bishop to a meeting. I gathered from hints dropped by Berrigan that relations with the bishop were strained for reasons he did not make clear.

At the meeting he was asked, in addition to his parochial duties, to take over as confessor and spiritual director to a convent. An elderly priest who lived in semi-retirement nearby was able to say Mass for them, but he was not considered to be fit enough for more exacting spiritual duties. Berrigan was deliberately vague to me about the location of this convent, but I gathered that it was in a fairly remote part of rural Lancashire and some distance from his own parish. Berrigan wondered why he had been chosen for the task, but the Bishop merely said that it was because Father Berrigan had a car, a rare commodity among Catholic priests in the 1950s.

His predecessor in the role had been a Father Coughlin who had withdrawn, apparently because of ill health. (Coughlin incidentally was not the man's real name; Father Berrigan told me he could not reveal it.) Berrigan asked the bishop if he might speak or write to Father Coughlin, but the bishop forbade any communication and refused to reveal Coughlin's whereabouts. There was something about the bishop's more than usually abrupt manner which made Berrigan feel that information was being withheld from him.

The following day Berrigan drove over to the convent which was called The House of the Sacred Heart. It stood in its own grounds on the edge of a large village which Berrigan called Crampton. It had high walls and was approached by a long gravel drive via a spiked wrought-iron gate which needed to be unlocked by one of the sisters. The house itself had been purpose built at the turn of the century of red brick in a plain, soulless style. The order of nuns which it served was contemplative though not utterly silent or enclosed. They conducted retreats, and they had attached to them what was known as a Magdalene House where unmarried girls who had become pregnant could be brought to have their children delivered and then taken away to be adopted. There, under the supervision of the nuns, the girls worked a laundry—the convent's chief source of income—until they were deemed fit to be released again into the community.

'We are talking about the 1950s,' said Berrigan, 'when attitudes were not as enlightened as they are now.' I nodded, acknowledging my friend's almost obsessive desire to give as accurate and fair an account as he possibly could.

His first impressions of The House of the Sacred Heart were contradictory. 'I felt I ought to have been more uplifted than I was. It was a fine day, bright with high clouds and a bit of a breeze, a good walking day. The place was spotlessly clean and neat; and the nuns I met showed cheerful faces. I was given what I could have described as a warm welcome; except that it left me cold. Perhaps the fault was mine. There was something too about the light in the convent which I did not care for. It is hard to describe except to say that the place was very cool and white, somehow unnaturally so. It reminded me of the light you get in a room when it has been snowing and the sun reflected off the snow throws a while glare on the walls and ceiling. I was shown into Mother Superior's office. I remember the one picture, a crudely coloured photograph of Pius XII, staring intensely at me out of that bespectacled skull of a face. Behind a desk Mother Superior smiled at me. She had regular features, and the typical nun's look of scrubbed agelessness, shorn of everyday human charm or ugliness.'

Berrigan found Mother Superior an admirable woman but not especially sympathetic. 'She was utterly devoted, efficient, unimaginative, a born organiser. Perfectly nice, but. . . . You find them in all denominations. In your church they'll be supervising bring and buy sales and flower rosters. . . .'

Berrigan hesitated a moment and I knew his thoughts. He was wondering if I felt that he was implying that my wife was like that.

'Margery was hopeless at flower rosters,' I said. 'Bring and buy sales left her cold.'

Berrigan smiled sheepishly, then went on: 'If that type has a fault it is a certain reluctance to face reality if a problem turns up which is beyond their capacity to deal with. Pretend it isn't there and it will go away was her philosophy. An inadequate one, as I discovered. But she was very friendly, and she knew how to treat me, without that creepy, servile respect that nuns often show towards a priest.'

After the interview with Mother Superior Father Berrigan took tea with the other sisters in their parlour. There were sixteen of them and Berrigan was introduced to every one individually. 'One small thing nagged at me. I can't say I was disturbed by it, but it did seem faintly mysterious. I had the odd impression that there was one nun in that parlour to whom I had not been introduced, and yet, when I counted them off, and memorised their names, I found that I had met them all. I put it down to nerves and unfamiliarity.

'When the tea party was over I asked if I might visit the girls in the Magdalene House. Mother Superior seemed a little surprised and disturbed by my perfectly reasonable request. I had been deputised to see to their spiritual needs as well as those of the sisters. Mother Superior took me through into their quarters.'

'The girls', as they were called, though some of them were in their late twenties, were housed in an annex, built slightly later than the main convent building. The ceilings were not so high, but the place had the same atmosphere of high polish and cleanliness, and Berrigan observed the identical quality of light that was in the convent. There were about a dozen girls who slept two to a room. The conditions under which they lived were not exactly harsh. They were clean, of course, and a degree of modest comfort was allowed them. They had a common-room which contained some easy chairs, a shelf full of improving books and a piano, but no radio or gramophone. Mother Superior explained that most of their time was taken up with work in the laundry or in cleaning and polishing the Convent. Berrigan gathered that the average stay in Magdalene House was six months.

'We find that they come to their senses very rapidly,' said Mother Superior. Berrigan had looked at her face to see if he could detect any signs of compassion, or even irony in her expression, but there was nothing. The girls seemed calm and well behaved, but there was something in their look that worried him. 'It was an expression common to nearly all of them,' said Berrigan, 'a sort of miserable resignation. All the fight had gone out of their faces. But underneath that there was something else; something I couldn't put my finger on immediately. Afterwards I realised that it was fear.'

Berrigan drove home in a heavy mood. The following Saturday, he was due there in the afternoon to hear the confessions of the community, and on the day in question, he felt a reluctance to set out on his journey which went well beyond the reasonable misgivings he felt about his new appointment. 'It was almost a physical force,' he said, 'as if someone were pressing down on my shoulders jamming me into the ground so that I couldn't move. I felt a terrible lassitude, of the kind I rarely felt in those days. Still, I went.'

Unlike the previous Saturday, when he had first seen The House of the Sacred Heart, the weather was overcast. Long lines of grey cloud, in Berrigan's phrase 'like dirty bolsters', lay over the landscape. It struck Berrigan as odd, uncanny even, that, though there were few electric lights on in the building the quality of the light, that blank and leprous white, was precisely the same as it had been the previous Saturday, even though the weather was quite different. He went to the convent chapel and made ready to hear the confession of the sisters.

At this point in the narration Father Berrigan allowed himself one of his charming, transforming smiles. 'Monsignor Knox once said that hearing the confession of nuns is like being nibbled to death by geese,' he said. 'Well, without claiming to be the expert on geese that poor Knox was, I would say that was about right. All the petty failings of humanity are there, but writ smaller. All the little nastinesses of the caged convent world came out.

'Well, all that I had expected. I was old enough in my profession to know that convents are not havens of serene sanctity. I had heard the confessions of the sixteen sisters and the Mother Superior and was preparing to leave the confessional when another slipped in to the box. I could see enough through the grill to know that it was a nun. But who was it? Was there another nun in the convent that I had not been told about; or was it one of the nuns I had heard slipping in again to tell me something she had omitted from her first confession? She said the "Bless Me, Father, for I have sinned" in a strange breathy voice, almost a whisper, that I did not recognise. The accent was Irish, but not, I thought, a genuine one. It sounded to me like stage Irish, self-conscious and mocking.

'Obviously, Bill, I can't tell you the substance of the confession. Even if I were released from the seal of the confessional I wouldn't, but that confession was a horror. Oh, I don't mean murders or anything dramatic like that, just an endless litany of cruelties inflicted on the inmates of the convent, mostly verbal, sometimes insidiously physical. Animals had been tortured too apparently. But the worst things had been done to those poor defenceless girls in Magdalene House. The recital was interspersed with the most terrible blasphemies. More than once I tried to stop her but she went on and on in this teasing mock Irish so that I began to feel that I was only the latest of her long line of victims. That was the worst of it. The creature on the other side of the grill had not only enjoyed committing her crimes, she was now taking pleasure in reciting them to me. When she had finished I began laboriously to admonish her before giving her the penance that was suitable to her. What it would have been I cannot think, because in the middle of my stumbling homily she left the confessional. I heard tripping feet running lightly over the stone of the chapel floor, then the chapel door clanged shut with a deafening reverberant echo.'

There was a long pause. Father Berrigan leaned back in his chair exhausted by his reliving of the ordeal. 'May I come back tomorrow night and tell you the rest?' he said.

&

The following night we had dinner together at a restaurant. He seemed more cheerful. As we walked back to my house he took up the story again. 'There was one thing I didn't tell you about which I should have done,' he said. 'There was something about my interview with the person I shall call the Seventeenth Sister that I had found exciting. Arousing even. The horror predominated, but I cannot deny the undercurrent of another feeling. It was what made my mind return to it time and again.'

Father Berrigan had made enquiries with the Mother Superior about the Seventeenth Sister, but she said that there were only sixteen sisters under her and that was that. He did not think that Reverend Mother was lying, but her dismissal of his story was abrupt to the point of rudeness. 'There is all the difference in the world between not knowing and not wanting to know,' was Berrigan's comment.

The only solution that Berrigan could think of to the problem of the Seventeenth Sister was that one of the girls in Magdalene House had been playing a trick on him. But then he heard their confessions and decided that this was out of the question. None of them had the spirit for it. The faults they confessed were even smaller and drearier than those of the nuns. Had a nun come twice to confession? And if so, why?

Berrigan was still pondering these questions as he walked to his car in the drive. 'As I was about to get into it,' he said. 'I was approached, rather furtively I thought, by Sister Joseph, one of the younger sisters. She was a small, almost dwarfish creature with prominent and badly arranged teeth. I sensed urgency in her manner, and fear. She told me that she had happened to overhear my conversation about the Seventeenth Sister with Mother Superior. She told me that not so long ago there had been another member of their community, Sister Assumpta, but that she had died. I tell you, I had no idea what to make of this, and I asked her what on earth she meant. She merely said: "Ask Father Coughlin. He's in St Francis Xavier's." Then she looked round sharply. I turned my eyes in the same direction and we saw Mother Superior standing on the steps of the convent. She had on a face, as they say, like thunder.'

By this time my walk with Father Berrigan had taken us back to my house. I invited him in for a drink. 'Is this all right?' he asked with a tentativeness which was quite uncharacteristic.

'Of course,' I said, opening the door. 'Tell me about St Francis Xavier's.'

Berrigan untensed and chuckled. 'So you've not heard of St Francis Xavier's? Well, there's no reason why you should, you being an apostate. We in Mother Church call it "the Priests' Nuthouse". Officially, it's a rest home for Catholic Clergy. It's where you go to convalesce, or if you have a breakdown, or sometimes if you are in disgrace and need some time and space to "consider your position", as they say.'

We sat down in the sitting room and he took a glass of whiskey from me.

'I wanted to know what was happening and I suspected that only Father Coughlin would or could give me an answer, so on Monday, my day off, I drove the two hundred or so miles to St Francis Xavier's in Hampshire.'

His journey was in vain: Father Coughlin had died two days previously. Berrigan found everybody very unwilling to discuss Coughlin. 'I gathered that he had had what we call "a bad death". You know what I mean. Personally, I think people pay far too much attention to how a man dies. It's how he lives that matters. Well, Coughlin had died in a way that everyone was reluctant to talk about, and I found myself under a strange cloud of suspicion for even asking about him.'

But his enquiries had not been entirely in vain because, a few days later, he received a package containing a child's school exercise book and a letter. The letter was from someone signing himself Brother Michael and Berrigan never knew whether he was one of the staff or an inmate of St Francis Xavier's. The letter informed him that Father Coughlin had been the victim of a 'succubus'. The term was familiar to me, but only as a relic of medieval superstition: a succubus being in legend an evil spirit which sleeps with its male victim in female form. Berrigan was as sceptical as I would have been about this information. 'As to the exercise book,' said Berrigan, 'I could make little or nothing of its contents. The letter told me that Coughlin had been writing in it during the last weeks of his life. The pencil script was partly indecipherable scrawl. Much of what could be read seemed to belong to an unknown language. The words "Alona

Shaga" occurred often. At the time I had no idea what that meant.'

Berrigan could find at least some confirmation of what Sister Joseph had hinted at in the frequent mention of 'Sister Assumpta'. Unfortunately the name was never incorporated into a coherent sentence, but was invariably followed by lines of meaningless scribble, or endlessly repeated syllables. Sometimes, close to where he had written the name, occurred the words, 'under the bed,' or 'on the bed', or, more rarely 'in the bed'. Once, after Coughlin had written the name and a string of syllables which looked like 'Babababababa . . .' he had scrawled the words: 'Her mouth wept cold water on my pillow.'

After he had told me this Father Berrigan had to pause and replenish his glass. I was aware that his narration was both a necessity and an ordeal, and could, to a certain extent, understand why it was both, but quite what made the horror of it so compelling was still a mystery to me. Having swallowed his whiskey, Berrigan steeled himself to continue.

'The last words of the exercise book were written in a childish hand which was still just recognisably Coughlin's. I know those words by heart. I can see them now. First there were four short sentences in Latin. *Abite procul hinc per misericordiam Christi! Noli succubere me, putida saga! Noli abripere me in abbyssum caliginis. Non sum ad te.* Then something indecipherable had been written. Then came the words: *Crist hav merci.* Those misspellings seemed and still seem heartrending to me. And with that the notebook came to an end.'

The words translated literally read, 'Go far from me, for the mercy of Christ! Do not sleep with me, foul witch! Do not carry me off into the pit of darkness. I do not belong to you!'

There was a long silence, as we both absorbed the meaning of these words. Then Berrigan rose abruptly. 'The final chapter will have to wait till tomorrow night. May I come to you at about nine?' I nodded and he left quickly.

ᢀ

The following evening, Father Berrigan arrived half an hour before his appointed time. I apologised to him because I had with me a student Bible study group which was due to leave at nine, but he said that he was more than happy to wait in my study until it was over. I had the feeling that he had deliberately arrived early in order to gather his resources for the final episode. Nevertheless his presence in the next room made me feel uneasy and contributed to my impatience with conducting the Bible study, never, in any case, a favourite part of my duties as University Chaplain. Perhaps the poor students sensed this, because we broke earlier than usual, and when I entered my study I think I took Father Berrigan by surprise. He was seated at my desk, his elbows on it, his head buried deep in his hands. When he looked up I saw a face suddenly twenty years older, lined by a worry and perplexity that I had never seen before. With what I imagine was a supreme effort, he reorganised his features into his familiar smile.

'Are you sure you want to go on with this?' I asked.

'Oh, yes. We must bring it to an end.'

So, I fetched the whiskey and the glasses, poured the drinks, sat down opposite him in my study and let him talk.

When Berrigan returned the following Saturday to the House of the Sacred Heart he decided to say nothing about the enquiries he had made. 'To tell the truth,' he said, 'I was a little ashamed of my suspicions. I wanted to believe that the unease I felt was imaginary. I heard the nuns' confessions. I waited for the Seventeenth Sister to put in an appearance, but she did not come. I felt frustrated rather than relieved. I wanted her to show her hand, you see, but she was too cunning for that. I began to feel that I might have been the victim of a delusion, even that the nuns who passed me in the white passages were looking at me strangely because I was insane. It was a relief to visit the girls in Magdalene House.'

By some hierarchical convention Berrigan did not hear the girls' confessions in the chapel, but in a small room reserved for the purpose in Magdalene House. He noticed that one of the girls called Aileen, who was notably more pious and serious than the others, had held herself back till all the other girls had made their confession. She came in last and, after he had given her absolution, she remained seated. She looked at him for a long time in silence with frightened eyes before she told her story.

On the Thursday afternoon of the previous week Aileen had gone into the convent chapel, had knelt in one of the choir stalls and had shut her eyes to pray. She had heard no-one enter the chapel but she felt the temperature drop, though she was not conscious of a draught coming from anywhere in particular. On opening her eyes again there was a nun sitting in the choir stalls opposite her. She did not recognise her, but this did not puzzle Aileen particularly because to her, she had told Father Berrigan with a hint of defiant contempt, one nun looked very like another. This one, she said, had a particularly nondescript face. What troubled Aileen was that the nun was staring at her; and this was odd because, unless they had done something bad, the girls were usually ignored by the nuns. It did not seem a malevolent stare to Aileen, nor was it kindly: it was merely steady, unblinking, insistent. Aileen, whose natural spirit had not been totally cowed by her surroundings, decided to stare back. Then the nun did something which sent Aileen into weeping hysterics even as she remembered it. What did she do?

It was a long time before Father Berrigan could get a coherent answer.

'She blew,' said Aileen eventually. 'She put her lips together and blew at me from the choir stalls opposite.' The strangeness of the action was horrible enough. The worst of it was that she actually felt the blast of the nun's breath across ten feet of convent chapel. At first Aileen thought this must just have been a hideous coincidence: a draught in the chapel had coincided with the nun's bizarre action. But each time the nun blew she felt a blast of damp icy air full in her face. After the third blast Aileen ran, and she had not been to the chapel since.

Aileen's story made Berrigan decide to tackle Mother Superior. He had anticipated a difficult interview but his expectations were exceeded by the reality. 'Perhaps,' he admitted, 'I got off on the wrong foot by immediately asking about Sister Assumpta. She virtually accused me of not minding my own business. She kept repeating the phrase: "We don't talk about Sister Assumpta." Well, I could see I was getting nowhere so I left. One other thing occurred. As I was getting into my car I happened to look back at the convent building. My eye became drawn to an upper window where I saw the face of a nun, pressed against the glass to such an extent that the nose and mouth were squashed and distorted. The tongue was out and, like a great pink slug, was smearing the glass. At first it puzzled me that any adult, let alone a nun, could do such a childish thing; then I realised. It must be Sister Assumpta. She was mocking me.'

I asked Berrigan how he could have been so sure it was her. He looked a little sheepish and admitted that he couldn't be sure. After a pause, he said: 'Everything I tell you is subjective. I can offer you no outside verification. All I have is my memories, and the best I can do is to be true to them.'

On the Monday of that week Berrigan had a call from his Bishop who had received a complaint about him from Mother Superior; he also knew about the visit to St Francis Xavier's. The Bishop told Berrigan that he was not on any account to make any further enquiries about either Sister Assumpta or Father Coughlin: they were both dead and that was an end of the matter. When Berrigan said to the Bishop that if he was to continue as confessor to the convent, he must know something of what had gone on, the bishop became very indignant but reluctantly vouchsafed him a few bare facts. Sister Assumpta had fallen sick while conducting mission work overseas. On her return to England she had come to the House of the Sacred Heart to recuperate. There she was believed to have formed an 'improper relationship' with Father Coughlin. Shortly after its discovery Sister Assumpta had been found drowned in the River Durden about half a mile from the convent. The coroner's jury had returned an open verdict. Had it been an accident? Had she jumped, or was she pushed? The Bishop was not prepared to say, and would not understand why these questions needed an answer. Father Berrigan was to stop this nonsense and continue his work at the House of the Sacred Heart.

'So I did go back the following Saturday,' said Berrigan, 'for the last time, as it turned out. This is what happened.

'I heard the nuns' confessions, as usual, and when this was over I felt the need to spend a little time praying in the chapel alone. I knelt down in one of the choir stalls and tried to take my mind down into myself, into the inner well of quiet, as I call it. I knew from the first that something was disturbing my efforts. I thought that it was my own wayward mind; I tried to untense myself, but slowly it was borne in on me that the unease came from an external source. A damp, rotten smell was beginning to pervade my senses, like old cabbages decaying in a wet cellar. The air became clammy. I looked up from my praying hands to see something black and slightly shiny dip behind the choir stall opposite me. It was humped and shaped like a human back, but who would be crouching in one of the chapel choir stalls? And why?

'I really can't describe to you my feelings. The memory of them has been blotted out, so that only the bare physical—if they were physical—facts remain. I remember the objective part of me thinking that it was like a waking dream because I found that I could neither move nor speak. I heard a sort of confused bumping coming from behind the choir stalls as if something was blundering about blindly, and there were long, gasping inhalations and exhalations of breath. Then it began to emerge from behind the choir stalls and crawled out into the aisle. It was without head or limbs but the size of a human being, a great lump made of black cloth like a nun's habit and wet, dreadfully wet. It oozed water as it inched its way towards me across the chapel floor, headless and black, but not without a purpose.'

Berrigan said nothing for a few moments, but just panted heavily for a while, as if he had been running hard and was out of breath.

'That was not the worst of it. That was only the physical manifestation, but I was aware that in it a force was concentrating, vibrating and growing. I would say it was like a pulse. It was an essence of some life form, deeply ancient and primitive. . . . But not primitive in the way that we normally mean, not in the sense of crude, or stupid. No. This was a higher form than us, essential, spiritual, above all, pure. It had a profound intelligence too, one that somehow knew what I was thinking almost before I did myself. But I haven't mentioned the essential fact. It was evil: pure, unadulterated malevolence, nothing added, nothing removed. It was the thing that had operated through that nun. I knew that. How, I can't tell you. Call it a guess. Call it intuition.

'Before that moment I had not understood the concept. I had known sin in many of its forms, some of them pretty awful. I had even met a murderer or two. But in that chapel I was confronting evil itself which, in all senses of the word, was unspeakable.'

After a long silence he suddenly laughed.

'You know the irony of it all? The next thing I remember I was in St Francis Xavier's. They told me I had had a nervous breakdown or some such.

'Slowly I began to piece together what had happened, but I doubt if I would be here today if it hadn't been for a very brave young woman. You remember I told you about Sister Joseph, the little nun with buck teeth who first mentioned the name of Sister Assumpta? Well, she defied her vow of obedience to come and see me. She said she felt responsible and guilty about not telling me more at the time. Bless her, wherever she is. Apparently I had been found lying in the aisle of the chapel in a pool of foul water. I was incoherent, sometimes violent. Only towards myself though, thank the Lord.'

'So, did Sister Joseph tell you more about Sister Assumpta?' I asked.

'She did. Not much, but perhaps enough. You see, Sister Assumpta had been a medical missionary in Western Samoa, highly respected, but when she came back everyone agreed she had changed in some way, not for the better. She was shunted from convent to convent, each time her presence causing trouble of some kind. People were vague: no definite accusation could be laid at her door, she was just trouble. Eventually she ended up at the House of the Sacred Heart, Crampton "on retreat". She was there for six months altogether. When I asked her about

Sister Assumpta, Sister Joseph said her memories were oddly vague, but she knew she had felt from the first that her presence was in some way disquieting and unwelcome. She believed Sister Assumpta's troublesomeness was connected with her time in Western Samoa. She could not be more specific.'

'And Father Coughlin?'

'Sister Joseph said she couldn't believe that there was anything going on between Father Coughlin and Sister Assumpta, because it was clear he couldn't stand her. Everyone remarked on it. But in the weeks before her death they had been seen together once or twice in odd places, and on the afternoon of Sister Assumpta's death Sister Joseph saw Coughlin walking quickly along the banks of the River Durden in which she was later found dead.'

'Did she tell the police?'

'No. No. What would have been the point?'

I let that pass. 'So, is the House of the Sacred Heart still there?' I asked.

'The community was disbanded soon after my little fiasco. No reason given.'

'How very discreet.'

Berrigan gave a half smile and bowed his head in acknowledgement of my implied criticism. 'When I was better I did some research and discovered that the Samoan tribes among which Sister Assumpta had worked had some strange and rather nasty customs. It gave me an unpleasant shock to read in some work of anthropology that they had a practise known as "Alona Shaga"—those two words which had occurred so frequently in Father Coughlin's demented exercise book. The words roughly mean "catching the dead man's breath". Apparently, if you are able to catch the last breath of a dying man in your mouth, especially if that man was himself a shaman of some sort, you are imbued with all kinds of powers from the spirit world. According to the Samoans you can start hurricanes, strike down your enemies just by breathing on them, all sorts. Only inundation in water can dampen the force of this power, so to speak. Rubbish of course, but there it is.' Berrigan spoke the last sentence with a forced casualness that carried no conviction. 'So,' he concluded briskly, 'that's my story.'

There was a pause. Berrigan looked at me with eyes that expressed a lifetime of exhaustion and pain. I was sure he needed to say something more even if he didn't want to, so I did not move but waited for him to speak again.

'Why it remains with me till today is that I found myself utterly powerless against it. Whatever it was. Oh, you might say, that is just a blow to your vanity. And perhaps it is. Perhaps. But I felt that I had been up against a force as absolute and inexorable as the love of God. And almost as powerful. . . . Sometimes —I can't help feeling—more powerful. . . . Not that I believe that, mind! But I felt. And I still feel. I suppose that makes me a sort of Manichee.'

'Feeling is not believing,' I said.

'I hope not,' said Father Berrigan.

Three weeks later a massive stroke ended his life.

THE COPPER WIG

You almost certainly will not have heard of, let alone read, Mr F. Harrison Budd's *Random Reminiscences of a Strolling Player* (privately printed, 1925): it is not a distinguished example of the genre. The observation is commonplace, the humour ponderous and the endless litany of parts played and press eulogies received tedious beyond belief. But, like nearly all the autobiographies I have come across, it contains one story worth preserving, and, as Mr Budd's literary executor, I consider it my duty to give this a wider audience. Though I have cut out the occasional irrelevant digression I have not rewritten anything. Budd's style is rather quaint perhaps but it gives us a flavour of the times he lived in and the circles in which he moved.

ꟈ

It was in the early Summer of 1893 that I was summoned to join Mr Alfred Manville's theatrical company at the town of Yarborough in the North of England. I would have preferred to wait for a London engagement—indeed Tree had promised me something in his next season—but my finances were perilously low, my landlady and tailor exigent, and my impatient youth could stand inactivity no longer. Besides, Manville had a fair reputation. He had once been known as 'the Macready of the North', but he was now content to manage the company, play the character roles and leave the leading parts to younger men.

Our tour of the Northern Circuit was to open with *One of the Best* and *Harbour Lights,* dramas made popular at the Adelphi Theatre by the ill-fated Mr William Terriss. I was engaged for a number of minor but not wholly negligible roles. The company was a comparatively small one, no more than a dozen or so players, but Manville, known by us all as 'the Guv'nor', produced on a lavish scale by the simple expedient of employing 'supers' in every town we visited to play very small parts and to populate the crowd scenes. These men and women, mostly enthusiastic amateurs, and often supplying their own costumes, would appear on stage for a pint of porter and the privilege of saying that they had once appeared in Mr Manville's company.

Perhaps for safety's sake, perhaps on the principle of 'divide and rule', the Guv'nor had engaged two leading men, Mr Edwin Marden and Mr Charles Warrington Fisher. They made an interesting and instructive contrast in character and talents. If Fisher was the subtler performer, Marden was the more dashing and undoubtedly the favourite with the public, largely perhaps because of his looks. For, though Fisher was by no means bad looking, Marden was half a head taller than him, wiry and muscular in build, and strikingly handsome. What perhaps distinguished them most, and advantaged Marden, was in the matter of hair. Fisher's hair was pale, fine and, to tell an unvarnished truth, receding, but Marden had a magnificent head of wavy, copper-coloured locks. Fisher often resorted to a wig, and while wigs are all very well, they can never compete with the genuine article. Audiences in those days could be very cruel on actors they detected wearing them. 'Remove your headpiece, sir, in front of a lady!' some wit from the gallery would cry in the midst of a tender scene.

Contrary to what one might expect, Marden and Fisher were not rivals in the normal sense of the word. They did not quarrel or divide the company into warring factions and they rarely spoke of one another except to pay compliments. Superficially they appeared to be on the best of terms, even to the extent of occasionally sharing lodgings, but under the surface they were very different beings. Marden was breezy, outgoing and addicted to long walks when he had the leisure; Fisher was more thoughtful and inward looking. If he took a walk it was to investigate sixpenny bookstalls in the town, or study the architecture of the local church.

Our first weeks were harmonious and successful. Marden and Fisher had equal status and billing in our first two plays, but I was conscious of a certain atmosphere developing between them when Mr Manville decided to put into the repertoire that fine drama *The Honour of the Tremaines*. This ever popular play was to be his chief attraction, and he decided to cast Marden in the leading role with Fisher supporting him as the hero's friend.

The play is in four acts but the great moment comes at the end of the third. In case anyone is unfamiliar with *The Honour of the Tremaines* I must, for purposes which will become evident, briefly summarise the plot. Apart from the first act, the scene is laid in India, where Roger Tremaine and his friend Hubert La Rose are officers in the Loamshire Regiment. Tremaine has come to India under a cloud, having in the first act taken the blame for an incident of cheating at the card table of which Roger Tremaine's elder brother the Marquess of Tremaine was actually guilty. Tremaine takes the guilt upon himself in order to protect the honour of the Tremaines and save the title from disgrace. In India he becomes popular with the regiment and falls in love with Emily, the Colonel's daughter. Unfortunately there is a rival for her heart in the shape of one Captain Frederick Vosper. Vosper, the villain of the piece, contrives that Tremaine should fall into the hands of Nazir Ali, a ferocious local bandit. So all is set for the great third act, the final scene of which is laid in the officer's mess of the Loamshires at Bangrapore. After dinner the conversation turns to the incident which drove Tremaine from England at which point Captain Vosper says: 'I say Tremaine is a blackguard!' Incensed by this, Tremaine's friend Hubert La Rose rises from the table and thunders: 'To any man who says that Roger Tremaine is a blackguard I give the lie!' Tremendous applause. But this fine moment is eclipsed by what follows, for through the double doors of the mess staggers a man in the tattered uniform of an officer of the Loamshires. It is Tremaine himself who has escaped from the clutches of Nazir Ali! 'I give the lie myself!' he cries and collapses onto the table. Tumultuous applause. Curtain. It was a moment, like 'I am Hawkshaw the detective!' in Tom Taylor's *Ticket of Leave Man,* which never failed.

When I say that it was Marden who took the role of Tremaine and Fisher who played his faithful friend Hubert La Rose, you can imagine what a gulf was fixed between them in the eyes of the public, despite their ostensibly equal standing in the company. For that part alone Marden became 'the idol of the ladies and the envy of the men'.

It has to be said that Marden took full advantage of the benefits conferred by the role. His success with the ladies of each town he visited was remarkable, a success he took with an easy careless arrogance which was not altogether likeable. He began to put on airs.

In Doncaster there occurred an incident which significantly worsened relations between Fisher and Marden. They had taken lodgings together at a Mrs Pardoe's. Mrs Pardoe had a daughter named Judith, a beautiful girl of nineteen, to whom Fisher was greatly attracted. Indeed, I believe that he had formed an attachment to her during a previous stay in the town and they had corresponded. However, the long and the short of it was that in the course of the week Marden managed to seduce the young lady and, worse still, boasted of the conquest to some of his cronies in the company. When they pointed out to him that his friend Fisher had an interest in that direction he winked. 'Ah, you see,' he said, pointing meaningfully to his magnificent locks, 'I won that race by a head'. The remark was accounted a great witticism in the company and was oft repeated. Not surprisingly when Fisher came to hear of it he was enraged. He said little at the time, but when Marden approached him at the end of the week and suggested they share lodgings once again, Fisher turned on his heel and stalked away from him in silence.

Relations between the two appreciably worsened in the ensuing weeks so that they barely spoke a word except on stage. The frost was greatly exacerbated by the extraordinary success of *The Honour of the Tremaines*. The Guv'nor dropped the other plays in his repertoire, and Marden's personal triumph was reflected in the billing. His name now appeared above the title and in letters twice as large as anyone else's (except, of course, the Guv'nor's).

However, by the time we reached Slowbridge, that drab and deleterious Midlands town, Fisher and Marden seemed to be on better terms. For the first time in many weeks they exchanged cordial greetings in the theatre. It appeared that Fisher had become reconciled to playing second fiddle, though, in the light of what happened next, I have my doubts.

On the Thursday evening of the Slowbridge week I was making up in a dressing room of the Regent Theatre with several of my fellow performers, when the call boy knocked to call the quarter, twenty minutes before curtain up. Unusually for him, having knocked he entered and announced to us that Mr Marden was not in his dressing room; indeed, had not come into the theatre at all. We said that he should tell Mr Manville, but the boy seemed fearful. No doubt he realised that he should have alerted the management when Marden had not arrived at the half. I agreed to go with the boy to beard the Guv'nor in his lair. When Manville heard the news he gave instructions that we should hold the curtain for no longer than five minutes in case Marden turned up, but that meanwhile Mr Fisher should prepare to take over the role of Tremaine, and I that of the hero's friend, Hubert La Rose. Mr Willington, the junior character man, was deputised to double my part, the small but showy role of Lieutenant Beauhampton, with that of his own, the comic Indian servant Babu. So it was. Marden failed to appear and we all went on and were word perfect in our altered parts.

Marden had disappeared without a trace. His movements on that day, as far as could be ascertained by the police, were as follows. The morning had been spent at his lodgings in Wendell Street. At noon he had ventured out for a walk and met Mr Fisher outside the White Hart Hotel in the centre of town and there they had lunch together. Witnesses declared that the two men had appeared to be on the most convivial terms. At two o'clock they left the White Hart together and then, according to Fisher, had gone their separate ways: Marden to walk by the canal, Fisher to examine the famous misericords in the choir stalls of Slowbridge church. After that there had been only one doubtful sighting of Marden. He had been seen by an itinerant match-seller from the other side of the canal running along the towpath, apparently in a state of some agitation. When asked if anyone had been following Marden the witness replied that he could not be sure.

Naturally some suspicion fell on Fisher, but no evidence could be found to contradict his account of events. Moreover, there was no body and so no certainty that there had been any foul play. Marden's disappearance cast a shadow over the company, but the great principle of 'the show must go on' prevailed. Only one member of the company was inconsolable and this was our leading lady Miss Rose Manville, the Guv'nor's daughter, with whom, it would appear, Marden had 'an understanding'.

Fisher took the role of Tremaine very well indeed and if he was not quite as dashing as Marden he was perhaps more soulful, especially in the scenes with Miss Manville. (Miss Manville, however, had a great aversion to Fisher though, trouper that she was, she never showed it on stage.) Fisher's wig, it was true, was not wholly satisfactory and often provoked a few derisive titters on his first entrance, but even this problem was solved.

Three weeks after Marden's disappearance we were playing at the Alhambra Theatre, Derby (now alas a cinematograph palace). On our first night there Fisher sent a note by the call boy summoning me to his dressing room. Fisher had befriended me and I had responded after a fashion. We had similar, bookish tastes, but there was always something remote about him that I could never get behind. Closeness was barred and companionship taken up and dropped very much at his whim.

That night, as I entered his dressing room, Fisher seemed to be in a state of high excitement. A square cardboard box with a printed label on the top was situated in the middle of his dressing table. His eyes glittered and he wore a gleeful smile which did not seem to me entirely pleasant.

'What do you think this is?' he asked, indicating the box. 'It came by carrier today!' Obviously baffled astonishment was called for and I duly obliged.

Like a conjurer performing an important trick, he removed the lid of the box with a flourish and from a nest of tissue paper drew forth a magnificent copper-coloured wig. Then, with another flourish, he placed the wig on his head. It was astonishing. Even without the gauze stuck down with spirit gum the hair looked as if it belonged to him. It was a triumph of the wigmaker's art. I congratulated him and he beamed exultantly. Once again I was conscious of something not quite nice about all this elation. I searched for a reason for my unease, and then it suddenly occurred to me: the hair was identical in colour and consistency to poor Marden's! For a moment my horror must have become apparent because he looked at me enquiringly.

'Are you going to wear that tonight?' I asked.

'Yes. Of course. Why not?'

'Well, if I were you,' I said, 'I'd show it to Miss Manville first, before you go on stage with her.'

'Why?'

I was amazed that he should ask, but somehow I could not tell him the true reason. The name of Marden would have stuck to my lips. Instead I reminded him of the theatrical etiquette which stipulated that if an actor was going to wear something radically different from his normal garb on stage, he should go round the dressing rooms and show his fellow performers beforehand. At this Fisher merely nodded, patted me on the back and went off in the direction of Miss Manville's dressing room.

About half a minute later I was standing in the backstage corridor when I heard a woman scream. I arrived outside Miss Manville's dressing room to find her being revived by her dresser with smelling salts. She had her hysterics but by the time the curtain went up she had recovered and, like the trouper she was, gave the usual admirable performance. However, she never again spoke a single word to Mr Fisher other than on stage.

Something else of note happened at Derby. Towards the end of the week news reached us that the body of a man had been found floating in a backwater of the Slowbridge Canal. There were signs that the body had been weighted down with stones, but that these weights had come loose and the corpse had floated to the surface. No watch or pocket book was found on the body to identify him, but the clothes were similar to the ones Marden had been wearing on the day he disappeared. Certain identification was impossible because of one dreadful fact: the head was missing. Indeed, despite extensive draggings of the canal and other searches, it was never found.

Our next few weeks were the most successful so far of the tour. The wig seemed to give Fisher a confidence he had never known before so that he managed to combine his own subtlety with some of Marden's dash. He became a firm favourite with the public, but off stage he remained his old subdued and introspective self.

One oddity about him that I noticed was that he would never let the wig out of his sight. Once the performance was over he would place the wig on its block, into the cardboard box and take it back to his lodgings. Sometimes he would wear it during the day. One morning I saw him from the back walking down Acker Street in Manchester. For a moment I could have sworn it was Marden. When I asked him who had made this wonderful wig for him he gave an evasive reply, and on looking for the label on the top of the cardboard box I noticed that it had been carefully removed.

I also began to notice something strange happening during the performance. There were moments when it seemed to me that Fisher's lines were spoken by two people at once. This was particularly the case during the third act which I have described. There were nights when that great curtain line 'I give the lie myself!' seemed to have an odd echo in the theatre, an echo which did not quite correspond with Fisher's intonation of the line. On one of these occasions I saw that Fisher too had noticed the echo. A split second before he crashed dramatically onto the mess table a terrible look of fear and rage passed across his face.

Fisher started to have an aversion to being alone and, when we reached Castleford, he asked me to rent with him what is known in theatrical parlance as a 'combined chatsby', a sitting room with two adjoining bedrooms. I was reluctant, but he seemed very anxious that I should join him, and his gratitude when I agreed was effusive and pathetic. In those days the landladies used to come to meet the theatrical Sunday trains to tout for custom on the platform. Fisher spent some time haggling with a number of these women before deciding on one of them.

We settled in to our digs late that morning and the landlady served us a passable Sunday dinner in our shared sitting room. After dinner Fisher urged me to accompany him on a walk, so we went out to tramp dully about the town. Though he seemed to need me to be with him, he was not much of a companion:

his conversation was desultory and monosyllabic. He led the way but in no particular direction as if bent only on filling the time strenuously between dinner and tea. I noticed also, rather to my relief, that he had given up wearing the wig during the day, settling for a grey bowler alone to cover his baldness.

By the time we had returned from our walk I was exhausted, but Fisher was still imbued with nervous energy. On entering the sitting room, Fisher, ahead of me, said, apparently to no one in particular: 'What did you do that for?'

Thinking he must mean me, I asked what he meant. He started, as if he had forgotten I was there. Then he pointed to the mantelpiece on which stood the copper wig on its wig block. It had its back to us, and it occurred to me that the thing could have been mistaken for a severed head.

'Did you put that there?' he asked me, but I knew that he knew that I hadn't. He did not wait for my denial but immediately went to the fireplace, snatched the wig off the mantelpiece and took it into his room. I was reminded irresistibly of a mother carrying a fractious child off to bed. From the bedroom I could hear what sounded like muttered scoldings. Fortunately at this moment our landlady came in with the tea. I began to wish devoutly that I had never accepted his offer of a combined chatsby.

My bedroom looked onto the street and on my first morning there I remember being woken before dawn by the clatter of clogs on cobbles as the mill workers went to the factory. It did not disturb me; in fact it gave me the selfish pleasure of knowing that I could turn over deliciously in bed and not think about work until the evening. I was warm and drowsy, safe in the knowledge that I would soon be asleep again, but something was preventing me. In my half-woken state it took me some time to identify the disturbance. It was voices, one clear, the other muffled, which seemed to come from the sitting room, or from Fisher's bedroom, which opened onto it. I tried to ignore the voices but I could not because there was something familiar about their rhythm and pace which tortured me. It was like hearing a tune that for the life of you you can't quite place. I crept to the door of my bedroom and opened it a crack.

The sitting room was empty, but Fisher's bedroom door was open and it was from there that the voices emanated. The clearer of the two voices was Fisher's. What he was saying was still indistinct, but I could recognise it because I knew it so well. It was Roger Tremaine's great speech from the last act of *The Honour of the Tremaines*:

> I say to you, Hubert, that a man's honour is like a precious jewel: once shattered it is never repaired. If a man has honour he will hold it dearer than life itself: for he gives it away at the cost of his immortal soul. Be he the poorest of the poor, the humblest of the humble, if a man has honour, he is a prince among men. But if he has lost it, then, be he as rich as Croesus, as mighty as a king, I declare him to be the vilest dog on earth.

Quite why Fisher should be rehearsing a speech he both knew and performed to perfection was a mystery. But the second voice was an even greater mystery. It seemed to be repeating the speech, though at times it anticipated Fisher. The sound of it was like a muffled groan, only the cadences of the speech being identifiable. It was as if someone or something was struggling to speak with a gag in its mouth. Who was it? What was happening? I put on my dressing gown and entered the sitting room. As soon as I did so the voices stopped and the door of Fisher's bedroom was slammed shut.

I heard those voices more than once during our week at Castleford, always at our digs, sometimes late at night, sometimes very early in the morning. I wondered at times whether I was dreaming them. Certainly they wove their way into my dreams which were of nameless things, things that were trying to struggle out of miserable dark holes into our world, things which even now I would give all my worldly goods to forget.

As for Fisher, I frankly avoided him. We had no quarrel; I took my meals with him at the digs, but even then I contrived to be reading a book or otherwise occupied, so that I would not be obliged to exchange too many words with him. I cannot altogether explain my feelings: it was nothing so simple as an aura of wickedness which repelled me. I can best express it by saying that Fisher seemed to me to be living in a different world to ours while still existing in this one. His eyes seemed to focus on points in empty space. He would suddenly address words to no-one in particular. They were often strange words belonging to a language of his own, ugly words of loathing and despair.

The easy explanation would be to say that Fisher had gone mad, whatever that may mean, but this would not cover all the facts. In the first place he gave an impeccable performance every night, and if one did speak to him on any subject he would answer as soberly and rationally as ever he did. Only his air of abstraction gave away the fact that a part of him was not attending to you at all.

And so we come to the last fateful night in Castleford. It began for me on a hopeful note. The matinee had been well received by a capacity house and I was beginning to look forward to the last week of our tour at Darlington, where I was determined at all costs not to share digs with Fisher.

After the matinee and before the evening performance I walked out of the theatre to get some fresh air. Fisher had gone out just ahead of me and I saw him walking along the narrow alleyway which led from the stage door to the street, head bowed, muttering something to an invisible presence below him and to his right. He might have been talking to an imaginary dog that trotted by his side. If it was so, the dog was clearly not behaving itself at all well. I waited to see which way he turned into the street, then I took the opposite route.

I returned to the theatre perhaps a little later than I intended, but refreshed, mainly, I think, because I had not seen Fisher. For the first time that week, I felt positively light-hearted. Then, as I walked down the dressing room corridor I became aware of a noise coming from Fisher's dressing room. It was that mumbling gagged voice again which had accompanied Fisher's recitation at the digs. It stopped me in my tracks, and all the unspoken horrors of that week threatened to return. I was determined not to let it. I would go and see Fisher and confront him. But with what? That I had not decided.

The dressing room door was ajar, I knocked and, receiving no response, I entered. All was silent and the room was empty, but on the table beside the mirror, its back towards me, was the copper wig on the wig block. I looked around more thoroughly and called Fisher's name, but there was no one there. A sensation of moist coldness crept over my skin. My eyes were drawn again to the wig. There were tiny beads of water on it that glistened like diamonds in the gaslight and it seemed almost imperceptibly to be trembling, as if shivering like me from the cold. Yet I could detect no other vibration to account for the movement. I watched transfixed as the wig shuddered almost like a living thing. Then it began to turn around towards me, as an object on a vibrating surface will turn, slowly, hesitantly at first, then with increasing deliberation. Suddenly I felt that of all the things in the world I did not want to see, I did not want to see the blank 'face' side of the wig block. I turned and ran from the room.

That was only the first of many strange happenings that night. Before curtain up Miss Manville had hysterics in her dressing room, claiming that she had seen Marden's disembodied head smiling at her in her dressing room mirror. During the performance Fisher seemed distracted. He was constantly adjusting his wig as if it gave him discomfort, and between the second and third acts I saw him drain a large glass of brandy and water in the wings. Not unusual for an actor, you may say, but Fisher was the most abstemious of men and never drank during a show.

We reached the last scene of the third act. There are moments on stage when one feels that a scene is not simply being played, but somehow lived by both actors and audience. This was such a moment. I felt as if I were actually in the officer's mess of the Loamshires at Bangrapore. I must have risen to the occasion because my line 'To any man who says that Roger Tremaine is a blackguard I give the lie!' was more than usually well received. Normally Fisher made his entrance as Tremaine with immaculate timing, just as the applause for my line was fading away, but on this night there was a hiatus before he staggered on in his tattered uniform. The pause before Fisher entered seemed horribly long to us on stage, but was probably barely noticed by the audience. 'I give the lie myself!' he cried, receiving the usual ovation. Then, instead of crashing dramatically onto the table, Fisher began reeling about clutching at his head. Something had gone hideously amiss. He seemed in agony and his eyes were starting from their sockets. I realised that he was desperately trying to tear his wig off, but to no avail. Little streams of blood began to pour from his temples just where the wig joined Fisher's head. He screamed in agony and, as he did so, a great torrent of blood gushed from under the wig join covering his face, hands and several nearby supers in gore. As he finally crashed onto the table and the curtain fell a great roar of applause burst from the audience. It was Fisher's last and greatest ovation. He never heard it because I am convinced he was dead before he had hit the table.

The last act of the play was cancelled that night and the Guv'nor went before the curtain to announce that upon application at the box office customers' money would be returned. Surprisingly few theatregoers took up this offer, however. As one of them remarked to me in the street the following morning in his blunt Northern way, he had got his shilling's worth.

No explanation could be discovered for the extraordinary and horrific death of Mr Fisher by either the men of science or of the law. The top of his skull had simply been crushed to a pulp as if it had been a rotten apple. At the inquest a verdict of Death by Misadventure was brought in. The only clue—if it can be called a clue—to the tragedy resided in a crumpled piece of paper found in the jacket Fisher was wearing on the day of his death. It was a bill, the tradesman in question being one, 'Jabez Wheeler, Superior Wig Maker of 12 Dock Street, Bermondsey'. No figures had been written on the bill side of the document, but on the reverse, the following had been scrawled in pencil:

> I find there are some additional costs still outstanding. Yours was an unusual request and mine an unusual talent to execute it. I also have a talent for silence, but silence comes at a price. J.W.

Upon investigation, 12 Dock Street turned out to be a deserted warehouse, and nobody in the district had ever heard of Mr Jabez Wheeler, Superior Wig Maker.

For our last week at Darlington I myself took the role of Roger Tremaine, but my heart was not in it. That third act curtain fell to only muted applause. When it was over I returned to London and was happy to accept the small role of an art student in a revival of *Trilby* with Sir Herbert Beerbohm Tree.

THE DREAMS OF CARDINAL VITTORINI

In the library of Wadham College, Oxford there is a small collection of manuscripts relating to one of its most famous alumni, the poet and rake, John Wilmot, Earl of Rochester. Perhaps the strangest of these papers is a single sheet of foolscap covered in dense, crabbed writing. Along the top in a rather larger hand is written: *This rendering of the* Responsoriae Foscarinenses *made for W of R by his Ldshp's humble svt Thom Wythorne, Anno 1678*. Wythorne was a fellow of Wadham, a secret Catholic and, it was alleged, both a Jesuit priest and a spy. He had known Rochester since they were both Commoners at

Wadham. The main body of the text details a kind of ritual, with a homily and responses, religious in form, but far from religious in character. Some of its language and ideas are strikingly similar to Rochester's poem 'Upon Nothing' which it undoubtedly influenced. As for the word 'Foscarinenses', I was intrigued because it seemed to throw light on a mysterious sentence to be found in John Aubrey's *Brief Lives*: *In his last sicknesse My Lord of Rochester was exceedingly paenitent and did confesse to Dr Burnet that before his paines drove him to repentance he had been Foscarine.* Some weeks of patient research yielded only a few bare facts about the Foscarines: that they were members of a heretical sect or secret society who first made their appearance at Rome towards the end of the sixteenth century and were all but wiped out there. A compulsive curiosity drove me to investigate further and took me to Rome which was where and how I uncovered the story of Cardinal Vittorini.

ℰ

The Spanish Inquisition is notorious, but the activities of the Inquisition in Rome during the 1560s and 1570s were no less bloody and far more secret. Its history is dominated by the strange and terrible figure of Cardinal Vittorini. There were those who said he was a saint. Moves were made soon after his death to have him beatified, then canonised, and his cause has recently been revived. His famous mystical work *The Means and Might of Spiritual Orison* (Benet of Canfield's translation of the title) is said to be a favourite with His Holiness. I have read it, and it certainly has a curious power: more a poem than a treatise.

He wrote a number of theological works, said to be models of their kind, and he was also a man of wide classical learning. His translation into ottava rima of Silius's *Punica* (an epic poem in seventeen books on Hannibal's invasion of Italy) is said to be better than the original though this could hardly be described as much of an achievement considering Silius's defects as a poet. Perhaps the Cardinal was attracted to the work because he had been christened Annibale. This may also explain why the present process of his beatification has been slowed down. A twenty-first-century Catholic Church can do without a Saint Hannibal.

The Cardinal was a great prince of the church. He had been born into the powerful Vittorini family which had sired, and, it was said, been sired by, many eminent churchmen. He became a bishop at the age of eighteen and a cardinal at twenty-eight. His palazzo in Rome was the centre of an enlightened and brilliant cultural circle of artists, poets and musicians. The finest painters decorated his reception chambers with frescoes, though his own private apartments were plain and Spartan. The finest food and wine was served at his banquets, but he himself touched little of it. Even on feast days he ate and drank modestly. He slept on bare boards for four hours a night and he was known to wear a hair shirt. His piety and asceticism were a byword.

In appearance he was spare and tall, with a stoop even in his thirties. The famous Titian portrait shows him seated, slightly hunched, head craning forward. He has a gaunt, melancholy face, not unlike some pictures you see of Dante, with a hooked nose and deep-set eyes. He seems to be looking intently at something in the far distance. But what is most arresting about the portrait is the hands. The eighty-year old Titian must have been fascinated by them because they are very carefully and brilliantly represented. One clutches the arm of his chair; the other rests pretentiously on a pile of books, presumably his own works. They are large, yet delicate with abnormally long fingers. The bones and sinews show vividly through the dry, almost transparent skin. These hands seem to be enjoying a separate and independent life, as if they were a grotesque pair of pet spiders that had just emerged from the Cardinal's sleeves.

Contemporary accounts of Cardinal Vittorini describe his voice as being low and his manner unfailingly courteous and gentle, if it is possible to be gentle without warmth. This was the only complaint that was regularly recorded of him. There was always a distance and detachment in his manner, and he had no intimate friendships.

In 1568 he was appointed by Pope Pius V to oversee the operation of the Holy Inquisition in Rome. Though the Cardinal was only thirty-three, this was generally regarded as an excellent appointment. His devotion to the True Faith was unquestioned, as were his piety and integrity. There were some who thought that he might be over-zealous, but they were few. Besides, in those days, when heresy was spreading through the Holy See of Rome itself, it was thought best to err on the side of rigour. It was the time of the Counter-Reformation when the church was beginning to wake from its corrupt, complacent slumbers. A new spirit was abroad and Cardinal Vittorini was its incarnate symbol.

The Cardinal soon found that the task which he had been set was not a congenial one; but being an ascetic, he found this very lack of congeniality to be an additional spur to his zeal. He had to oversee the interrogation of countless people, most of them as incapable of heresy as they were of orthodoxy. A life of privilege and culture had prepared him for almost everything except an encounter with the uneducated mind. He found such meetings profoundly disturbing: he was fully equipped to fight heresy, but not ignorance. Ignorance was the foe without a face; and it was everywhere.

But then His Eminence the Cardinal began to be beset by another and far more troubling threat to his spiritual life. There are a number of documents in the Vatican archives relating to this crisis which can be found among the papers collected for his original beatification process. It was only with the greatest difficulty that I persuaded the Director of the Vatican Archive, the very charming and courteous Monsignor Dossi, to let me see these papers. I am fully aware that my releasing some of them to the general public will be seen in some quarters as a breach of trust, but I believe that my action is justified for reasons which I hope will become clear.

The most important of the papers was written by Brother Benedetto, a Capuchin Friar who was the Cardinal's chaplain and secretary. He was one of the few men who could possibly have been described as being close to the Cardinal, and for this reason alone his story carries conviction. There is another reason, though. It is clear from other documents in the Vittorini file that Fra Benedetto wrote what he did under duress, in compliance with his vow of obedience. Orders had come from the Pope himself that a narrative of the Cardinal's last days should be given and that no detail should be spared. Fra Benedetto, therefore, felt bound to tell the truth in spite of the fact that he was devoted to the Cardinal and anxious to put the best possible construction on his words and actions. What follows is his story, and it will be interspersed with other documents where relevant.

℘

My memorial must begin in the Autumn of the year 1572. One night in, I think, late September, His Eminence was sitting at dinner with a select company. I myself was present. The hour was late and much excellent wine had been drunk, though not, I must add, by my master, who kept to his rule of extreme moderation. Among the company was the eminent poet Alessandro

Andrei whose immortal *Somnum Iamblichi* is, I suppose, admired by all men of taste and learning. Signor Andrei was discussing the works of Porphyry, a favourite subject of his, when he happened to mention that there was a group of men and women in Rome—he called them a sect—who were devoted to the teachings of Porphyry and Plotinus. They called themselves Ignotists, and taking as their premise the idea of Plotinus that God was unknowable, they worshipped Ignorance as a god and indulged in all kinds of curious practices. At this His Eminence stiffened. It was normal at these banquets for the Cardinal to be at his most carefree, and to allow conversation to wander where it would without consideration for the strictest propriety; but Signor Andrei had entered a sphere in which His Eminence's most sacred obligations were engaged. Andrei himself immediately became aware of this and fell silent. Soon afterwards His Eminence retired for the night and the party was dismissed.

The following morning Signor Andrei was summoned to the Palazzo Vittorini and was there questioned by the Cardinal in private, I being the only other person present. His Eminence first satisfied himself that Andrei was in no way a party to the doings of these Ignotists. This was a relief to the Cardinal, for he was a great admirer of the poet's incomparable verses. He then asked Andrei to tell him everything he knew about the Ignotists and Andrei was very willing to oblige.

Several times during the interview Signor Andrei was seen to tremble violently. On one of these occasions my master the Cardinal stopped his interrogation and asked gently if he was suffering from the ague. Signor Andrei replied no, that it was merely anxiety. I find it hard to believe that it was fear of the Cardinal that made him tremble because His Eminence never once raised his voice to him or showed the slightest sign of anger. He was, as usual, earnest and persistent, but he was always softly spoken.

The facts about this sect which Signor Andrei revealed to us were as follows. The Ignotists were led by a man named Ascanio Foscari, a Venetian by birth, who sometimes styled himself 'Count Foscari'. He was a notorious libertine and lived in a most extravagant style without any known source of money. Around him he had gathered a number of bravos, all equally dissolute, but distinguished, so it was said, by some wit. Women too, from all classes, were among his associates. Foscari himself was reckoned to be a man of learning and had spent several years in a seminary before being expelled for licentious behaviour. The practices of the Ignotists were both vile and curious. They would assemble in a cellar or ruined church where they would offer worship to the god they called Agnoia, which means unknowing or ignorance; but sometimes they changed the name of their god and called it Outis, No-one, or even Ouden, Nothing. According to them God created the world out of Nothing and that therefore nothing, or Chaos, preceded God and deserved to be worshipped before him. Many of their ceremonies were plainly blasphemous and in mockery of those of Holy Mother Church. Sometimes they bowed low to a casket which on being opened was seen to contain nothing, or 'Divine Darkness', as they called it. Clearly this ritual mocked the reverence due to the ciborium which holds the blessed sacrament. On one occasion, Andrei told us, they dressed an ape as the Virgin Mary and carried it about in procession; on another they crucified a small black dog. They did this, they said, to show that all forms and ceremonies were vain and meaningless, and that they had no regard for the common forms of decency. They also have no belief in the immortality of the soul and as a hymn sing those verses from the chorus of Seneca's *Troades* which begin:

> After death nothing is, and death itself is nothing...

They also had secret signs and passwords by which they recognised each other. One, I must repeat because it became a strange source of torment to my master, the Cardinal. When one Ignotist met another he would often greet him with the words:

> 'Of what cannot be spoken . . .'
> To which the other would reply:
> 'Of that let no man speak.'

Signor Andrei's descriptions were so clear that I thought he must have been more closely connected with the sect than he made out, but I held my tongue. His Eminence had undertaken to trust his word that he had not taken part in any of their rites, and there was an end of it. When Andrei had finished his account, the Cardinal dismissed him and, immediately summoning his officers, told them to find out these Ignotists with all speed, and especially their leader, Foscari.

The sect was discovered to be more widespread than Signor Andrei had implied and there were as many women as men to be found in its ranks. Indeed, women were regarded as in all respects equal to men within the cult. A large number of both sexes were taken to the dungeons of the Castel Sant Angelo and there put to the question [i.e. tortured].

His Eminence himself conducted many of the interrogations. The results were unsatisfactory because whenever any Ignotist was put to the question he or she would admit to anything simply to stop the pain. Their stories were fantastic and contradicted one another. When asked to reveal their confederates they often gave many names of people who were plainly above suspicion. This made His Eminence the Cardinal very angry. It has been said that in his wrath he had several Ignotists summarily put to death, but I do not believe this to be the case. It is true that some died from their wounds after being put to the question; but none of them departed this life without the ministrations of a priest. I myself attended several of them *in extremis*. They declared themselves penitent before me, but, alas, so carelessly that I was compelled to doubt their sincerity.

Though many Ignotists were discovered and arrested, their leader Foscari evaded capture. His Eminence sent out men into all parts of Italy, but could find no trace of him. His agents in France and Spain were equally unsuccessful. It is most likely that he took refuge in his native city of Venice where the authorities, as ever, showed themselves very unwilling to assist the Cardinal in his holy work. These frustrations drove my master nearly to distraction, and he lost much of his customary composure.

One of the last people to be taken in this purge of Ignotists was a young lady of noble family, Katerina Vernazza, who had a reputation for piety, beauty and wit. It was said that she could compose impromptu a sonnet that other poets might have laboured over for a month. Though His Eminence had never met her—he never allowed women guests at his dinner table—he knew of her good reputation and was very astonished that she was named as an Ignotist. At first he did not believe his informers, but the assertion was confirmed from many sources. Moreover, it was alleged that she had been Foscari's mistress.

When La Vernazza was arrested many papers and treatises were found in her house which showed beyond doubt that she was a follower of Foscari. In particular, the Cardinal's men found a document known as the 'Homily and Responses', of which I have cause to regret that it was not immediately burned.

His Eminence took a particular interest in La Vernazza's case, since he believed her to be essentially virtuous, but led astray by the evil Count Foscari. He interviewed her many times, at first very gently and patiently, but when he found that this did not yield satisfactory results he felt obliged to put her to the question. He was very reluctant to inflict pain on this noble young lady, but, as usual, he put the sacred cause of Mother Church above his own petty scruples. There is no doubt, however, that these interrogations contributed greatly to the mental anguish of the Cardinal.

Fra Benedetto does not explain why they caused Vittorini such anguish. A clue is to be found in the surviving records of the Ignotist interrogations. These are fragmentary and only two of Vernazza's many interrogations survive, the second and later one under torture. The following extracts are taken from them. I have followed without modification the style in which the inquisitions were recorded. The interrogator is, as usual, not named, but 'His Eminence' can only be Vittorini himself:

> On the 19th November 1572 at the Castel Sant Angelo. Katerina Vernazza.
>
> - Asked if she knew the man known as Foscari?
> - She had some acquaintance with him.
> - If she and he had been lovers?
> - It was impossible to define the word lover, for love takes many forms.
> - If she had committed fornication with him?
> - These were mere words. 'Lover', 'fornication', they had no meaning except as people gave them meaning.
> - That La Vernazza understood quite well the meaning of these words.

- Indeed. Far better than His Eminence. But what business was it of his? She understood that she was here on a charge of heresy not fornication.

His Eminence then warned the said Katerina Vernazza to show respect to the Office of the Holy Inquisition. To which she replied that respect for the office did not imply respect for the officers. After a short while the interrogation was then resumed.

- Asked if the Ignotists worshipped a god called Agnoia?
- Replied that God had many names and no name. For did not the Apostle Paul himself commend the Athenians for their worship of the Unknown God?
- If Ignorance was not worshipped by the Ignotists?
- Ignorance must be acknowledged, for the most eminent and orthodox divines have said that God is unknowable.
- If she knew of a rite of the Ignotists known as the 'Homily and Responses'?
- She knew of many homilies and many responses for the ways in which God may be worshipped were many and various.
- If thereby she meant that one way of worshipping God was as good as another?
- That His Eminence knew well that her assertion contained no such implication in reason or reality. . . .'

And so on. This sparring continues for several pages with La Vernazza more than holding her own against the Cardinal. He returned more than once to her relations with Foscari but got the same dusty response. By the time of the second interview it has become an obsession.

On 3rd January 1573 at the Castel Sant Angelo. Katerina Vernazza was brought to the Question. Disrobed, she was laid on the frame and tied to it by the legs and arms. Was shown the fire and the irons heating in them.

- La Vernazza persisted that she was guilty of no sacrilege or blasphemy. Asked why she had been brought here?

- Exhorted to tell the truth. The irons were brought to her and shown for the second time.

- Ah, my God! Will tell the whole truth.

- If it was true that she enjoyed relations with Foscari in the presence of others?

- Before God, it was a lie told against her by her enemies.

- Before God? What God? The God of the Ignotists, or the one true God?

- There is only one true God.

- If it was true that a black dog was crucified in a rite of the Ignotists?

- It was not a black dog.

- What was it then?

- It was a creature of the mind. It exists, but only as each one perceives it.

The first application of the heated irons to the left leg. Exhorted to tell the truth.

- Ah! God have Mercy! What must she say? The black dog was there in all of us. Even in the mind of His Eminence. There must be a sacrifice so that its true meaning may become apparent.

- Must not waste time with such triflings. What were her relations with Foscari?

- They were as His Eminence imagined them to be.

The second application. Cried out—

- Ah, God! Ah, God! May His Eminence know such agony. May His Eminence know what he will not let himself know. May his dreams speak to him.

During the rest of the interrogation nothing of importance is said. The Cardinal presses Vernazza again and again about her relations with Foscari to which she returns ambiguous replies. The irons are applied several more times. Despite the clinical official language in which it is couched, the account of Vernazza's interrogation is almost unbearably painful to read. Some days later Vernazza died as a result of her ordeal. Other Ignotists were handed over to the secular arm and burned alive on the Campo de' Fiori. Fra Benedetto relates what happened next:

It may be said that His Eminence took all these incidents too much to heart, but it was in his nature to pursue his duty with the utmost zeal and with no thought to himself. It is true that the matter of the Ignotists preyed on his mind, so that they invaded not only his waking, but also his sleeping moments. He brooded over the meaning of a number of their writings, mostly composed by Foscari, and in particular the one called the 'Homily and Responses'. He read it many times and when I suggested he put it away or burned it, he replied that he must fathom its mystery. If he did that, he said, he could root out Ignotism for ever.

It was very shortly after the death of Vernazza that the Cardinal began to be plagued by dreams. He would tell them to me because he said that relating them relieved him of some of the burden they placed on his spirit. Two in particular troubled him, because, unlike most dreams, they did not shift and change shape but held to one place and one consistent narrative. Their meanings, however, were very dark and neither I nor His Eminence could guess at them.

In the first dream he found himself walking along a stony path in a great wide valley. The sun was high and hot, the place waterless and barren. But this was at first a joyous dream, because he had a companion on his journey, our Blessed Saviour himself. His Eminence's face lit up when he told this part of the story. Our Saviour walked on his right and just a little ahead of him, but would often turn round to give him words of comfort and encouragement. His Eminence said that if only he could remember those words that Our Saviour spoke to him, all the agonies of his spirit would be laid to rest.

As they walked along, His Eminence trying with all his strength to go faster to catch up with the Saviour, and the Saviour urging him onwards with sweet words, His Eminence told me that he noticed that something had come up beside him on his left hand. It was a small black dog. There was nothing unusual about the creature, except its utter and complete blackness. (His Eminence was not sure of the breed—his knowledge of dogs, he freely confessed to me, was limited—but he said it had a squat nose, a round barrel of a body and little thin legs.) It trotted briskly, never more than three feet away, always keeping exact pace with him, however fast he walked. Otherwise it seemed to take no notice of him. His Eminence said that, as the journey went on, he began to feel a peculiar and quite unreasonable horror of this creature. Several times he thought he might draw the Saviour's attention to the little dog, but something prevented him. (Something like shame, he said.)

Presently they came to the end of the valley and to the foot of a high mountain. A rocky path wound upwards to the summit, and there Our Saviour left His Eminence saying that the Cardinal must make the ascent alone. Mourning the departure of his Divine Companion, His Eminence began the difficult climb and was further distressed to find that the little dog went with him. He tried to send it away, but it took no notice.

As he climbed up the path, the dog kept pace with him, but was now much closer, almost under his feet at times. A horror of touching it with any part of his body prevented His Eminence from physically attacking it. The stones he threw always missed the animal. He became possessed by the idea of escaping it, to the exclusion of all other thoughts. He started to run. The little dog ran behind him and began to emit sounds. They were not barks, His Eminence said; they were not the sounds that any dog might make. Though inarticulate, they were human in character, like the cries of a woman in pain. As he told me about this, my master the Cardinal covered his eyes in horror.

In his dream the Cardinal continued to run faster up the hill, but in no way could escape the dog. Suddenly, ahead of him on the path, was a great black hole, but His Eminence was running so fast that he could not prevent himself from falling headlong into it. Then he entered a great yawning darkness in which all sense of distance and direction vanished. The end of it only came when he awoke in his own bedroom.

The second dream began as a continuation of the first. He was falling down a dark hole. Reasoning with himself, he became convinced that he had died. Then suddenly, as happens in dreams, he found himself descending the steep steps into the dungeons of the Castel Sant Angelo. He still believed that he had died since the staircase that he descended was not quite like the one he knew in the real Castel Sant Angelo, firstly because there were many more steps. In the second place there was something curious about the walls. They were soft, warm and viscous to the touch. They felt like flayed flesh and shuddered as if a living pulse was moving through them. His Eminence said he had the feeling of walking through the organs of a vast body.

Something compelled him to continue to descend the steps towards the chamber where heretics and recreants are put to the Question. It occurred to him that, now he was dead, perhaps he was going to be punished for the pain he had inflicted on those he had tortured. He began to feel a great terror that, as soon as he entered the chamber, devils would seize him and bind him down, but he went on, trusting in a righteous God. When he came into the dungeon he found it to be deserted except for two figures bound and ready to be put to the question. One was La Vernazza, the other was a man with a leather mask over his face whom the Cardinal by instinct knew to be Foscari. The instruments were heating in the brazier. His Eminence waited to be bound down and tortured himself, but no-one came. Vernazza and Foscari remained silent, staring at him. Presently he saw one of the instruments, now red hot at its end, lift itself out of the brazier and come towards him, the handle towards his hand. Then he knew that he was destined to complete in the afterlife the work he had begun on earth. He approached the two bound figures and begged them very earnestly, as they valued their immortal souls, to confess their sins and errors. The figures remained silent and so the Cardinal felt it necessary to cause the pain which, in life, he was always reluctant to inflict. He had never used the instruments in person before, but he did so now.

His Eminence told me that what happened then filled him with an unbearable sickness and horror which lasted long after he had woken up. Each time he scorched the flesh of his victims with the burning iron they did not cry out in pain. They sighed with pleasure, giggled, laughed and uttered blasphemies such as he had read in the Homily and Responses. Perplexed and frantic, His Eminence began to strike Foscari and Vernazza all over with the burning irons. He stabbed them, he flung hot coals over them, burning himself in the process; but the more he attacked them the more they laughed and uttered blasphemies. Then he realised that he was in Hell, because in Hell there is no justice, but everyone is tortured in the way that is most terrible to themselves.

Despite the torment to his mind that these dreams gave him, His Eminence never relented in his pursuit of the heretical Ignotists. He succeeded in wiping the stain of their presence from the face of Rome; but, ever zealous for God and his Holy Church, he remained unsatisfied because he had not captured their leader Foscari.

Foscari was never heard of again, unless one counts the rumour that reached us some years later that he was lecturing on Natural Philosophy at the University of Leyden under the name of Doctor Foscarin and that he had a number of followers who called themselves Foscarines.

ഌ

In reading this account I became convinced that the *Responsoriae Foscarinenses* which had been translated and presented to Rochester by Thomas Wythorne were the 'Homily and Responses' referred to by Fra Benedetto. The version handed down to us is obviously inexact and tainted by later accretions but it gives us some understanding of the mind of the Ignotists, or Foscarines whom I take to be one and the same sect. It also, in an oblique way, offers us an insight into the mind of Cardinal Vittorini, because this text must have struck some answering chord in his mind to have preyed upon it so.

The text begins with a rather muddled account of a ritual, much of it childishly unpleasant and sadistic. This short extract is quite sufficient to give some idea of it:

> Then shall the black dogge be brought forth and after he be made to eat of his turds and drink of his pisse, he shall be beheaded and put upon the crosse that all may adore him.

Shortly after this occur the words: 'Then shall the homily be spoken'. I quote in full what follows:

> THE HOMILY UPON NOTHING
>
> He that hath ears to heare, let him heare. Last night I lay with a whore. I was very eager for her. I entered her lustily and strove to carry my heart up to the place where her soul had been if she had one. I thought to have found out some great secret by her and so went to it with a will. But having spent everything and got nothing in return but a weak spasme of pleasure, rank shame and doubtless some disease, I lay back and it came to passe that, as I slept in the harlott's bed, behold I saw a vision and I dreamed a dreame. Lo, methought I was dead and passed out of my fleshly habiliments and was a spirit free from the torment of the body and the pleasures thereof. And it came to passe that I was carried out beyond this world which seemed as I looked back to be a very mean thing, no more than a flake of ashe turning in a sunbeam. And I was carried out beyond the sunne and the planets and the crystall sphere of starres. And I stood on the edge of a great abysme into which on a sudden I was throwne with a great rushing and roaring of a mighty wind. And it came to passe presently that I seemed to enter a great temple. And, behold, the floor was of jet and the great columnes were of ebonie which reached into a vaulte hung with shadow. And I came up to a Great Throne which was of the blackest

ebonie and canopied with the cloudes of night, and upon this throne in fantastick triumph sate—

All replye: NOTHING.

And behold, he had on him a crowne of black iron, studded with jet, and around him he had on an inky cloake of everlasting darknesse, and his eyes were twin pools of vacancy. And lo, I saw that in one hand he held a shadowy sphere in which flickered fitfully a few rebellious lights. And then I saw that the sphere was the Universe which I had left with its starres and the sunne and all the wheeling planets. And it came to passe that, as I looked, the Great Nothing who held the shadowy sphere did breathe on it with his dusky lips and, of a sudden, the fitful lights were all extinguished for ever, eternally, and, behold there was nothing left but onlie—

All replye: NOTHING.

And it came to passe that I heard a mightie voice like unto the great silence which filles the void. And the voice said: What art thou? And I said: I am a man an't please you. What art thou? And the voice replyed—

All replye: NOTHING.

Then the voice said: Lo, I have called you out of Nothing and into Nothing shalt thou go everlastingly. And I said: What is Life? And the voice replyed—

All replye: NOTHING.

Verily, it is a greate emptinesse which some have thought to be something, but that is a delusion. For it is but a dreame. Nay not even that, but the dreame of a dreame. Thy life, mortall man, and the life of all things is but a frail candle in my hand. The light shines in darknesse, but the darknesse comprehendeth it. It is squeezed between my black thumb and forefinger and then is out for ever. Think not, o man, that even within the pale confines of thy world I am not ever there. For in the midst of light, you are in darknesse. You will find me under the cassocks of priests, and the gownes of scholars, and in the heads of grave politicians there am I also. Show me the promise of a King and I shall be there. Show me the truth of a Frenchman, Spaniard's dispatch, Dane's wit, whore's vowes: I am in them all. Then what of me? I said. And the voice replyed: Lo, you are my sonne, my onlie sonne in whom I am well pleased. And the Great Nothing that sate upon the throne of ebonie stretched out his black hand to grasp me. But I cried out a great crye and started awake. And the whore who laid beside me said: What ails you, chuck? And I said: It was a dreame. Then the drab did aske: What did you dreame of? And I answered—

All replye: NOTHING.

For the final episode in the story of Cardinal Vittorini, we rely again on the narrative of Brother Benedetto:

I am now compelled by my vow of obedience to say something about the Cardinal's last days on earth. That the end came suddenly, swiftly and mysteriously is well known, but there have been many stories told about it which are quite untrue and a monstrous insult to my master's memory. This is the whole truth of what happened.

One exceedingly hot day in the June of 1573 His Eminence was travelling by carriage to visit the Convent of Barnabite nuns in Trastevere. He frequently visited them to give them wise spiritual counsel, and to be refreshed by the simple humility of their holy lives. It was, he once said to me, so much the pleasantest of his sacred duties that he wondered whether he should forego it for the good of his soul.

As his carriage entered the Piazza dei Miracoli a little black dog ran straight across his path in front of the carriage horses who took fright. They reared up, upsetting the carriage and throwing His Eminence violently onto the stone pavement. He sustained some bad cuts and bruises to his left leg because the paving stones where he fell were uneven and badly set. Nevertheless he was helped back into the carriage which had sustained no irrevocable damage and went on his way. At the Barnabite Convent the nuns tenderly washed and bound up his wounds.

He gave no further thought to his injuries until the following morning when he found that the pain they gave him had not diminished but greatly increased. When the bandages were taken off, his leg was seen to be covered with black pustules. The wounds gaped and gave off a nauseous stench. Physicians were sent for. Some prescribed hot poultices, some cold compresses, some leeches and some fumigatories. All were applied, but though they added much to His Eminence's agony they did nothing to aid his recovery. Throughout this ordeal he showed the most exemplary fortitude, but when night came the poisons in his leg began to affect his brain. He suffered the most extraordinary delusions. At one moment he believed that his room was filled with small black dogs, the size of rats, at another that he was being embraced by a great black snail. His delusions were many and various, but the colour black was a constant feature.

The following morning his left leg had turned a dark purple colour and the wounds constantly oozed a malodorous yellow liquid. A surgeon came and declared that the leg must be immediately amputated to prevent the infection spreading further. This operation was then performed with the greatest possible speed and skill. His Eminence again showed great courage and only cried out once. Even this cry was in the form of a prayer to God that he might have mercy on his soul.

Though the amputation was performed quickly and the stump immediately cauterised, the Cardinal had been greatly weakened by the loss of blood. Moreover the poison which had entered his system from the leg still affected his mind. He now suffered from the most curious delusion that we who stood about him were all creatures of his imagination, that even his physical surroundings were an hallucination, and that he was the only sentient, living being in the universe.

I thought it was right at this point to send for a priest to bring him Extreme Unction. I asked for Father Mattei of St John Lateran, an old friend of the Cardinal's and a most pious and holy man. When I told the Cardinal that Father Mattei was coming he was suddenly seized with a furious terror. Why had I summoned Father Mattei? He was an old man and his mind wandered. He would forget to bring the holy oil for extreme unction. His ciborium would be empty and there would be no sacrament for him to receive. He kept asking the time; he seemed possessed by the idea that time was slipping away from him, like, as he said, 'water from a man's hand'. With great difficulty we calmed his mind on these matters, but with each hour that passed he was becoming weaker.

When Father Mattei arrived, His Eminence was at first convinced that this was not his old friend but Count Foscari in disguise. We convinced him that it was not so; or, at least, the Cardinal professed to us that he no longer believed Father Mattei to be an impostor. So we left the Cardinal's room. Then Father Mattei went in to administer the last rites to His Eminence and to hear his confession alone. When he came out from the Cardinal's room he went away quickly without a word. Within a week he too was dead.

Then came the last death agony of Cardinal Vittorini. He seemed at first calmer. He said to me that he regretted having mistaken Father Mattei for Foscari because he was now convinced that Count Foscari did not exist. He said that Foscari had been invented by the Ignotists and that they, having imagined him so fervently, succeeded in persuading others and then finally themselves that he existed. All this the Cardinal explained to us so smoothly and rationally, so like his old self, that I had to force myself to remember that he was not in his right mind.

Then he gathered his servants and associates about him to give them his final blessing. Having done so he gave a long sigh and uttered these words: 'Where he is, I shall be also. Where he is not, I also shall not be.' To whom he referred is not certain. Many who heard him believe that he was talking of his Blessed Saviour, and I will not disagree with them. But he said these words with such anguish in his voice that my heart troubles me.

After this he said only one thing more. At about three in the morning he sat up in bed, rigid and with open eyes suffused with blood. Then he cried out so loudly that it could be heard in the antechamber and beyond: '*Deus, Deus, ut quid derelequisti me?*' ['My God, My God, why hast thou forsaken me?' Vulgate translation.] Having said this he at once lay back on the bed and, after he had made a convulsion so violent that the bed shook with it, he sighed a last long rattling breath and gave up his spirit.

To those who would contend that my most revered and pious master died in an agony of unholy despair, I would say this: his last words were those of Our Blessed Saviour himself upon the cross. I cannot tell in what state His Eminence Cardinal Annibale Vittorini went to meet his maker, I can only say that I, Brother Benedetto of the Capuchin Order, pray daily for the repose of his soul.

8)

There is only one thing to add which may shed some light on the Cardinal's strange behaviour. In his book *The Means and Might of Spiritual Orison*, a work which, but for Cardinal Vittorini's unassailable reputation for orthodoxy, might not have escaped censure for Quietism in the century after his, the following passage occurs (I am using Benet of Canfield's translation):

> As we ascend to the highest sphere of Spiritual Orison we enter into a Divine Darkness which is the very darkness in which God stands, he being the source of all light and so not lit by any Thing. And there we may know Nothing and see Nothing, for any image that we may see and any sound that we may hear is false, for Nothing can represent that which is Infinite. By this means we may dwell in the Abyss of the Divine Essence and the nothingness of things, by annihilation only. For only by unknowing may we approach the Unknown, and only by not seeing may we perceive the Truth which cannot be spoken. And of what cannot be spoken, let no man speak.